A PRACTICAL
GUIDE TO DATING
A DEMON

A PRACTICAL GUIDE TO DATING A DEMON

HANNAH REYNOLDS

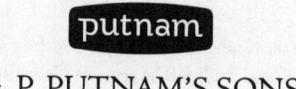

G. P. PUTNAM'S SONS

G. P. PUTNAM'S SONS
An imprint of Penguin Random House LLC
1745 Broadway, New York, NY 10019
penguinrandomhouse.com

Edited by Gretchen Durning
Design by Rebecca Aidlin
Text set in Centaur Now Text

Library of Congress Cataloging-in-Publication Data

Names: Reynolds, Hannah, 1988- author
Title: A practical guide to dating a demon / Hannah Reynolds.
Description: New York : G.P. Putnam's Sons, [2026] | Audience: Ages 14 years and up |
Summary: Naomi, a studious scholarship girl at a magical academy, accidentally summons a charming demon fiancé and must team up with him to uncover the source of mysterious magical disruptions in her city.
Identifiers: LCCN 2025027118 (print) | LCCN 2025027119 (ebook) |
ISBN 9780593859032 trade paperback | ISBN 9780593859049 epub
Subjects: CYAC: Romance stories | Demons—Fiction | Betrothal—Fiction |
Magic—Fiction | LCGFT: Fiction | Paranormal fiction | Novels
Classification: LCC PZ7.I.R4865 Pr 2026 (print) |
LCC PZ7.I.R4865 (ebook) | DDC [Fic]—dc23
LC record available at https://lccn.loc.gov/2025027118
LC ebook record available at https://lccn.loc.gov/2025027119

Manufactured in the United States of America
LSCC

ISBN 9780593859032
1st Printing

The authorized representative in the EU for product safety and compliance is Penguin Random House Ireland, Morrison Chambers, 32 Nassau Street, Dublin D02 YH68, Ireland, https://eu-contact.penguin.ie.

*To everyone who longed for magic powers,
then learned to fight for their dreams through
hard work and perseverance*

ONE

IN THE CITY OF TALUM, THE WINDS WERE STRONG, THE MAGIC thick, and everyone knew each other's business.

My floormate, Leah, nudged me as we crossed campus. It was late in the day—the setting sun painted the Lyceum's marble buildings a tawny gold, and warblers sung from leafy branches as students laughed and shouted. "Your latest suitor," Leah said with a wicked grin.

I groaned. Sure enough, a boy in a gray blazer lingered before the open brass gate. Beyond, a land bridge led from the Lyceum's peninsula to the rest of the island. Everyone crossed here to leave campus, so it was a great place to catch someone. "Let's hide."

"Too late." Leah's brown eyes were bright, her expression impish. "What number are we up to now?"

"I'm not telling." We slowed, other students swirling around us. The majority of us wore school-issued blazers made of twill-worsted wool to protect against the winds. They varied in color based on which of the five Lyceum schools we attended, but the gold emblem emblazoned on the breast remained the same—an open book against a stylized tree. Leah and I wore blue, for the School of Humanities, paired with sensible blouses and trousers tucked into sturdy boots.

Leah smirked. "Eight, is it?"

"Seven," I corrected quickly, as though one fewer were any better. Leah cackled while the boy caught sight of us.

Ephraim was reed-thin with freckles stark against his pale face. We had the same Old Cinnaian language class, and we'd worked together on a project last week. He seemed smart and nice enough, save an irritating habit of second-guessing my work.

"Naomi." He wiped damp hands on his pants and swallowed hard enough to bob the amulet around his neck. "Hi."

My father's advice about confronting mice back home flashed through my mind: *They're more scared of you than you are of them.* I suppressed a sigh. "Hey, Ephraim."

"Well, I'm off." Leah sounded delighted to leave me in this awkward situation, which would make a good story for her tomorrow. "You two have fun."

I shot her a pleading look. If she stayed, maybe I'd avoid Ephraim's inevitable question. "Aren't we walking home together?"

She shook her head, the crystal studs in her ears glinting in the early-autumn light. "I have a date."

We'd both been in Talum only a month, but Leah had already gone on more dates than I had in my entire life. Admittedly, I'd been on none. I was torn between admiration and exhaustion at her social life. "Right. See you later."

"I'll walk you home." Ephraim spoke unsmilingly, as though a graver utterance had never been made. He was a serious boy, as all these gray-blazered School of Government boys seemed to be. Their school's main requirement seemed to be a dour expression and the inability to take a joke—or a hint.

I tried not to sound pained. "Sure."

We crossed the land bridge over the Lersach River into Issachar Quarter—the Scholars' Quarter—where students and academics lived in shoulder-to-shoulder buildings above bookshops and cheap pubs. I decided to nudge Ephraim and get this over fast. "What's up?"

"Oh. Uh." He gave me an appraising look as we turned up Avenue de Bedzin, which cut through Issachar Quarter like an artery. Wind tugged at our clothes. City fashion favored trousers instead of long skirts like back home; without weights in the hem, skirts could easily gust up. People usually wore their hair either short or braided, and I'd bound my own long brown curls in the student style of four braids knotted at the nape.

But despite my best efforts at looking presentable, my ragged shirt had come untucked from my secondhand trousers, and the sole of one boot was half-detached. Even the frayed red string around my wrist looked ready to disintegrate. Like the amulet around my neck, I wore it to protect against demons. Superstition said if it fell off, you were about to meet your spouse.

I hoped Ephraim noticed the bracelet was still securely tied.

He cleared his throat, obviously steeling himself against my dismal appearance. "Are you going with anyone to the graduation festival?"

And there it was.

I wish I could say seven boys had asked me to the Lyceum's festival because of my dazzling beauty and wit, or for my skill at languages, which had landed me my scholarship.

This was not the case.

"No, Ephraim," I said tiredly. "I'm not going with anyone to the festival."

4 ~ HANNAH REYNOLDS

"Really." Ephraim braced his shoulders. I could almost taste his nervous anticipation. "You're not?"

"Nope." The avenue opened onto one of the quarter's main squares, where loud music and rowdy debates drifted from pubs. We cut across the plaza, passing elderly folk playing games of strategy. Globes of neshem-powered light blazed in wrought iron lamps to hold back the darkness. Children chased each other around the bronze statues at the plaza's center, which depicted the three primordial beasts of ancient mythology: the Behemoth, a desert-dwelling monster; the Leviathan, a sea serpent with piercing eyes and brilliant scales; and the Ziz, a griffin-like bird with a wingspan capable of blocking out the sun.

Ephraim took my hand and pulled me to a stop, his skin clammy with sweat. "Would you like to go with me?"

Oy. I tugged my hand from his grasp and kept walking. "Thanks, but no."

Ephraim followed, sounding surprised. "Are you waiting for someone else to ask?"

All the boys did this—they wouldn't take a simple no for an answer. They'd all pressed on against my every excuse. Well, almost every excuse.

If it hadn't been so infuriating, it might have been flattering— except I knew it wasn't me they were interested in. It was an introduction to my aunt—a member of the Great Council—that made them so desperate to bring me to the festival where she would be in attendance.

To deter my unwanted suitors, I'd settled on a stronger deterrent, one girls in my village had used for ages. I'd first dropped it glibly, a sarcastic whim born more out of frustration than expectation it would work. "I can't go with anyone."

"Why not?" Ephraim thrust his chin forward.

"Because I'm already spoken for." Around us, a fresh easterly wind tugged at the fronds of palm trees in the plaza. A few birds took flight, though most remained. A small blue-and-orange kingfisher swiveled its head and looked, I swear, right at me. "I'm betrothed."

Ephraim looked skeptical. City folk thought eighteen was young for an engagement, except in unusual circumstances. "To whom?"

I smiled sharply. Because my circumstance was most unusual and impossible to argue against. "To a demon."

I wasn't, obviously, betrothed to a demon.

The lie was so silly I had a difficult time keeping a straight face each time I told it. I'd been shocked it'd worked, actually. But people don't mess with demons, especially not city folk. At home, everyone has crossed paths with demons a time or two at the border market, where they traded strange feathers or stones, but Talumizans had almost no exposure.

It's not like I was an expert. I knew the basics: Demons lived in the vast plains in the center of Ena-Cinnai, between the western port cities, like Naborre, and the Lersach River. Some said demons had their own cities in the desert, carved into towering limestone cliffs. Others said they inhabited the cities of ancient human civilizations who'd dared to press into the wilderness only to pay the price with death and ruin. Since the long-standing treaty between humans and demons prevented us from entering their lands, we knew very little.

Just enough to make us blanch, as Ephraim did now. "A demon?"

"Yes." I turned onto one of the streets branching off the plaza like spokes on a wheel. It sloped down toward the edge of the island, toward the dorms. "He's terribly jealous."

"Huh." Ephraim sounded stumped. "What's his name?"

"Um." No one had ever asked for a name before. I cast about. "It's Daziel." Many demons' names ended in *-iel*, didn't they? "The demon Daziel is my betrothed," I said again, trying to sound convincing.

"How did you meet?"

Wow, this boy really wanted details. Usually, people backed off immediately. I'd never spun an in-depth story before, and I floundered. "I'm from one of the northwestern plains villages, close to the borderlands. I was . . . out picking flowers . . . and I wandered too close to the wilderness, and there he was. Daziel, my demon betrothed. And we fell madly in love."

Inwardly, I winced. I was too busy minding my three younger sisters to go out gathering flowers. Plus, I wasn't stupid enough to linger by the border.

Ephraim, apparently, didn't have a high enough opinion of my intelligence to find this suspicious. "I didn't know demons and humans could marry."

Could humans and demons marry? Another thing to which I had no answer. The grandmothers in my village—some with a knowing gleam in their eyes—had warned us about how seductive demons could be. It wasn't impossible a village girl had run off with a demon before. "I'm sure it'll be fine."

"What do you even talk about? With a demon?" When I glanced at Ephraim with likely wild eyes, he held up his hands. "Sorry. Didn't mean to pry. Mazel tov. When's the wedding?"

I let out a sigh of relief. "It's a long engagement. Not until after I graduate."

He nodded thoughtfully, then refocused. "So, do you have any single sisters or cousins?"

~ ~ ~

THE WIND PICKED UP after I ditched Ephraim, chimes pealing out as the eastern breeze strengthened. I'd sailed down the Lersach into Talum a month ago, when gentle, humid winds carried memories of sun-soaked summer days. Now, as autumn edged in, the winds had abandoned their warmth, though I'd been told the bitterly cold Trio Winds wouldn't arrive until winter.

The winds influenced everything here, from fashion to architecture. Testylier House, my residence hall, was a five-story sandstone building with thick walls to block out the wind. The roof barely sloped so the winds would have difficulty peeling tiles away.

The door to Testylier House bore the same emblem as my jacket—an open book against a tree. Inside the foyer, a few worn but presentable chairs stood by the mailboxes. A desk took up most of the space, behind which the dorm's guardienne, Madame Hadar, often sat. Her sharp eyes caught everything.

I opened my mailbox, anticipation surging at the sight of a beat-up packet with Mom's handwriting. A creamy white envelope, which I ignored, lay alongside it. I ripped open the packet as I started up the stairs to the fifth floor, where I lived with Leah and two other scholarship students.

Two giggling girls came flying around the bend, their arms linked. They wore long coats with flaring skirts, much more fashionable than our school blazers, and kitten heel lace-up boots I coveted on a soul-deep level. The three of us pulled to an awkward stop.

"Oh, hello." Élodie bat Amit straightened the sleeves of her royal blue coat. Birra Shachar said nothing, fixing her gaze over my shoulder. They'd piled their hair high and embellished it with jewels and flowers. You'd need wire frames, hair pads, a jar of mousse, and a thousand pins—all of them enchanted—to secure it against the winds. In Talum, the styles of the rich seemed to exist to show they had the resources to be impractical.

My aunt had suggested I befriend girls like these, Talumizans from powerful families, but we had nothing in common, save family members with the same job.

Aunt Tirtzah served as one of the six representatives of the Judahite tribe on the Great Sanhedrin, the highest court in the land. I only grasped how important people considered my aunt when strangers went out of their way to be nice—or invite me to the graduation festival. She had a palatial house on Society Hill, the most exclusive neighborhood in the city. But the house was hers only as long as she served on the Sanhedrin. She wasn't really wealthy, not like these two. And these girls knew it.

"Hi." I forced a smile. "How are you two?"

"Great," Élodie said. "Heading out for the evening."

"We got invited to a party at the Rocks," Birra burst out, as though she couldn't help herself. I tried to keep my stab of jealousy off my face. The Rocks lay on the southern side of the island, and I'd never heard of first-years attending the upperclassman parties there.

"What are you up to?" Élodie asked, scrupulously polite. She was in the School of Government, and I'd have been shocked if she didn't run for the Sanhedrin herself one day.

"Studying." If I didn't maintain high grades, I'd lose my scholarship and be sent home. "I have an Intro to T3 test tomorrow."

They both winced. Intro to Theurgy and Thaumaturgy Theory was required for first-years and unanimously hated. "Good luck," Élodie said, and the two of them were gone.

Continuing up the stairs, I skimmed my family's letters hungrily. Dad reported on his current woodworking project and asked about my classes; Grandma gossiped about neighbors and my sisters; Mom said everyone loved and missed me, reminded me to eat well and get enough sleep, and asked if I'd made friends.

I swallowed hard. I wouldn't tell my family and worry them, but it hadn't been easy to adjust to life as a Lyceum student. I loved Talum, and I'd been lucky to bond with the girls on my floor, but I felt out of my depth at school. While I might have been the most dedicated student in my village, I was nothing special at the Lyceum. Dad had tried to warn me, but I'd been too excited to listen.

Dad had grown up in Talum. He'd left at seventeen to become a sailor, to his parents' dismay, then met my mother on leave in Port Naborre and never gone back. He knew what the city was like—and he had been right. The brightest student in a high plains village was considered deeply mediocre at the fabled Lyceum. I had an ear for languages—my mother's mother had spoken to me in her singsong southern dialect since I was a child, and I'd picked up foreign tongues from sailors in Port Naborre—but I didn't have eighteen years of formal study.

Sighing ruefully, I skimmed my sisters' letters, though the last envelope nagged at me. Better to get it over with fast. I ripped it open.

Dear Naomi,

I am hosting a festive gathering next month, on the 22nd. I will send a carriage for you at six. Please confirm you have an appropriate outfit. If not, I will send something.

Aunt Tirtzah

My stomach clenched. I'd met my aunt only once, and I wasn't eager to repeat the experience. Also, what did "an appropriate outfit" entail?

A skittering up the stairs distracted me. I had no time for unwanted suitors, a looming exam, *and* a mouse. Cautiously, I took another step—and saw something glowing red with a long tail whip around the bend.

I blinked. Surely I hadn't seen a salamander. Salamanders—according to legend—were born from stone calcite burned for seven years in fires built of myrtle wood. They died as soon as they were removed, their blood used to make one impervious to flame. It'd been a long day; I was imagining things.

At the top of the stairs, a worn carpet lined the wooden floor, threadbare from thousands of footsteps over the years. Lights glowed in old-fashioned brass sconces, etched with the standard spell for lighting; the four of us had a schedule for painting them every morning with neshem oil so they didn't run out of power. At the end of the hall was my favorite detail: stained glass windows depicting olive trees.

Four doors faced each other, leading into matching sets of rooms. As I neared mine, I slowed. Something was off. Light glowed from the crack beneath the door, and I never left my lamps on. A faint scent, like the wind blowing off the desert, made the back of my neck prickle.

Had Leah been home, I'd have knocked on her door, but she was gone, and so were the others—Jelan and Gilli had a late class today. If I was smarter, more cautious, or less tired, I would have called in reinforcements—the gendarme, or a rabbi, or someone from one of the other floors at least. But wasn't it usually your imagination when you suspected a villain was hiding in your shower? I braced myself and opened the door.

Someone was sitting on the sofa.

The air around him wobbled, distorted like the shimmer above a fire. His bronze skin glowed from within. Perched on his shoulder sat a small, luminous red salamander.

When I entered, he looked up from the book in his lap, which I recognized as a present from my mother: *A Household Guide to Demons*. His eyes were a pure, glossy black, no whites, no irises. His mouth turned up at the corners. "Hello, darling," he said, and his voice sounded like smoke, silvery and strange. "Welcome home."

TWO

STUDENTS AT THE LYCEUM OF TALUM BELONGED TO ONE OF five schools: the School of Science, the School of Humanities, the School of Engineering, the School of Government, or the School of Religious Studies. Each taught students to write new spells and adjust old ones in their specialization. My yearlong scholarship came from the School of Humanities.

Which meant, notably, I had no clue how to defend myself except through biting social commentary and deflective humor. So instead of tossing out a banishment or containment spell, I defaulted to my baser instincts.

I screamed.

The demon winced and covered his ears. The salamander darted beneath the neckline of his crisp white shirt.

"Who are you?" I looked around frantically. It turned out I didn't own weapons. The living room consisted of soft, pretty things—the thick carpet, several throw pillows and blankets, curtains. I had a lamp with an outrageous fringed shade, but it was on the other side of the room—next to the demon. Besides, it was large and unwieldy and I might be too weak to swing it. "What do you want?"

"I'm Daziel."

"What?" How did he get in here? I glanced at the mezuzah on my doorframe, which should have kept demons out. It appeared intact. Pressing my palm to my collarbone, I felt the firm disk of my amulet, still there. What had I done wrong? My gaze caught on my mirror, which I'd lugged from a thrift market to the tram and up the stairs. Mom had said I should redo a mirror's protective castings every six months or keep it covered, and I hadn't. "Did you come through the mirror? What about the wards?"

"Don't worry about those," the demon said, as though I'd been concerned he might get accidentally locked out. "As your betrothed, I have the right to your space."

My *betrothed*.

Oh.

This was bad. My mother had told me that naming a demon risked drawing one's attention. I'd thought I was being clever, but now I realized I'd been very, very stupid.

Taking a deep breath, I studied the demon before me. He looked my age and mostly human, save the fathomless black eyes. Faint lines formed a pattern of shimmery feathers along his neck, disappearing under his shirt collar. His nails were black and came to a point like talons. Gleaming black stones filled the gauges in his ears, and a giant ring with red stones encircled his right pointer finger. No necklace, unlike most Ena-Cinnaians, who wore amulets both for protection and to show our tribal allegiance—like the Naphtali amethyst around my own neck.

A wild demon, I suspected—as intelligent and savvy as a human but chaotic, prone to mischief and capricious behavior.

I tried to remember what *A Household Guide to Demons* said about ridding one's home of a wild demon, but I'd barely flipped through the book. I fell back on childhood spells, more superstition than magic, singing a protective song my grandmother had taught me for when I walked alone outside the village.

The demon blinked and didn't move.

Okay. Fine. Sidling along the wall, I snatched from my bookcase a miniature shofar Dad had given me when I was twelve. When I blew it, the ram's horn emitted a piercing sound, but the demon didn't flee.

Instead, he frowned. "You're very loud."

The audacity. "You broke into my rooms." I blew the shofar again, louder. When I tried a third time, no sound came out. I stared at the shofar, betrayed and bewildered, before transferring my gaze to the demon. "What did you do?"

"Do you want the technical explanation about how I stopped the molecules from vibrating?" I couldn't tell if he was in earnest or teasing me—I thought it might be the latter, but he was too inhuman to read. "I find usually humans don't."

"What?" I had no idea what he was talking about. I had no idea what was happening. I had no idea I was so bad in a crisis. "What are you *doing* here? You can't just make things not work. That's— unsettling. And rude."

"Sorry." He didn't sound apologetic; he sounded put out. The little salamander popped out of his shirt and curled up in a ball on his shoulder, resting its narrow head on its hindquarters. Its eyes were as black and glossy as the demon's. "But *I* think it's rude to cast spells to banish shedim with malicious intent when I have none."

Demons weren't always malicious, but they might accidentally ruin your life for the entertainment value. Especially wild demons, known for seeking larks and pleasure at any cost.

On the other hand, Ena-Cinnaian demons upheld the same laws of hospitality and good behavior as humans did. They considered themselves scrupulously polite. This demon had called me rude, so maybe I should backpedal. I softened my voice. "Do you mind sharing why you're here? Is there something I can help you with?"

"I'm visiting."

Right. Because that was normal, demons visiting the Scholars' Quarter. "If you need a place to stay, you could try one of the local inns. The Drowned Pelican at the end of the street is supposed to be very nice."

He turned his gaze to me. Unnervingly, when his onyx eyes moved, iridescent color crossed them like light striking black mother-of-pearl. "Why would I stay at an inn instead of here, with my betrothed?"

Unease curdled my stomach. I started shaking my head and didn't stop. "That's just a story I tell to get guys off my back."

"You said 'I'm already betrothed' and 'to the demon Daziel.'" He smiled, incisors sharp like a carnivore's. "We are madly in love."

A horrible thought burbled up. If this demon's name really was Daziel, I might have accidentally summoned him. Which could be very bad.

Millennia ago, humans and demons warred. Demons consumed human vitality, and humans bound demons for their power. Demons were pure magic, while humans could only manipulate magic. Spellcasters used bound demons to power letterform magic instead of using neshem crystals as we did today. The demon wars led to the empty cities in the wilderness—and a treaty renewed every twenty years.

Summoning a demon *probably* wasn't illegal by itself, though what did I know—it could be against the treaty. It was *definitely* illegal to bind demons. "You're not bound to me or anything, are you?"

The demon tilted his head; one of his dark curls fell across his forehead. "Isn't a betrothal a type of bind?"

"I release you," I said once hurriedly, then twice more to make sure. "I release you. I release you." I opened the door to the hallway. "You're free! I'm *so* sorry."

He stared at me. The tiny salamander stared at me. "I was joking. I meant—because it's a vow? Vows bind you together?"

"Demons joke?" That was almost as startling as anything else. I glanced out the door. What if I lured him outside, like a pesky fly, then ran back inside and closed the door?

He frowned. "Where are you going?"

"Just—a nighttime stroll." I took a few steps. "Maybe you want to come with me?"

For a moment I didn't think he'd fall for it, but then he flowed to his feet and followed me over the room's threshold and into the hall. I backed up to the stairwell. He took another step too, and another. Wow. Okay, this was working. I smiled, tentative relief growing, and he began to smile back.

Then I lurched forward and past him in a mad dash toward my rooms. I slammed the door so hard the clap reverberated up my arms and in my ears.

But I'd done it, the demon's surprised expression etched into my mind.

Letting out short, fast breaths of relief, I turned the lock. It'd worked. I'd vanquished a demon.

I turned around and saw the demon sitting on the couch.

My mouth dropped open. "You're kidding me."

He looked irritated. "That was also rude."

"It wasn't—" I swallowed my words. I wasn't getting into a fight about courtesy. "Look. I'm sure I'm very—flattered—by your attention, but there's been a misunderstanding. You're not my betrothed. I don't want a betrothed! Like, thank you for coming out here, I appreciate you taking the time, but if you could just . . . go, that'd be great."

His tone and expression were perfectly pleasant, as though this was a normal situation. "We *are* betrothed."

Surely this demon didn't *actually* think we were engaged?

Okay. If there was a demon in my rooms who wouldn't leave, *I* needed to leave. I could go to Madame Hadar, the guardienne. If she didn't know banishment spells, she should at least know who to contact. I wouldn't be thrilled to approach her—her nephew had asked me out, and admitting I'd lied about a demon betrothed wouldn't look great—but needs must.

Or maybe Gilli and Jelan were home by now. I wasn't used to asking others for help—I was used to being the oldest sister, the one in charge—but this problem was too big for me alone.

I headed back to the door.

"I'm not following you this time." He sounded worried and sulky, and his arms crossed tightly over his chest.

"Fine." I felt a little better, a little more in control. It was hard to fear a pouting boy, no matter his species. "But I know better than to stay in my rooms with a demon." I grabbed my keys and headed out.

Sure enough, the demon Daziel followed, scowling as I knocked on Gilli's door. "Why are you—"

It swung open. A petite, pretty girl stood there in white lounge-wear. She'd threaded ribbons through her pigtails and tied them in a bow at the top of her head.

"Naomi, hi," Gilli said with a sweet smile. When we'd first met during move-in, I thought her earnestness might grate on me, but she turned out to be inescapably endearing. "What's up? Want to come in?"

"Thanks." I felt an awkward shyness. Though I liked Gilli and Jelan, we'd only known each other a month, and we hadn't spent as much time together as me and Leah; mostly, we were either in separate duos or a group. "I'm having a bit of a night."

Inside, Jelan sat in an armchair. She wore half her hair shaved and the rest kept in a tight coiled braid. I'd only ever seen her in black, save her red School of Engineering blazer. While Gilli's family seemed to have some money—her mother was a navigator, a coveted position aboard ships—I suspected Jelan needed every last bit of her scholarship.

"What's going—" Gilli began, then froze, gaping.

"Hello," Daziel said.

Gilli shrieked. Jelan grabbed a protective bowl from the book-case. Speaking in a low, steady tone, she began turning it up and over, as though capturing something inside.

"This is Daziel," I said.

"I'm Naomi's betrothed," Daziel said brightly.

"What?" Gilli said, which was a fair reaction, because it was also mine. Then her face transformed, like a theatergoer's when the farm boy was revealed to be the prince. "Oh my god. Your *demon betrothed*."

Jelan hesitated in her casting.

"He's not," I protested. "You guys know it's a fake excuse."

"Right," Gilli said uncertainly, looking back and forth between us. "But . . . he is a demon. Who says he's your betrothed. And you say you have a demon betrothed."

"I'm lying! We're both lying! We're not betrothed!"

"We are betrothed," Daziel said cheerfully.

The girls exchanged bewildered glances. Neither Gilli nor Jelan were likely to have practical knowledge of demons. Gilli's family lived right outside Talum, while Jelan came from the capital city of Maurino, Ena-Cinnai's southern neighbor. Cities were heavily warded against mazzikin—small spirits—and usually avoided by wild demons, like Daziel, who preferred space and nature. High demons occasionally visited cities for society entertainments or treaty negotiations, but ordinary folk had nothing to do with them. Besides, high demons knew how to behave in human society—they might be more powerful than their kindred, but they were also more predictable, and so not as alarming.

"Can I crash with you tonight?" I asked Gilli. "I can't figure out how to banish him."

"Have you tried, um, blowing a shofar and spitting?" Gilli asked.

"The shofar, yeah, but not spitting."

Daziel looked astonished. "Are you going to *spit* on me?"

"No?" Gilli responded timidly. Which, also fair. It was one thing to read about spitting on a demon and quite another to spit on a very real one.

"I won't spit if you leave," I said. "Which you should, because even if you're allowed in my rooms, it can't be proper for you to be in Gilli's uninvited."

He frowned, but he couldn't dispute that, not if he cared about hospitality. "You won't stay here forever. I can wait at home."

I almost choked. At home? Meaning *my* rooms? Presumptuous. "I might stay here tonight, though."

He scowled, looking as petty as my sister Adina. This felt weirdly reassuring—the more he reminded me of a teenage boy and the less of a strange, magical creature, the more sure-footed I felt. "Since you're *so* insistent on avoiding me, even though I came *all* the way out here to be with you—we could strike a bargain."

This didn't assuage my wariness. "What kind of bargain?"

"I don't think you're supposed to strike bargains with demons," Gilli whispered. Jelan shook her head.

He smiled, all sharp teeth and black eyes. Not so human after all. He held out a round red fruit: a pomegranate, which he definitely hadn't been holding a moment before. "Accept this gift. Then I'll leave."

I loved pomegranates. They were high on my list of favorite fruits. But there were a lot of stories about people eating fruit, and I couldn't remember any ending positively.

"Am I missing something?" I asked my friends. "Because on the surface, this sounds good." I narrowed my eyes at Daziel. "Is the pomegranate bespelled? Do I have to eat it?"

"It'd be a waste of a perfectly good pomegranate if you didn't," Daziel said with some asperity. "But no. And it's not bespelled. It's not magical. It's a pomegranate."

I glanced at Jelan, for she was one of the smartest people I'd met. "How good are demons at lying?"

"Very good."

"A rude and baseless stereotype," Daziel scoffed. "Will you accept it?"

I hesitated. "You'll leave if I do?"

He nodded.

I took the fruit.

Daziel smiled. And vanished.

Sheer relief descended. It hadn't been a trick. I hadn't made a terrible call, dooming myself and my friends. He'd kept his word and left.

"Wow," Gilli said faintly. She leaned over, her nose close to the pomegranate as she examined it, the lavender bow in her hair fluttering. "Do we eat it?"

"No," Jelan said.

"No," I agreed.

"I was just asking." Gilli made a face, then turned earnest. "Want to stay here tonight?"

I nodded fervently. "Please."

A few hours later, right before losing consciousness on Gilli's couch, I reached up to check on my amulet, as I often did, then down to touch the red string tied around my wrist, the one my grandmother had given me before I left home. The one offering protection from demons. The one old story spinners said would fall off when you were about to meet your husband.

It was gone.

THREE

"THIS IS FINE," I MUTTERED THE NEXT MORNING, RETURNING to my rooms after Gilli and Jelan left for class. "I'm so fine. No demons anywhere."

This evening, I would demon-proof the place, but for now, I didn't even have time to shower if I wanted both to eat breakfast and to run through my Intro to Theurgy and Thaumaturgy Theory exam flash cards again. I rubbed neshem oil on the charaktêres on my comb, muttered the spell, then raked the teeth through my greasy curls. It restored them to halfway decent shape. As I braided my hair back into one thick plait—no time for anything else—I glanced out my window at the wind flag raised on the weather pole. Tan with white stripes: a medium-strength dry wind from the west. The clouds swirled slightly too vibrant a pink against the blue sky, making me frown. Though I'd only been in Talum a month, I'd noticed the strangeness of the winds and weather, and the whole student body talked nonstop about how something must be off with the magic that governed the natural world.

I tried not to think about it, nor about my missing bracelet. It wasn't as though red string would have kept the demon away when everything else failed. And the silly old story about meeting your husband after losing your bracelet didn't mean anything. Grandma said when she'd met Grandpa, she'd yanked her string off, marched up to him, then acted shocked to find it gone. You made your own destiny.

It just shook me up, that was all.

Fully dressed, I stepped out of my bedroom—and found Daziel sitting on the sofa, once more reading *A Household Guide to Demons*, his red salamander resting on his shoulder.

"No!" I cried, half-inclined to stomp my foot. I was infuriated instead of scared—hard to be alarmed by a boy reading a book with a friendly-looking lizard.

But he had promised to leave me alone.

Daziel looked up. His face was just as strange as yesterday—the planes and angles a little too sharp, the pure blackness of his eyes unnerving. But it was impossible to deny how strikingly handsome he was, too, even if it unsettled me. "Good morning."

I supposed this was why you were supposed to ward against demons—they were notoriously difficult to get rid of. "You can't be here." I pulled on my boots and started lacing them up. "You promised to leave."

"I didn't specify for how long."

I grabbed my blazer off the hook, exasperated. This was like arguing with my youngest sister, Selah, who thought arguments were about semantics instead of the heart of the matter. "I take it you're a law student, then."

He answered my snipe as though I'd been serious. "Shedim study the laws, but that isn't my specialty."

"What's your specialty, irritating people?" I stomped into the hall.

Daziel followed me to the stairs and down, his footsteps unnervingly light. "I can carry your bag."

I clutched it tighter. No way I was handing over my possessions, no matter how much they weighed. Also, I didn't want to give him a reason to feel less guilty about being a pain. "No. It's mine."

"It looks heavy."

"I carry it every day. It's fine."

He narrowed his eyes. Apparently I'd finally managed to annoy him. "Are you always this unaccepting of help?"

"Are you always this hard to get rid of?"

As we reached the third-floor landing, the door to the stairwell swung open. I froze. Oh no. How was I supposed to explain a demon walking down the stairs with me at seven thirty in the morning?

Élodie stepped out. She glanced up, her composed expression morphing into one of abject surprise and, worse, alarm. Her mouth fell open. "Naomi . . . ?"

I grimaced. "Hey."

"Um—who—I mean—" She swallowed and schooled her expression. Apparently, Élodie, unlike me, had mastered politeness in unexpected situations. This made me grumpy. "Honored to meet you. I'm Élodie bat Amit."

"One of Naomi's friends?" Daziel bowed. "The honor is mine."

Élodie's gaze flickered to me, her shock deepening, I expected, at the logical conclusion that this demon was my betrothed. Unexpectedly, satisfaction flared through me. While boys might buy my excuse, girls saw through it. Élodie and Birra definitely knew I'd made everything up. *You know*, Birra had said pityingly, after I turned down a boy in our Intro to Household Magic class, *you don't have to lie. Henri's a great guy, and it's not like you're going to get anyone better. Especially not* . . . She'd looked me up and down, as though my very being made the reason self-evident. *Well, you know.*

Yet now I'd provided incontestable proof of a demon betrothed. And while humans were wary of demons, we were also fascinated by them—they were, after all, powerful, magical beings. Catching the attention of one might be foolhardy but also undeniably thrilling.

Still, much as I liked showing Élodie up, I should swallow my pride and ask for her help. She was one of the best spellcasters in our year. I took a deep breath. Dad always said the sooner you admitted your mistake, the sooner you could move on.

Then Élodie smiled at Daziel. "It's so funny, no one believed Naomi when she said she was betrothed to a demon. But here you are!"

My pride snapped into place. I couldn't do it. Daziel seemed more nuisance than danger, and Élodie was more annoying still. "Here we are," I said shortly. "Excuse us. We're running late."

Daziel followed me, leaving, no doubt, a bewildered Élodie behind. Madame Hadar wasn't behind her desk in the entranceway, so I couldn't ask her for help; plus, I didn't want to with Élodie in earshot. Frustrated, I slammed my shoulder into Testylier House's door to open it against the winds.

Dad said the winds hadn't been like this when he grew up, but in the last few years they'd increased in ferocity. Even without the wind flags, you could tell the direction they came from by their scents: The northern wind carried marshy loam and sea salt from the delta; the east wind, the forests; the west, the faintest hint of the wilderness. The south required no gentle hints—when the southern winds blew, they carried rain and thunder and lightning. There were other winds, too—the harsh Trio Winds of winter; the dry Maestril of spring; the rare Corisoc, which covered everything in a layer of fine red dust from the southern deserts. And while I found their wild strength intoxicating, it definitely wasn't normal.

"Where are we going?" Daziel asked. The salamander poked his head out of Daziel's shirt, his small black tongue darting out as though he could taste the winds.

"The boulangerie. Then school." If Daziel was here because he thought we were affianced, maybe the best way to get rid of him was to be blunt. "Look, I'm sorry, but I'm breaking up with you."

"What?" He stopped in his tracks. Walkers parted around us—a pair of middle-aged women with pumping arms, a pack of schoolchildren in matching uniforms, a businessman who gave us a dirty look, then stumbled back when he realized what Daziel was. "You're what?"

"I'm dumping you. I'm ending our betrothal."

Daziel swallowed and blinked rapidly. He sounded, of all things, lost and a little wounded. "Why? Have I offended you?"

"You did break into my rooms." This was absurd. I refused to feel bad for having boundaries. I started walking again, and he fell in beside me. "It wasn't a real betrothal. We don't even know each other."

He made a frustrated sound. "That's what the betrothal period is for. And I do know you. Your name is Naomi bat Yardena. You're from the Naphtali tribe, near Foillefw." I didn't recognize the word; I wondered if it was a demon name for the high plains near my village. "My name is Daziel, son of Cathmeus, son of Khasmodai. I am apprenticed to the stone-garden keepers."

"What does that mean?"

"I tend rocks."

"Sounds . . . enthralling." We passed a stone wall draped with bougainvillea. The flowers matched the pink clouds so unnervingly I almost tripped, certain they'd been red yesterday. Maybe I'd been mistaken—or maybe magic was getting even stranger in Talum.

He gave me a wry smile that transcended species. "Yes, I feel similarly."

I recognized the droll, exasperated note in his voice—it reminded me of my own when I'd told my parents how badly I wanted to see the world beyond our village. "Is that why you're here? You're bored. You somehow heard me say your name, and you were like, 'Great excuse. Peace out, wilderness.' How old are you?"

He set his jaw mulishly, like I'd challenged his brilliant plan. "I have eighteen winters. I've almost reached my majority."

My age, then. I felt a touch of sympathy, though not enough to let myself get dragged into his escape plans. "Don't you have somewhere else to go? What are you going to do here—follow me everywhere?"

"We can explore the city." He sounded hopeful. "There's supposed to be dancing and opera and food enveloped in boiling oil."

Had he never tasted donuts, or falafel, or fries? Now I genuinely felt bad for him. And I did yearn to explore the rest of Talum, since so far, I'd barely left the Scholars' Quarter. But I imagined exploring it with a demon would cause chaos. "I have school."

We reached the bakery, where a long line snaked out the door. When we joined the end, the customers shot Daziel alarmed looks—notable, since Talumizans made a big deal of never being surprised by anything. Once I saw the grand duke's cousin on her way to the opera, and all my friends from outside Talum gaped, while the city kids acted almost sick with ennui.

I noticed they could precisely describe her outfit later, though.

"I don't mind school," Daziel said cheerfully. "At home, we study constantly. I am considered the top of the lykeion."

"Cool," I said. "Congrats. Isn't your family going to miss you?"

"I have seven brothers and six sisters. It will be some time before they notice my absence."

And I'd thought having three sisters was a lot. "That's . . . a lot of siblings."

Another wry smile. "I am aware."

We reached the front of the line. A display of mouthwatering pastries greeted us—lemon tartlets with tightly clustered raspberries, chocolate-glazed éclairs, canelés with caramelized crusts. Unfortunately, they'd all set me back far too dearly, so I stuck with the order within my student budget. "A black coffee, please. And a demi baguette."

"I, too, will have a black coffee and a demi baguette," Daziel said. He peered at the case and pointed. "Also, these seven pastries."

"What?" Choked amusement caught in my throat. If this had been happening to anyone but me, I'd have found it hilarious, but as it was, I couldn't decide if Daziel's comical demeanor outweighed the preposterous situation. "You don't need seven pastries."

"I do." He sounded deadly serious. "This one has chocolate, and this one has nuts, and this one has fruit. It is necessary."

The server bagged Daziel's seven pastries, apparently more willing to face my wrath than a demon's. Still—"I can't afford to buy you seven pastries."

The server placed our coffees and baguettes next to the large white pastry bag. Daziel took everything but one coffee and smiled at me. "It's all right. We do not need to pay."

"Uh, yes, we do."

"No, we don't."

"No, you don't," the server said dreamily.

I gaped at her, then reluctantly smacked a few bills down and grabbed my coffee before running after Daziel. "You can't *bespell* people."

"I didn't." Daziel lifted his baguette, and the salamander nibbled on the corner. "I spoke. Am I not allowed to speak?"

"No." I grabbed my own baguette from him and took an angry bite, breaking through the flaky crust into yeasty, warm crumb. "No speaking."

He sighed again, mournful. "If that is what you wish."

Above us, in their sandstone tower, city bells started ringing the quarter-to melody. I took a long sip of coffee, warming against the morning chill, and I picked up my pace. So did Daziel, perfectly serene in his light jog, as though he was merely taking long steps. "Why are we running?"

So much for not talking. "I'm late. Professor Haik is a stickler; he doesn't allow you to reschedule exams unless you submit a request in advance."

"What if you're sick?"

"Don't be sick."

We arrived at the land bridge. Students and horses and neshem-powered carriages crammed the avenue over the water. I led the way at a brisk clip, winding between bulkier, slower groups.

We were halfway before we got stuck, trapped behind a delivery cart piled high with crates of oranges and lemons, and hemmed in by a pack of schoolchildren and their beleaguered teachers, who were apparently taking them on a field trip to the Lyceum.

I heard the cawing first. It came in a wave, a loud, shrieking mass of noise, underscored by asynchronous flapping. In confusion, I—and everyone else—looked up. From the east, sweeping over and down from Talum's four hills, came a clamoring, jarring cloud, like a blanket pulled across the sky.

At first, I couldn't parse the horde above me. Then I realized it was a thousand—ten thousand, a hundred thousand?—birds, flying above and below each other, enough layers to block out the daylight. Their wings beat in a massive undulating patchwork. All types: sparrows and eagles, hummingbirds and falcons. They shrieked and cawed, their volume as varied as their type, trills and hoots and chirps and harsh *kak-kak-kak*s. It made me think of a war cry. Or a warning.

As they dove closer, people shrieked, crouching low and holding bags over their heads. Horses reared, adding unhappy neighs to the cacophony, and people scrambled away from their hooves. Someone tripped into me, and I lost balance, my coffee jostled out of my grip, the precious liquid arcing away as I fell. I barely got out a hand to keep my face from smashing into the pavement. Pain sliced through my palm and jarred up my arm. I lay there, stunned, then rolled over to watch the shadow above beating with a hundred thousand wings.

Of all the unsettling, magic-touched things I'd seen in Talum, this was the strangest. I couldn't imagine it boded well.

Then the birds were gone, leaving disarray behind. The kids—eight, nine years old—screamed and ducked away from the teachers, who tried to wrangle them to safety. A horse kicked dangerously at the air. The cart harnessed to it began to tip, the fruit inside spilling from their crates to the ground.

Daziel ran in to help, grabbing the horse by the back of its neck and pulling it down to all fours. He said something, and the horse went very still, only its flaring nostrils indicating any discomfort. I staggered upright and grabbed the cart edge to stabilize it, as a pair of hip-high children stared at me with large, unblinking eyes. A few oranges rolled between their feet.

I looked over at Daziel, surprised. I wouldn't have expected a wild demon to help calm the chaos—but maybe I was being unfair.

Around us, people rose from crouches. Clothes were tugged back into place; items from spilled rucksacks gathered. Daziel released the horse and wove his way through the crowd, passing children and students and merchants until he'd reached the edge of the land bridge, where the breakwater fell several yards into the river. He stood ramrod straight, staring at the cloud as it dwindled on the horizon. His salamander crept up to his shoulder and made distressed squeaks.

With one finger, Daziel absently stroked the salamander's spine, calming him. "You all right, Paz?"

The salamander nodded.

Okay, so the salamander could understand us. Or him. Good to know. Not something to find unnerving at all.

"What's going on?" My voice trembled, which I disliked. I was used to being steady and capable, to being the one who reassured my younger siblings. "What happened?"

Daziel held his body with a particular stillness, like a cat watching a bauble on a string, trying to decide when to pounce. "The birds have left the city of Talum."

"What do you mean?" I could hear the agitation in my voice and tried to tamp it down. "For how long? *All* the birds?"

"I don't know," he said. "It's not good."

"I didn't think it was." My tone came out worried instead of pithy. "What's going on? Is this—are you connected to this?"

"No," he said, voice troubled. "But I don't like it." He focused on me and frowned. "You're hurt."

I followed his gaze and realized my hand was scraped and bloody from my fall. Tiny pebbles had embedded themselves in my skin, and a jagged cut crossed my palm. "Ew."

"Let me see." He reached out, and I realized he wanted me to put my own hand within his black talons. I hesitated. He was a demon, unreasonable and unpredictable. But he'd calmed the horse, protecting children he had no reason to care about. He was a demon, but he was also a boy who pouted and wanted an unreasonable number of pastries and to see the world. A stranger, but maybe no stranger than the boys I'd met at school.

I placed my hand in his.

He sandwiched my hand between his, firm, intimate. An itch grew around the stinging cut. I tried to pull away, but Daziel was unmovable. Liquid heat replaced the itch, like water from a hot shower. The cut became hotter and hotter until all sensation vanished, and I felt fine again. I pulled my hand out from his, and the cut was gone.

"Neat trick," I said, unnerved. I'd never seen magic done without letters or speech. "Thanks."

Daziel tilted his head, and I realized he'd clocked my alarm when his brow furrowed. He rummaged in his satchel and pulled out the white bakery bag, from which he extracted a croissant with almond slivers. He held it out, and there was something hopeful and tentative about the gesture. "Have a pastry?"

The kindness of the offer, of comfort in the form of food, softened me. "Can I have a chocolate one?"

Nodding, he replaced the almond and extended another with two bars of chocolate folded into the buttery dough.

I stuffed half the croissant in my mouth and immediately felt better. Now what? Were a demon visitor and a weird surge of birds excuses for missing my test? Probably not. "Come on," I said, and we were off, sprinting across the rest of the land bridge and into the wide, open campus of the fabled Lyceum. I led him past manicured lawns and fountains, down paths lined by pillared buildings and olive trees. I ignored the students staring at Daziel as the bells began to toll.

I reached the building where my Theory class took place, pounding up the stairwell, Daziel right behind me. I careened around a corner so fast someone yelled. The ninth bell had tolled out its final long, indomitable note when I burst, panting, into the stadium-style lecture hall. The other students—all forty-nine—turned toward the noise from their seats.

I checked if they were staring at Daziel, but when I looked behind me, the demon was gone.

FOUR

ADIFFERENT STUDENT MIGHT HAVE INTERRUPTED THE exam and declared, "I am beset by a demon, and I cannot get rid of him."

Not me. Daziel was gone, and so I'd consider the problem of him solved for now; if I'd learned anything since arriving at the Lyceum, it was I could only juggle what was immediately in front of me. Right now, I needed to get through this test. My scholarship depended on maintaining high grades, and Theory was my hardest class.

Alongside my cryptography seminar, I was taking six classes—half of them language courses, and then the three classes required for every first-year: Intro to Theurgy and Thaumaturgy Theory, Intro to Household Magics, and Intro to Spellwriting.

Everyone in Ena-Cinnai used spells, but not everyone knew how to tweak them or write new ones. Letterform magic required writing or carving charaktêres into objects, then painting the charaktêres with neshem oil—a strange, shimmering substance made from crystals mined in the caves beneath the city and the mountains of the south—and reciting the words out loud. I'd seen spells for everything from floating heavy materials to changing your shoes' color. You could buy window shades with a spell pre-carved to make them open when the sun arrived or hand warmers with a spell ready to activate to protect against chilly nights.

The best place to learn to write new spells was the Lyceum, which most students attended for two or three years. Students took their learnings home, or to an apprenticeship, or into more specialized education. In Intro to Spellwriting, we learned the three major spell languages, and in Intro to Theurgy and Thaumaturgy Theory, the theory behind each.

After the exam, I exited warily, half expecting Daziel to appear in the hall. When he didn't, I let out a sigh of relief and headed to my next classes. I had Keft I, the study of a hieroglyphic language from before the twelve tribes joined together, then Old Cinnaian, the precursor to modern Ena-Cinnaian.

I did my best to stay focused, but a poke in the back of my shoulder distracted me from Professor Isserlis's lecture. "Hey, Bat Yardena," someone whispered as Isserlis went on about the construct state of possessive nouns in Old Cinnaian. I turned to see Noam Dimkov holding a pencil. "I heard there was a demon with you this morning."

Next to him, two girls watched with avaricious expressions. Gossip flowed at the Lyceum as steadily as the Lersach, and anything fresh spread like wildfire.

"And?" I whispered back.

"How come you know a demon?" he asked.

One of the girls leaned forward—Ami or Ani. We only had this class together, and we'd never spoken. "I heard you're betrothed."

"Something to share with the class?" Professor Isserlis cut in. Relieved, I faced front.

Unfortunately, Noam decided this *was* worth sharing with the class. "Bat Yardena's boyfriend is in town. He's a demon."

Great. Perfect. I noticed Ephraim listening from a few rows over and forced a smile. "Yup."

Professor Isserlis squinted like she wasn't sure what to do. I could practically see the thoughts running through her mind: Humans didn't date demons. But I was from the distant high plains, and who knew what people did there? Also, students were untrustworthy, and we could be pulling an elaborate prank or using "demon" as slang.

She decided, as so many adults did, to ignore us. "How . . . open. Perhaps you should discuss it on your own time. As I was saying, this differs from modern Ena-Cinnaian's use of the construct state because instead of changing the end of a noun, we usually add a preposition. Though as you can see on page 104, this is not always the case . . ."

WHEN CLASS ENDED, I hurried out, hoping to escape more questions. The breeze was cool as I crossed the Linguistics Quad. Morning glories added a splash of purple to the white marble buildings rearing against a painfully blue sky. Something felt off, though, and it took me a moment to figure out what: There were no warblers, no terns, no birds of any kind.

Eerie.

Dozens of food stalls lined the main lunch courtyard. Back home, I'd mostly eaten local food: beans and barley, artichokes and turnips, berries and mint. A few shops in Port Naborre catered to sailors from the Taro Islands, the first land you reached when sailing east—they had rich rice dishes with seafood and cold soups made from blended vegetables. Otherwise, I hadn't tried much from beyond Ena-Cinnai. The variety of food in Talum had thrilled me: stews with spices I'd never tasted, fruits I'd never heard of. Today I bought a carton of cold sesame noodles with shredded cucumbers and carrots, then made my way toward the corner where my friends usually sat.

My attention caught on Daziel waving his arms from an otherwise empty table. Of course. The surrounding tables were also empty, but beyond those students gathered. People craned their necks and whispered. Apparently the vaunted Talumizan indifference only went so far.

"Naomi!" Daziel called, as though maybe his waving and existence had been inconspicuous. "Over here!"

I made my way over, grumpy. I could find a professor and make a fuss, ask them to help me banish him—and thereby annihilate my tale of a demon betrothed. Or . . . I could try to pretend in public this was normal and Daziel *was* my betrothed. Then I could banish him later. It would strengthen my ruse so completely no one would ever bother me about meeting my aunt again.

Trying to act nonchalant, I carried my noodles to Daziel's table. I eyed the gyro he ate as I sat. He had a whole spread of food lined up: breaded mushrooms, fries, fruit salad, and a tiny cake. "How did you pay for these?"

He took a huge bite of the gyro, tzatziki smearing across his face, and gave me a wide-eyed shrug.

"You're supposed to give them money! After you order but before you take the food."

"I *know* how money works," he said haughtily. But he did peer very closely at the coins I pulled out.

Once more, I wasn't sure whether to be amused or annoyed.

But the situation was ridiculous, and the more I watched Daziel cover himself with tzatziki, the more hilarious it became. My shoulders started quaking, and then laughter burst out. I folded my arms on the table and hid my face in them, shaking with amusement.

"Are you all right?" Daziel sounded genuinely concerned.

"Who's to say." I couldn't stop laughing. I'd done this to myself. No—my aunt had! No, I would blame the School of Government boys, so obsessed with meeting a member of the Sanhedrin that they'd driven me to this.

"Oh my god."

I lifted my head at Leah's voice. My friend stood a few feet away, her braids coiled around her head, her mouth parted.

I smiled weakly. "Hey."

Daziel beamed at Leah. "Hello. I'm Daziel, Naomi's betrothed."

Leah came from one of the many silk farms lining the shores of the Lersach River, so I hoped she'd be less nervous than city folk about demons. Sure enough, she dropped down beside me without hesitating, fixing her gaze on Daziel as she pulled her lunch from her satchel. "What's happening?"

I offered a wry smile. "I've made a terrible mistake. I've summoned a demon, and I can't get rid of him."

She unpacked a neat box filled with small bites and dipping sauces. "Explain."

I tried my best. Daziel pouted as I did, which left him looking particularly boyish. His shimmer, I realized, had lessened, though not enough anyone would mistake him for human.

"What kind of demon are you?" Leah asked him.

"The best kind." Daziel flashed her a smile full of sharp teeth.

There were between three and twelve types of demons—scholars couldn't seem to agree. But essentially, there were (1) the mazzikin, (2) wild demons, and (3) high demons. The mazzikin were small spirits: thousands of invisible creatures up to no good, bound to make you trip or give you zits or infiltrate your bathrooms (bathrooms were always getting infested with mazzikin). I'd dealt with their symptoms plenty of times back home.

There were high demons, rare as mazzikin were numerous. They ruled over the rest and struck treaties with humans; they were said to look human, too, save more beautiful and terrifying.

Then there were wild demons. The common citizens, if you would, able to shape-shift into human form but not as well as high demons. Some were cruel, some helpful, some morally ambivalent. They were mischievous and pesky and confusing. Daziel's black eyes and talons, the faded feather pattern on his skin, made it clear he was a wild demon—but whether he belonged to a specific type was beyond me.

Gilli and Jelan arrived before Leah could press further, Jelan focusing on Daziel as she sat. She wore her customary black beneath her red School of Engineering blazer. "He's still here."

"I am," Daziel agreed. "Hello again, Naomi's friends."

"We should maybe tell a professor?" Gilli said nervously. As always, I was impressed by Gilli's delicate outfit, this time a lacy pink dress and matching headband. Gilli was one of the few girls I knew who bothered to sew weights into dress hems instead of wearing pants. Her ensemble, paired with her yellow School of Science blazer—Gilli was training to be a healer—was springlike.

I shook my head. "I'd rather not make a fuss. I'll try again to-night, after classes. It might be silly," I added, flushing, "but I don't want Ephraim and the others to figure out I was lying."

"We can come over around eight and help," Jelan said in her low, steady voice as she brushed neshem oil over her clay pot containing veggie chili, which would heat the bowl and thus her lunch. She activated the spell in the same calm tones.

I felt bad about taking up their time. "You don't have to—"

"Of course we do," Leah said. "That's what friends are for."

AFTER LUNCH—THROUGH WHICH DAZIEL moped performatively as the rest of us discussed potential banishment strategies—Daziel followed me across campus. Much of the Lyceum had been built in the last three hundred years, but not all. A thousand years ago, Talumizans constructed the Keep as a defensive outlook along the peninsula's west coast. The walls were thick, the interior cool, and the views insurmountable. It had six floors, each a single room, and belonged to the linguistics department in the School of Humanities.

My thighs burned as I spiraled up. No one had told me moving to Talum would mean quite so many hills and stairs. Stepping off on the fifth floor, we entered a room where narrow, tall windows let in light. Books packed the shelves between them. Tables filled the center of the room, and a few chairs lined the edges. It was cozy but not cramped; the high ceiling made it feel larger than the square footage. From one window, you could see the hills of the city rising to the east, while the other three windows looked out on the river. This was my favorite place in the entire

Lyceum—and the materials within were the reason I'd applied here in the first place.

"No distractions," I warned Daziel. "I have to concentrate."

He flashed a sharp smile. "Am I distracting? I'm flattered."

"You weren't supposed to be." I looked away, flushed. Was he flirting? I didn't know how to flirt with humans, let alone demons. Everyone back home felt like siblings, and if any local boys had been attracted to anyone, it was always my sister Adina. The people who'd shown interest in Talum only wanted my aunt's attention.

Not that I was developing a complex or anything.

"What are you working on?" Daziel looked at the scroll fragments covering the tables. Paz emerged and hopped from Daziel's shoulder to one of the bookcases and began scampering about, chirping excitedly.

It made me smile. "We're trying to reconstruct old scrolls."

"Hm?"

I pulled out a drawer below the closest table, showing him fragments of parchment held between glass plates. "These were found in spelled urns in the genizah at Zerach. Professor Altschuler went on an expedition there three years ago. He and a few colleagues have been trying to put the scrolls together ever since." I'd read about the expedition in the news and had followed the story ever since. When I realized that the lead scholar worked here, at the Lyceum, I'd applied immediately and won a scholarship to assist with the translation.

Daziel bent to study the fragments. "What's the language— Old Cinnaian?"

"Nope. We call it Language X, and we think it was the language spoken here before Old Cinnaian—maybe two, three thousand years ago. None of the characters are familiar, and until we can piece the fragments together, it's tricky to make calls about grammar and syntax. It could be encoded, or spelled so we can't read it. And it's possible not all the fragments are here—some might have decayed or been buried elsewhere—so even if we can decipher the language, we might not be able to read the text. But we're going to try."

Daziel trailed a finger over the glass, one black talon coming to a stop under a fragment with a spiral character. "You're doing it all yourself?"

"Professor Altschuler has four students and some staff. I work on this three days a week, and there's a weekly seminar. He's given me a reading course to get up to snuff on different cryptography methods. I don't suppose you recognize the characters?"

He bent over, looking closely at the whirls and dots. Regret colored his voice when he answered. "No. I'm sorry. I can understand living languages, but this one is well and truly dead."

I waved it off, trying to swallow my disappointment. "It'd be too much of a break if you knew them."

"How are you trying to put it together?"

I touched one of the fragments on the tabletop. "See these? They aren't the actual fragments—those are in the glass plates. We created replicas. This way, we can rearrange them without touching the fragile originals. We try spells, of course, but it's just as likely we'll put the pieces together through manual labor."

"I'm exhausted just listening to you."

I laughed. "It's fun. It's like a jigsaw puzzle."

I'd always loved puzzles, like I'd always loved languages—the satisfaction of putting pieces together intoxicated me. Deciphering an unknown language would be the grandest puzzle of all. But it would also be the hardest, like doing a jigsaw puzzle without an image to guide you.

The art of deciphering an unknown language is not an easy one, Professor Altschuler had said when I'd first arrived in his office. He was so tall and so thin, it stretched one's belief, with thick hair and salt-and-pepper scruff. *We know nothing about the characters, not whether they're ideograms or have phonetic values or a third option we've not yet dreamed of.*

I hadn't known half the things he mentioned, but I'd learned. Ideograms referred to symbols representing ideas or concepts—like a pig or a sheaf of wheat—and phonetic values meant symbols signified a sound, like in most modern alphabets. I learned the first steps we'd take after putting the scrolls together—how we'd analyze every character, each word, and their placement and frequency. I wanted to know everything. I wanted to have the keys to unlock this ancient secret. I wanted to be the person to turn said key.

"Why do you care so much?" Daziel asked. "You don't know what's in the scrolls, do you?"

My parents had asked me the same question, baffled and frustrated by my fixation. I struggled to explain. "There's knowledge hidden here. History. We don't know what, but it might tell us about a lost civilization, our ancestors—and the feat itself! Solving this would be incredible." Flushing, I turned back to the scraps, worried I'd embarrassed myself by being too enthusiastic.

"Interesting." Daziel sounded thoughtful. I looked up, unsure what he meant. "What you're doing takes determination and perseverance. I'm impressed."

I ducked my head. "We'll see. I've only been at this a month."

He flashed me a smile, sharp and bright. "Take the compliment, yonati."

I paused at the endearment.

And I remembered something my father had told me once—to be careful in the city of Talum, for there were many kinds of danger.

FIVE

EVEN WITH MY FRIENDS' HELP, I FAILED TO BANISH DAZIEL.

"We could go to Madame Hadar," Jelan suggested after three hours of trying. Well, Jelan, Leah, and I had tried—Gilli had gotten distracted when Daziel asked her to show him how to crochet. Admittedly, teaching someone to crochet looked more fun than trying to banish them.

We'd removed all the mirrors from my rooms. We'd tried capturing Daziel via incantation bowl. I threw a thrift market ring at him, based on lore that rings could capture demons. He caught it and slid it on, smiling. I even spat at him, which was a horrible experience for everyone involved.

"It's fine," I said wearily. We were in my living room. Leah, Jelan, and I were exhausted, while Gilli and Daziel chattered about crochet hooks. "I can go to a professor or a rabbi tomorrow. I think if I get something written up, it'll dissolve the supposed betrothal."

"You can sleep in my room tonight," Leah offered.

"Thanks," I said. "Give me a minute to get my stuff, and I'll come over."

After the girls left, Daziel shot me an extremely miffed look. Which was unfair, given *I* should be miffed by his continued presence. I ignored him, stuffing items into my tote.

A minute later, someone knocked. I went to the door, expecting one of my floormates had forgotten something. When I opened it, Élodie and Birra stood there.

My heart sank. I didn't have the energy to deal with them now, not after a day as long as a week.

"Hi," I said warily, opening the door a scant sliver.

Which didn't prevent Daziel from popping up behind me. "Hello."

Sighing, I opened the door wider and waited for the girls to make up an excuse about why they'd come. They didn't bother. Élodie nudged Birra, who gaped at Daziel.

"We wanted to introduce ourselves properly," Élodie said, ignoring me in favor of Daziel. "And welcome you to Testylier House."

He's leaving, I wanted to say, but I swallowed the words.

Birra managed a polite greeting too, though it clearly pained her. Then, unable to resist, she shot out, "You're not allowed to have boys in your rooms after visiting hours."

My eyes narrowed. Feeling petty and knowing this was a bad idea, I said, "If you're affianced, you are."

"True." Élodie widened her eyes with false innocence. "Where's your ring?"

Daziel held up his hand, surprising all of us. The ring I'd thrown at him earlier—a cheap band set with colored glass— circled his middle finger, looking wildly out of place next to the signet ring on his pointer finger. The massive stone there definitely wasn't glass.

"That doesn't look like an engagement ring," Birra said accusingly when Daziel pointed to mine.

"It's the ring my beloved gave me," Daziel said. "And thus I treasure it."

Now the girls looked at me like I gave horrible gifts. I glared at Daziel. I hadn't been trying to *give* him the ring, I'd been trying to *banish* him.

Birra looked at my hand. "You're not wearing a ring."

"We made a formal verbal affirmation," Daziel said. "Then we exchanged gifts symbolizing our love, upon the acceptance of which the betrothal is confirmed. The ring came from Naomi. My gift was different."

"What, like pearls?" Élodie frowned thoughtfully. "Or a pome-granate?"

I'd forgotten about the blasted pomegranate.

I wanted to curse. I even *knew*, sort of, that pomegranates were associated with love and fertility, but like a secondary definition. Mostly I thought of them as symbols of righteous order.

"Yes." Daziel bared his teeth. "Precisely."

"If you guys don't mind," I said tightly, trying to keep my seething under the surface, "Daziel and I have to talk."

Birra scowled. "Did you tell Madame Hadar? Even if you *are* betrothed, you have to clear things with her. And fill out a form."

"I'm working on it."

"Hmph," she said, and I had no doubt she'd be on her way to Madame Hadar's momentarily.

I closed the door, then pulled Daziel by his arm into my bed-room as a safeguard against eavesdroppers. Closing my door, I whirled on Daziel. "You tricked me."

"I'm honored you've invited me into your chamber." His gaze landed on a bra lying on the floor. His mouth twitched, making me very aware he was a teenage boy.

I shoved the bra in a drawer, my cheeks hot. "You *knew* I didn't know what the pomegranate meant."

His black gaze snapped back to mine. "You shouldn't have accepted it, then."

My mouth fell open. "Excuse me, *you're* the one who tricked me into it!"

He arched his brows. "Is it a trick if I asked and you accepted?"

I glared at him. He was infuriating. "Yes. It is."

I stomped out of my rooms, grabbing *A Household Guide to Demons* on the way. Daziel certainly didn't need it, except for a laugh.

"Good night," he said behind me, sounding peeved. As though he thought I was being rude and wanted to make a point of his own good manners.

I refused to let him think he had better manners than me. "Good night," I snapped back. Unfortunately, slamming the door as I left probably undermined my attempt to be polite.

Leah made me up a bed on the sofa, since our own were too small to share unless you were as in love as Jelan and Gilli. After she went to bed, I flipped through the book my mother had given me, rereading sections as though they'd offer more help the second time around. I paged through the chapter on rings, my gaze catching on a footnote I'd skimmed over before: *In Levin's* A Case for the Augmentative Power of Artifacts, *he argues a ring's ability to affect a demon is directly linked to the quality and craftsmanship of the ring itself, refracted and amplified by material and maker's skill . . .*

I considered this. I'd never heard of any such thing, but I'd only been at the Lyceum a month. Perhaps a fancier ring would do a better job at banishing Daziel?

The memory of Daziel holding up his hand flashed in my mind. Next to my cheap band had been a heavy signet ring.

It wouldn't be easy to obtain the ring, then carve it with any sort of spell. But Daziel might be asleep right now; Leah definitely was, from her tragically loud snores. If there was ever a moment to slip off someone's ring, it would be when they were unconscious.

Taking a deep breath, I padded to Leah's door, opening it slowly so the hinges wouldn't creak. I slipped across the hall, pausing outside my own door. No light spilled from beneath, and when I pressed my ear close, I heard only silence.

Okay. Here went nothing.

Slowly, pulse pounding in my ears and anxiety turning my hands sweaty, I slid my key into the lock and pulled the door open with the carefulness of a surgeon. The living room was dark, and I closed the door quickly, breathing as quietly as possible as my eyes adjusted. Moonlight spilled in, soft and silver.

Daziel lay curled up in a nest of blankets on the floor. Smoke rings floated up from his nostrils, carrying the scent of scorched dust.

I crept to his side, my fearful nerves growing as I crouched low. He breathed slowly, slower than a human. Paz rested on his chest, rising and falling.

His hand with the ring lay flung out to his side. His fingers, long and talon-tipped, curled up slightly in sleep.

I twisted the ring, ever so slowly, trying to slide it with the least amount of friction up to his knuckle. It stuck there, and my racing heart felt like it might explode. I wasn't cut out for this. My gaze flicked to his to make sure he was still asleep.

Daziel stared back at me unblinking.

I yelped and stumbled back. Surprise and sharp dismay burned through me. He was, after all, a demon, and I didn't know how he would react.

He sat up in one sinuous twist. "If you're so desperate for a ring from me, yonati, you have only to ask."

"I—no," I said, my mortification edged with fear. While Daziel during the day was friendly and wide-eyed, Daziel angry was the deepest shadows of night.

He pulled the ring off his finger and offered it to me in one smooth movement. His eyes were almost more red than black, his voice low and hard, and I remembered demons were creatures of fire and ash. "Put it on if you want it so badly. We can say the vows right here. I'm sure there's no other reason you'd attempt to take my seal from my hand."

Something crackled through me, making my hairs stand straight. I recognized embarrassment and discomfort and maybe a hint of alarm, but something else too, a distinct awareness of how intensely he'd focused on me. In the soft moonlight he looked un-nervingly beautiful, and a hot and heady current swirled through my body. I swallowed and straightened, stuttering slightly. "N-no. I don't want that. I just don't know how to make you leave!"

At my outburst, he nodded and leaned back a bit, putting more space between us as he slid his ring back on. Then he tossed a ball of light into the air, which increased in brightness until it illuminated the room as well as any lamp. For a minute we regarded each other in a troubled détente, him in his rumpled nightshirt and with an unruly mess of curls, me in an overlarge sweater, my hair unbraided.

Finally, Daziel spoke, much calmer than before, though he managed to sound both wounded and offended. Not unlike my sister Adina when I'd told her she had to do the same number of chores as everyone else. "I don't know why you're so set on banishment. You've been telling everyone about me for weeks, but now that I'm here, you're mad."

I couldn't believe I had to explain this. "You're not supposed to exist. The *idea* of you existing made my life easier. You actually existing doesn't."

He frowned. "How did the idea of me make your life easier?"

My head fell back against the sofa. I felt exhausted now, the rush of fear and heat draining away. "Government School boys kept asking me out, hoping to meet my aunt. A fake betrothed stopped them."

"A real betrothed will be even more effective, then."

I made a face. "Having a demon infesting my rooms isn't the right trade-off for peace."

He perked up. "You'd like to negotiate a different trade?"

"Nope." I drew back, wary. "You're not supposed to make deals with demons."

"Why not? You 'invented' me to make your life easier. Let me. I can keep unwanted suitors at bay. I can even help with your schoolwork. You study languages, yes? I might not understand the scrolls, but I understand living languages. You study those as well."

The offer was surprisingly good. I'd done study sessions with my classmates, but since none of us truly grasped the languages we were learning, we often ended as confused as we'd started. A fluent Keft or Tzorybia speaker would make an excellent tutor.

Still. He was a stranger and a demon. "No bargains. No deals. I'm no fool."

"No fun, either," he muttered, sounding aggrieved. He blew out a breath, twisting the rings on his fingers. When he caught me watching, he separated his hands quickly. I wondered if he'd been chastised as a child for hand-wringing. "Look. Did you always know you'd attend the Lyceum?"

Growing up, I'd dreamed of leaving home the way a human in the desert dreams of water, the way a trapped bird dreams of the open sky. But I hadn't expected anything. I shook my head. "If I hadn't gotten my scholarship, I doubt I'd have left." My father was a courier, my mother a seamstress, and my grandmother harvested saffron from crocuses. I'd probably have wound up helping one of them.

He nodded. "I always wanted to travel—I thought I would. My father said he'd take me with him. My father . . ." Daziel tensed slightly, and when he continued it was with a lightness I suspected was false. "Always said more than he meant, I think. It took me a while to realize that."

I didn't want to feel any sympathy for him, but my chest twisted. My parents had never fallen short of my expectations. I'd been lucky.

"Anyway." Daziel shook off any low spirits. "I decided I'd explore on my own. Especially when my parents made noises about me taking on more of the family business."

"Rocks?"

He smiled wryly. "Rocks. A more tedious responsibility than I'm keen on."

Who'd have thought I'd have fellow feeling for a demon? Apparently growing up had some universals. "I get it. But . . . why not stay at inns? Why drag me into this?"

He blinked as though confused. "They'd find me."

I was equally confused. "How is staying with me any different? You think they wouldn't look for you in a girls' dorm?"

Understanding dawned on Daziel's face. "Shedim can sense the location of those they're connected to," he explained. "If someone has a claim on your location—as a parent does on a child's—you can only be shielded by someone with an equal claim. Like a betrothed. According to the treaty rules, shedim can't track humans without permission. Since I am betrothed to you, I am hidden from them."

It took me a moment to process this, and as I did, my mouth fell open. "Are you serious?"

He nodded.

But that meant . . . if he was only shielded by someone with an equal claim . . . "We're not actually betrothed."

He stared at me.

No. Oh *no*. The ring, the pomegranate. No wonder he had worked so hard to get me to accept the fruit. My stomach sank. "We *are* actually betrothed?"

"At least fifty percent."

What the hell. "I'd like to be *un*betrothed. One hundred percent."

He winced. "That's more complicated. To deter demons from entering betrothals casually."

"Complicated?" Daziel was making it sound like betrothals for demons were magical bindings. My breathing came faster. "How complicated?"

Paz cheeped, nervous-sounding, and squirreled himself away down the back of Daziel's collar while Daziel scratched his ear and examined the ceiling. "Can I get back to you?"

I was going to wring his neck. "And there's effects to being be-trothed? *Magical* effects, like this location thing?"

"Several." Daziel looked confused, as though this was obvious. "Depending on how far along the betrothal is."

"Human betrothals don't have magical effects," I said from between gritted teeth, because apparently that needed to be clari-fied. "What are they?"

He shrugged. "Location-finding. Magic-sharing. Health-sharing—like with your hand."

This was too much. I focused on the first bit, location-sharing—and blocking. "What were you going to do if some random girl *didn't* claim you were betrothed?"

"No plan." He plumped up a few cushions, looking ready to go back to bed. "I just grabbed the opportunity."

I closed my eyes briefly. "If I can't break up with you on my own, how do we undo this betrothal?"

"We'll have to get it signed off by one of our rabbis and one of yours. And have a court of law approve of the dissolution. And, uh, undergo a period of reflection where we perform ceremonies to help the magic untangle."

I tried to convey, wordlessly, my renewed desire for neck-wringing.

"Or you can let me stay," he said hopefully as he slid more hor-izontally into his blankets. "I'll help you with schoolwork, I'll fend off unwanted suitors, I'll—I'll clean!"

Nothing about this boy filled me with confidence he knew how to clean. "I told you, I'm not striking a deal with a demon."

He rolled his eyes. "It doesn't have to be a formal deal. It can be . . . an exchange of services. Your service: a place to stay and not ending the betrothal immediately. My services: My brilliant company. Apartment-decorating. Fashion advice—"

Rude. "Thanks, I've got the picture." I rubbed my forehead. Maybe I was so sleep-deprived I couldn't think straight, but letting him stay didn't sound so bad. Much easier than hunting down multiple rabbis and petitioning the court, which sounded exhausting. I was so busy with my classes and maintaining my grades for my scholarship . . . Maybe it wouldn't hurt to wait until after the term was over to figure out how to untangle this. "Help studying, then. Flash cards and quizzing me on theory and language. Chores, maybe, if you don't break anything."

"I'm not going to break anything." He sounded offended.

I thought about it. I could handle a roommate—I'd always shared a room with my sisters. A boy would be different, but he could stay in the living room.

Someone to clean, to run errands . . . no more unwanted suitors hunting me . . .

And a language tutor. Being taught by an expert . . . that was an edge scholarship students could rarely afford. I was good at languages, maybe even great, but so were many people here. If I wanted to win Professor Altschuler's esteem, and a scholarship for a second year at the Lyceum, this could be an incredible opportunity.

Besides, it sounded like I didn't have much of a choice until I found both human and demon clergy members and performed whatever ceremonies were necessary to untangle this magic.

Still, I hesitated. It might be wildly foolish, not to mention dangerous, letting a demon into my life.

"Please," he said. Maybe he could see how I was on the edge, ready to teeter in either direction. "I can't go home yet. I only just left. I haven't seen anything. I won't be a bother. You'll barely know I'm here. Please. I don't know if I'll get another chance."

Maybe it was naive, but I believed him. "There'd have to be ground rules. You can't do anything weird."

From his curled-up position in his nest, he pulled a face. "I would never."

"And it's not a formalized deal. Just an . . . agreement."

He nodded. "Of course."

What the hell. If I was stuck with him until we dissolved this betrothal, I might as well get something out of it. "Let me go tell Leah not to worry. And tomorrow we'll see Madame Hadar about getting you approved to stay overnight."

SIX

I TOSSED AND TURNED ALL NIGHT—MY SLEEP PATTERNS NOT helped by a bizarre storm that rolled through in the early hours of the morning, whipping the winds and raising the heat to near unbearable temperatures before it broke just before dawn. I woke next to the sweet scent of ground coffee beans. Amazing. Less amazing was needing to put on a bra before entering the living room. I gathered the clothes I planned to change into post-shower—in the bathroom; I wasn't ready to cross the living room in a towel—then cautiously opened my door.

"Good morning?" My words ended in a question mark. The living room was recognizable but—better somehow? The rug seemed brighter, and the floorboards gleamed. And the nest of cushions and blankets on the floor—where Daziel had slept—contained vibrant blankets I definitely didn't own and pillows with silk cases. There were plants I hadn't had before: a pear tree bearing fruit in the corner and ivy hanging from the ceiling.

"Good morning," Daziel said, distracting me from trying to determine how the ivy was attached. I was becoming slowly used to his appearance, to the sharp black nails, the pattern of feathers on his neck, though every time I saw it anew, it was somewhat startling, his inhuman beauty distracting. Today he wore a light gray outfit, crisply ironed (with what iron?). "Did you sleep well?"

"Um—the storm woke me," I said, taken aback by both the change in my apartment, his politeness, and the fact that in addition to coffee he'd somehow acquired a spread of croissants.

His head snapped up, a little too quickly to be human. "You too?"

"It was weird, right? And the heat . . . Any idea what caused it?"

He shook his head. "I've heard of similar occurrences—but the conditions are usually different. It was . . . unsettling."

I was unsettled that the magic in Talum was strange enough to unsettle a demon. I smiled awkwardly and retreated to the bathroom, where I showered, dressed, and questioned all my life choices.

Not enough to refuse the coffee and croissants when I re-emerged, though. "How did you pay for these?" I asked, breaking off the corner of one golden brown crescent, buttery flakes clinging to my fingers. I recognized the bag they'd come in; they were from the fancy boulangerie. "*Did* you pay?"

"Of course." He sounded affronted, then started coughing.

My concern grew as his cough worsened in roughness and volume. "Are you okay?"

He waved a hand but didn't stop.

I'd heard if you were coughing, you couldn't be choking because you could still move air through your airways. Still, I touched his arm. "Do you want me to pound on your back?"

He curled forward and gave one final, horrific cough. Something large and shiny hurtled out of his mouth and into his hand.

He held it up triumphantly. "Ta-da!"

It was a polished, multifaceted green stone. It looked like it should be showcased in a crown, not covered in saliva. I blinked rapidly, not knowing what else to do with my surprise. "Did you—is that—an emerald?"

He wiped the saliva away on his trousers. "I paid," he said happily.

"What?" I swallowed. "We can't—people don't *pay* with emeralds. How—where did it come from? Is that, like, your breakfast?" At his smile, I winced, deciding I didn't need the details. "Did it *hurt* coming up?"

He beamed. "Are you concerned for my welfare, Naomi?"

"No! I mean—I'm curious. Grossed out a bit, but curious."

"I think you are," he mused. There was a glint to his eyes, a delight in teasing me. "You worried I was choking. You stroked my arm."

"Let's move on," I said. "Thank you for breakfast. Maybe take any more jewels you cough up to a jeweler's instead of paying with them directly."

"Noted," Daziel said. "What is our plan for today?"

I finished a second croissant—they were very good—then began loading my rucksack with the relevant folders and books. "My first class is at nine." When he didn't respond, I clarified: "School."

"Again?"

His outraged tone stole a smile from me. "That's how I feel too."

Leah and I walked to the Lyceum together on Mondays, Wednesdays, and Fridays, so I knocked on her door. When she opened it, she dragged her hand against her brow in exaggerated relief. Last night, when I'd woken her to say I was letting Daziel stay, I'd asked if I was making a terrible mistake. She'd looked dubious, and said, "Probably. But I can hear you through the walls if you scream."

I offered her a croissant. "Good morning."

She considered it. "Is it bespelled?"

"I don't think so. I recognized the bakery bag. I'm not taking any chances with my new pear tree, though."

We headed to school, Daziel behind us. Leah had no qualms about handing him her rucksack to carry, and after a moment, I did too. "You don't seem to be murdered," she said. "Seduced? Aren't demons into seducing people?"

"I suppose coffee and croissants are a form of seduction." Maybe I could become the kind of person who airily spoke about seduction. It should be easy to joke about, as Daziel wasn't trying to seduce me, just use me to hide from his parents.

I wondered what it would look like if he tried to seduce me.

Leah let out a thoughtful hum, and I shut down my thoughts. "Maybe *I* should pretend to be betrothed to a demon."

Daziel followed me to my classes. In addition to Old Cinnaian and hieroglyphic Keft, I studied Tzorybia, the language of a sprawling northeastern empire that had been one of the premier centers of scholarship for centuries and in whose tongue much modern scholarship had been done. These classes didn't interest Daziel. He slept through them, curled up on the floor in pools of sunlight, Paz draped over his head. I didn't say anything, and neither did the other students or professors. It seemed wiser not to.

They watched, though. It had been twenty-four hours since Daziel first stepped on campus, and the entire student population now knew about him. Both casual acquaintances and people I'd never talked to stopped by to say hello, expressions bright with curiosity. "I didn't realize you were betrothed," Sara Apter from my Intro to T3 class said, leaning over from her desk. "How'd you guys meet?"

"Picking flowers," I said. Best stick to one lie.

Overall, people didn't seem to view Daziel with too much fear or suspicion. Since I'd theoretically vetted him, and because he didn't pay anyone but me any attention, they mostly left him alone, as one would anyone's guest.

They did stare a lot more, though.

The only class Daziel showed interest in was Intro to Spellwriting. "This is how you write your spells?" he asked, studying my worksheet on Taro Islands seals. Most spells in the countries surrounding the Long Sea used the thirty charaktêres of ring letters, but students at the Lyceum also learned the seals used in the Taro Islands and the far-off Green Continent, along with the seven symbolic string letters used by eastern civilizations. "You make things so complicated."

I felt vaguely insulted on humanity's behalf. "And how do you do it?"

"We just ask for what we want. It seems much easier."

"Well, excuse me for being from a species not imbued with magic."

"You are excused," he said politely, which made me want to kick him.

He proved to be an able tutor, though, making good on his promise to help with my language studies. He was almost too tough, forcing me to complete practice after practice, insisting I work on my Old Cinnaian *L* until he deemed it passable. "No one even speaks Old Cinnaian anymore," I muttered, irritated. "Why do I have to say the *L* correctly?"

"Scholars speak it," Daziel said. "Their keeping it alive is the only reason I can understand it. And if you want to honor it, you will speak it correctly."

I narrowed my eyes at him, and he looked embarrassed. "Sorry. My tutors were—exacting."

"Hmph," I said. "Well. I'll *try* to say the *L* right."

On Friday, he followed me to my cryptography seminar. Anxiety wound my nerves tight as we made our way to the Keep. I cared about my work on the scrolls more than anything else—I needed this interaction to go well, but I had no idea how my professor or his other three students would react to Daziel.

Most importantly, I needed Professor Altschuler's respect—or at least for him to consider me a worthwhile, serious student. He'd accepted me to the Lyceum, and he would decide if I received a scholarship next year. If I wasn't talented or valuable enough, he might dismiss me.

"You have to behave," I told Daziel as we approached the Keep, in the same tone I used to tell Michal not to so obviously sneak food on fasting days or Adina not to flirt during shivas. "No weird stuff. Professor Altschuler is tough."

It was nearing four and the last hour of classes for the day. We climbed the Keep's stairs, stopping at the fourth floor, where Professor Altschuler taught his cryptography seminar. I took a steadying breath, gazing out the windows at rain dripping from the flat sky into the blue-gray river.

"When have I ever done anything weird?" said the person who'd spent this morning talking an acorn into sprouting into the tiniest oak in one of my coffee mugs. Admittedly, I hadn't minded. But it warranted a warning glance as we stepped into the room.

Professor Altschuler's three other students were inside, spread as far as possible from each other in the dozen seats. The professor hadn't arrived yet, which was standard—none of us would dare be late for this class.

"Hi, guys." I tried not to sound nervous. One would think since the four of us spent so much time together, we'd have formed a fast friendship. Instead, we were wary rivals. "This is Daziel. He's visiting."

All three glanced up. I was the only first-year of the bunch—Yael and Stefan were in their third year, Gidon in his second—and I wasn't used to having their undivided attention. I looked first to Yael. Elegant and intimidating, she was the scion of a wealthy family and usually impossible to ruffle. Now, though, she looked astonished. Fine lines crumpled her brow, and she ran a hand through her short blond hair.

"Whoa." Stefan examined Daziel with interest. He was the most sociable of our cohort, a partier when he wasn't working on the scrolls, and I got the feeling he found the rest of us tediously boring. "I did not see this coming."

Gidon, younger than the others and more timid, stayed silent, but his wide eyes proved he was equally as intrigued.

"Is he—" Yael said to me, then realized that was rude and addressed Daziel directly. "Are you going to be helping Naomi?"

Are you more competition? she meant.

"Daziel's coming to all my classes." Like always, I was torn between wanting to impress Yael and wanting to reassure her I wasn't a threat for Professor Altschuler's regard. Of all our cohort, she was the one I wanted to like me.

The door creaked and we all stiffened. The professor swept in, talking as he moved. "Today we will be discussing—"

He stopped abruptly, staring.

"This is Daziel." Maybe if I acted totally normal, everything would proceed as usual.

"I'd heard you were keeping company with a demon," Professor Altschuler said, "but I'd hoped it to be rumor."

I hesitated. I'd only dealt with student reactions to Daziel so far. A few professors had lit incense, since demons were supposed to hate strong scents, and one brought in a potted kero masa tree, the shadow of which was supposed to harm demons. But no one had thrown a fit. You might as well yell at a cat or curse the strengthening winds. Besides, banishing a demon was probably above an academic's pay grade.

"Not rumor," I said. "He's very real. I thought it'd be all right if he sat in today?"

"No."

Taken aback by the professor's sharpness, I added, "He won't interfere—"

The professor ignored me, his gaze trained on Daziel's. "You should leave."

"I don't want to," Daziel said in a silk-smooth voice.

My stomach twisted, bile rising. I didn't think my skills in handling my little sisters' fights would help me manage this situation.

"If you don't depart at my request," Professor Altschuler said, voice like ice, "Bylaw 174 permits me to cast banishment—"

"Bylaw 174 permits such *after* 'reasonable attempts at discourse,' which have not occurred," Daziel interrupted.

Altschuler's jaw twitched. "I have told you what I want—"

"And I've told you what I want." Daziel moved sinuously closer to the professor. My brain said he must have stepped, but I wasn't sure that was what I'd seen; it felt more like fog rolling over the hills, until he stood right in front of Professor Altschuler. "Perhaps we must compromise."

The professor's lips drew up in a sneer.

"*Daziel.*" I grabbed his arm and shot Professor Altschuler an apologetic grimace. "I'm sorry. One second." I pulled at Daziel's arm. For a moment, I thought he might resist; tugging at him felt like trying to drag a heated pillar. Then he softened and followed me into the stairwell.

Where he drew to a stop, all ruffled pride. "You're going to take that man's side?"

"I'm not taking a side." I pulled him down a bend in the spiral staircase so we weren't so easy to overhear. "He's my professor. He's in charge."

"You made me leave."

"I need my scholarship. I can't afford to piss him off."

"You don't mind pissing *me* off."

"It's his classroom."

Daziel scowled. "You're my betrothed."

That gave me pause. Because while our betrothal was only technical, Daziel's statement made me realize I was the only person he really knew in Talum. The only person he could expect to stand up for him. "I'm sorry. But you're not one of his students—I think he's allowed to say nonstudents can't be in his classroom."

"Fine." Daziel's ears twitched, and he vanished.

SEVEN

I FLINCHED, SURPRISED BY DAZIEL'S ABRUPT DISAPPEARANCE. Guilt followed. I hadn't expected Daziel to be so insulted—or hurt?—that he left. I'd thought I was being reasonable. But the professor had been rude, and Daziel didn't have anywhere else to go.

"I'm sorry," I said softly, in case Daziel could still hear me. With a sigh, I headed back to the classroom.

Professor Altschuler was nowhere in sight, but my cohort swiveled in my direction. "He wants you in the scroll room," Yael said.

Swallowing, I nodded and headed up a floor. I knocked twice before entering. "You wanted to see me?"

Professor Altschuler stood, gazing downriver. From here, you could see the uninhabited islet west of Talum, a black streak dividing the blue of river and sky.

He turned, his gaunt expression even more drawn than usual, his face half-silhouetted by the setting sun. "It is not safe to consort with demons," he said. "They are not human, even if they take human form. They do not reason the way we do, or have the same morals." His lips tightened briefly. "I am given to understand they offer certain . . . carnal pleasure—"

Horrible, I hated this, no. "It's not like that," I said hurriedly, because even if it *had* been, I'd rather jump out the window than discuss my sex life with a professor. "We're—it's—he's my tutor. He's nice."

Professor Altschuler regarded me as though he'd never met such an imbecile. "Demons are not 'nice.'"

I swallowed. The majority of humans would probably describe demons as mischievous or dangerous, but maybe that was because humans and demons usually encountered each other in more stressful situations than hanging out on the sofa. "Daziel's nice."

"Daziel," he repeated. He ran his fingers along his bookcase, stopping at a thick, weathered tome. "Did he tell you his lineage?"

"Yes." He definitely did. "Daziel, son of . . ."

Well, no one ever called me detail-oriented.

Professor Altschuler sighed and released the book. "You are making a mistake."

Was I? Or was the professor? In the last five days, Daziel had been nothing but funny and thoughtful and annoying. Maybe I was making a mistake, but maybe the professor was prejudiced.

An unpleasant silent stretched, and the professor's expression soured when he realized I wasn't going to agree with him. "Your personal life is not my concern, but you cannot bring the demon back to my seminar," he snapped. "I won't have him in my class or meddling with my scrolls."

I nodded, and we headed back to the classroom, where Professor Altschuler set out the parameters for a new technopaignia spell he wanted to try. Technopaignia spells were written in the shape of an object to strengthen the magic. In this case, we'd write the spell in the shape of scrolls, hoping to remind the fragments of what they'd once been.

Like with each new spell, our cohort's job would be carving

charaktêres into a large piece of plywood, then painting the words with neshem oil. For complicated spells like this, spellcasters often carved charaktêres into porous materials, which absorbed more neshem then clay or glass or paper. This created reserves for the spell to draw on so the caster didn't need to scramble in the middle to add more. We'd layer paper over the plywood so the neshem wouldn't dampen the fragments, which we'd place on top.

"Is everything all right?" Yael asked once the professor had departed. We divided the spell in quadrants and began writing out the charaktêres before carving them with our stylos, to make sure the spacing worked. "With the demon?"

Her concern unnerved me. Things had to look bad for her to ask me the first personal question since we'd met. "We're fine."

"How long have you known each other?"

"Um . . ." With Stefan in the room, I didn't want to admit I'd made up the betrothal. He'd been one of the first to ask me out; though not in the School of Government, he came from a high-ranked family in Aolong, and I figured he'd been told to make connections here. He'd backed off quick after learning about my demon betrothed, though.

"A year. Though we don't see each other often. The engagement was—sudden."

Silence fell, as per usual. But Yael had opened the door for conversation. Maybe we could be friends. I cast about for something to discuss. Maybe we could get past the competition between us—

"How can you still be so slow at writing charaktêres?" Stefan asked me. "Man, the candidates must have been rough your year."

Never mind.

When we finished preparing for the spell, Professor Altschuler returned with a colleague and three of his staff. All nine of us read the spell together.

It didn't work.

"Failures can be as useful as successes," Professor bat Rachel said, aiming for a positive spin. But we'd had enough failures here.

Dismissed, I headed out, my stomach twisted. The spell hadn't worked, I didn't know if I'd have a scholarship next year, and on top of everything, I'd hurt Daziel's feelings.

An unsettling, lukewarm rain started to fall. The rainy season wasn't due for another few weeks, but thick, plump droplets burst on my shoulders and the pavement like slow tears. At least it wasn't too cold, though the rain increased from a slow patter to a fast and soaking downfall. I ducked under a shop's awning to wait it out. Everything looked dark and shiny, the world washed clean and smelling of petrichor.

"Fine," Daziel said. I jumped, looking wildly around before locating the demon seated on the top of a wrought iron lamp. His face was shadowed, but a familiar loftiness shaded his voice. "I accept your apology."

Relief washed through me, tinged by pique that he'd reappeared in the haughtiest possible manner. I shot him an arch look, relieved to be back to trading quips. "Did I apologize?"

He jumped down, landing lightly on his feet. "Earlier."

So he had been listening, and it had mattered to him. I studied him, this strange, wild boy. "I'm sorry I didn't tell Professor Altschuler not to be a jerk."

He shrugged. He wore a scarf thrown haphazardly over his shoulders, new shoes in a buttery dark leather, and silver cuffs around his wrists.

"Did you go shopping?"

"I asked a gentleman who shared my box at the opera where he had acquired his coat, and he recommended an establishment."

I blinked several times, not sure which part of this to respond to first. "You went to the *opera*?"

"At first I went in because everyone was well dressed and the building so pretty, but then I stayed because I was amazed." He still looked amazed. "The drama! The vocal acrobatics! The costumes! Afterward, I wanted to look as sharp as everyone else."

My lips quirked up. Of course he had.

He lifted an umbrella I hadn't noticed and stepped out into the downpour. Impossibly, when rain hit the umbrella, it slid off in a long arc, creating a dry dome at least six feet in diameter.

I stepped under the dome, which moved with us as we walked. I craned my neck to take it in, trying not to gape. "How are you stopping the rain?"

"Magic. Shall we head home?"

Human magic couldn't do anything like this. "We're not headed home." I grinned, not without trepidation. "It's Friday. We're going to the pub."

Wonderment slid over Daziel's face, as though I'd announced I was taking him to a ball on Society Hill. "I have never been to a pub before!"

I snorted and led him through the winding streets of the Scholars' Quarter, stopping at a wooden door, which couldn't muffle the storm of noise behind it. "Get ready, then. And stay close."

I pushed the door open into the packed pub. With beer both cheap and good, people always crowded in here, and it'd become my friends' de facto meeting place. Rain dripped off the people closest to the door, while musicians strummed their guitars and heckled their listeners into tossing coins. I elbowed my way past students with sloshing pints, the floor already sticky beneath my feet.

My friends squeezed around a table in the back—my floor-mates, along with Ezra and Hiram. We'd met the boys during orientation, and we'd all bonded over being scholarship students. Ezra was loud and boisterous, with an opinion on everything. He had uncontrollable black hair, large ears, and he asked a hundred questions a minute. He was in the School of Humanities, like me and Leah, though he complained about the government so much I wondered why he wasn't in school to change it. Hiram was quieter, shorter, and very handsome, with a tendency toward dour pronouncements. He came from the Taro Islands, like so many sailors did in Port Naborre, and spoke with a soft, lyrical accent. Like Gilli, he'd enrolled in the School of Science.

Nerves tightened my chest as we approached. I hadn't known the boys long enough to know how they'd react to Daziel, and I didn't want to mess up this new friendship group. Back home, I hadn't had a group like this. I had my sisters, and I was friendly with my age group in the village—Abel and Hila and Keren and Mendel—but I'd always felt too intense around them, like I cared too much. This group fit me, and I didn't want to mess it up.

"Hi, guys." I slid onto the edge of the bench, bumping Leah's hips with mine to encourage her to squeeze down. Daziel perched next to me. I gave a floppy wave, trying to swallow my nerves. "This is Daziel."

They'd heard of him already, of course, but Hiram and I shared no classes, and Ezra and I only had class on Mondays. "I thought you were joking," Ezra said, astonishment clear. "You're actually betrothed to a demon?"

Daziel leaned forward, beaming—happy, I suspected, to tease some gullible humans. "We are."

The boys drew back.

I accepted the glasses of cheap ale Leah pushed over, passing one to Daziel. I needed to set the situation straight. "We're not really betrothed. He's just hanging around a bit."

"Technically, we're *really* betrothed," Daziel said. I was so used to him sounding chipper that I could identify an undercurrent of irritation. He didn't like me refuting the betrothal, then.

"He's a demon." Hiram sounded suspicious. "Why are you here?"

"To delight in the company of my betrothed and her friends." Daziel's glib expression slipped when he sipped his ale. He made a face. "What is this?"

"It's ale," Ezra said. "Don't demons drink ale?"

"Can demons get drunk?" Gilli asked.

"On starlight and moonbeams."

My friends stared at him, then at me.

"He's joking," I said. My lips twitched. Daziel was exasperating, no doubt about it, but I could see how everyone being constantly agog at your existence might prod one into light teasing. "He thinks he's funnier than he is."

Daziel looked affronted. "I am *very* funny."

"He's here to see Talum," I told Hiram. "He'd never left home and wanted to explore."

This broke the ice, particularly for Hiram, who also loved exploring. Then Daziel asked about the colors Ezra wore, which set the boys off on an overly excited explanation of knockball. "You should join our league!" Ezra cried. Ezra was forever trying to recruit people to the club team he captained, which was, by all accounts, actively bad.

"Are you serious right now?" Leah asked.

Daziel tilted his head. "What's knockball?"

"It's the best," Ezra said. "A thinking man's sport, smart, heady. You'd love it. Demons are fast, right?"

"You can't have a demon on your team," Leah said. She flicked a peanut shell at Ezra from the wreckage on the table. "That's cheating!"

"That's discrimination," Ezra said, all superior. "God, Leah, I didn't realize how prejudiced you were."

"I am very fast," Daziel said, looking back and forth between my friends. "With excellent reflexes."

"Sweet," Ezra said. "Practices are twice a week on Charing Field—I'll get Naomi the details."

Across the room, the musicians returned from a break and burst into an energetic rendition of the popular ballad "Where Has My Love Gone?"—only, they'd tweaked it to be "Where Have the Birds Gone?"

Leah winced. "Too soon."

"Fast turnaround, though," Ezra said. "Kind of impressive."

"Has anyone seen a bird since Tuesday?" Jelan asked.

Everyone shook their head. "Kaylee Shatterly in my Intro to T3 class said her pet parakeet banged his head against his cage over and over until she was afraid he'd kill himself, so she let him go, and he flew away with the mass," Leah said.

Dark.

The door to the pub opened, and more people gusted in with the rain and wind. Gilli frowned prettily. I committed to frowning in the mirror later and seeing if I could do the same instead of looking like a gremlin. "It's one more strange thing, isn't it?" she said. "The birds flying off. The heat the other night. The winds being so strong."

Ezra thumped his beer glass emphatically on the table. "It's obvious something's off with magic. The Sanhedrin needs to investigate it. Or if they can't figure out the source of the problem, they need to protect people, put shields up or something against the too-strong winds."

"What's the Sanhedrin?" Daziel asked.

Another roar from the group, this one disbelieving. Even I shot him a look askance. "The Sanhedrin?" Leah repeated. "The Council? It runs the city?"

Daziel picked up his cup and idly took a bite of it. Glass crunched under his teeth. "We don't pay much attention to your politics."

"Daziel!" I cried. Not understanding money and politics was one thing, but this was a step too far. "You can't eat glasses!"

"Why not?" He looked confused.

"It's not an ice cream cone, mate," Ezra said. "They're not edible."

"Come on, you pay some attention," Leah said. This was how all conversations went at the Lyceum: students talking over and under each other, three conversations at once. Luckily, I'd been trained by having three sisters. "There's a treaty. It gets renewed every twenty years."

"No offense," Daziel said smugly, "but I think your lot pays far more attention to us than we do to you."

I almost grinned at how pleased he sounded. Of course we paid attention! Demons were magical and rare! I didn't want to give him the satisfaction of impressing *me* so easily, though, so I rolled my eyes. He grinned back.

"You're a wild demon, though," Ezra said. "Do you know what's going on with the magic? It's the natural-world magic that's off, not letterform. Wild demons are close to the natural world, right?"

Leah turned to Daziel sharply. "*Do* you know? Because if the rains and winds continue to be unpredictable, it could affect my family's silk harvest. *Every* family's harvest. My parents are freaking out."

"Shedim don't control natural magic," Daziel said, his voice gentle. "Natural magic is controlled by the primordial beasts. I'm sorry."

Our waitress came over, a beleaguered woman who must have subsisted on her irritation at students, because it certainly wasn't on tips. "You lot buying anything else?"

"Have I told you how beautiful you look tonight, Sophie?" Ezra said.

She regarded him stonily. "You need to purchase something if you want to keep sitting here."

"We'll get mixed nuts. You are *stunning*, Sophie."

"You need to get more than mixed nuts."

"Two orders of mixed nuts?"

"Out," Sophie said.

"Sophie, we have a *demon* with us," Ezra said, as though saying *please let us stay*.

Sophie examined Daziel. She did not look impressed. "And is the demon paying for food?"

Daziel smiled. "I am happy to." He pulled at the obsidian-black nail on his pinkie. Blood welled up in the bed as the nail began to detach.

Good lord. Was he serious? Nails were not an acceptable form of currency, and I didn't want to be responsible for bits of demon floating around the black market. I batted Daziel's shoulder, and he turned to me, startled, letting go of his nail.

"He is most definitely not," I said firmly. "Sorry! We're leaving now." I dragged Daziel out of the pub behind me. Maybe it would be more work than I thought, managing this demon.

EIGHT

As I walked to the Keep a little more than two weeks later, I kept noticing the result of the birds' absence. Beetles everywhere. A disconcerting number of cobwebs. The lack of birdsong I hadn't realized I expected.

I reached the Keep, climbing swiftly to the fifth floor. Paz accompanied me. Daziel was at knockball practice, having taken to the game immediately—he'd announced after his first practice he planned to become a professional player. Who would have expected a demon to be so sporty?

Paz, on the other hand, was not charmed. He disliked all the running around, preferring to stay curled on someone's shoulder, so on knockball days he stayed with me.

No one else was in the scroll room; it was six, and while I often ran into the others at odd times, it wasn't unusual to be here alone. We all came as our schedules allowed. I bent over the replicated fragments, moving them round and round. So many of them looked identical—how could we manually match them together? Surely a spell would be better, if only we could get one to work. But despite every attempt, we'd come no closer the whole time I'd been at the Lyceum.

I shifted a few fragments, then sat back with a sigh, gazing out the window. To the west, the Lersach River ran dark green, and on the far shore, the vineyards and mulberry trees of the silk farms rippled in the wind. I stroked Paz's head. He snoozed gently, little rings of smoke rising from his snout.

When I looked back at the scrolls, the fragments I'd grouped together had separated. I blinked. How was that possible? I must have only thought I'd put them together. I tried again, then moved to a different section. When I looked back, my earlier attempts had been undone.

Was I losing my mind? What was going on?

As I worked, wind howled past the windows, rain smacking big, loose droplets against the glass. I bent my head closer to the parchment, then glanced at the windows—all tightly closed. No way for any wind to slip inside.

So why did I now feel it swirling around my ankles, tugging at my feet? I looked down, baffled. It felt like the wind was inside me, blowing me toward the door. Urging me to go outside.

I hesitated.

The wind kept tugging.

Slowly, I rose—just to see what would happen. It led me across the room, and I paused in the doorway. This was probably a bad idea, following a force I didn't understand. Probably I should ignore the strange tugging wind. Following it would be impulsive and irrational.

But illogical or not, I felt like I could sense the wind's yearning. And I was too curious to ignore it. After all, how many people had ever been pulled by the wind before? How could I resist?

Paz cheeped, uncertain. I stroked his head. "It's okay," I murmured. "We're not going to do anything dangerous. We're just going to . . . walk." I could stop anytime I liked if it felt like things were getting risky.

Pulling on my blazer, I left the Keep. The wind tugged at my braids, pushed against my calves, steered me by my back. I hadn't felt such a strong wind yet. Maybe this was the Clo, the first of the Trio Winds, which came in early winter. They were supposed to be so strong and fierce they could brush the whole world clean.

I had no problem letting it lead me across campus and over the land bridge. I hesitated when it led me out of the Scholars' Quarter into the larger city beyond. The rain had grown from droplets to a steady drizzle, and part of me wanted to go home, to be safe and dry.

But then I would always wonder.

I walked for over two hours, even as the rain increased, even as I started to shiver in the cold and the wet. Water dripped over my eyes and mouth. Paz made nervous sounds, and I moved him to the inside pocket of my blazer, murmuring comforting words. I could have given up—I wasn't trapped in the wind's thrall—but every time I considered stopping, I also thought about how rare this was and how it might never happen again. I was driven by the same kernel of curiosity that made me want to decipher the scrolls: a desperate curiosity, a longing for knowledge. I wanted to know what the wind whispered. I didn't want to turn my back and spend the rest of my life wondering.

The wind and rain stopped.

I was in a city park I'd never visited. Larger than most, so big you could almost believe you weren't in a city—a deception helped by the valley in the center and the sides rimming it that almost hid the rest of Talum. On the crest of a hill in the distance stood a tiny gazebo; to my left, the rocky hillside opened to reveal a cave. I entered, breathing in the cool scent of running water and growing green things, complementary to the rain dripping off me. A waterfall trickled down the glazed black rock, collecting in a shallow pool that must have then drained into the earth. The water ran over a carving of three gazelles running. This was, I realized, the Naphtali Quarter, my mother's people. I'd never visited before. Above the gazelles the three Great Beasts had been carved in sharp relief—the massive land beast, the Behemoth; the sea monster, the Leviathan; and the ruler of the air, the Ziz.

And there, in the shadows tucked away in the craggy rock face, a deeper shadow caught my attention. I stepped toward it, my breath quickening. There was an intensity to the blackness unlike any I'd seen before.

Paz started cheeping, but I kept moving forward, fascinated by the opening leading deeper inside the cave.

"What are you doing?"

I spun. Daziel stood in the cave's entrance, his face pale. I'd never seen him look worried before. Paz chirped in delight and jumped over to Daziel's arm.

"Betrayer," I murmured, then to Daziel, "I'm listening to the wind. I think it wanted to show me—"

When I turned, the opening was gone. I blinked. "There was a crack. Right there."

Daziel crouched where I gestured, pressing his hand to the wall. Paz scampered up his shoulder, diffusely lighting the area with a warm orangish glow.

Daziel turned back to me, gaze focused. "Why did you listen to the wind?"

I spread my hands, surprised by his intensity. "Who could ignore it?"

He didn't smile at my teasing tone. "This whole city was built by people who try to ignore it. You don't live with the wind; you live against it. You build stone walls to keep it out, you talk about shields—"

"That's not fair," I interrupted, stung by his admonishing tone. I hated being scolded—and *Daziel* was supposed to be the one baffled by norms and customs. Him lecturing me unbalanced our dynamic. "Talumizans are proud of the winds. The Maestril, the spring wind, is part of the ecosystem. It blows away the grit other winds blow in and dries out the earth for the harvest."

"But why did you follow this one?"

I didn't understand why he was harrying me over this. "Don't you think if most people felt the wind tugging them, they'd want to know why?"

"People with sense would think strange magic best ignored."

I couldn't argue there, so I looked back where the crack had been. "What do you think it was? The opening."

"I don't know."

"I've heard the whole island is riddled with caves," I said. "The winds and river made them thousands of years ago, they say— there's networks everywhere."

"Then I'd assume it led into the caves," Daziel said. "Do you think, perhaps, you'd be willing to give up following the winds and head home for tonight?"

I still had no idea what had drawn me here, what—if anything— the wind wanted. Maybe it was all in my head. "I wish I knew what it was. Or at least knew it was *something*."

"I suspect it'd be like picking at a scab. Best not to. And maybe don't wander off after the wind without letting me know in the future."

I scoffed. "I don't need a minder."

"No?" He looked aggrieved. "Because you definitely would have gone into those caves if I hadn't been here."

"Oh my god," I said, infuriated. "I'm capable of making my own decisions. I don't need you lecturing me about safety."

Daziel's expression was fierce. "You're too impulsive, Naomi. You want to wander into a dark cave without any idea what's there. You follow the winds through a storm. You let a stranger stay with you with no concern for your safety!"

I felt like I'd been jabbed in a soft spot. I lifted my chin, embarrassed and hurt. "Would you rather I hadn't taken you in?"

His black eyes sparked. "I'd rather you don't put yourself in positions where you're endangered all the time. You trust too easily."

"Are you telling me I'm in danger from you?" I shot back. If he was going to insult me, I'd give back the same. "That you'd hurt me?"

"I could." He stepped closer. His heat warmed me like a caress, and copper gleamed across his eyes. "Did you ever consider that?"

My stomach clenched. I hadn't taken the idea seriously after the first day or two, and I felt foolish to be called out on how maybe I should have. But it was hard to stay wary of someone who quizzed you on flash cards and cleaned the bathroom and made coffee every morning. Any wariness I'd had regarding him had been firmly dismantled as he learned to crochet with Gilli and played knockball with the boys. "Yes," I said testily, embarrassed even more. "Why are you making this into a big deal?"

He closed his eyes and took a deep breath, clearly trying to calm himself down. I'd never seen him so serious before, save the night I'd tried to take his seal, and then he'd been angry rather than grave. Now I watched as he forcibly relaxed his jaw. When he opened his eyes they were still bright but the opaline glint across them had softened. "I'm sorry," he said, voice restrained. "I just wish you'd take your safety more seriously."

"Why do you even care about my safety?" It was odd to hear him talk like *he* wanted to take care of *me* instead of me making sure he wasn't chomping chunks out of pint glasses.

"Are you serious?" His brow furrowed, and his mouth pressed into a firm line.

It took the wind out of my sails to realize he did care about my safety, that he'd yelled because he'd been genuinely worried. It left me feeling wrong-footed by this whole interaction, like I'd discovered a new side of Daziel. "Do you really think I should be worried about the winds pulling on me?" I asked. "Are *you* worried?"

He turned his frown toward the carvings of the Ziz, the Behemoth, and the Leviathan. "The birds have left Talum. The winds are behaving oddly. There's heat storms and strange rain and flowers blooming out of season. I think everyone should be worried."

His bluntness alarmed me. "What do you think is going on?"

He shrugged. "I think we should all pay attention to anything odd, and if there's strange magic, don't tackle it by yourself."

"Okay," I said slowly. It didn't seem positive if a demon from the wilderness was worried about the magic. "I'll keep that in mind."

NINE

"I KNEW IT," LEAH SAID THE NEXT DAY WHEN I TOLD HER WHAT Daziel had said. We were in the Testylier House common room, where we'd curled up on the most comfortable couch before the fireplace and wrapped a cozy blue blanket around our legs. Each of us clasped a mug of mint tea, a plate of spice biscuits on the table before us, while outside a storm lashed at the windows. "Ezra's right, the Sanhedrin should be figuring out why the magic is off and fixing it."

I put my tea down so I could rub her arm gently. "Are you worried about your family?"

She nodded. "I'm not so worried about the autumn winds being off, but it's more if the Maestril also acts differently. We depend on the Maestril—it dries out the soil soaked by rains all winter and blows away the dust brought in by the Trio Winds. It's like clockwork. But . . ." She sounded defeated. "Nothing else is normal this year, so what if the Maestril isn't either?"

The riverlands produced the nation's silk, wine, and olive oil— Ena-Cinnai's major exports. If their harvests failed, it wouldn't just bankrupt families like Leah's; it would hit the whole nation. "I'm sure the Maestril will be fine."

She pressed her lips together. "I hope so."

Marie, a girl from the fourth floor, stuck her head into the common room. Water dripped from her white School of Religious Studies blazer, and her hair was plastered to her head; she'd clearly just come in. "Naomi? There's a courier here for you."

Leah and I exchanged curious glances. I'd never had a package delivered before, only letters from my family.

"Thanks," I said, climbing out from beneath my blanket and heading into the foyer, Leah beside me. A woman stood there in the brown-and-green outfit of the courier service, a slightly damp-looking rectangular package at her feet. "Hi? I'm Naomi bat Yardena."

The courier scrounged a pad out of her waterproof satchel and held it out, rainwater forming puddles around her. "Sign here, please."

I did, glancing at the returnee's address as I did so. "Oh no."

"What?" Leah leaned over my shoulder to see. "Who's it from?"

"My aunt." I smiled weakly at the courier as she departed. "I completely forgot she told me to come to a party she's hosting this weekend." The idea of being presented to my aunt's colleagues and peers made me sick. I imagined they'd be adult versions of Élodie and Birra, dressed brilliantly and sneering politely. "And she told me to confirm I had a decent outfit or she'd send something."

"Amazing." Leah eyed the package with excitement. If she hadn't been the eldest child and expected to take over her family's silk farm, I imagined she might want to do something in fashion. "Do you think it was a passive-aggressive slam, like 'you *definitely* don't have something,' or was it supposed to be nice?"

"No idea. I barely know her. To be fair, I definitely don't have anything fit for Society Hill." I'd happily accept an outfit from my aunt if it meant I could fade into the party's background instead of being the poor relation who stuck out like a sore thumb.

Leah smirked. "You could borrow something from Élodie or Birra."

"I'd rather stab my eyes out, thank you."

We took the package back to the common room, placing it on a coffee table and peeling back the brown paper. A white box lay within, emblazoned with the seal of a house of design I didn't recognize.

"Oh my god," said one of the other girls in the room, Suri, who sat with another fourth-floor girl, Danielle. "Is that from Shoshana's?"

"I don't know?" I said. "My aunt sent it over."

The two girls joined us, kneeling on the other side of the coffee table. "It definitely is," Suri said, examining the box's seal.

"Nice," Leah said. "I bet you can resell it for a ton."

I undid the strings and lifted away the box's top to reveal white paper folded around the outfit. Untucking it, I glimpsed the fabric within—navy silk with silver threading and glinting seed pearls. I lifted out the first piece, a high-necked top, and Leah pulled out the matching billowy pants with the classic cinched ankles of Talum fashion to protect against the wind.

"Your aunt has *taste*." Leah sounded astonished. "This cut only just came into style."

"It's tiny," I said, holding the top against my front.

"That's fashion."

"Look at this threadwork," Danielle said. "It's impeccable."

I murmured in agreement, then refocused. "What if I'm cold?"

"That is also fashion." Leah slid the pants through her fingers.

"You must suffer for it. Look at how luminous this is. This silk is really good quality. Do you have shoes to wear with it? Ideally silver."

"I have a pair," Suri said. "When are you wearing it? I can bring them over anytime."

Daziel hopped out of the mirror above the fireplace, landing softly on the floor. Everyone flinched, then pretended not to; we were Talumizans, or we wanted to be, and we refused to be startled by anything.

Perhaps because we were looking at clothing, I noticed his: burgundy pants and a matching silk scarf held in place by a dazzling stick pin. He'd thrown his jacket over his shoulder with faux nonchalance; I was sure he was going for a rakish air, and it made me grin. He'd nailed it. I noticed Suri and Danielle noticing, which, confusingly, sent a twinge of pride through me.

Daziel practically quivered with excitement as he took in the fine silver embroidery done on the top's high collar. He ran his fingers across the silk. "Stunning. Where are we going?"

The mere idea of Daziel interacting with my aunt gave me hives. "Not *we*," I said firmly. "I'm going to my aunt's this weekend."

"I will escort you," Daziel said happily.

"No." I doubled down on my firmness. "This is a family thing. I can't deal with you at the same time." I imagined my aunt's dour expression and, worse, her writing a missive to my parents. Horrible. "You'll stay here."

DAZIEL SULKED FOR THE rest of the week. It was very trying. He sighed endlessly, muttered asides to Paz, and draped himself across my couch like the world was ending.

"Have you changed your mind?" he asked Saturday night as I got ready. Leah had come over and was helping me paint my eyelids with kohl and silver shimmer.

"It's a lost cause," Leah told him. "She's stubborn."

I pulled a face. "I wouldn't say *stubborn*. What about determined?"

"Two sides of the same coin."

"I will be on my best behavior," Daziel pleaded. He was currently hanging—upside down from his knees—from a chandelier he'd installed in our living room. Would I be fined for that? Probably.

"Why don't you go see if any of the boys want a pickup game of knockball?" I suggested.

Daziel dropped to the floor, twisting in the air to land on his feet like a cat. The resemblance intensified when he hissed at me. "I am not a *child* to be appeased by *games*."

I raised my hands, suppressing my laughter to keep from disrupting Leah's work. "Just a suggestion."

He flopped onto the sofa, pouting. "What if there are suitors you need to deter?"

"If they've been invited to my aunt's, I doubt they'll need me for an introduction to her."

"Plus," Leah said, "maybe there'll be some hot guys there who *don't* want you for your aunt."

"Are you joking?" Daziel snapped.

"Are you jealous?" I retorted. He had no business being sharp with me about other guys. We weren't together. He had no right to act possessive like a child unwilling to share his toys.

"Oops," Leah said, grinning at me. "This sounds like a conversation for you to have when I'm not here. I'm done! You look amazing, I did great."

I checked out her work in the mirror. She'd made my eyes look dark and intriguing, my lips ruby, my skin poreless; she'd coaxed my hair into a six-strand crown with silver studs embedded against my dark braids. I hugged her. "You really did. Thanks."

After she left, I went into my bedroom to change. The top, with its high neckline and sleeveless cut, exposed my shoulders, arms, and half my midriff. The pants laced high on my waist, though, leaving only a thin strip of skin. The legs were wide and comfortable, yards of rippling navy silk. The silver embroidery on the ankle cuffs and waist shimmered like stars against the night. I looked like a different version of me, an elegant, more confident one.

When I came back out, I sent a sidelong glance at Daziel. It was silly to want him to say anything—what did it matter if he liked my outfit or appearance?

Daziel had never indicated any interest in me; he focused on knockball and training me in languages and had never given me a single compliment on my appearance or the smallest hint of a smoldering eye.

Which was fine. It wasn't like I wanted his romantic interest. God, no, the attention of a demon was a recipe for disaster. It was only that we lived together and spent all our time together. We were—friends, I supposed, and it was natural to care about your friends' opinions.

"What do you think?" I asked.

He ran his gaze over me, his own rather haughty and ruffled. "You'll do, I suppose."

His uncaring tone struck at my heart. "Fine," I said, hating how snippy I sounded but unable to help myself, not sure how else to bandage over the wound he'd inflicted. Would it have been so difficult to say I looked pretty? *I* didn't have any problem acknowledging Daziel was exquisitely beautiful. I mean, I hadn't told him so to his face, but his ego was big enough, wasn't it? I slung my blazer on, keeping my chin lifted and trying not to let it wobble. "I'm off, then."

I headed out. A slow, dull drizzle had begun. Thankfully, my aunt had sent a carriage. The driver, a balding man in his sixties wearing a diamond amulet of the Zebulun tribe, introduced himself as Samuel.

This was a neshem-powered carriage, which meant it needed no horses; the inner machinery had been carved with charaktêres and wrapped in piping. An ingenious technology pumped neshem oil through the pipes so the spell kept working. The driver had to continuously turn a wheel to add neshem throughout the drive, plus manage other knobs for turns and speed.

I peered hungrily out the window as we left Issachar Quarter. The city's thirteen arrondissements were named after the twelve tribes that had come together to form Ena-Cinnai—except for Roynes Quarter, colloquially known as Society Hill, site of the Politicians' Quarter and the seat of the Great Sanhedrin. I'd only been here once before, my very first day in Talum, when my aunt greeted me. Neither of us had known what to do with the other.

We climbed high up the hill, the view over the rest of the city likely stunning on clearer days, and wound along a wide avenue to my aunt's house. Like all the buildings in Talum, it faced south to protect against the northern winds. It was built from the yellow-orange sandstone popular to the river region. The roof, like all roofs here, sloped shallowly to keep the winds from stealing tiles.

There, the similarities with the local architecture ended.

Because Aunt Tirtzah's house was owned by the Judahite tribe for their representatives, it'd been built to display the power and wealth of the tribe. The windows weren't small, but large and spelled against breaking. The structure surrounded an interior courtyard with a spelled glass dome that closed on blustery nights. Cypresses lined the property, hearty trees often used as windbreaks—but inside, delicate plants signaled wealth and power.

The door flew open, and Chava, my aunt's assistant, scowled at me. She was a round-faced woman in her midtwenties wearing a neat black sheath and a bold-shouldered jacket. "*There* you are."

"Hi?" I blinked at her.

"The councilwoman wants you in the garden immediately," Chava said, voice dire. She took my arm and steered me inside. Confused, and a little alarmed, I allowed her to tow me to the courtyard. Was I late? Had I messed up already? But I was wearing the outfit my aunt had sent, and I'd arrived in her carriage. What was going on?

Winding flowers twined over the rose arbor at the entrance to the garden courtyard, writhing like a mass of snakes. The glass dome above the space had been closed. I could see rain bursting upon it, but the spell on the glass transformed the pelting drops to muted genteel music.

Almond and apricot trees lined the garden's pathways, and rosemary shrubs grew along the border. There were extravagant flowers in bloom: great swaths of lavender and colorful lilies. I'd heard some spellcasters specialized in succinct spells and impossibly small writing so they could carve strength and life into seeds to make them bloom out of season.

The guests were equally colorful, in wispy fabrics spelled to withstand the winds—yet another display of wealth. The women had high, teetering hairstyles. The men twisted silk cravats around their necks and wore long coats with exquisite embroidery. I felt small and self-conscious. I didn't belong here. I didn't know how to interact with the wealthy and beautiful, and I wasn't sure I wanted to, either.

At the center of the courtyard clustered a thick clump of people, their attention turned inward. The other guests darted glances their way. In fact, the whole party seemed aimed at the center, as was often the case when someone far more important than everyone else attended a gathering. Unease raised the hairs on the back of my neck. A member of the grand duke's family, perhaps. A famed writer or singer, the likes of which these politicians rarely encountered?

No. Of course not.

There, at the very center, revealed by shifts and turns, stood an impeccably dressed young man in a green silk coat with brass buttons, supple fawn-colored boots, and a white cravat. Black stones winked in his ears, and a small red salamander curled on his shoulder.

My stomach sank.

"Ah, darling," Daziel called across the garden, beaming like he'd just delivered the choicest of pastries. He raised a flute of champagne in my direction as I swallowed against the knot in my throat. "There you are."

TEN

O F COURSE DAZIEL HADN'T LISTENED. OF COURSE HE'D decided to show up at the event where I already felt out of my element, where I was worried about being an embarrassment to my aunt and humiliating myself by acting like a country bumpkin. Of course he was distractingly handsome in his elegant outfit, each detail lovingly tended. And of course he looked entirely too pleased with himself, as though appearing at my aunt's house was a delightful joke.

Not so my aunt. I couldn't read her expression—politicians practiced their poker faces—but she hardly looked happy. The guests were easier, their gazes sticky with curiosity.

I marched toward Daziel, watching his smile widen. He looked like he belonged on Society Hill more than I did. As he crossed the garden to meet me, he shed onlookers as though his very presence pushed them back.

"Hello," he said brightly when we met. "Surprise!"

"I told you not to come." Anger warmed me, and I felt embarrassment over being so rattled. How was I supposed to explain a demon to my aunt? I was nervous enough about fitting in. "This is my *aunt's*."

"I like a party. And I wanted to meet her." He smiled over my shoulder. "Hello, aunt."

I turned, finding Aunt Tirtzah behind me. She was in her forties, tall, and she wore a simple navy shift and silver bangles. She gave Daziel a tense smile before pinning me with her steely gaze. "Both of you, come."

She headed for the exit. Daziel made a polite *after you* gesture, which made me scowl even harder. It should be illegal for him to look so handsome and be so relaxed when I was so angry. We followed my aunt out of the courtyard, down the high-ceilinged halls of her home, and into her private study.

It was an airy room with whitewashed walls and bookshelves of political treatises with excruciatingly long titles. She sat behind a desk that looked impossible to move, so large and sturdy I wondered if it'd been constructed within the room. "Sit."

We sat. I perched on the edge of a velvet chair before her desk, unwilling to let my spine slouch at all.

"Are you mad?" Daziel asked me, sotto voce, as Aunt Tirtzah studied us.

"Obviously."

He looked confused. "Why?"

This was why Daziel made me want to pull my hair out. He could be *so smart* and also such an idiot. "I told you not to come. This is my *family*. It's private."

Aunt Tirtzah spoke, voice crisp. "Tell me why this—young man—showed up in my house, claiming to be betrothed to my niece."

"We're not really betrothed," I said. "He's staying with me for a bit."

Daziel set his chin mulishly, and I sensed the words coming before he said them. "We're betrothed."

I glared at him. "Daziel!"

He glared back. "You don't need to deny it *so aggressively* all the time."

"Start from the beginning," my aunt said.

Chastened—was this how my younger sisters always felt?—I laced my fingers together. "I accidentally summoned him."

Even my stone-faced aunt couldn't keep a flicker of horror from her face. "You *summoned* him?"

"I didn't bind him!" I said quickly. "I just said his name. It was an honest mistake."

Aunt Tirtzah looked increasingly pained as I explained the situation, though she tried to school her expression to a bland politeness. "Have you slept together?" she asked at the end, through a smile of ground teeth.

I flushed and refused to look at Daziel. No reason to get overheated and awkward. No need for my heart to gallop in my chest when I recalled his intensity when he got protective or the glint in his eyes when he teased me. "No."

"Exchanged gifts?"

"A pomegranate," I admitted reluctantly. "And a ring. Sort of."

Daziel held up his hand and wiggled his fingers, the cheap ring I'd thrown at him flashing.

"I cannot," Aunt Tirtzah muttered. Then she pinned me with her gaze. "Is there a reason you didn't tell me this immediately?"

"Um." I hesitated, feeling awkward. "It only happened a month ago."

She looked almost hurt, then nodded briskly. "I'd appreciate,

in the future, if you let me know about any magical entangle-
ments you find yourself in."

I nodded, trying to look obedient. My hands squeezed each
other hard enough to hurt.

Her fingers tapped ceaselessly against the desk. "To make sure
I have this clear. Your betrothal is binding, but you're not planning to either banish him *or* marry him?"

When she put it like that, it sounded like I had no idea what I
was doing. Which. I did not. "I'm waiting until after the graduation festival," I said. "Then we'll part ways."

Aunt Tirtzah rubbed her forehead. "What are you getting out
of this?" she asked Daziel.

He smiled, showing his teeth. "Croissants."

She closed her eyes, looking pained. When she opened them,
she'd become more focused. "This is the largest social event I've
hosted in half a year, and I don't want it to be a disaster."

"I don't want to make it a disaster," I said quickly.

"If you don't," she said, iron in her voice as she leaned forward,
"the two of you will go out there and dance and mingle, and the
three of us will behave as though we've all known about this betrothal for ages. What are you called, here in the human lands?"

He inclined his head slightly. "Daziel bar Cathmeus."

She repeated it to herself as though committing it to memory,
then added, "Send in Chava and wait in the hall."

We did. Once her assistant had closed the office door, I didn't
know where to look, cringing as my aunt's words replayed themselves in my mind. *Have you slept together?* What a mortifying
question.

But when I snuck a look at Daziel, he appeared remorseful,
clearly not dwelling on the same part of the conversation as me.

Which, fine. I didn't want him focused on sleeping with me anyway.

He twisted his signet ring and gazed at the floor. "I'm sorry. I knew you didn't want me here. I should have respected your wishes."

"Then why didn't you?"

He frowned. "I didn't realize how serious you were, I suppose. How much it would upset you. I'm used to statements being challenges. Games. You weren't playing a game, and while I mostly knew that . . . I'm still getting used to how serious humans can be. How deeply you feel things."

"Don't you feel things deeply?" I asked, baffled. "You were very serious the night with the winds and the caves."

"Yes," he said slowly. "But . . . we don't hold on to things as long as humans do? I'm used to people getting upset but not staying upset." He bowed his head. "You're the first human I've known. I'm still getting used to it."

"Well, you're the first demon," I said wryly. "So I guess we're equal."

"Shayd."

"Shayd," I corrected. The singular of "shedim," the term Daziel used for demons. "I'm sorry. Is 'demon' rude?"

He shrugged. "It's incorrect. And has negative connotations."

I nodded, embarrassed. "Sorry."

"Shall we strike a deal?" he asked, his mood shifting. Well, he *had* just mentioned he didn't hang on to things as long as humans. "Since we are here, let us endeavor to have fun. It *is* a party."

"A party for stuffy politicians," I said wryly. There'd barely been anyone under forty in the courtyard.

He raised his brows, black eyes gleaming. "You're not up for it?"

Ha. I'd turned both collecting crocus flowers and being silent into games for my sisters. If anyone could make a boring party a good time, it was me. "I can handle it."

He tilted his head consideringly, then smiled, sharp and bright as a knife. "You look very beautiful tonight."

His unexpected words stabbed me, leaving me hot and breathless. My whole body warmed from my forehead to my palms. I didn't want to care, but I felt a fluttering in my stomach, a delight and uncertainty I didn't know how to handle. The back of my neck prickled. He thought I was *beautiful*.

Instead of saying thank you like a normal person and potentially revealing how much the compliment meant to me, I scowled. "Why didn't you say that earlier?"

"I was mad at you," he said cheerfully. "I didn't want to be nice."

I wasn't sure whether to scream or laugh. In the end, I kicked his shin lightly, and he grinned at me so fondly I thought my heart might burst.

The door opened, and Aunt Tirtzah and Chava reappeared. "Let's go, then," my aunt said, marching into the hall.

The four of us returned to the garden courtyard, Chava peeling away. Aunt Tirtzah walked confidently through the guests until she reached a clump of well-dressed men and women in their sixties and seventies. I was glad; I wasn't ready to look Daziel in the eye again. *Beautiful.*

"Messieurs and madames, may I introduce my niece, Naomi bat Yardena, and her betrothed, the shayd Daziel bar Cathmeus."

A man with an impressive coiffure and twenty years on the others recovered from his shock first. "Enchanted, mademoiselle. And—honored guest—I believe we crossed paths at the opera last week."

Amusement welled within me, and I felt a bit more normal. Of course they had.

"Which one?" Daziel said, which was how I learned he'd attended *multiple* operas.

"*The Sons of Har Chermon*. I believe . . . you were accompanied by a cat?" The gentleman glanced at me, as though maybe I'd been the cat in question.

A crack of lightning drew everyone's attention upward to the dome shielding the garden. The guests stared at the night sky until thunder rumbled. As though it was the permission they'd waited for, everyone then returned to their dancing and talking.

"It's a beautiful dome," a lady in orange silk said to Aunt Tirtzah, who inclined her head graciously. The dome was a wild extravagance, but that was the purpose of parties like this, to show off your resources and taste.

"If only Bar Asher had one yesterday," one of the men said. "The storm completely decimated their garden party."

"Were you there?" someone else asked. "I heard it was carnage, everything flooded."

"You should have seen it—chairs strewn across the lawn, everyone chasing after napkins and scarves."

"It's hardly the only strange thing going on," said a man with a weak chin and a strong mustache. "Did you hear the first maelstrom stopped spinning last week? It started up again a few hours later, but still quite alarming."

My eyes widened. The three maelstroms guarded the northern entrance of the Lersach River from the Long Sea. Only Ena-Cinnaian sailors knew how to navigate the whirlpools. They kept their secrets in rutters, guides explaining exactly how to sail, used by navigators like Gilli's mom. Because of this, only Ena-Cinnaians could enter the river's delta and sail down to Talum. Foreigners landed in port cities, then crossed overland to the river and continued on domestic ships.

I remembered my voyage here, my ship navigating the safe currents through the maelstroms, listening as sailors raised their voices in the traditional song requesting safe passage from the Leviathan, the Behemoth, and the Ziz. I'd told myself we'd be safe, that the sailors had done this a hundred times, but I'd been terrified all the same.

"If the winds are off, why not the maelstroms?" a man with a cravat said.

An elderly man with a sheaf of silver hair turned to Daziel. "What do your people think of these changes?"

Daziel smiled without teeth. He took my hand and lifted it to his lips, pressing a kiss to it. I almost wrenched my hand from his in surprise. "I care only about my betrothed. Shall we get a drink, yonati?"

He dropped my hand and sauntered off. With a hurried apology to my aunt's guests, I followed.

"I think we can do better than that for fun," Daziel said lightly when I caught up to him on the lantern-lit garden path. The silver-tinged leaves of olive trees shimmered above us.

I watched him, curious. He'd clearly been displeased, but I wasn't sure why. "It irritated you, them asking what your people think about the maelstroms."

His expression hardened. "I'm not an emissary. I'm not here to answer politicians' questions."

"True." I couldn't argue much, given how sick I was of government students hounding me to get close to my aunt; like Daziel, I had no desire to be sucked into politics against my will. But in my case, I was treated as a pawn, and in Daziel's . . . "It's an interesting opportunity, though, isn't it? You're the only shayd here. They'd listen to you. You could make an impact."

"They won't listen to me. They'll listen to my elders at the treaty renewal but not me."

We reached the bar and asked for two lemonades. "Maybe not officially, but everyone's aware of the power shedim have. They wouldn't ignore you, even if you're young."

He raised his brows. "Very shrewd. Planning to follow your aunt into the Sanhedrin?"

I made a face. "You don't have to want to be a politician to want to have a voice."

"And what would you say, with your voice?" he asked lightly.

I shrugged, accepting my drink from the bartender and taking a sip of the crisp lemonade. "You've heard Ezra say politicians aren't doing enough to figure out why magic's off. Maybe you could be a bridge, get humans and shedim to work together to figure out what's going on."

"Maybe we should get married."

I choked on my drink and started coughing uncontrollably. He'd sounded *serious*, though I knew he couldn't be. "Excuse me?"

He grinned, eyes gleaming with a teasing glint. "If you're so keen to be a bridge. It probably would be savvy."

This boy found getting under my skin far too amusing. "You're hilarious."

"I have often thought so," he said. "I'm glad you agree."

I barely suppressed the childish urge to stick out my tongue. If the way he was grinning indicated anything, he could tell. "Come," he said. "Let's dance."

"No," I said, in danger of pouting.

He plucked my drink away and deposited both our glasses on a passing server's tray. Then he took my hands, his own warm as heated rocks, and widened his eyes. I was very conscious of his fingers wrapped around mine. His exaggeratedly hopeful expression was ridiculous, but it made me smile. "*Please*, Naomi."

I glanced toward the middle of the garden, where couples danced around a fountain. It looked fun, but I felt too self-conscious to join. "I don't know society dances."

"Neither do I. So we won't dance them." He pulled me close, his hands firmly wrapping around my waist. My stomach swooped, a strange, tantalizing fall. I caught my arms around his neck, and then we were twirling.

I'd danced at home with boys, but always ones I'd known my whole life, boys who felt like brothers. They had been group and line dances, too, where you occasionally twirled your partner but spent most of the time in circles or squares. This was different. This was a couple's dance, with Daziel's hands at the small of my back.

I didn't know where to focus or how tightly to hold on to Daziel. But he held me securely, his grip above my hips firm, the heat of his hands burning through the thin silk of my waistband. I tried to look over his shoulder, only for my gaze to catch on Paz nestled under Daziel's collar, seeming as delighted as a tiny lizard could.

It made me laugh, which helped me relax. Being held by Daziel as he swept me along in dreamlike steps was strangely thrilling. We weren't dancing like the others. I didn't know the steps, but my body managed them anyway, pulling me through the motions. It was not a human dance—different parts of it were far too fast, others too slow—and I shouldn't have been able to follow the way I did. But I didn't care. It was too much fun.

We danced for an hour, maybe more. Dancing with Daziel was intoxicating, the rush of energy, the joy in his eyes, the way he threw his whole body into the movements. Though we spent every day together, we'd rarely been so close before, and I was intimately aware of the way his body framed mine, how we lined up, how his heat enveloped me. It felt both heady and dangerous, and I wasn't sure if I was glad the rules of dancing and public decorum kept us apart or if I regretted them.

When we paused, it was only because I needed to catch my breath—Daziel wasn't even breathing hard. I gulped down two glasses of water while he barely touched one.

"You're a very good dancer," a woman said wistfully when I sat on the same bench as her at the edge of the courtyard. She looked a decade older than us but had a timidness I recognized from my sister Michal, who could be shy apart from family.

Daziel threw me a questioning look, and I nodded. "Would you like to dance?"

Her eyes widened before narrowing, and she drew her shoulders back tightly. "I wasn't angling for an invitation."

He shrugged. "You looked like you wanted to dance. Naomi can't keep going. She doesn't have the stamina."

"Thanks," I said wryly.

He looked at me, surprised. "It wasn't an insult. It's because you're a human."

This boy. I wasn't offended, but I imagined if someone didn't know him, they would be. Laughter bubbled up in me. "You're not helping yourself."

The woman had loosened up enough to look amused. "If you don't mind. I'd love to dance."

"Excellent." Daziel took her hand and swept her off to the dance floor. As they left, Paz crept up the back of Daziel's collar and leaped from him to me, landing with a wobble on my shoulder.

I laughed and stroked his head. "Good job, you."

Paz licked my cheek in a happy greeting, then scrambled down my arm, wrapping his limber body and tail around my wrist.

Idly scanning the room, I caught my aunt watching me. I looked away—I don't know why, instinct not to be perceived by authority figures?—then back. A mistake. She beckoned me imperiously, and I could do nothing but head over.

She excused herself from her group and led me along a courtyard path lined with apricot trees. "It's kind of your demon to dance with the wallflowers." She made it sound like *What's his ulterior motive?*

"He's not mine," I said, flushing again. Good lord, I'd blushed more tonight than in the last year. "And he says the proper term is 'shayd.'"

"Mm," she said noncommittedly. "You say he's been here for a month?"

I nodded.

She sighed. "I should have known. I'm sorry I haven't been better about seeing you."

"Oh," I said, surprised. "It's okay. You're busy."

She looked gutted. "It was wrong of me. You're family. You don't know anyone else here."

"I've made friends," I said. "And don't worry about Daziel. He's not dangerous."

Her forehead crinkled, and the corners of her mouth turned down. "There are multiple forms of danger."

She looked and sounded so like my father I couldn't bear it. I stared at my feet. "Is the Sanhedrin trying to figure out why the magic is off—why the winds are strengthening, the maelstroms weakening? People are worried."

"Ah." She pinched the skin between her thumb and forefinger. "Many divisions are working on understanding what's happening, but no one knows why yet. Are *you* worried?"

I shrugged. "My friend Leah says if the winds are too rough, and if the Maestril is too weak, it could ruin her family's silk harvest. And everyone's worried about the lack of birds. The cobwebs and bugs everywhere are getting out of control."

"Right." She nodded. "We don't understand natural magic— the workings of the earth, sea, sky—the way we understand letter-form. It's not something humans control; it's the domain of the primordial beasts. While the Council is trying to understand why natural magic is misbehaving, we haven't yet figured it out."

"How can it be the primordial beasts' domain? How do they control it?" I believed in the existence of the Leviathan and Behemoth and Ziz in a vague, unchecked way, the way I believed in cosmology and prophets and divine speech—they existed, probably. The rabbis could likely explain very thoroughly, but I didn't really care. I'd never thought of them having an impact on my life.

"We don't know," Aunt Tirtzah said. "We know so little. We don't even know if the beasts have forms like shedim or if they're more . . . metaphysical. The study of natural magic has historically been ignored since it's difficult for humans to harness, so it's quite the pivot for the Council to now try to understand it."

"When do they think they'll know?"

Her shoulders slumped slightly. "I'm not sure."

This was not reassuring. I looked away, watching Daziel spin his partner, who laughed with delight. "Can I ask you a question?"

"Of course."

"Can you not mention Daziel to my parents?"

Aunt Tirtzah didn't answer for a moment; I was too embarrassed by my request to look at her. "They're your parents," she finally said. "They need to know what's happening in your life."

"But nothing's happening." I gave her a pleading look. I almost said, *Let's make a deal*—maybe I was spending too much time with Daziel. "And they're such worriers. They're already worried about me being here in the big, scary city."

"I can't keep secrets from them," she said, sounding on firmer ground.

"But you don't even talk to them that often. You and Dad send letters once a year."

She sucked in a breath, and I immediately felt bad. I hadn't meant to hurt her feelings. I softened my voice. "Please. Did you want your parents involved in every part of your life?"

Some of the tension drained out of her. "Your parents are less strict than your grandparents were."

"Just think about it," I begged. "If you decide they need to know, I'll tell them. But I don't want to upset them about something small."

She pressed her lips together. "I'll consider it."

"Thank you," I said, relieved, and gave her an impulsive hug. She was clearly startled, frozen for a moment before tentatively patting my back.

Daziel came up to us, smiling. He swept an elaborate bow, the kind that spoke of years of training plus a natural elegance. "Councilor Bat Tovah," he said. "May I have this dance?"

Her brows went up. "Are you a charmer or a politician?"

"I am a dancer," he said, offering my aunt his hand. Shaking her head ruefully, she allowed herself to be led onto the dance floor.

They floated around the floor, talking but not seriously, based on their expressions. Daziel twirled my aunt, and she laughed, something I hadn't heard before.

Daziel was as strange and unpredictable as the winds, infuriating and engaging and amusing. Nothing like I'd expected when he'd first arrived. I would never have expected him to apologize. To empathize. To *care*.

I watched them dance for another song, and then I went over to join in.

ELEVEN

WHEN I WENT INTO THE LIVING ROOM THE NEXT MORNING, Daziel was already awake. A pot of coffee steamed on the narrow counter, and a plate piled high with fluffy pancakes stood beside fig jam and ricotta cheese.

"Wow." I sank onto one of the counter stools, admiring a new plant, a strange spiky red thing with a white flower blooming out of it. Did this flower look like it could kill me? Maybe! I decided to ignore it and inhaled the buttery scent of the freshly made pancakes. "This smells delicious."

Daziel looked nervous. "I have never made pancakes before. But your aunt's housekeeper gave me the recipe, and I think they came out all right."

"You asked my aunt's housekeeper for a pancake recipe?" I echoed, baffled. "When?"

He looked down. "When you were in the restroom. I wanted to make up for showing up at your aunt's unannounced."

I was startled and touched. I hadn't expected another apology after last night—I hadn't needed one—but I appreciated it. "Thanks. I guess I don't mind if I get pancakes out of it." I pulled several of the steaming flapjacks onto a plate and covered them in the ricotta and fig jam. The combination of sweet and savory on the buttery pancakes were decadent. "It tastes *amazing*. Do you cook at home?"

Daziel laughed, louder than usual, seeming relieved I'd liked them. "No. Maybe I'll try more when I return." Relaxed now, he tried his own bite. His eyes widened. "These *are* good."

We ate and drank our coffee companionably. I gazed out the window, at the blue wind flag indicating an eastern breeze, before my attention dipped to my living room, which now hosted a veritable forest along with new mirrors, paintings, and what I suspected was the beginning of a rock garden in the corner.

"Are those new cushions?" I asked, noticing the velvet pillows tucked into Daziel's blanket nest: deep-jewel-toned with buttons, nothing like the faded old things I'd owned.

"Hm?" He glanced over at his nest. "Oh. No. I just encouraged them to be their best self."

I raised my brows. "What?"

He shrugged, feeding Paz a tiny square of pancake. "You know. I asked what they wanted to be."

"I do not know. Are you saying those are my old cushions? What did you do to them?"

"I told them to be what they desired." He picked up my empty coffee mug. "This mug, for example, wants to hold lots of coffee and be a soothing shape."

Before my eyes, the coffee mug doubled in size. It bulged in the middle, forming a pleasing round body, and its handle developed a pretty little flourish. The chip in the lip disappeared.

"There," Daziel said, sounding satisfied.

I stared at the mug, astonished, then at the beautiful couch pillows. I didn't know inanimate objects had opinions. "Do all inanimate objects have shapes they want to be?"

"To a degree."

My mind ran wild. Did my bed yearn to be elegant, or my rug brighter and thicker?

Or ...

I caught my breath. Could Daziel ask the scroll fragments to be what they wanted? "Do you know in advance what form they'll take?"

"Nope," Daziel said cheerfully. "It's whatever they want. Sometimes it goes poorly."

Oof. What if the scroll fragments didn't want to be scrolls but dust instead? *That*'d be a disaster.

But it was an interesting way to think, considering what an inanimate object wanted. We'd kept trying to force the fragments back to scrolls, but they didn't budge. Could they want to be anything else? What did scroll fragments want to be except scrolls?

Maybe being a scroll wasn't enough to draw on. What if there was something stronger? Something with more energy than being a scroll, something the fragments would like more? Something more alive?

Like being alive.

The fragments were made of parchment.

Parchment was skin.

I froze, unwilling to move, barely willing to breathe until I'd finished thinking this through. Until I'd determined if this was as big as I thought it might be. How was parchment made? Was the parchment of a scroll made from multiple animals or one?

"Naomi? Are you all right? You look—"

"Shh," I said. "I'm figuring something out."

Say it was the same animal. How much parchment came from one animal? I had no idea. Even so, imagine ... "I could ask the parchment to be calves again. We keep trying to make it return to its shape as a scroll—but what if we asked it to return its skin to its shape as a *calf* ?"

Daziel raised his brows. "It's worth a shot."

"How do you ask things to take the form they want most?" Though human magic was wildly different than shedim magic, perhaps I could draw on his style, use its influence to write a letterform spell. "I know you said you can't tell in advance, but if you wanted to influence their form, how would you try?"

Daziel considered. "I'd suggest . . . trying to awaken the fragments' memory of their former life. Something like 'Go back to when you were a young calf. Feel the stretch of your skin across your muscles, the shiver in the wind, the dryness in the sun, itching, smoothness. Be *aware*.' Then ask it to come back together. Though I shouldn't try it, because they might literally turn back into a calf. A zombie calf."

His phrasing sounded so different from the technical way I was used to spells—different enough, maybe, to work. I gripped my coffee so hard I thought I might break the brand-new mug. Certainly all the spells we'd been trying so far hadn't worked. What if this did?

He watched me sharply. "Do you think you have something?"

"Yes," I said, feeling heady with hope. "I do."

MONDAY MORNING, I HEADED toward Professor Altschuler's office before classes started. Everything was soaking wet; the rainy season had arrived in earnest, with another storm sweeping in during the night, the strong wind wrenching branches from trees and scattering leaves on the ground. More worms than usual covered the pavement and lawns with no birds to eat them up. And a fog covered everything as I crossed campus, thick and heavy, swirls of mist hanging low to the ground, the world around me gray and blurred.

I entered the Keep, spiraling up to the professor's office and knocking. My stomach ground against itself. Daziel had looked worried when I barely ate breakfast, but I'd been too nervous. He'd offered to come, but I'd told him to go back to sleep; Paz, instead, had curled up in my shirt pocket, his warmth welcome against my chest.

"Enter."

"Hi," I said, trying to sound confident, instantly undercutting it with an apology. "Sorry to show up so early. I wanted to talk to you about something?"

The professor gestured me to a seat before his desk.

I took it, my back very straight. Professor Altschuler looked like he'd been up for hours, his hands stained with ink, his coffee mug empty. "I have a theory about the scrolls. We've been trying to call them back to their original forms as texts, but . . . what if we called them to their forms as calves? As parchment?"

The professor stopped looking at the paper in front of him, lifted his head, and stared at me.

"Sorry," I said nervously. "Is that stupid?"

"No," he growled, his thin face getting thinner. "It's *obvious*."

"Oh." The word snuck out of me, timid and embarrassed. Did "obvious" mean he'd already tried it? "Sorry—"

"Obvious, yet we all missed it." He shook his head, then focused his dark gaze on me. "Good work, Miss Bat Yardena."

Oh. Phew. I almost sagged with relief at his compliment. Then elation filled me. He liked it. He thought it had potential. Hopefully this would go toward convincing him to renew my scholarship for a second year. I wasn't ready to go home yet.

I handed over a folded piece of paper from my satchel. "I wrote a spell to try it. It's unorthodox," I admitted. "More poetic than usual."

He scanned the paper. His brows didn't shoot up—he rarely showed so much emotion—but I could see an arch to them, a slight purse of his lips. "Very pretty," he murmured. "Very . . . different." He pinned me once more with his eyes. "I hear you're still spending time with that demon."

"Shayd, sir," I said. "That's what they call themselves."

"I hope you understand that the work we're doing is confidential. Not to be shared with anyone."

"Of course," I said, though discussing the work with Daziel was what had gotten me this far. "I understand."

"Yet he had a hand in this? It has the—theatrical flair—one associates with their kind."

I stiffened, offended both on Daziel's behalf and at the idea I would claim someone else's work. "I wrote it. I asked what his jumping-off point would be. He thinks about magic differently than I do. It makes me more creative. He's helpful, you know."

"Hm." Professor Altschuler held on to my paper, and I began to regret not having made a copy. "I'd hate to have to take you off the project because your loyalties were unclear."

So much for impressing him enough that he'd renew my scholarship on the spot. "They're not unclear, sir."

"Good. See that they remain so." Professor Altschuler circled several sections in red. "Rewrite this in a technopaigniac form and add refrains here and here. That will strengthen the magic. Your beginning is too long, and your middle bridge too short. I'll expect a revised version in two weeks." He extended the paper back.

I tucked it inside my folder. "Thank you. I'll have it done."

He gave me a brisk nod of dismissal, and I left, walking through the mist toward the campus boulangerie. I still felt the high of Professor Altschuler's all-too-rare praise, but it was dampened by his brusqueness and his disdain for shedim.

As I left the boulangerie, Daziel fell into step from nowhere, taking one of the croissants from my hand. "Did it go well?"

I didn't startle as I led him up the steps to the library. Apparently I'd gotten used to his appearances. "Well enough. He likes the idea."

"Good." Daziel craned his neck back, taking in the library's pedimental sculpture, which could just be seen through the fog. It showed the symbols of the twelve tribes interacting. The sun, moon, and stars of Issachar took center stage, while my tribe's symbol, the gazelle, leaped gracefully in the left corner. "We've not been in here before."

"It's the library." I hadn't come here since Daziel appeared, finding the idea of keeping him quietly entertained too stressful. But sometimes a girl needed to do research, like when she had a major spell to write. "You have to be quiet."

"You have so many rules," Daziel said. But softly.

The front doors opened into a spacious atrium, all white marble and gleaming statues of scholars. I led him into the main hall, where wooden beams arched high above endless stacks of books. Tables clustered in the center, surrounded by green velvet chairs, almost all filled by students and piles of books—plus, often, the surreptitious remnants of lunch.

Through the stacks we went, into a hall built three hundred

years ago. Burnished wooden shelves held heavy treatises; narrow windows let in slats of light, and the ceiling arched in a dome. Chandeliers hung all down the long hall above wooden tables with brass lamps, and more students filled these seats, quieter than in the main hall.

I found us a spot at the edge of one of the tables. Daziel settled across from me. He spoke sotto voce, scanning the room around us. "So this is where the books live."

I smiled, pulling notebooks from my rucksack. "I'll be right back. I have to get a few more."

He came with me. *Refrains for Revealing*, *Advanced Technopaigniac Forms*, and a dusty old title called *The Elegant Cast*, which discussed writing spells inspired by foreign languages. All of which would hopefully help me figure out how to amend the spell as Professor Altschuler had requested.

Daziel carried them back to the old hall. "You don't have to stay," I whispered to him. "I'll be here a couple of hours. You could play knockball or whatever."

Daziel shrugged. "I have some work to do too."

At home I often worked in companionable silence with Daziel, usually while he read or crocheted or, recently, tried out recipes. Yet I had no idea what library-appropriate work he had. Foiled by my curiosity, I kept glancing over. I wasn't the only person covertly watching him—so were half the other students. While they'd become used to him enough not to stare, sidelong looks and murmurs still followed him wherever he went.

Daziel cupped his hands together. When he pulled them apart, a ball of light hovered between them. He began playing with it the way a cat toys with yarn.

I leaned forward, mystified. Looking at the bright sphere didn't hurt the way looking at the sun did, but it didn't feel comfortable, either. Like the blurred distortion around Daziel, it looked *off*, like there was something behind or beneath it I couldn't understand.

"What's that?" I finally whispered across the table.

"Magic," he whispered back. "Why are we whispering?"

"The quiet thing."

"Right, right."

Magic, he'd said—but shedim magic, not letterform. "Why's it look like that?"

He paused in his motions and appeared intrigued. "How's it look?"

I watched the threads expand and contract. "Like you're pulling at a ball of shimmering light. Does it look different to you?"

"Shedim retinas are different than humans', so yes. We can see a different range of particles than you can. And we have what you might call thaumaturgical sensing."

"You can sense magic."

"Essentially."

"So, what do you see?"

He looked at the light. "Mess. You know how wool is combed before being spun? I'm essentially combing my magic. Neatening it up, keeping it aligned and tidy."

"That's *your* magic?"

He nodded, looking amused. "Some of it. Interesting you can see it. Humans usually can't." He turned to the closest student, a boy at the table behind us wearing a red Engineering blazer. "Can you see anything between my hands?"

The boy flinched, stared at Daziel, looked at me, then shook his head very quickly.

Daziel nodded, satisfied. "See?"

I swallowed, fixing on the very distinct golden glow. I wasn't a huge fan of being able to see things other humans couldn't. "An effect of the betrothal?"

"Probably."

Great. "You don't have, say, a *list* of all the things that might happen to me because of the betrothal?"

"Nope," Daziel said cheerfully. "Since you're a human, I have no idea."

Cool.

I SPENT THE REST of the week improving the spell. Daziel was unexpectedly easygoing about my lack of attention, perhaps due to knockball season ramping up; he attended his biweekly practices with great fervor and often went out with Ezra and other teammates afterward to discuss strategy.

One afternoon, when he was at practice and I was trying to figure out how to trim the beginning of the spell without losing any pertinent information, a bell in my rooms chimed.

The bell connected to a panel in the lobby of Testylier House. When a visitor wrote their name in the clay tab downstairs, then pressed a resident's name, the writing appeared in the resident's matching tab upstairs. Such spells couldn't work over great distances without shocking amounts of neshem, but they were useful within the same building. *Tirtzah bat Tovah*, my tab read.

I slid my feet into my dorm slippers and spared a glance for my hair before darting out the door. This was it, then. She'd decided whether to tell my parents about Daziel.

Downstairs, I found Aunt Tirtzah in the receiving parlor, reading a briefing. I tried to take in the room from her perspective. It was very much a student parlor, worn furniture, faded wallpaper, glow globes thirty years out of style. Two windows looked out at the street, where students hurried by. "Hi, Aunt Tirtzah."

She put away her papers. "Naomi. Hello."

"Can I get you something to drink? Tea, coffee, water?"

"Tea would be lovely."

I set the water to boil and offered her the parlor's eclectic mix of teas to choose from. She selected chamomile, and I followed her lead. I could use some soothing.

"I'm sorry to impinge upon you." She regarded the basic furnishings in a way that made me suspect she was sorry to subject herself to student housing. "I'm here to talk about Daziel."

"I figured."

"You're in over your head."

I winced. "You're going to tell my parents?"

"Frankly, I should do more than that. I should banish him."

Startlement jumped through me, then anger. That wasn't her call to make. "That seems excessive."

"Is it?" she returned, more forcefully than I'd expected. "Naomi, you have no idea what he might do to you, out of amusement or by accident. If this is because you wish to have a tutor so you can maintain the grades for your scholarship—I can afford a tutor." She sighed, rubbing her forehead. "Unfortunately, I don't have the money for your tuition, or I'd pay it outright. But I can help navigate loans. You can live with me, and you won't have to pay for housing."

I lowered my head, embarrassed she'd do so much for me. "Thank you." The water boiled, and I poured us both our tea. "But you don't have to."

"That makes it sound like it's not about your bargain, then," she said heavily. "It's about him."

I bit my lip. I should probably tell her about how the betrothal bound us together; she'd probably help nullify it. But for some reason, I was reluctant. Daziel was an infuriating demon, but he was *my* infuriating demon, and our arrangement worked. "It's complicated."

She rubbed her nose. "I'm not unaware of the appeal of unique or forbidden romances. I was eighteen once. But the two of you have no future. I say this not to be hurtful but to set your expectations. Sleep with him, laugh with him—"

"I'm not sleeping with him!" I interrupted, mortified to have this brought up again. My mortification doubled when my aunt gave me a pitying look. It wasn't clear if she pitied me for *not* having sex or if she thought I was lying.

"Enjoy your time—but remember he's not going to stay. He'll be gone with the winds."

"Why are you even talking to me, then?" I said bitterly. "If you've made up your mind to banish him?"

She studied her mug. "Because I haven't. I *should* banish him and tell your parents. As your aunt, I should protect you from inevitable heartbreak, and potentially worse."

I straightened, curious. This wasn't the turn I'd expected our conversation to take. "But?"

"But I'm also a Judahite representative on the Sanhedrin. And having a shayd in my corner is leverage. People who don't normally socialize with me will accept invitations if it means they might meet a shayd."

This shocked me more than it should have. "You're as bad as

the classmates who asked me out so they could meet you. You want to use me."

"If it leverages me connections so I can make more allies and pass better laws? Yes." She stirred her tea. "You're worried about the weakening maelstroms, the strengthening winds, the birds disappearing?"

I nodded.

She gave me a grim smile. "So am I. I've been trying to raise funding and awareness and get more research into what's happening. As long as you're not in actual danger, yes, I'm willing to use you. Your inevitable heartbreak?" She gave a one-shouldered shrug. "I'll accept that as collateral damage."

Brutal. I was almost impressed.

At that moment, Daziel walked past the parlor door toward the stairs, then doubled back on seeing us. He was kitted out in his knockball clothes, his equipment bag slung over his shoulder, bright athletic shoes on his feet. "Hi."

Aunt Tirtzah stared. He couldn't look less dangerous if he'd tried. He looked like a Lyceum student badly in need of a shower. Which should have made me wrinkle my nose, but his sporty, sweaty demeanor worked for him. "I know," I said to my aunt. "He's very confusing."

"You play knockball?" Aunt Tirtzah asked.

"Middle back," he said cheerfully. He leaned his bag against the wall—definitely not something the dorm guardienne would approve of—and swung a chair around to sit in backward. "You a fan? What's your team?"

"The Green Sparrows."

I gaped at my aunt. "*You* follow knockball?"

She cast me a droll look. "I do have hobbies."

"Naomi hates knockball." Daziel snagged my tea and drained it in several long gulps. He slipped the lip of the mug into his mouth as though ready to chomp down, then caught my side-eye and hastily put it on the table.

"I don't hate it." I removed the mug from his reach, overly aware of how intimate sharing a drink looked. "It's just not my thing."

"Naomi only likes things more than a century old."

"Knockball was created in the 5540s," Aunt Tirtzah said. "So it's a hundred and twenty years old."

"Really?" Curiosity piqued, I tried to imagine students in old-fashioned uniforms knocking about a ball.

Daziel and Aunt Tirtzah laughed, and I bumped Daziel with my shoulder. "Leave me alone," I grumbled, but I was smiling.

He grinned back, but the grin faded as he turned to Aunt Tirtzah. "You think I'm a threat to Naomi."

"Are you?"

"No. We're betrothed. Any threat to her is a threat to me. I am beholden to protect her."

I scrunched up my nose. "That's a little paternalistic."

He frowned. "How is it paternalistic to say I want to keep you safe?"

"Because I'm responsible for my own safety."

Now he looked full-on irritated. "Oh, and you're so good at safeguarding yourself?"

I glared at him, peeved he'd alluded to my run-in with the winds before my aunt. "I've survived this long."

"All right," Aunt Tirtzah interrupted, looking back and forth between us. "Daziel, I'll be frank. You seem like a nice boy, but your kind have a reputation for mischievousness. If you're going to continue staying with Naomi without any interference on my part, I'm going to request you attend twice-monthly events at mine."

Daziel perked up. "Parties?"

I should have anticipated Daziel would be thrilled by this turn of events.

Aunt Tirtzah raised her brows. "Occasionally. Also luncheons and dinners."

Daziel smiled. "And what do I get?"

"Not banished."

He grinned. "Fair enough. I warn you, though, I am not easy to banish."

"I wouldn't challenge me," Tirtzah said calmly. Probably Sanhedrin members were better spellcasters than Lyceum students.

"Also, she'll tell my parents," I said. "Which might be worse."

Daziel dealt me a mock-hurt look. His hair was particularly disarrayed today from practice, and my fingers itched to comb it into place. "You haven't told your parents about me?"

I rolled my eyes. "Have you told yours?"

Daziel ignored this. "I'll make a deal. For each visit, we see a new part of Talum."

Given my aunt had threatened to banish him if he said no, I didn't think *I* was the person he should bargain with—but it sounded fun. "Deal. Unless I have an exam to study for."

He groaned. "You *always* have an exam." He appealed to my aunt. "Can't you do something about it?"

She regarded him from above her tea. "About . . . exams?"

"They are the bane of my existence," he said, a touch melodramatically. "Do you know, she refused to go see *The Barber and the Violinist*, playing for *three nights only*, because of an *exam*?"

"Actually, I think that was because I had to finish an essay for my Keft class."

He sighed. "*I* could have written the essay."

"I don't let him," I told my aunt quickly. "He helps me study but doesn't do any of my work."

"I would never," Daziel said disdainfully, despite having literally just said he would. "It is *so tedious*."

Aunt Tirtzah stood, biting back a smile. "I'll see you in a fortnight."

TWELVE

AT THE END OF THE NEXT WEEK, I NERVOUSLY PRESENTED my revised spell to the other cryptography students. I couldn't imagine they'd want to spend an entire afternoon working on my spell, an honor only Yael had received since I'd been here. Their expressions ranged from bored to murderous as I passed out copies. "We can read it over and get to work," I said. "Unless anyone has questions about the spell itself?"

"Why's it written fancy?" Stefan rubbed his abs, the jeweled bangles on his wrists clanging together—in Aolong, they wore spelled bracelets instead of amulets. He touched his muscles often, as though to make sure they were still there. "You trying to be a poet? Transferring to the literature department?"

"No," I said, flustered, hands going to my braids to loosen them instinctively, before reminding myself that would make my hair look terrible. I locked my hands behind my back. "I wanted to try something new."

"It's ... poetic. Elemental," Yael said, studying the text. "Shedim work with the elements, don't they? That's why they live in cliffs carved by wind and rivers."

Gidon stared at Yael. "Isn't that just a rumor?"

The three of them looked at me. I shrugged. "I don't know."

Gidon looked surprised. "You don't know where your be-trothed lives?"

This would have been embarrassing had Daziel really been my betrothed. I was embarrassed a little, anyway. I knew so many small, intimate details about Daziel—how he looked when he first woke up; that his favorite scent was the low-lying shrub gar-rigue; he was bizarrely averse to kidney beans; he twisted his sig-net ring when nervous; sometimes he hummed to Paz when he thought they were alone. But the larger facts of his life—many of those I didn't know.

"It's an interesting tactic," Yael said, still studying the spell. "Different."

Professor Altschuler tapped his podium. "I'll meet you in the scroll room at seven. I expect the materials to be prepared by then." He swept out.

"At *seven*," Gidon groaned. Three hours from now, if we didn't pause to eat.

"You better not be wasting our time, Bat Yardena," Stefan said.

"Leave her alone," Yael said dismissively. "You're just jealous Professor Altschuler hasn't tried any of your spells."

"Course I am. She's a *first-year*. How can she know anything?"

I bristled. At home, people considered me competent, the per-son to look up to. I hated being the newest and untrusted. I lifted my chin in Stefan's direction. "Do you not like the spell? Because I think it's worth trying."

He heaved a sigh and turned toward the door. "Yeah, it's a pretty good idea," he said, so easily I wondered if maybe he didn't think I was an idiot after all.

We pulled plywood from the storage closet. Then we divided

the spell into quarters and set to work penciling the charaktêres in charcoal before chiseling them.

Plywood wasn't hard to carve, especially with our sharp metal stylos, but it still took over two hours to space the charaktêres correctly and carve them. By the end, our hands ached. While everyone else did wrist exercises, Gidon unscrewed a jar of neshem oil, the liquid the color of moonlight on water. The four of us dipped in our brushes and painted the spell.

We finished preparing three minutes before seven, our dinner the almonds and carrots Gidon always had on him. Despite our growling stomachs, we straightened as Professor Altschuler swept in.

"Evening," he said. Stefan started choking on an almond; we all ignored him. "Is everything prepared?"

"Yes, sir," Yael said, and I felt a little salty. It was my spell. I wanted the credit.

Still, I felt nervous when Professor Altschuler turned to me. "Miss Bat Yardena. If you'll do the honors?"

I nodded and took a deep breath. More voices were always better—each strengthened the spell—but one person always led. They set the pace, and everyone looked to them. If it were a song, they would be the one carrying the melody.

I'd led a million simple spells with my sisters, but I'd never led one at school. *Just pretend it's me, Adina, Michal, and Selah*, I told myself. I pictured them: Adina, always quick-tongued and irritated with me; Michal, dreamy and earnest; Selah, serious and solid. I began.

"'Remember when you were a young thing,'" I read. The other four—Professor Altschuler included—joined in. "'When you had hooves and horns and you ran through the grasses.'"

First iterations of new spells rarely worked. Most spells were rewritten a hundred times until the most effective word order had been found to channel magic. First attempts at a complicated spell got tangled, the magic knotted. It would stop moving, and the spellwriters would take another crack at ironing the words out.

Sometimes, if a spell was only a tad rough, you could use more neshem. The sheer force of power would scrape the magic through, like extra water forcing a mill to turn. But most people didn't have endless neshem to spend. Even with extra trills added to strengthen the magic—multiple voices, refrains, melodies, dancing—words were the most important part of a spell.

Basically, I knew better than to expect a first attempt to work.

I still hoped. Who doesn't want to be a prodigy, even if they've showed no prodigious talents before? This spell was so different from any we'd tried. Maybe it *would* work.

"'Remember when your skin was taut and pulled tight over your bones . . .'"

With this amount of neshem, you could feel it in the air when it activated against the charaktêres. Something shifted as we spoke, the magic waking up. It followed the words I read out loud, weaving through each charaktêre the neshem had seeped into. I exchanged wild, startled looks with Yael and Gidon and Stefan to see if they felt it too. They looked back with shock.

It was working.

"'Come once more to that form, to your body as it was, with your skin supple and smooth . . .'"

The magic tangled. Disappointment jolted through me, followed by a stubborn refusal to admit defeat. I kept reading, trying to force the magic through. But the more I pushed, the more it knotted, refusing to flow. Desperate, I moved toward the neshem jar, thinking if I slathered more on the charaktêres it might add enough power to push through. Professor Altschuler caught my eye and shook his head.

The spell was broken.

Blinking back disappointment, I faded to a stop. No one looked at me. Professor Altschuler grunted low in his throat and swept out of the room.

"Sorry, everyone." I stared at my feet. I'd failed. I'd been so conceitedly hopeful, but all I'd done was waste their time.

"What are you sorry for?" Yael said shortly. "I've been working on this for years, and this was more effective than anything I've done so far."

I looked up, shocked she wasn't mad. A bud of hope uncurled in my chest.

"It worked until here." She pointed to the section where the magic had slowed to a murky trickle. "When you described it being parchment. It liked when you were describing being a calf— that was strong. The transition's where it stuck."

"Maybe you weren't specific enough." Stefan leaned beside Yael, shoulder to shoulder, his black hair striking against her blond, their blue School of Humanities blazers identical. It struck me how often they'd workshopped spells together—almost three years now. I was so used to thinking of Yael as serious and Stefan as off-the-cuff. I'd never considered how well they must know each other. "Maybe we need to describe the calf being killed, the hide tanned and turned to parchment. Bridge from calf to parchment scraps. We're not trying to get a multidimensional sculpture of the calf, we still want it to be parchment."

I nodded slowly. I'd been willing to give up too quickly because I was nervous and embarrassed, because Professor Altschuler had walked out on us—but I wasn't a savant to land it on the first try. I was steady, determined, and driven, and I would keep trying, and maybe that was worth the same amount as being brilliant. "I'll work on it."

"We'll all work on it," Yael said. "Four minds are better than one."

My eyes must have widened, because she lifted her brows challengingly. None of us had ever collaborated—we all wanted to stand out.

But ... four minds *were* better than one. We'd have better odds of success. Besides, they all knew the spell now. They'd have their own jumping-off points to try.

My thought startled me, how territorial it was. It made me realize maybe *I'd* been as standoffish as I'd imagined they were.

I didn't want to be standoffish and competitive and isolated and alone. "Okay," I said. "Together."

DAZIEL SPENT OVER AN hour getting ready for my aunt's first luncheon.

"Is *this* why you went to her party without me?" I teased. I'd been ready for thirty minutes, and he'd spent the same time coaxing his hair into perfect curls. I sat cross-legged on the couch, Paz asleep on my knee, and alternated between Old Cinnaian language exercises and watching Daziel. Rain fell outside, but it was cozy within; I had a blanket draped over my legs, and two candles burned in the exquisite pair of carved bronze lanterns Daziel had brought home.

"I've never been invited to a human luncheon before," he said.

"I want to look right. And no, of course not, I went without you because I wanted to shock you with my sudden appearance."

"Glad we've got that cleared up," I said dryly. "You look good. You don't need to keep tinkering."

"I don't want to look *good*," he sniffed. "I want to look *astounding*."

I smothered a smile. "You look astounding."

I'd said the words automatically, but as I watched Daziel study himself in the mirror, I studied him too. His outfit was exquisite, a crisply ironed green jacket over trousers the silvery green of olive trees. But my eyes caught on his face, which had become so familiar to me I no longer found the solid black of his eyes jarring or the shimmer around his body disconcerting. Instead, I noticed how very beautiful he was.

I looked away, feeling overly warm. I'd known he was attractive from the start—his inhuman beauty had stood out—but it felt weirdly intimate to notice his looks now that I knew him so well. It felt less objective and more intimate, a flush of attraction heating my whole body. I stared downward, unusual shyness washing over me. It wouldn't do me any good to find Daziel attractive. He was my roommate and my tutor, and that was it. As my aunt had said, the two of us had no future. And I had my spellwriting and grades to focus on.

Besides, he'd never acted interested, save calling me beautiful a couple of weeks ago—and even then he might have just been being polite. I wasn't going to dash my heart on uncertain shores.

"Do you think I can wear these ear cuffs with these shoes?" he asked. "Because you're not supposed to mix metals."

Nice that we were both having our own private crises. The cuffs in question were long strands of gold curving over the helix of his ear. The shoes were black with silver detailing. "I don't think any-one will notice."

His expression made it clear I'd answered incorrectly. "Obvi-ously people will *notice*. It's more if it looks *bad*."

"Wear different shoes, then."

"So it does look bad?" He sounded agonized as he turned back to the mirror. A new mirror, full-length. He hadn't liked the pre-vious short one I had in the living room. When he'd brought this one home, I'd asked if it was because he wanted an easier ledge or whatever to step through when traveling by mirror. He'd said no, he just wanted a full-length mirror.

I bit back a smile. "It looks great."

"You're no help at all." He kicked off the shoes in frustration. "The problem is I only have six other pairs of shoes—"

"I'm sorry, what? Where?"

He reached into the mirror, which I'd never seen him do be-fore. His arm slid unsettlingly through the glass, and he pulled out a brown leather pair. "This goes better with the gold, but I'm not sure it's the right material for the rain."

Eventually, I hauled him out of the apartment and into my aunt's carriage. He was still fussing when we arrived, but he stopped upon entering the dining hall, throwing back his shoul-ders and lifting his head like the proudest peacock in the land. I stifled my smile.

My aunt looked up. "There they are. My niece, Naomi bat Yardena, my brother's firstborn, and her betrothed, the shayd Daziel bar Cathmeus."

Four adults turned: two men and two women. My aunt had said people who wouldn't normally dine with her would to meet

Daziel. This group looked older than my aunt, in their sixties, and they wore more expensive clothing, less interestingly made. They looked the way I pictured Élodie's and Birra's families, I thought, a touch unkindly.

"Why, Tirtzah," one of the men said. "I shouldn't have doubted you."

Tirtzah's polite smile looked pained. "This is Councilor Monteux and her husband, Monsieur Bar Henri, and the Doctors Bernard."

"Nice to meet you," I said.

For the most part, the lunch was fine. Which is not to say it wasn't awkward. "We've not been so lucky to have a shayd staying in Talum for a long stretch before," Councilor Monteux said. "Usually the visits are as though your kind are blown here and away."

"Perhaps we could tempt you to visit our home," her husband said. "Throw a ball, perhaps inspired by the shedim fashions."

Daziel smiled pleasantly. "No."

They looked taken aback. "No? Do you have a particular objection? I'm sure we could address it."

"I don't want to."

Aunt Tirtzah closed her eyes briefly. "Monsieur!" she said with forced cheer. "Have you tried the roasted sprouts? The honey-mustard glaze is exquisite."

On the wall across from me, a line of ladybugs crawled toward the open window. The rain was slowing, at least, and I could see the sun trying to fight its way out from behind the wall of clouds. "Is there any news about the birds?" I asked.

The adults shifted. "I thought we weren't going to speak of politics, Tirtzah," one of the men said with a false-sounding laugh.

"My apologies," my aunt said, and changed the subject. I grimaced into my food. I hadn't realized it would be political to talk about the birds.

Under the table, Daziel found my hand and squeezed it.

When lunch finally ended, I was as excited as Daziel to flee the scene. Samuel dropped us off on Temple Hill. It was the highest point in the Levite Quarter and the second highest of the city's four hills. The rain had come to a complete stop, though the pavement was wet and gleaming. The air was cool, and I was glad to have brought a bulky sweater to bundle up in.

I'd never been to Temple Hill before, though it'd been inevitable I'd visit—everyone eventually made their way here. Talum housed many temples—with twelve tribes, everyone thought they should have their own, and that was just Ena-Cinnai locals, not to mention the people from all over the continent who had built their own houses of worship in the city.

The Temple, though, was different. It had been built two thousand years ago, during the human-demon wars. Harnessing the power of shedim allowed for incredible feats—path-jumping, which allowed a person to travel great distances; construction of massive structures; wars of epic scale. All done through stealing magic from Daziel's people.

All the streets here funneled people upward toward the Temple, though shopkeepers did their best to distract potential customers. Towering over the cafés and shops, the white stone of the Temple's walls always gleamed in the cool winter sun, the gilded column capitals almost blinding.

We wandered up the streets until we reached the hill's peak. Though it had been raining an hour before, it was still a weekend, and the tourists were out in spades. A long line wound from the entrance of the Temple complex, which Daziel declined to wait in. He walked to the front, smiled his sharp-toothed smile, and they handed us pins to mark we'd paid the entrance fee (we had not) and waved us right in.

The complex was larger than I'd expected—I'd imagined it as a single building, but instead more than a dozen covered the hilltop, some with trickling fountains, others with statues. There was a small amphitheater, a tour guide speaking to her group where the stage had once been. Everything seemed bright and clean after the rain, almost ruthlessly so, as though it had been freshly washed for us.

Daziel was unusually quiet. It took me a while to realize, as I was wowed by the beauty of the place, the contrast of white stone and newly blue sky. "Are you okay?"

"It's strange." He trailed a hand over a fluted column. "Built by shedim but to human tastes."

Of course. I was embarrassed I hadn't realized this earlier. "Does it make you angry? Seeing what humans used your people to do?"

He looked at me, too quickly for a human to move, his speed jarring. I didn't usually startle him into that. "Yes."

"Do you hate it?"

He tilted his head. Paz popped his own head out, tilted as well. "It's very beautiful. But yes. I think I might. I think I might burn it to the ground if I didn't think it would get you in trouble."

"I appreciate your forbearance." I paused, then added more seriously, "I'm sorry if it's painful."

"I wanted to see it. It feels important to . . . bear witness to what they did."

We wandered, silent for a few minutes. From so high, we could see all of Talum: the great plazas, spice markets, and public buildings. We could see the other hills—Society Hill, with its private residences and the glimmering dome of the Hall of the Sanhedrin; Lyra's Seat, green and lush, the highest point in the city; Diamond Hill, where the grand duke kept his palace, though his family had long ago lost all political power and now had only riches and social clout. We could see the Lyceum jutting out on its peninsula, and even the black bar of the Keep, tiny from this distance.

"I'm sorry if it's too much," I said as we leaned against a wall taking in the view. The Lersach River cut like a ribbon north and south, and we could make out the curve of the uninhabited islet off Talum's west coast, then the vineyards along the far bank. Sunset was already on its way, despite the hour not yet being four, and it painted the world gold. "Everyone treating you differently because you're a shayd, here and at my aunt's."

Both our forearms rested on the stone, and our shoulders brushed. His warmth bled into me. "It's sweet how much your aunt cares about you."

"She does?"

"Clearly." He paused. "Will your parents visit you?"

"I'll go home this summer, and maybe they'll come for my graduation, but I don't expect before then."

"I'll have to go home with you in summer, then."

I started. I'd never imagined Daziel meeting my family. Now I pictured Daziel on the high plains and the stir he would cause. People would be meticulously polite, even if they tried to banish him. He'd get on with my sisters, because he was basically a child himself, and my mother because he'd help with chores without her asking. Dad would like him too. And my grandmother always appreciated a good-looking, well-dressed young man.

He'd fit in perfectly.

"Do you miss your family?" I asked. "What are they like?"

"My father is distant. My mother . . ." Daziel's eyes narrowed in concentration. "Not very maternal."

"No?" I asked, surprised. I knew, without any doubt or sentimentality, my mother would fight a bear for me and my sisters. A demon. "How so?"

"It's not such a . . . procedure for her . . . as it is for human women to have children. And she has so many. We aren't as interesting as other things in her life."

I stared. "What's more interesting than your kids?"

"What isn't?" His smile didn't seem sad or self-pitying. "I'm used to it. And I'm trying to become interesting."

"*I* think you're interesting." I was offended on his behalf. Daziel was one of the most interesting people I knew. Not just because he was a shayd but because of his curiosity about the world around him, his delight in beautiful things, the way he listened and tried to make me happy.

He smiled, and a warmth bloomed in my chest. "Thank you," he said, pressing his shoulder more firmly into mine. I smiled back, and we watched the oranges and golds of the setting sun in silence.

THIRTEEN

"**D**ID YOU HEAR ABOUT THE EARTHQUAKE IN ILTHALIT?" Ezra said a few weeks later at our usual pub. The temperature had continued to drop, and the students around us layered coats on top of sweaters and knotted scarves around necks. The heavy rains were worse than previous years, people said. They caused flooding by the river shore, including at the Lyceum. Some of the administrative offices had to be hurriedly closed and moved to higher grounds.

Yet I loved the rain, as I loved the wind. I loved watching the silver rain dash against the river, loved listening to it from the cozy safety of the Keep or my rooms as I worked on endless iterations of the spell to restore the scrolls. Daziel wasn't as charmed, grumbling when knockball practices were canceled. I tried to entertain him with baking projects, and we explored Talum after my aunt's luncheons—though we stuck to indoor activities, like museums and coffee shops and the pub.

Jelan nodded in response to Ezra's question. "Killed over a hundred people. They've had tremors there in the past, but not so far north—they didn't have the infrastructure for it."

"Which would you rather have," Hiram mused, passing around beers, "our rains and winds or an earthquake, or the heat wave they're having in the south?"

"That's a horrible game," Gilli said, appalled. "I'd rather everything was normal."

"Okay," Hiram said, rolling his eyes. "But if you *had* to choose?"

"Our rains," Leah said. "At least we can stay inside."

"I'd rather have the heat," Ezra said. "I'm sick of the gray. And this means natural magic is weird *everywhere*."

Hiram, who was from the Taro Islands, nodded. "My parents wrote that refugees stopped by on their way to Tzorybium from even farther west. From a city now completely uninhabitable."

The conversation got under my skin, and I was still uneasy when Daziel and I arrived home a few hours later. "It's strange, isn't it?" I said. "How things are going wrong not just here but everywhere."

"Yeah." Daziel looked distressed by my depression and changed the subject abruptly. "How's the spell going?"

I groaned. "We're making progress—yesterday, we inched the magic through three-quarters of the spell. But we're low on neshem. The professor is trying to get more, but until then, we might not be able to test more iterations."

"If you need magic, you can have some of mine."

I jerked my head up. "What? You can . . . give it to me?"

He looked blasé, as though he hadn't just offered something unheard of. "In theory." Light gathered around his fingers. "Hold your hands out."

I did, and he tried to hand a golden bundle to me. It dissolved into my skin, and I yelped at the shock.

"Sorry." Daziel looked equally surprised. "Uh . . . let me try a different way."

We tried for hours, until we figured out how he could hand his magic to me, though we couldn't figure out how to contain it. I practiced directing it into small spells around the apartment. *You could make a killing off this on the black market,* I almost said, except that was the thing, wasn't it: Humans had made a killing, of shedim, off this thousands of years ago. "Thank you for trusting me with this," I said.

He looked up, our gazes connecting. There was an urgency in the way he held himself and in his voice, as though he wanted to make sure he conveyed enough gravity. "I trust you."

"I trust you too," I said, surprised by his intensity.

THE NEXT DAY, ON too little sleep but not minding, I made my way through my language classes and Household Magic. After weeks of rain, the weather today was bizarrely good, the sky as blue as a summer day, the temperature uncomfortably warm. We passed people in shorts, having unseasonable picnics. Startlingly large butterflies with jewel-bright wings fluttered about, safe without their biggest predator.

At three, I headed to the Keep. Though we had to re-carve charaktêres and rearrange the fragments each time we tried a new spell, though it was exhausting and tedious, I was still excited by each attempt.

I'd never worked so closely with anyone as I now did with Yael and Gidon and Stefan. Even among my new friends at the Lyceum, I'd never had peers who cared about precisely the same thing as I did. It filled a gap I hadn't known existed, the ability to speak the same language about a passion.

"Here's my latest," Gidon said as I joined the other three. By now our group had become familiar: Yael's intensity and leader-ship; Stefan constantly tossing whatever round thing was at hand in the air; the way Gidon, lanky and still growing, always had small pieces of fruit and nuts for snacking. "We switch the eighth and ninth paragraphs, where the magic got stuck last time, and add a line describing texture."

"It's a good idea," Yael said, "but we don't have enough neshem."

I steeled myself. "Daziel offered to let us use some of his magic."

Yael blinked. "How?"

"He'll come here, and we've figured out how to transfer it to me, and I'll direct it into the spell."

Stefan started laughing from his prone position on the floor. "That is *ridiculous*. You figured out how to take a demon's magic out of him? *What?*"

Yael reacted more calmly, but I caught a hint of a frown. "Is it legal?"

Binding shedim wasn't legal. Accepting freely given magic? "I don't see why not."

"I'm down," Stefan said. "I'm so tired."

Gidon shrugged. "Same."

Yael met my gaze. "Is it safe? Do you trust him?"

I trust you, he'd said, so fiercely. I trusted him too, trusted his support and his steadiness and his openness. "Yes."

She let out a long breath. "Fine. Let's do it."

"I'm going to call him here," I warned, so as not to startle them, and said his name three times.

He appeared.

Gidon jumped, and Yael's eyes widened. "Shit," Stefan said. "Is he always listening?"

"Just when people say my name," Daziel said. "Or if I'm eavesdropping."

"Did you add the last part just so we know we're never safe?" Stefan asked.

Daziel grinned, sharp. "I like to keep people on their toes."

"Metaphorically, I am *very* on my toes," Stefan said without shifting from the floor.

We carved our latest spell into plywood. In the beginning, Professor Altschuler had attended every attempt, but no longer, not when we'd tried so many and they'd all failed.

We began reading. Daziel passed his magic to me, and I directed it into the spell. It was stronger and more volatile than using neshem, a bonfire instead of a match. It made me nervous but not enough to stop.

The magic gathered and built as we read. It moved through the words easily. We hit the first couple of points where it'd been sticky in the last few iterations—not stopped, but if the spell had been a river, this was where the magic started to get clogged with sticks and logs.

The magic kept going, smooth as silk.

We exchanged cautiously hopeful looks. But we'd gotten this far before, if not so easily. Now we approached the bridge, which we'd changed in this rendition with Gidon's paragraph swap. We hit the point where we'd been blocked last time, bracing ourselves.

The magic kept flowing.

My tentative hope heightened. My breath came faster, the thump of my heart deeper in my ears. The magic never stopped building. It didn't plateau, didn't stick. It kept going.

It flowed through the entire spell. The crescendo built, one we'd never reached before, and the four of us exchanged wide-eyed looks. My legs shook with the effort, and my throat squeezed tight.

Yael held out a hand—*hold it*—as we reached the final stanza. We dragged the words out, letting the magic build into one final surge. The fragments trembled, their edges fluttering. "'Remember, remember,'" we said, our excitement palpable, glancing at each other as though to confirm we were all seeing this. "'Remember when you ran through the grass.'"

Slowly, so slowly I thought I might be imagining it out of sheer hope, the fragments began to shuffle. I wanted to stop breathing, but I needed breath to speak, and I needed to speak the spell. "'Remember, remember,'" I said, my voice blending into three others. Gidon reached out and grabbed my hand, squeezing hard, and I squeezed back.

"'Now.'"

On the final word, the magic swept out of us. The edges of the fragments glowed and started to tremble. Then the golden light bled inward, saturating each fragment until they gleamed like polished coins under the afternoon sun. They lifted off the table, hovering, then began to spin as though whipped up by a tornado. My mouth gaped, my neck craned back, as the fragments formed a frenzied cyclone, their light brightening until I couldn't make out individual pieces. Then, with a burst so sharp and white, I flinched and closed my eyes, they drifted down like feathers, nestling against each other with clear intent. Each jagged piece aligned with others until they spread out in eight separate scrolls.

For a breath, no one said anything. No one moved.

"Oh my god," Yael finally said, and I tore my gaze from the

parchment—actual parchment, not fragments—to her. Her eyes gleamed with repressed tears. "It worked."

"It worked," I repeated, too surprised to say anything original. Something about articulating it made it crack through my stunned surprise. "It—*worked*. We did it!"

Yael started laughing, and Stefan let out a whoop. Gidon bent in half, hands on his thighs, breathing in and out very quickly.

Then we were all yelling and gasping with relief. I threw my arms around Yael, and after a surprised second, she embraced me in return. The boys piled on until we were all laughing. I caught sight of Daziel hovering on the edges. "Daziel, get in here!"

His eyes widened, true shock in them, but the others weren't waiting. They opened their arms and pulled him in. Yael was kissing cheeks, including Daziel's, and Stefan knuckled Gidon's and Daziel's heads. Daziel met my gaze across the circle, his own wide and bewildered and filled with an unexpected vulnerability. It hit me in the gut.

The noise must have carried, because a minute later the door scraped open. Professor Altschuler stood there. We fell silent, children before an authoritarian father. Daziel vanished.

Professor Altschuler observed the eight scrolls, joined together, with only the faintest hint of where they'd once been torn. We watched him prowl around the tables, breath bated.

"This was your spell, Miss Bat Yardena?"

"It's based on my original, but we all worked on the improvements—"

"It originated in the one you showed me?"

I hesitated, looking at the others. "Yes."

"Very nice. Congratulations. The rest of you—" He shook his

head. "I'm disappointed. You're further along in your studies. You should have been able to come up with this."

Yael stared at her feet, blinking, while Stefan set his face grimly, and Gidon stared out the window, looking defeated. I felt horribly uncomfortable, even though this was part and parcel of Professor Altschuler's behavior.

"There will be a chance to make up for it," the professor continued, as though bestowing a magnanimous gift. "Whoever makes a step in deciphering the text itself, if you do it by the Lumière Festival next month . . . you will receive a seat at my table at graduation. Good night, students. Miss Bat Yardena, stay a moment."

The other three filed out.

"Good job," Professor Altschuler said. "But this is not the time to rest on your laurels."

"I know." I shifted. "Professor Altschuler, I'm sorry, but—this wasn't just my success. The others worked on this as much as I did. I can't take more credit than any of them."

His brows rose slightly. "You won't win yourself any accolades by giving away what recognition you receive."

"I'm not trying to. But I mean it. This was a group effort."

"Groups have leaders."

"If we have a leader, it's Yael. She's the one who organizes us. I'm sorry," I said, scarcely believing what I was saying. "I need to go."

"Excuse me?"

"No, excuse me," I said. "Good night."

I bolted, running out the door, down the hall. I could see the other three, not together, all walking toward the exit. "Guys!" I called. "Yael! Gidon! Stefan!"

Yael turned first, then Gidon, and lastly Stefan, as though unable to resist the group. I caught up to them, huffing slightly. "What we did there—that was amazing."

They stared.

"I'm sorry—I mean, *I'm* not sorry. It's not my fault that Professor Altschuler is a jerk—but he is. I wish he hadn't singled me out. This is our success. We all did it."

"I mean," Yael said, somewhat grudgingly, "you came up with the theory for the spell."

"I did. But you all helped." I paused, nervous they would reject my peace offering. "Do you guys want to grab a drink? Celebrate?"

They looked at me. Looked at each other. A hesitant moment, as we all tried to decide if we could transition from allies to something stronger. To the start of being friends.

"Yes," Yael said. "And call Daziel back. We couldn't have done it without his help."

A smile blossomed on my face. Once more, I said Daziel's name three times, and together the five of us headed out.

FOURTEEN

THE NEXT MORNING, EVERYONE WITH ANY RELATION TO the scrolls crammed into the fifth-floor Keep room. Outside, under a strange orange sky, waves surged through the Lersach, crashing against the shore. Earlier, as I'd crossed the land bridge, I couldn't tell if the rain fell down or up. I'd told myself it was the spray whipped off the river, but it wasn't clear.

Inside, though, everyone focused on the scrolls, quivering with excitement. Professor Altschuler stood at the front of the room, and even he couldn't keep the glee from his voice. He strode back and forth, as though unable to contain himself. "We will analyze every word in each scroll and across the scrolls—their frequency, their location, their similarity to other words." He looked at my cohort. "Who can tell me the first question to ask when faced with an undeciphered language in a foreign alphabet?"

All four of us shot our hands up. We'd been well trained on what to ask once the scrolls had been re-created; any one of us could have put together a checklist.

"Stefan," Professor Altschuler said. After my outburst last night, I was no longer his pet, but I didn't care—I had no desire to be separated out from the others, envied and isolated.

"We have to determine which way the words run," Stefan said. "Left to right, right to left, up to down, or vice versa."

"Excellent. How can you tell?" He gestured at Yael.

"By the alignment of the text," she said. "Where it's even and where it's crammed."

He nodded. "And what have you seen?"

"Right to left," we chanted in unison. The characters on the right side of the scrolls were full and round, as though the writer had all the space in the world, but on the left margin the characters squeezed together.

"Excellent. We will begin with an analysis of individual words and characters. We will number each scroll, each line, each word, each character, and track how many of each appears in each individual scroll and the scrolls combined." He turned to the classroom easel. "Here is the breakdown of who will work on each scroll."

The difficulty with deciphering Language X was twofold; first, we didn't know the alphabet, and secondly, even if we did, we'd need to translate the words.

Most countries around the Long Sea used the same letters, meaning people could sound out foreign words even if they couldn't understand them. But we didn't know the phonetics of Language X characters, and we'd yet to identify a language family it belonged to. It seemed likely that before we could translate words, we would focus on phonetics.

We dove in. This was the moment we'd waited for and been warned about: for the puzzle we were trying to solve to be the text, not the material. We'd been told a thousand times how hard it would be, how lost languages didn't give up their secrets easily— especially not when they'd held them close for so long.

We didn't care. We were hungry for discovery and desperate to prove ourselves. In the first week, we whipped through the sixteen thousand words in the scrolls and created a master list containing all of them. The scrolls contained thirty-five hundred unique words, half of which were used only once. Twenty-two were used over a hundred times—articles, we expected. The language had thirty-two characters, for which we were writing a finding spell that would count and categorize each.

It felt like both so much information and none at all. It was like a sea, and we were adrift upon it. The more we looked at the scrolls, the more water our tiny boat took on. We drowned again and again, sank to the bottom, and cried in defeat. Yet we shared the ability to resurrect ourselves. Not to keep from drowning in the first place—that would have been too much to ask—but to come back to life, to claw our way to the top of the sea. And if we found the surface frozen over, well, we'd scrape our nails against it, ignore the chips of ice, persevere.

"This is a very elaborate and slightly melodramatic metaphor," Daziel said when I shared it one Saturday morning two weeks in. He was happy for me but also bored. This, evidenced by him whining, "I'm bored." The rain had finally let up, swept away by the arrival of the Clo, the first and most common of the Trio Winds.

The Clo signaled winter, drier and chillier than autumn, and with winter came preparations for the Lumière Festival. The residents of Testylier House strung up twinkling lights and ornaments in the common spaces. Gilli and Leah physically dragged me from my books to participate. We scattered candles around the common room and loaded up the sofas with blankets. Someone was always mulling wine or cider in the kitchen, and one of the fourth-floor girls, Marie, left out day-old croissants and the occasional tart from the bakery where she worked.

"I thought you were learning to bake donuts," I murmured to Daziel absently. We were in the common room, and I was rushing through my Tzorybia language worksheets so I could get back to the scrolls. A mug of apple-cinnamon tea steamed on the table before me.

"I've already mastered donuts."

I looked up, warned by his petulant tone that I wouldn't be able to brush him aside. "Wasn't Gilli showing you a new crochet stitch?"

"I don't want to crochet. I don't want to bake or play knockball. I want to do something with my betrothed, who isn't paying me any attention at all." He crossed his arms. "Besides, you need a break. You haven't slept more than five hours all week."

An exaggeration, but I saw his point. My brain wouldn't be sharp if I didn't rest. "Okay. What do you want to do?"

He brightened so much I felt bad; he clearly hadn't expected me to give in. "The Lyceum's winter holiday market starts today."

Within an hour, we'd collected Gilli, Jelan, and Leah and were headed to the school's peninsula for the fair, passing shops and pubs charmingly decorated for the Lumière Festival. Windows held candles and glowing ornaments; the scents of hot cocoa and cookies wafted through the air.

The holiday fair had been set up in the central courtyard of the Lyceum, right inside the gates from the land bridge. Dozens of stalls ringed the perimeter, selling sweaters and mulled wine and cinnamon buns and spelled hand warmers. Overnight, a skating rink had sprung up. An exorbitant amount of neshem must be needed to keep the water frozen. I wondered how the spell worked, since natural elements were so difficult to affect—a massive spell written on the bottom of the rink?

"Don't overthink it." Leah tugged my arm. "Let's go!"

We rented skates and laced them up, laughing nervously and leaning against each other as we tottered onto the ice. None of us had ever skated much—here in the south, all rinks were artificial, and even up north, it didn't often get cold enough for water to freeze. Giggling and shouting, we wobbled around the packed rink, smiling at classmates and trying not to take anyone with us whenever we fell.

Daziel took my hand, lacing his fingers through mine. A jolt ran through me, my stomach swooping. In the nearly four months he'd been here, I'd become used to Daziel touching me to get my attention; I was used to smacking his shoulder when he said something ridiculous. This was different, touching only to touch. Scarier. His palm was warm, and his body beside mine radiated heat in the chilly afternoon.

I was paying more attention to the feeling of our hands against each other than to staying upright on skates. I stumbled, and yanked on Daziel's hand to stabilize myself, spinning to an awkward stop before him. My gaze flew to his in apology for pulling him briefly off balance. I was almost afraid, as though it would remind him we were holding hands, like if he remembered he might want to stop.

Gold slid across his eyes, his expression soft in a way I'd never seen before. Like he was looking at me not to deliver a retort but just to look, full of delight and familiarity and tenderness. My breath quickened, and my heart started pounding. I was so aware of how close we were, how easy it would be to close the space between us. How warm his hand was and how warm the rest of him would be.

Then our friends returned from their latest loop, almost colliding with us. Daziel's hand fell away. I felt its loss, my lungs constricting as though the air had thinned.

"Let's get hot cocoa!" Gilli cried, looping her arm through mine. Trying to smile and not look as shaky as I felt, I clambered out of the rink with her. Daziel dropped behind to talk to Jelan.

I stretched my hand, though, the physicality of Daziel's fingers laced through mine lingering. Their heat, his strength.

For the first time in weeks, the scrolls were no longer top of my mind.

Armed with hot chocolate and a dozen chocolate-glazed donuts, we found a table in the busy seating area behind the rink. "Does it ever snow here?" I asked the other girls. I felt too shy to look at Daziel now, though he sat right next to me. His thigh pressed against mine as we squeezed onto the benches. "Back home, we get a few inches, but since Talum is so much farther south, I wasn't sure."

"Nope," Gilli said, licking chocolate off her fingers. "Which is too bad, since snow seems so romantic."

"It's cold enough as it is," Jelan grumbled. She wore a red hat Gilli had crocheted pulled over her ears, and a bigger jacket than the rest of us—this was the first winter she'd experienced outside her semi-arid country, and she wasn't loving it.

"Snow is pretty magical," I agreed, actively not looking at Daziel. "Especially for something that isn't actually magic."

We chattered until we'd drained our cups and only crumbs remained of the donuts. "My hot cocoa is gone," I said mournfully. To no one, really.

Okay—to Daziel, whose mouth twitched. "Anyone else?" he

asked, and the girls cheerfully handed over their empty mugs. Daziel gave me a slightly woebegone look, then headed back to the cocoa tent. The mugs bobbed behind him like a trail of ducklings.

Gilli leaned her head against my shoulder. She'd done her braids in loops behind her ears, and her blue velvet hat matched her coat. "You and Daziel seem cozy."

I looked up at the pale blue sky and smiled. I felt warm and soft—cozy, one might say—in a way I wasn't used to, making the whole world seem like a kinder place. "Yeah."

"I noticed he held your hand while we were skating."

"Did he?" Leah leaned forward. "I missed that."

"Shh," I said, despite Daziel being too far away to hear. My cheeks blazed. My friends noticing embarrassed me, like I'd had a vulnerable underside revealed. But I also felt gratified they thought it worth discussing; if so, maybe it *had* meant something. Still, I didn't want to make too big a deal out of this, not when Daziel might have done it absentmindedly. Shedim might hold hands as a matter of course. "It doesn't mean anything."

"Your blush means something," Leah teased. Her amber earrings twinkled in the sunlight, as playful as her tone.

"Has anything happened between you two yet?" Gilli asked, as though it was a foregone conclusion something would.

"Of course not." My friends waited, clearly deeming this not enough information, so I babbled on. "We're just roommates. He's not interested in me."

Leah rolled her eyes. "Okay."

I frowned at her. "Besides, I don't have time for romance. The work on the scrolls is ramping up, and I need to make sure Professor Altschuler is impressed enough to renew my scholarship. I irritated him a few weeks ago."

My floormates looked unimpressed. "There's always time for romance," Gilli said. "But it doesn't magically happen. You need to make a move."

"Who even says I *want* something to happen?" I didn't. Probably. Well, not if Daziel didn't.

Leah snorted. Gilli pursed her mouth. Even Jelan, who usually avoided these conversations, couldn't contain her amusement.

I unbuttoned my blazer, overly hot. I wouldn't even need the warmth from a second hot cocoa. "Why do I need to be the one to make a move? He could."

"He's clearly obsessed with you," Leah said. "He's getting you *and* your friends cocoa at this very moment."

"You're his friends too."

"Do you not like him?" Gilli sounded confused. "You spend all your time together and act like an old married couple. But if you don't like him . . ."

This was such a surreal conversation. "I like him. But . . . he thinks of me as a friend." Anything more than friendship was terrifying. How did one even *make* a move?

"Do you think of him as just a friend?" Leah asked. "You *must* think he's hot. He's objectively more attractive than any human."

"Attraction is subjective," I said, peeking at where Daziel still waited patiently in line. He'd been assailed by two science students in their yellow blazers but didn't look like he minded. And he did look strikingly handsome. "Though fine, yes. But we *live* together. What if it went horribly? We'd be *trapped*." Any shift in our relationship would impact so much of my life.

Gilli shot Jelan a meaningful look. "What if it went wonderfully?"

"No." I understood what she meant, but their situation was different. "You two still have separate rooms. Space. Daziel and I have no space."

"What you do already have is a relationship," Jelan said practically. "You eat together, study, socialize. You look out for each other. You do everything anyone in a romantic relationship does except the romance." She raised her thick brows. "If you're both attracted to each other, you should see if the romance is as strong as everything else you have."

I stared at Jelan, stunned. I'd never heard her say so many words in one go, and they resonated deeply. I loved spending time with Daziel. My favorite part of every day was having breakfast or walking to school or unwinding on the sofa at night together. I loved when we went out exploring, spending an afternoon poking about the city, wandering into tiny shops and trying new cafés and joking about absolutely nothing for hours.

But what if that wasn't his favorite thing? What if he had other things he preferred to me? Or what if he liked everything we did, liked spending time together, but that was where it stopped? On his side, we could be better as friends. Because Jelan had dropped a key truth—we should try a romance if we were *both* attracted to each other.

"What if he doesn't like me back?" I whispered, the darkest fear I had, the one that curled around my heart so snugly I wasn't sure it could be dislodged. "What if he doesn't want me?"

"Please. Is that what you're worried about? That boy wants you," Leah said firmly.

Gilli burst into giggles, and the rest of us started laughing too, which was how Daziel found us a minute later. He put our cocoas down. "What'd I miss?"

"Nothing," I told him as he scooted in next to me on the bench, his body warm, lined fully up with mine, thigh to shoulder. A sizzle of desire, of anticipation, of hope ran through me. I wasn't sure I believed Leah, but one thing was clear—my feelings for Daziel were far stronger than I'd realized. And like anything under pressure, they were bound to eventually come out, on purpose or not. "Nothing at all."

THE LYCEUM GAVE STUDENTS a few days off for the Lumière Festival, though people only headed home if they lived close to the city. Leah would be at her family's silk farm, a two-day trip downriver; Jelan and Gilli were spending the holiday with Gilli's parents, just an hour south. Since it took a week to reach my village, I'd stay here at the end of the month.

Or, more accurately, go to Aunt Tirtzah's.

The Lumière Festival had been celebrated for thousands of years in the countries edging the Long Sea. It was one of the six new years, and the second-most popular, after the civil new year (though the trees and the harvest were also beloved). Everyone wore yellows, oranges, and reds and lit all the lanterns and candles they owned.

I borrowed an outfit from Leah before she left—a red jumpsuit with long sleeves and a structured orange jacket. I had an orange silk ribbon from my mother, which matched nicely. I wove it into a braid crown, examining the results critically in my bedroom mirror.

I didn't think Daziel would be so blown away by my effort he'd confess his desire, but I wouldn't mind if he took a little notice.

I stepped into the living room. Daziel, too, had dressed for the holiday, but unlike anything I'd ever seen—at first his jacket and trousers looked white, but when he moved, they glimmered with all the colors of fire, as though woven with iridescent thread. I pulled to a stop. "That's a gorgeous outfit."

He looked pleased. His gaze pulled over mine, and I grew hot, my skin tight with awareness. He stepped forward, and I caught my breath. He ran a finger over the stitching on the jacket's cuff. A shiver ran over me. "So is yours."

Ducking my head, I murmured a thanks and hurried to put on my shoes.

When Daziel and I arrived at my aunt's, I was surprised to find her alone. I thought it'd be like the luncheons, where we were mainly there to impress her political acquaintances.

"Oh," I said, blinking. "Are we early?"

"It's just us." She smiled awkwardly. While we'd dressed up, she'd worn a more casual outfit than I'd ever seen, a mustard-yellow gown and an oversize beige cardigan. She wore her hair loose—a sign she didn't plan to leave the house.

"Oh! I didn't realize . . ." I trailed off, even more embarrassed now.

"Come in." She led us to one of the less formal parlors. Bowls of candied fruits and nuts sat on the round table between several chairs, along with a pitcher of iced tea and fresh oranges and pears. My aunt pushed her hair behind her ear, an unusual sign of discomfort from her. "I gave my staff the week off, so I'm afraid nothing might be any good . . ."

"Thank you for having us," Daziel said, because he clearly had better manners than me.

"Thank you," I echoed hurriedly. "I'm sure it'll be delicious."

She gave us a grateful smile.

It was too early for dinner, so we munched on almonds and candied orange peels. Aunt Tirtzah asked us about classes, and Daziel, to my surprise and amusement, answered as though he were taking the same ones as I did, filling her in on the theory we were currently struggling through in Intro to T3 and the latest group project from Household Magics.

"How is your knockball team doing?" Aunt Tirtzah asked.

Daziel brightened. "We have our first interschool game in two weeks. So far, it's just been Humanities School games, but we won our championship, and so we'll be playing the School of Engineering next."

"How exciting," Aunt Tirtzah said. "Naomi, do you enjoy the games?"

Her question struck me in the gut, leaving me quietly devastated. It'd never occurred to me to go to a game. Should I have? Had not going hurt Daziel's feelings?

"Naomi's very busy," Daziel said quickly, which made me suspect it had. "She doesn't have time to go to the games."

"Not even the championship?" Aunt Tirtzah sounded taken aback. I felt the same, my chest pounding. I hadn't realized Daziel had had a championship game.

"It's fine," Daziel said. I stared at him, stomach twisting, and he reached over and squeezed my hand lightning fast. "It's fine."

Aunt Tirtzah changed the topic, asking me how the decipherment was going. "I read an interview with your professor in the papers a few days ago," she said. "Everyone is fascinated by what the scrolls might contain."

It was not fine. But I managed to answer my aunt. I told her about the scrolls up until dinner. We heated up ratatouille and paired it with garlic soup and fresh bread. For dessert, we had nougat and honey cake and jam-filled donuts.

Then we carried my aunt's lights out into her garden, placing them in a giant circle around us near the fountain. The glass dome was open, and we craned our necks back, taking in the moon and a few bright planets, before beginning to light the candles and lamps.

"How do your families celebrate?" Aunt Tirtzah asked.

I answered first. "The whole village does the Lumière ceremony together. We walk an hour outside, so there's no artificial light, and sing the old songs surrounded by candles. We have a chaotic family celebration the second night—Dad fries up all sorts of things; he's currently into zucchini fritters—and Michal and Grandma and I decorate, and Mom and Adina make cookies." I smiled, the memories bittersweet. I'd never missed a holiday before. "Selah—she's eleven—organizes everyone, whether we need organization or not." I noticed how intently Aunt Tirtzah was listening. I strove for an offhand tone. "You could come one year."

She smiled too brightly. "It's a long trip. And—I wouldn't want to impose."

Except she wouldn't be imposing, because she was family. *Why haven't you ever visited?* I wanted to ask, but I wasn't brave enough. She was the adult. It was her prerogative to decide she didn't want to see her brother's family, not mine to question her. "What about you?" I asked Daziel. Though humans and shedim were inherently different, our religious and ceremonial observances were often the same. "How do you celebrate?"

"We set candles adrift on the winds, and there are light and sound displays. There's dancing and feasting." His black eyes connected with mine, bright with flecks of gold. He smiled. "But I like these family meals more."

I smiled at him, then hesitantly turned to my aunt. "How did you and—your parents spend the festival?" I stumbled over how to refer to my paternal grandparents.

"They were shopkeepers," Aunt Tirtzah said. We finished lighting the candles and sat cross-legged on the ground, watching the flames flicker. "It was always a very busy time for them. Still, on the second or third night, we'd manage a few minutes of candle lighting. My own grandparents—your great-grandparents—lived in the Judahite arrondissement, and we'd visit them."

Her words raised questions I'd never thought of. "Are there other relatives?"

She smiled sadly. "Almost no one is left."

Ena-Cinnai was so big on family—I certainly had plenty of cousins back on the plains—that it felt strange I hadn't known about any over here. Sadness washed over me that my aunt didn't have people to spend the holidays with.

"Anyway," my aunt said briskly, reaching into the satchel she'd brought outside and lifting gift bags from within. She passed one to me and one to Daziel. "These are for the two of you."

"Oh," I said surprised. "Thanks."

"This is incredibly kind of you," Daziel said softly.

We unpacked popcorn with chocolate and caramel, a pair of

gloves each, and a candle. "Thank you so much," I said, touched
and sorry I hadn't gotten her anything.

"It's nothing," she said briskly. "Just a few trinkets."

Maybe she'd never felt invited to visit the plains.

When the chill became uncomfortable, we headed inside. It
was late, past ten. "We should be getting home," I said, then hesitated. Aunt Tirtzah had sent her staff home, and I wasn't sure the
tram would be operating today.

She hesitated too. "If you wish—you could stay the night—"

I glanced at Daziel, unwilling to commit him to anything without talking it over first. "We didn't bring any of our things—but
if your driver is gone—"

She smiled. "As it turns out, I'm perfectly capable of driving a
neshem carriage myself."

She drove us back to Testylier House, all three of us crowded
on the driver's bench, my aunt explaining the dials and levers.
The sky was unexpectedly clear still. When I watched her drive
away, I felt a small pang in my chest at the thought she might be
lonely.

Still, I was delighted to be home, ready to curl up in bed and
sleep forever, happily sated by dinner and family. I collapsed on
the sofa, yawning so widely my mouth hurt.

"I have a gift for you," Daziel said shyly.

This perked me up. Who didn't love an unexpected gift?
"You do?"

Sitting beside me, he handed over a poorly wrapped bundle. I
pulled it apart to reveal a teal-and-pink crocheted scarf, the colors
familiar from seeing them wound around Daziel's crochet hook.

There was a strange wrenching in my heart. I smiled at him, my
cheeks hurting. "It's beautiful."

"You like it?" He sounded hesitant. "It's not very professional. I tried, but I'm not very good."

"Yes. Absolutely." I wrapped the scarf around my neck, feeling as warmed as though it was a giant blanket, then impulsively squeezed Daziel's hand. He stared down with surprise. Then he smiled, brighter than the moon.

My throat went dry. I didn't recognize the feeling in me, the strange bubbling sensation fizzing through every part of my body.

Or maybe I did. Like Jelan had said, we'd spent the last several months cooking and laughing and studying, and though I kept reminding him we weren't really betrothed, we felt like a couple. I *wanted* us to be a couple. I wanted to lean against him, to curl into his side when we read on the sofa. When we walked to class, I wanted to hold hands.

I wanted to kiss him.

I cleared my throat. "I'm sorry I didn't get you anything."

"Maybe later I'll ask you for a gift," he said softly.

"Why not now?" I asked just as softly. The space between us felt alive, crackling with energy.

He tilted his head. I was aware of the depth of his eyes, the length of his lashes, the firmness of his mouth. His skin seemed to contain an extra glow, a burnished gold radiating health.

Paz burst out from under a pillow, chirping excitedly as he spied a beetle in the corner of the room and dashed after it.

We burst into laughter, the moment broken. "I should get ready for bed," I said, pulling back. My heart raced as I brushed my teeth and washed my face, as I undid my braids and combed my hair. Both Daziel and my aunt had been so kind tonight. They felt like family. It made sense my aunt did, but Daziel—

Daziel felt like family in a very different way.

When I came out, he was curled up in his nest of blankets and cushions. It struck me how I'd never seen him in a state of undress—even though he owned a million outfits, I'd never seen him change from one to another. Daziel had always been very careful not to make me uncomfortable inside my own home.

The words burst out quickly, tumbling together. "I'm sorry I haven't been to one of your knockball games."

He looked up with unnatural speed. "It's fine."

"I don't think it is. I feel awful." He did so many nice things for me, I wanted to do something nice for him too. I wanted to show I cared. "Do you . . . Should I come to your next?"

He stared with obvious surprise. "Do you want to? I know sports aren't your thing."

Oh no. I shoved my hands in my pockets. He didn't want me there. This had been a stupid idea. And he definitely couldn't be interested in me if he didn't even want me at his game. "Right. I shouldn't have suggested it."

"No, I—Naomi." He took a deep breath, a hint of vulnerability on his face. "Yes. I'd like you to come."

"Oh," I said, more upbeat but still nervous. "Okay. I'll be there."

"Okay."

Feeling giddy and confused and a million other things, I turned toward my door. Daziel's voice stopped me. "Naomi."

I paused. "Yes?"

He hesitated. "Your hair looks very beautiful down."

My breath caught. "Thank you," I said, before throwing myself into my room, where I lay staring at the ceiling, my heart ramming against my chest with confusion and intensity.

I didn't sleep for a very long time.

FIFTEEN

I SHOWED UP AT THE PITCH AT TWO ON GAME DAY, DAZIEL'S scarf wrapped around my neck. I hadn't been to these fields before—they weren't on the Lyceum peninsula but where Issachar Quarter sloped down to the Lersach River. The fields were separated from the water by an abundance of mimosa trees, their bright yellow blossoms swaying under the pale winter sky.

A sparse crowd had gathered on the bleachers. I stood uncertainly on the sidelines, trying to decide if I should grab a seat or find Daziel. I was unaccountably nervous. Though we spent so much time together, it was *together*, going from one place to another—it felt stranger to separately enter a space he belonged in.

Daziel bounded over from a group of players on the field. He wore a blue uniform I'd never seen before, with white stripes on the shoulders and down the sides—the School of Humanities club knockball team. I'd only ever seen his practice clothes.

"You came! Come meet the team." Daziel grabbed my hand and towed me toward a loose crew of others. Paz jumped from my shoulder to Daziel's and chittered excitedly as he ran up and over Daziel's head.

"Are you sure? I don't want to get in the way before the game or anything . . ."

"I want you to meet them." He bubbled over with excitement,

and my shyness increased as we approached his teammates. I knew some of these boys—like Ezra, of course—but most were strangers. For the first time I'd be in the position of being Daziel's betrothed instead of the other way around.

"This is Naomi," Daziel proclaimed, interrupting their huddle, beaming proudly. Everyone ignored us, which was about what I'd expected.

Everyone had their residence hall written on the back of their jersey, beneath their team name, the Fiercest Figs. I peeked at Daziel's. It said *Testylier House*.

The sweetness of this was so sudden and intense I had to blink very rapidly to maintain my composure.

"Here's the deal," Ezra said, in his element as team captain. "The other guys are faster, stronger, and smarter than us."

"Isn't this supposed to be a pep talk?" I murmured to Daziel.

"It's a 'here's the deal' talk," Ezra said. "But you know what we have that they don't have?"

"Spirit?" I suggested.

Ezra glared. "Your input is unnecessary. What we *do* have," he continued, "is no fear of pain."

"What," I said under my breath.

"No pain!" the boys all cried, like (1) this made sense and (2) was something to be proud of. "No pain!"

I looked at Daziel. Like the rest of them, he was pumping his fist in the air, looking delighted. "No pain!"

The corners of my mouth quirked up. Okay. This was kind of cute. Bizarre. But cute.

Ezra delivered a not-very-empowering speech about how they'd win no matter what, even if it meant playing dirty, then backtracked and said they couldn't play dirty because they already had two strikes, and also the other team played dirtier and one of their front men had a nasty habit of kicking knees, stay away from him. Then, with a final "No pain!" they clapped their hands together and looked toward the other team on the opposite end of the field.

Daziel kept holding on to my hand, even though I suspected the game was about to start. I tugged free. "I think I better go. Have fun, okay?"

"It is not about *fun*," Daziel said seriously. "It is about *winning*."

We were going to have to have a talk later about Ezra's speech-making. "Hm. Good luck, then."

"Hey," a voice called from the other team as I started toward the bleachers. "Is that—do you guys have the demon?"

I stiffened and turned.

The opposing team approached en masse, matching scowls to go with their matching red uniforms. The boy wearing the captain's epaulets stepped forward. "You can't have a demon play."

"Whatever," Ezra said dismissively. "It's fine."

"It's *not* fine," the opposing captain said. "That's cheating."

"Don't be ridiculous. He's not even any good." Ezra used the same tone as when he decried the Sanhedrin's ability to do anything. "He gets distracted half the time."

"I don't!" Daziel protested.

"Look!" Ezra pointed behind Daziel. "A tabby cat."

Daziel turned.

This didn't appease the School of Engineering's team. The fight snowballed until the umpire made his way over, besieged as each side made their case. He was a slim man with ginger hair and a cleft chin. He took one look at Daziel and shook his head. "It'd be an unfair advantage."

I'd stayed uninvolved until then, but at this, anger bubbled up. "Oh, come on. This is ridiculous. He's played in the games within the School of Humanities."

"Who the hell are you?" one of the boys on the other team asked.

"She's his betrothed," Ezra said, "so be nice."

"He just wants to have fun," I said. I wanted to hit something. Who were these guys to police who played?

Daziel's shoulders drooped. "No, I understand."

"You can stay within human limits!"

"He could be within human limits and still be better than any of us," someone on the other team retorted. "It'd be like hiring a ringer."

Daziel stepped back. "You should sub Colin in for me," he told Ezra. "Good luck, everybody." Shoulders slumped, he walked off the field.

Sending a fierce glare at everyone, I hurried after his dejected figure. "Come on," I said, determined to cheer him up. "Let's get out of here."

He shook his head. I could practically hear the morose music playing about him. "I should watch the team. Cheer them on."

Watching other people do something I couldn't sounded horrible. "Are you sure?"

He nodded. "It's the right thing to do."

So I watched the first knockball game of my life, trying to offer support to Daziel supporting his team. He stared intensely at the field, shouting encouragement at his teammates.

"Are you okay?" I asked halfway through.

He mustered up a smile. "Yeah. For sure. Go, Ezra!" He cheered as Ezra slapped at the ball.

I took his hand and squeezed.

I'd never paid much attention to knockball before. Still, I knew the basics. One ball, two teams, nine players on each. Zones where different body parts were allowed in play—heads, feet, hands. Three ways to score and one to lose points. Three goal zones, one decided randomly just before play.

Knowing rules didn't mean I knew anything about strategy. People had tried to explain it to me before, but I'd always tuned out. It was easier with Daziel. His excitement was infectious, and he shared the plays like he was whispering secrets—"Ah, they must be trying Brown's Route. It's a sneaky one . . ."

Daziel's team won. Not, as far as I could tell, because they were better than the other team but through pure luck. I turned to Daziel. "Congrats?"

He'd managed to be fairly upbeat through the game, despite the longing on his face. But now, as he watched his friends jump on each other and hug, the depressed creases in his brows deepened. "Are you okay?" I asked again.

"I just really wanted to play," he said in a small, forlorn voice.

I bit the inside of my cheek, hard, to keep from viciously going after the other team. "You know what? Let's climb Lyra's Seat."

Daziel lifted his head with bewilderment, then spoke as though afraid to hope. "It's the weekend. You like to spend weekends getting ahead on homework."

"I'm done already," I lied.

His eyes widened. "Really?"

"Let's do it."

Lyra's Seat was the highest of Talum's four hills, on the north-most peak. We took the tram, arriving as the sun started to sink. We climbed it in the cold, and harsh wind kept whipping past us, yet we couldn't stop laughing. At the top, we could see all of Talum spread out before us, glowing in the twilight.

WHEN WE GOT HOME, it was pitch black, and we were exhausted. We fell onto the sofa, wrangling the blanket over our legs, letting them fall against each other.

"Thank you for today," Daziel said.

"I didn't really do anything."

His black eyes met mine—so unnerving once, and now so dear. "You wanted me to be happy. That's something."

I looked away. I did want him to be happy. It almost hurt, how much it mattered to me.

When had I started caring about him so deeply?

And what was I going to do about it?

Winter was the bleakest time of year, not just in Talum but all of Ena-Cinnai, the days short, the nights long. The temperature dipped below freezing in the night as the season deepened, and we often woke to frost covering the Lyceum lawns. Students exhaled white puffs of air as they hurried across campus.

The Trio Winds intensified. Though the second wind, the Ver, came less often than the Clo, it was far worse. It blazed down from the northeast and tore shingles from rooftops. Then the Den arrived, and when it collided with one of the other winds, it created gales so fierce they howled together like dogs pursuing a wild hunt.

The Maestril was worse, I'd been told by proud locals. Like the Trio Winds, the Maestril was bitter and violent, but it was helpful, too. It dried out the soil for the harvests and churned the river, which improved its ecosystem. When the Maestril left, it carried away the dirt and grit of winter in a golden haze—so beautiful, locals bragged, artists came from all corners of the continent to try to capture it during the two weeks it blew.

"But this year, the Trio Winds are as fierce as the Maestril," Leah told me one day as we walked to class in the bitterly cold dawn. She sounded stressed; she'd had a letter from her parents describing the wreckage the Trio Winds were causing. "Only, they're more chaotic. And if the Maestril doesn't function like usual . . . I don't know."

"When's it supposed to arrive?" I asked. "Spring?"

She nodded. "You can smell it on the air even earlier. When spring begins, it settles in and really blows."

The Trio Winds howled as the winter weeks bled into each other. To my disappointment, Daziel and I continued without change as well. I'd hoped we were building toward something, but maybe I'd been mistaken, or maybe neither of us were brave enough to try. Now, though, I was excruciatingly aware of every time our hands brushed, or our eyes held an extra beat, or our legs touched on the sofa.

I spent most of my time in the Keep, trying and failing to make any progress with Language X. "Even if we *can* make sense of articles and common verbs, how are we going to figure out unique words?" Stefan said mournfully as our cohort gathered one Saturday afternoon. The weekends were often best for working, with no other classes to distract us. Outside, the Ver shrieked down the Lersach, unsettling in its rage, and from the windows we could see violent waves. "They could be adjectives or weird verbs or names—there's no way to know."

"Names," Yael mused, moving her pen in circles on a scrap of paper, as though hoping ideas would spring forth. "That would be useful. If we could find, say, 'Stefan' in Language X, then we could pronounce those characters."

Stefan laughed. We were at the point of exhaustion where everything seemed funny. "It *should* say 'Stefan' in there."

"Not 'Stefan,'" Gidon said suddenly. He had pulled out a bag of dates, and I was wondering if I could steal one. "But what about—the name of an ancient king? Ena-Cinnai was ruled by royalty twenty-five hundred years ago. Maybe the king's name is there—or 'Talum.'"

"Talum wasn't founded yet," Yael said, but absently, as though correcting a mistake through sheer force of habit rather than because she was focusing on it.

Because she was probably focusing, as I was, on the potential of this idea. This could be a breakthrough. While we could potentially translate words based on frequency—in our language, the most common words were "the," "be," "to," "of," and "and," with much of our work so far based on theorizing similar frequencies in Language X—we still wouldn't know phonetics. If we could match a name from Ena-Cinnaian to Language X, we would be able to pronounce letters.

"It doesn't have to be a king's name," I said slowly. "If we could figure out *any* word—probably a proper noun—that's remained unchanged all these years, we could match Language X characters to ours."

"Are there going to be any?" Stefan asked skeptically. "Pronunciations probably shifted over two thousand years."

"Do you have a better idea?" I asked.

Stefan shrugged. Apparently not.

For a few minutes, we racked our brains. Stefan took one of Gidon's dates, so I did too, and we stood around, munching on them and staring at each other. I couldn't think of a single ancient noun. Surely nouns existed. Probably.

"The tribes," Gidon said.

Right. Of course. Old things *did* exist. "Place names," I added. "I can pull a map from the library, and we can see what's stayed unchanged."

"The Great Beasts," Stefan added. "Other religious stuff, probably? Shedim?"

"Good." Yael's pencil stilled, and she ripped off her page of doodles to leave a fresh new page. "Let's make a list."

"You're distracted," Daziel said a few hours later, probably not for the first time. "What's going on?"

"Sorry." I returned to slicing the pears I'd picked from the pear tree in the corner. They weren't seasonal, but they were very sweet. "We're trying something new. We're coming up with words that might have stayed the same for thousands of years—ancient nouns."

Daziel looked confused. "Ancient nouns? Like what? Why?"

I brought the pear slices over to the couch, very aware of the space between us as I sat. "If a word was pronounced the same way millennia ago as now, we could match our version to Language X's

and extrapolate which Language X characters phonetically corre-
spond to ours. So we're looking at ancient cities, stuff like that." I
snagged a library book I'd left on the coffee table, flipping to a
map of the world from three thousand years ago. "Not tons of
places have been around that long, but Aolong has, and Tzorybium. If the scrolls mention a noun we still use and match it, it
could be a game changer." I sighed. "Of course, we'd have to be
able to match them in the first place."

"Huh." He leaned forward, his shoulder almost brushing mine.
If I tilted slightly to the right, we would touch. "You need a word
that's . . . distinctive. So you can recognize it."

I munched on the crisp pear. As I licked the juice off my
fingers, I caught Daziel watching and looked away, flushing. "Exactly. But what's distinctive?"

Daziel looked as intrigued as I'd been a few hours ago, but his
brain was still fresh tonight. "You've made a list of unchanged
proper nouns?"

"That's what we started, yeah."

He nodded thoughtfully. "Are any of them . . . different?
Unique?"

"How do you mean?" I rubbed my forehead. More than anything, I wanted to lean against Daziel's shoulder and have *him* rub
my head. Why was it so hard to figure out if he liked me? This was
driving me mad. I'd thought he might, but hadn't I obviously
shown my own interest, going to his game? If he knew I liked him,
and he also liked me, why wouldn't he do something? "My brain
hurts so much."

He took a pear slice. "Hyphenated? Like 'Ena-Cinnai.'"

Leah had told me going to his game wasn't the clear indicator I
thought. I supposed I could say something, but if he rejected me

we'd be trapped in these tiny rooms and it could ruin our entire friendship, and there'd be no way I could focus on the scrolls. "'Ena-Cinnai' isn't old enough."

"I mean something that looks different. Something you could recognize without needing to know the characters themselves. By recognizing a pattern. Something with four O's in a row or whatever."

A pattern. I racked my brain, willing to entertain this because it wasn't like I had any better ideas, and I needed some distraction from my yearning to press my body against his. I thought through the proper nouns we'd written down so far. The tribes. Ancient royalty. A few ancient places. The Great Beasts.

Wait.

My stomach hollowed out, and my head felt light.

"Ziz," I whispered. Two sounds but three letters—because it was two letters, one repeated. "'Ziz' is a palindrome," I breathed, the realization hitting me with blunt force, leaving me shaking with excitement. "If we have a three-character palindrome . . ."

You didn't need to understand a language to recognize a palindrome.

I broke out in sweat, then shook my head. "It's wildly unlikely one of the scrolls would mention the Ziz."

Daziel shrugged. "Okay."

"But . . . on the off chance . . . or if there's *another* palindrome in there we could match to a proper noun . . ."

He laughed. "You're dying to run to the Keep and check right now, aren't you?"

"I mean, yeah!"

"It's past nine bells."

"Please," I begged, more to be funny than anything else. Making Daziel laugh always lit a delighted spark within me.

He grinned, his eyes gleaming with silver amusement, and sure enough, it sent a thrill through me. "I'm surprised you haven't left yet."

If I'd been a more spontaneous person, I would have pressed my lips to his right then. But while Daziel had called me impulsive, it turned out that only applied to my physical safety, not my heart's.

So I channeled my energy into dashing to the Keep. We ran into Yael and Stefan leaving a pub on our way there, bundled up in sweaters beneath their blazers and hats pulled over their ears. Yael looked surprised, but no more so than me to see the two of them together. "Where are you going?" she asked.

"The Keep," I said. "It's probably nothing, but . . ."

They both went on alert. "But what?" Stefan asked.

"The name 'Ziz'—it's a palindrome. We could recognize a palindrome in Language X."

I watched as the realization hit them, the hope they desperately tried to temper. "It's super unlikely the Ziz is mentioned," Stefan finally said.

"Super unlikely," I agreed.

"Let's go," Yael said, and started running.

Gidon was alone in the scroll room, still working, when the four of us burst in. He startled, looking a bit like an upright grasshopper. "What's going on?"

"Ziz," I said.

"What?"

"Don't you people take breaks?" Daziel asked, looking at the two cups of coffee next to Gidon's desk. "Gidon, did you even have dinner?"

"It's a palindrome." I strode to the reference binder containing the thirty-five hundred words in the scrolls. I could probably modify a spell to sort them by character length, but I didn't have the patience. Instead, I started paging through, scanning for three-character words.

Gidon's mouth parted with understanding.

My cohort crowded around me, our heads almost knocking as we scanned Yael's neat handwriting. We wanted a short palindrome. We wanted—

Gidon let out a strange sound, half a laugh and half a sob. He jutted his finger halfway down the first column on the third page. "There. A palindrome. A three-character palindrome."

זיז

Stefan grasped Yael's shoulder, squeezing tight, and she didn't seem to mind; she was beaming too. "Ziz," he said, and then we were all saying it, staring at the letters we hadn't been able to pronounce before, that we had eked meaning out of. Now we could *understand* two of the letters, something we'd never been able to do. We could pull sound from characters silenced for thousands of years.

"Ziz," we said, like a chorus of insects. We were laughing and cheering, and I caught a few suspiciously gleaming eyes. *"Ziz."*

Beside each word in the binder, a number showed how often it occurred. "Ziz" showed up fifteen times, a startling frequency for an uncommon word. Also, unexpectedly, an asterisk marked it as a word included in one of the scrolls' headings.

"Here," Daziel said, pointing. We gathered to look at the heading he indicated, and we let out another round of congratulatory hollers.

We should have known we were being too loud, especially given the closeness of Professor Altschuler's office. Yet we couldn't help ourselves, lost in excitement, unable to stifle our happiness about connecting a few scant dots.

So we shouldn't have been surprised when someone else entered the room, though I didn't think any of us noticed him until he spoke—and not for the first time, if the volume of his voice was any indication.

"What," Professor Altschuler said, staring at us, and now finally we quieted and stared back, "is going on?"

I flinched, my heart thudding. I felt like I'd been caught robbing a museum or plagiarizing a paper. But no, we'd done something *good*. "We've found a word. Well. We can't confirm it. But a guess. A three-letter palindrome we think might be 'Ziz.'"

For a moment, I wasn't sure if Professor Altschuler had heard me. He stood very, very still, and then he drifted over to the scroll. Gidon pointed out the palindrome in the heading.

The professor closed his eyes. A look of almost ecstatic relief crossed his face, smoothing lines away and making him look much younger. "Then we have *Z* and *I*," he breathed. His hand flexed, as though he didn't know what to do with the energy within him. I realized, for maybe the first time, Altschuler cared about this the way my cohort did—he too longed to unearth hidden secrets, to bring the unknown to light.

"Next we need other words that might contain *Z* and *I*," Yael said. "We should start looking—"

"Not now," Professor Altschuler said. "It's nine thirty on a Saturday, and I have places to be. We'll return to this tomorrow." He gestured for us to leave the room before him.

"But, Professor—"

"We're on a roll—"

"We're not tired, I promise—"

"Out," Professor Altschuler said firmly. "I'll see you in the morning."

Banished, we stood outside the scroll room, buzzing with energy and stumped on what to do next. Then I started laughing. "Do you think he's afraid we're going to steal his discovery?"

Stefan let out a hoot and shot me a look of appreciation. "Honestly, yes."

"What are we going to do now?" Gidon looked like he might tear his hair out.

"Easy," Stefan said. "We're going to fucking celebrate."

SIXTEEN

TALUM WAS SHAPED LIKE A KIDNEY BEAN, LONG AND CURVED at both ends. The wealthiest lived on the hills for the views, or along the soft beaches of the east coast. On the southern tip of the isle lay the craggiest, least accessible part: the Rocks.

Geologists weren't sure what had formed Talum, but they suspected a volcano, which had left behind both the main island and an islet, uninhabited save for a herd of sheep and red succulents. The glossy rock of the islet and the Rocks was difficult to build on, and therefore uninteresting to the law-abiding, wealthy denizens of Talum. But because the Rocks were riddled with caves and hidden beaches, it was the perfect place for wild parties.

I'd never been invited to a party at the Rocks before.

Stefan led the five of us across the island on the tram, disembarking in the leatherworking district. From there, we followed progressively narrower streets, then ducked between two decrepit houses whose barren yards turned rocky, then to glazed rock itself as we left the neighborhood behind.

For fifteen minutes, we scrambled over the jet-blue rocks. There was nothing on this side of the island—no trees or houses—to protect us from the racing wind, and it scoured our skin, cold and fierce. Was it the best idea in the world to have an outdoor party in deep winter? Maybe not.

"There," Stefan said, sounding satisfied as we reached the edge of a cliff. "Welcome to the Rocks."

Before us, the rocks canted down toward a sandy cove, cut off from the rest of the shoreline by the cliffs. Bonfires lit the beach, and music drifted up, drums and bells, the thrumming melody resonating deep in my bones. In the night-dark river, a floating plank bridge led twenty yards offshore to a wooden platform with a bar. People crowded it, dancing and blowing green smoke circles through pipes.

I shivered, wrapping the scarf Daziel had made me more securely around my neck, the air cold and sharp in my lungs. This wasn't my comfort zone. I was not cool enough for this.

"Let's go." Stefan bounced down the stairs cut into the rocky cliffside, and the rest of us followed. He led us to a bonfire, where we stood close enough for warmth against the chill and the right distance from the music for it not to overwhelm. Yael and Stefan looked entirely at ease, Daziel sanguinely unimpressed, and Gidon and I kept shooting each other shocked *what are we doing here* looks.

It was cold with the wind off the river and the chill of the night, even with the fire and our warmth spells. Some people sewed spells into their jackets, but neshem could ruin fabric, so people usually carried porous stones, the heat spells slowly pulling on neshem and dispersing heat.

Then there were less magical ways to stay warm. Stefan lifted a bottle of champagne from his satchel and poured it into tiny cups. "Cheers! We did it!"

"To Naomi." Yael raised a cup, and I felt a rush of gratification and shyness at her words. If I lived a hundred years, I doubted I would be as composed and serene as she was. "Who figured out the palindrome."

"It was really Daziel," I said. He stood beside me, heat radiating off him. Unlike the rest of us, who'd bundled ourselves so thoroughly as to abandon fashion, he'd carefully arranged his scarf around his shoulders to appear careless. It accentuated his neck rather than cocooned it, the long bronze column strong and elegant in a way I hadn't realized necks could be. "He thought about looking for a pattern we could recognize in Language X."

"To Naomi *and* Daziel, then," Yael said, a small smile on her mouth. Her short blond hair had been completely hidden by a giant white hat. "The most unlikely pair of cryptographers."

"Cheers!" We clinked our drinks together. I looked at Daziel. He smiled with such warmth my stomach clenched, and goose bumps flared along the back of my neck and down my arms. He made me feel like he saw me.

Like he delighted in me.

"And congrats to all of us," Yael said. "We pulled off something no one else managed. Something we've been working toward for *years*. Two things, actually—repairing the scrolls and cracking the first hurdle."

"Cheers!" we all cried again. The bubbly was going straight to my head, and I drank a little extra to warm myself against the night. I wanted to nestle into Daziel's warmth with an almost physical yearning. I held myself back, still too wary and shy to risk rejection. Though, maybe, with the moonlight and the confidence from tonight's discovery, I could be brave.

"What's that?" Gidon asked the older two, nodding at the platform across the water, with the bar and the floating haze above it.

Daziel was the one who answered. "Menthaloc."

Though the smoke wasn't familiar, I recognized the name.

Menthaloc: a hallucinogen I hadn't known existed before I came to Talum.

"You like?" Stefan asked him. "We could get some."

"No," Daziel said. Firmly.

"I'm game," Gidon said.

Yael was watching Daziel. She, I expected, had also noted Daziel's certainty and wondered what was behind it. "I'm good," she said when the boys turned to her.

When Gidon and Stefan headed to the pontoon bridge, I found I had no idea what to say now that Daziel and I were alone with just Yael. I admired her more than anyone, but maybe that was what robbed me of anything interesting to say.

Daziel glanced at me, and I widened my eyes, trying to convey my panic at trying to be cool. He suppressed a smile and turned to Yael. "So, how'd you end up interested in cryptography?"

"My parents know Professor Altschuler's family," she said. "Growing up, I heard about all his expeditions, and they fascinated me."

Oh, phew, I could relate here. Dad had raised me on tales of the sprawling empire of Tzorybium, where buildings had gold-plated ceilings, and descriptions of the tropical islands of Aolong, where mist and rain were as measured as clockwork. He'd told me of the red sand deserts to the far south and of temples topping rock formations to the north. I wanted my world to be as wide as his. "My dad was a sailor, and he told me all sorts of stories about his travels. It's what made me start learning languages in the first place."

At my side, Daziel slipped his hand around my fingers and squeezed.

A rush of almost-painful gratefulness welled behind my eyes, thankfulness for Daziel's support, and joy that he *wanted* to support me. I squeezed his hand back.

Surely tonight, by the river under a bright moon, I could be bold enough for romance.

Eventually, a few of Yael's friends joined us, and at some point, Gidon and Stefan returned, notably giddier. By the time the moon had reached its zenith, Daziel and I had wandered off for more drinks. I kept staring at him, at the way he glowed from within, at the dark wells of his eyes, the gleam of gold on the surface. He was so beautiful. And he had called *me* beautiful, twice, and crocheted me a scarf and laced his fingers through mine. Maybe he was also shy. Maybe I did need to be the one to say something.

We refilled our cups, then sat on a rocky boulder high up on the beach, nestled against the cliffs. We looked out at the cove, the river, the crowded platform in the distance. The stars twinkled above us, their winter light colder than usual.

A gentle breeze floated by. Wind tugged at my ankles. It smelled like summer, like green growth. Where was that scent coming from? I turned, trying to catch the direction. It shouldn't smell like summer.

But my gaze locked back on Daziel as I turned my head, and I forgot about the tugging wind. I'd never found myself as captivated by anyone before. "Tell me something. What do you really look like?"

"Does it matter?"

It didn't *matter* so much as it intrigued me. I knew parts of Daziel so well—his tastes in food and outfits, the crinkle in his brow when he was upset, the way he really liked munching on glass when he thought he could get away with it. But I didn't know what he actually looked like. "Indulge me."

He hesitated, twisting his signet ring distractedly. "I don't want to scare you. Humans are notoriously high-strung about appearances."

I didn't want to be grouped in with humans; I wanted to be me, unique. I nudged his shoulder with mine, trying to put him at ease. "Do you have a tail?"

"Hm."

I took the noise as an affirmation. Which, admittedly, not my favorite. "Wings?"

He didn't say anything.

"Chicken feet?" I teased. The small spirits were said to have chicken feet; one way to tell if you had an infestation was to scatter ash on your floor and look for tracks in the morning.

He frowned. "I don't have chicken feet."

"That's good," I said with mock relief. "I don't think I can get behind chicken feet."

He examined his talons with deep concentration. "I do have a rear dewclaw."

"I'm sorry, what?" While I was aware not only chicken had vestigial claws protruding from the backs of their legs—dogs did as well—I found it unappetizing.

He gestured to the back of his foot. "It's to help with climbing."

"Where are you climbing?"

He shrugged.

Okay, moving on. "What about a beak?"

He touched his nose primly. "I would call it noble and full of character, not a beak."

I narrowed my eyes. "Is it a beak or not? Is it made of—what are beaks made of?"

"Bone," Daziel said. "Covered by a thin sheath of keratin." At my blank look, he extended his hand, black talons gleaming. "The protein that covers hair and makes up fingernails.

"Really?" I placed my hand next to his, aware of the scant space between them. "What do you think is the biggest difference between humans and shedim?"

He shot me a look, a grin slowly growing, but didn't say anything. I frowned. "What?"

"Don't be mad."

I got ready to be mad. "Tell me."

He smiled. "There's a pureness among humans. A naivete. An earnestness. I like it."

My mouth fell open, and I pushed his shoulder. It didn't help that I was, in fact, feeling fairly earnest toward him at the moment. "*You're* earnest! You get wide-eyed over donuts and the opera."

He looked wry. "Yes. But. Maybe it's how kind you all are? We're kind," he said quickly. "But it's not the same. It's not as ... intentional, perhaps."

I frowned, not understanding what he meant. I didn't like being called naive and earnest—the description sounded childlike. And I didn't want to be seen as a child. I drew one knee up to my chest, trying to sound blasé and intellectually curious, not like I cared. "Do you mean about relationships? Have your previous relationships been so unearnest?"

A grin blossomed slowly on his face. "Why do you want to know?"

Maybe he wasn't as shy as I was, after all. "I'm just trying to understand."

No innocence on his face now, much closer to wickedness, though I could hear how carefully he picked his words. "I think shedim are more sexually open than humans. We don't tie sex to emotions as often as humans do. Maybe that's part of it."

"We're open," I protested, feeling defensive. I was using the human "we," given I had minimal experience at being open or closed. Was that why he hadn't kissed me? He thought I'd get too attached? "At least here, in Ena-Cinnai, we're not like in Tzorybium." In the northwestern continent, across the Long Sea, people were more conservative: no sex before marriage, more reserved clothing, restrictive beliefs around gender.

"All right," he said. "But for shedim, the pleasure in the moment is often enough for an interaction. We don't dwell on it overmuch."

I parsed this. "What, so you're great at one-night stands? So's half the Lyceum."

His teeth flashed in the night as his smile grew even more. "And which half are you?"

One-night stands weren't an experience I had any knowledge of, as Daziel likely knew, given he'd lived with me for five months. "Which half are *you*?"

His black eyes hooded, and the smile lines on either side of his mouth deepened. "I'm not having any. I'm betrothed."

"Only technically," I said, aware I sounded petty.

"Yes." He reached out, slowly wrapping his finger around a curl that had sprung loose from my braid crown. My heart thudded in my throat. Our eyes locked on each other's, and a silkiness entered his voice. "Only technically."

A shiver went through my whole body, a clenching that seemed reserved for Daziel. It was a response to the depth of Daziel's voice and the cant of his body and the way he looked at me, along with how much I liked his humor and slyness and sweetness. Liquid heat spread through me, and my cheeks burned.

But he didn't kiss me.

Kiss him yourself, you fool, the wiser part of me said, the part that advised my younger sisters and was good at being practical and brave, especially for other people. But there was another voice, my aunt's, droll and dry: *You have no future. Inevitable heartbreak.*

If I was going to make this leap, I needed him to jump with me. I needed to know if he wanted it too, if I had been mistaken or not about the attraction between us. "You know how I know this isn't a real betrothal?"

"Do tell." His voice was still soft. Intimate. His gaze never strayed from mine.

"Because you haven't courted me." I tried to sound airy and theoretical, still too scared to give too much away. "You haven't kissed me."

The words hung in the air. When he didn't respond, I wanted to snatch them back, pretend I'd never said them. Why had I brought this up? I should have buried these feelings.

No. I needed to know.

His gaze pulled over me. There was something heated in it, something I wouldn't have thought I'd be able to detect from obsidian eyes, but it turned out this kind of look transcended species. "Do you want me to kiss you?"

Yes, I wanted to say, but it wasn't right, not yet. I didn't want to lay bare such a raw, vulnerable desire without knowing how he felt. I didn't want to be the only one to own up to the yearning coiled inside me. "I'm just saying, if our betrothal was genuine, you would have shown more interest."

"Ah," he said, a smile unfurling. "Making you coffee and bringing you croissants and plants isn't showing interest? Spending all my time with you? With your friends and family?"

My heart started pounding so forcefully I could hear it. Maybe he did like me. Maybe this could work. "You could just be being nice."

"Trust me." His hand fell from my hair, and his gaze slid to the moon's reflection on the water. His jaw tensed. "I'm not being nice."

"Aren't you?"

He picked up my hand. He'd done this before, so many times—when he begged me to make him a cup of tea so he didn't have to get up from the couch, when he was bored and wanted something to fiddle with, when he wanted to convey warmth or support. It'd never felt like he was trying to seduce me. His hand was warm, but when his thumb stroked the center of my palm, I shivered.

"What if I wasn't nice?" he asked. "How mad would you be?"

The odd note in his voice made me frown. "What do you mean?"

Then the first shriek carried from across the water.

SEVENTEEN

R AIN BROKE OVER US, DRENCHING ME AND DAZIEL SO completely and suddenly that I screamed. He threw up a shield, large enough to stop the rain a foot above us and send it arcing away.

A storm had arrived, with such ferocity and suddenness we hadn't had warning to flee. People ran back across the floating bridge from the platform, hampered by the increasingly rough water, and the bonfires sizzled out. Shouts cut through the rain as people searched for their friends.

I'd never seen river waves like this, so tall and wild. They reminded me of the ocean back home. And not Port Naborre's protected bay, but farther down the coast where the land jutted into the water and the sea fought back. These waves were ten feet tall and crested with whitecaps. And they were angry.

"Come on," someone shouted. "We can enter the caves from the staircase!"

Most people ran toward the promise of safety but not all. To my shock, I saw Élodie run past me in the opposite direction, toward the bridge.

"Élodie?" I shouted after her. I hadn't even known she was here.

The other Testylier House girl turned. *"Naomi?"* She sounded insultingly shocked by my presence but refocused, gesturing toward the platform. "Birra's out there."

I felt a pang of empathy. I didn't like the rich girls, but if Leah had been on the platform, I'd panic. I peered through the rain. It was too fierce to see well, but I could make out people on the raft—at least half a dozen. As for the causeway . . . I winced. The waves had broken it into at least three parts and submerged one.

"We have to fix the bridge," I said.

"Using what spell?" Élodie shot back, desperation turning her voice mean. "Do you know one? Or would you have me write one on the spot?"

Shoot. I turned to Daziel, who'd just warded off the rain in a completely inhuman way. "Can you do something?"

His dark eyes were impenetrable. "What?"

"We can't let them die. You have different magic than us. Able to affect natural elements, faster, bigger—"

"More volatile," he said. "And I don't care about them not dying; I care about *you* not dying."

But there was something in his face, in his tone, that made me think he could do something. He did have an idea. "*Please*, Daziel. They could drown."

Daziel's gaze transferred briefly to Élodie before returning to mine. "It's too dangerous."

"There's half a dozen people out there." I nervously eyed the rising waters. "We could get more people. Make a human chain and go into the water."

"You'd help them even if it put you at risk?"

"We have to do *something*."

Daziel cursed low under his breath. His gaze on mine seemed

to weigh me, to go deeper than his usual laissez-faire attitude. "Are you sure?"

His demeanor unsettled me, but I nodded.

He kept studying me for a long moment. Then he spoke, decisively, as though coming to a grave decision. "We need a stylo."

Some people kept stylos on them in case they had to write impromptu spells, along with flasks of neshem oil, but most of us didn't. I'd only taken spelled hand warmers and a glow globe today. I looked at Élodie. She shook her head miserably. "Nothing."

I looked around wildly for someone else to ask, but almost everyone had run for shelter. "We could use your—nails. On a rock?"

Daziel shut his eyes, looking pained, then shook his head. "Come away," he said, and started down the beach.

I followed him, and Élodie followed me, her brow heavily furrowed. "Where are you going?" she called.

Daziel looked back at her. His voice changed, turning cold and authoritarian, something I hadn't heard from him before—except almost, when I had tried to take his seal and when I had followed the winds. "This is private. I'm willing to share some things with my betrothed but not other humans."

Élodie looked torn. The storm had destroyed her pretty hairdo, despite the obviously expensive spells holding it upright. Ignoring Daziel, she addressed me. "Naomi, I don't know about this. He's a demon."

Daziel glared at her. "If I do this, it's only because Naomi asked. It's nothing to me if a few humans die."

This alarmed me, but I decided to shelve it for later. "Look," I said to Élodie, "if we can save them, we need to make every possible attempt."

She looked torn. When it came down to it, apparently, Élodie might not like me, but she still worried about my safety. "Let me stay. I won't tell anyone what you do."

"No." Daziel sounded rudely aristocratic and walked away.

"It'll be okay," I told her, though Daziel's manner had also set me on edge. What *was* he going to do, that he didn't want any other humans to see?

He paused once we reached the water's edge, where the waves lapped hungrily against the glossy black beach. The wind tore at us. I started to bend, looking for a large rock on which we could scratch charaktêres.

Daziel stopped me gently. His voice, now that we were alone, was soft, and his gaze apprehensive. "This must be written on your skin."

"What?" Alarm shot through me. Oh. Wow. My *skin*? Because that sounded a lot like—if it *broke* my skin . . .

He didn't say anything. Wind curled his hair. The feathered markings on his neck looked more real than usual.

Carving in skin meant blood magic.

Blood magic was dangerous, and illegal.

More shouts sounded across the river. Through the rain, I could make out people clinging to the wildly rocking platform. "We'll be able to save them?" I confirmed, and he nodded. I steeled myself. "Okay. Do it."

I expected him to raise a hand, but instead there was a terrible ripping noise, and two dark shapes unfolded behind Daziel. They were so unexpected I didn't understand what was happening, couldn't comprehend the dark membrane and the tendons dividing it. When they whipped toward me, I shrieked and jumped.

He grabbed my arm to keep me from bolting, and I stared, wide-eyed, at the appendages sprouting from his back. Breath tore through me in ragged bursts, and panic clawed at the back of my mind—some vestigial reaction telling me I was in danger. "Those are wings," I said, in case Daziel hadn't noticed.

"Privacy." The wings swept forward, forming a tight, secure cocoon with only the two of us inside. The world was immediately tinted red. He tugged me closer by my forearm, then gently pulled down the sleeve of my blazer, then my cardigan. He pushed up my shirt sleeve to bare my shoulder and bicep.

Chills rose on my skin despite the heat streaming off Daziel. This suddenly seemed like a very bad idea. My voice came out high-pitched. "Maybe we could fly to pick everyone up? If ... you can fly?"

"Too many people," he said shortly, and raised his hand. His talons looked so, so sharp, and I closed my eyes, reminding myself to breathe.

A slicing pain cut through my shoulder, and I shrieked. He stopped immediately. "Can you do this?" he asked, his voice terribly adult and serious. "We don't need to. But it is the only way I can think of to save them."

I swallowed. Okay, then. What was a little pain in the face of people's lives? "Yes."

I forced my eyes open, focusing on his wings tenting us, wrapping us in a dark, private world. He carved something I couldn't see into my shoulder, the pain real but not impossible, leaving behind a burning sensation. I concentrated on breathing. It was warm in here, insulated against the winds, and I wondered if he could wrap himself up like this and sleep in the wilderness.

It was beautiful, too, in the strangest way, like being inside a temple. Light didn't so much filter through his wings as emanate from them, a steady glow allowing me to see Daziel's features, so different from a human's. So ethereally beautiful.

"Repeat after me," Daziel said. "'Calm the water and form a bridge from the platform to the shore.'"

It wasn't a spell, not as letterform magic worked. Spells were more specific. A spell would have described what calm meant, would have specified the square footage. This was more the high-level takeaway of what a spell would do.

But if I'd learned anything from Daziel, it was shedim had very different magic than humans. "Calm the water and form a bridge from the platform to the shore."

Magic ripped through me, a dizzying, sickening amount. It billowed through my body, disorienting me. I clutched Daziel's arms. I felt like I was teetering on a rope a thousand feet above a gorge, or inhaling a sunset. My body was being blown out in every direction.

And blown from it was stillness.

The first hint was the silence. The howling of the wind calmed, the dash of the waves lessened, and the sounds of human panic vanished. Daziel uncurled his wings. In my peripheral vision, I saw the eerie flatness of the water, the people on the platform. The rain kept falling, slashing through the sky, but there were no waves, no dangerous swells.

"Hold it," Daziel said. "Breathe through it."

I didn't have the capacity to respond. Magic lurched through my body, knocking against the walls of my stomach, the back of my knees, the side of my throat. I felt distended and unreal, like it might bubble out of me, explode my body.

A bridge took shape. I'd said the words, but I hadn't pictured a specific sort of bridge—what kind could form, with nothing to form from? Yet it was from nothing the bridge appeared—from the air itself. It shimmered in the distance, as though becoming more concentrated. Then a structure coalesced in one great rush, the color like cloudy blocks of ice. It started by the platform, then skimmed over the water toward us, growing as it went, accompanied by handrails made of the same concentrated nothing. When it reached the shore, I could see it more clearly, this grayish glass-like structure, solid and unnerving.

"Cross!" Élodie screamed from down the beach. "Birra, cross!"

It took a moment—I imagine no one trusted the sudden, bizarre stillness around them, let alone this strange bridge. The back of my neck prickled. This was far outside the scope of anything human magic could do, and how could you trust something you didn't understand? But then one of the figures started running across the transparent platform, and others followed. I watched them dash toward us, breathing as Daziel had instructed, magic thrumming through me.

In. Out. In. Out.

My vision was going. The people on the bridge were getting smaller and smaller. Did my knees work? Daziel had wings.

Had I performed blood magic? Had I bound a demon? Had I broken the law and a two-thousand-year-old treaty?

Runners emerged, staggering up the beach, soaking wet. I closed my eyes. I couldn't watch anymore. I had to concentrate on holding the magic, on not letting it rip me apart into a thousand fleshy, bloody bits. Like the scrolls. My head hurt. Was it supposed to hurt?"

"Naomi." A light female voice spoke my name. Élodie. "Everyone's safe."

That was good. Breathing was good.

A hand on my shoulder. A deeper female voice. "Naomi, are you all right?"

I knew that voice. Opened my eyes. Yael, soaked to the bone. Had she been on the raft? She looked like an otter. Where was her other otter to hold her hand?

"Let it go," Daziel said.

Let it go? How? I'd never handled magic like this. The more it streamed through me, the more I felt like I was merely a vessel meant to be poured through, to accept and process and deliver magic, spreading stillness across the world.

"Say 'stop,'" Daziel said.

My stomach hurt. Like those years growing up when the harvest had been bad and my belly ground against itself, searching for something to eat.

"Say 'stop' *now*."

He sounded serious. He must really want me to do . . . what? What did he want me to do? My whole body seemed to be centering toward something, like a flame, and it wanted to keep burning and burning and burning . . .

"Naomi." Daziel's talons dug into my forearms. "*Naomi*. Say 'stop.'"

That was it. That was what he wanted. I had to open my mouth. Had to push sound through my vocal cords . . .

"Stop," I managed.

Like a puppeteer cutting a marionette's string, the magic snapped out of me. I collapsed. Daziel caught me, arms circling my waist and pulling me so my head rested on his shoulder. I was drained and empty and lightheaded, too exhausted to be confused. At my side, Élodie, Birra, and Yael stared at me with tremulous expressions. I looked beyond them. The bridge dissipated in a gust, swirls of white drifting away and dissolving.

"Leave," he barked at the others. "Get everyone to the caves."

Élodie swallowed but didn't move. Yael stepped forward, her patrician features grimly set. "Let her go."

"*Leave*," he said, and they were blown backward. His wings snapped shut, cocooning us again. He slashed a hot talon against the marks on my skin, in one direction, then the other, forming a bloody X that the heat of his claw seared shut even as he made it. I screamed, both from pain and surprise. Then he reeled his wings back, revealing Yael and Élodie chanting spells. Birra held a rock and wound her arm to throw it.

"I'm not harming her," Daziel said, sounding furious.

"Let go of her," Yael demanded. She held a stylo in one hand, a clay tablet in another—of course she'd always be prepared to cast.

Élodie's gaze had transferred to the waves, which were wild once again. "The beach is going to be underwater soon."

"What did you do to her?" Yael asked, face pale. "That wasn't normal. You shouldn't have been able to do that."

"I saved your life," Daziel snapped. To me, he asked, "Can you walk?"

"Yes." I took a step, and my knee collapsed. I gazed at it, baffled. Why wasn't my knee working? How odd.

Cursing, Daziel scooped me up. The others followed, and we caught up with the students from the platform as they scrambled up the glossy stairs carved in the cliff, which the rain had turned dangerous.

"This way," Yael said once we'd gone two-thirds of the way up. She led us out on a small but sturdy ledge and through a tall, slanted opening into a large cavern.

Fifty drenched students huddled inside, illuminated by glow lights. Puddles covered the ground. The cave was clearly often used—people had pulled out crates of supplies and were making tea—but it had the look of a disaster zone right now.

Daziel touched my shirt. It sizzled dry.

"Thanks," I said, grateful to be dry, wanting to curl up into him for added warmth. Instead, I glanced at the group next to me, soaked through. I'd been about to ask if he'd dry them too, but Élodie spoke first.

"How did you do that?" she asked. "You didn't write any charaktêres. You shouldn't have been able to affect the water and air like that."

He'd written something, though. On my shoulder. In blood.

"Natural magic is different than letterform," he said shortly.

"True," Yael said, her voice steady, her gaze piercing. "But wild shedim still don't have that kind of power. Wild shedim can't control the elements with such totality. I've never read of anything like this."

I looked down so they couldn't read the unease on my face. A wild shayd hadn't cast the spell; *I* had, hidden from view.

Daziel didn't reveal a hint of what I feared we'd done. "You think human texts contain all possibilities?" he tossed off.

Desperate to stop my classmates from pushing further, I changed the topic. "Daziel, can you dry everyone?" To the others, I said, "You'll get sick if he doesn't."

Yael kept frowning, but she stepped forward, her fine blond hair plastered to her head. *Do you trust him?* she'd asked me two months ago. Now she knew Daziel, had spent hours with him in the Keep, had gone to the pub with him. I hoped she trusted him too, even if she knew something strange had happened.

198 ~ HANNAH REYNOLDS

Daziel touched Yael's shoulder. Her clothes fluttered as water evaporated, sizzling into the air around her. The short strands of her hair fluffed up so she looked like a duckling in spring. She kept her gaze pinned on his face, like she was trying to read the truth there, but he looked behind her, bored, signaling someone else to come forward.

A few moments later, Stefan and Gidon hurried up. "You both all right?" Stefan asked, looking worried. Gidon, to my shock, hugged me tightly, then Yael, then Daziel.

I drew her aside as the boys grilled Daziel on events as he kept drying students. "Hi."

"He's more powerful than he should be," she said with no pre-amble.

I tried to maintain a neutral expression. "He's right, though. We don't know everything about what shedim can do."

"A wild shayd couldn't perform that spell." She sounded certain.

Part of me wanted to tell her what had happened, but I had no idea of the repercussions of a binding, even if both parties had agreed. I needed to talk to Daziel about this before anyone else. I hadn't even known shedim could bind humans; I'd thought only humans did the binding. "Don't worry," I told Yael. "I trust him."

Her gaze slid back from Daziel to me, and I wondered how much she guessed. "So you've said. But be careful."

We stayed in the cave for an hour, until the rain slowed. Then, slipping and sliding, we made our way back across the rocks to the leatherworking neighborhood, then the tram. It was an hour more before we reached Testylier House, where Daziel and I said reserved good-nights to Élodie and Birra as we left them at their floor.

My door hadn't even finished closing before I'd collapsed on the sofa. "What a night."

"Don't *ever* do that again," Daziel hissed.

I lifted my head a smidgeon, shocked. "Excuse me? What?"

"You risked your *life*."

"People could have died—"

"I don't care about people," he snapped. "I care about you."

I stared, astonished. "Well, *I* care about people."

He took a deep breath and reined himself in. "I know. I know it's not in your nature to leave people behind. But that was dangerous, Naomi."

I considered this. There was a lot to consider, really. "What was the spell we did?"

His steady gaze held mine. "What do you think?"

I gnawed at my lower lip. I knew it even if I didn't want to say it. His abilities were so different from the way humans handled magic. We couldn't affect things on such a large scale. We couldn't affect elements. And we needed to write our spells and use neshem.

I forced the words out. "Was it a binding? The blood magic? Is that why—we didn't need a proper spell, or neshem?"

He didn't look away.

My stomach hollowed out. It had been. "Is it—still—?"

"No," he said flatly. "I broke it."

The X he'd carved. I absorbed this, remembering the way the magic had flowed through me, how there had been so much of it, how it had needed so much less direction than a spell written and cast by humans. "That's why people used to bind shedim," I said in a low voice, feeling sick. I'd always heard how powerful spellcasters had been when they bound shedim; I didn't like having personal experience. "You're an inexhaustible source of magic."

"Not inexhaustible," he said. "Eventually, we die."

My gut clenched at the truth of that. "It didn't feel great to me, either. Heady and addictive—but I couldn't let go. It felt like it might drain me."

He winced. "I hadn't realized it'd hit you like that."

I started pacing, thinking hard, while Daziel leaned against the counter, watching. "The old stories say only the most powerful spellcasters bound shedim. I'd thought they became powerful from stealing your magic, but maybe they already needed to be strong to funnel it."

"Maybe. I don't know."

"Why did we need the binding, though? Why couldn't you have done it on your own?"

"Shedim don't have the precise control humans have. If I'd told the water to calm, I have no idea what would have happened—like I didn't know what form your cushions would take when I encouraged them to be their best selves. The river could have iced over or drowned the people who jumped in. The wind could have been calmed by being depleted of oxygen. I can be specific on a small scale—like drying clothes—but not on a large one."

I shuddered. No wonder shedim had a reputation for thriving on pandemonium—not being able to predict their magic's behavior probably bred comfort with chaos. "But I wasn't precise, either."

"You didn't need to be. In a binding, the force of shedim magic can be funneled into human precision and cast using more words than shedim but fewer than humans would. It's why bindings are so powerful."

"And you bound me," I said slowly. "I didn't know it could go in either direction. Though I guess there's not much motivation for shedim to bind humans, unless they could control what humans said."

Daziel held himself very still.

Realization seeped through me. I recalled all the people happy to let Daziel have pastries for free or attend the opera or have a new outfit. When he suggested things, humans listened. "*Can shedim control what humans say?*"

He lifted his shoulders in the smallest shrug. "We can sometimes . . . influence humans." He seemed to debate whether or not to say the next part. "In a binding—control can be wrested by the more powerful of the pair."

So binding could go either way. I hadn't been taught that in school, and I wondered if it was because humans didn't want to look weak or because shedim didn't want to reveal their ability.

His gaze finally fell. "I'm sorry I didn't discuss it with you first."

"I'm not." My voice became a bare whisper, mixing with the moonlight and the breeze. I stepped toward him. He'd done something illegal and dangerous, and he'd done it because I begged him to save the students on the platform. "You did it because I asked you to."

His gaze flickered back up. We stood very close, a scant foot apart, and his intense expression sparked an answering fire in me. "I would do anything you asked."

I bit my lip, a frisson of anticipation dancing through me. "Anything?"

His eyes, always so dark, sparked with iridescent light. He knew what I was asking, or what I would ask. He gave a minuscule tilt of his head. "Anything."

My whole body had been taken over by the beating of my heart. My pulse pounded in my neck, and each separate breath felt heavy. Heat coursed beneath my skin. "You asked if I wanted you to kiss me." My tongue darted out to lick my dry lips, and I swallowed, hard. "Yes. I do."

"Is that so," he said softly. He brushed his fingertips against my cheek, curved them over the shell of my ear. "Why?"

A burst of heat and shivers and something I didn't recognize radiated from his touch. Like I'd had a taste of a new flavor I'd never tried, and I wanted more of it almost desperately.

I shrugged. My throat had closed up; I couldn't get a single word out.

"You *like* me." A smile broke the intensity of his expression, teasing the corners of his lips.

I made a face. "You're all right."

His grin widened, and he stroked his hand down my neck, sending bolts of sensation through my entire body. "You're madly in love with me."

I hadn't had much romantic experience. At home, I'd been too focused on my schoolwork to start anything, so I'd only shared a few kisses at festivals in Port Naborre—where if anything went sideways, I wouldn't have to see them again. But I knew enough to raise my face and lean forward.

Daziel hesitated.

I felt like he'd plunged his hand into my chest and twisted. But I made myself speak, even though my voice came out small. "You don't actually have to kiss me if you don't want to."

He groaned. "I want to. I really do. I'm trying to restrain myself."

"Why?"

He closed his eyes briefly, black lashes sweeping across his cheeks. He looked strangely pained, but when he reopened them, his eyes were clear. "Good question."

He lowered his head, and his lips met mine.

Heat and delight sparked through me, so powerful I thought I might gasp and lose my balance. Instead, I leaned into the kiss, clinging to Daziel's shoulders, pulling my body flush to his.

For a heartbeat, he went still. Then he pushed against me, all heat and desire, every hard line of his body pressing against the soft curves of mine. I felt like if he wasn't holding me up, I would collapse, like my bones had turned to rivers of flame. I held on to him, not entirely sure how to do this, determined to try. His mouth angled against mine, opening it, and I did gasp now and lost track of everything but feeling.

He drew back, breathing hard.

I gazed up at him. It was astonishing how beautiful I found his face, how familiar and perfect it was to me, how I knew each line of it so deeply and thought they met in perfect harmony. "I do," I said. "In case it wasn't clear. Like you."

He kissed me again, kissed me until we were both breathless and weak and on fire. Kissed until his hand slid under the hem of my shirt and I was the one to pull back, my face red.

Daziel's hand stilled. He looked a little red too, embarrassed and pleased and happy. "Right," he said. "It's late. Should we go to bed?"

I raised my brows. I could tease this boy, I realized. He was mine to tease and kiss and laugh with. "Together?" I asked archly.

He looked startled, as I'd hoped. Then we were both laughing, so hard I had to sit down, and he did too. Nothing was funny, really, but I was so absolutely happy, joy spilled out of me. Maybe we were relieved, too, to be home and safe after the long night.

And that happiness and my security in it gave me the courage to say what I did want. "I, um . . . I'd like to sleep out here tonight," I said. "On the couch. It was a long day, and . . . I think I'd feel better." Being near him.

He squeezed my hand. "I'd feel better too."

I brought out a blanket and a pillow for the couch, and Daziel curled up in his nest, and we talked of nothing in the darkness until we fell asleep.

I woke to the stringent tones of the dorm's guardienne, Madame Hadar. "Miss Bat Yardena! Naomi, open up!"

Confused and half-asleep, I sat up, my blanket falling away. I was on the couch, where I'd slept as soundly as I did in bed. Someone banged on my door. I glanced at Daziel—who stretched and blinked with the confusion of someone who never woke abruptly—then wrapped my blanket around my shoulders and headed to the door.

I opened it to find Madame Hadar and a man in the silver uniform of a civil servant, backed by several members of the gendarme. The civil servant wore amulets around his wrists and neck, and metal toggles closed his blazer. The gendarmes had modified their uniforms the same way—all protective measures against shedim.

"What's going on?" I instinctively used my body to block the doorway.

"These people would like to speak to your guest." Madame Hadar's eyes were a little wild, and her nerves woke my own.

"Lord Daziel." The civil servant looked past me. "The Sanhedrin would like to speak with you. If you would come with us, please."

"What?" The *Sanhedrin*? The governing council? I looked back and forth between the guardienne and civil servant. "Why do they want to talk to Daziel?" I frowned. My aunt's friends had always referred to Daziel as "honored guest." "Why are you calling him 'Lord'?"

Daziel came to stand behind me. "I expect the invitation is not optional?"

The man smiled thinly, the kind of smile bureaucrats everywhere seemed to have perfected, where it never reached the eyes. "They await your earliest convenience."

"You can't bang on our door at—" I glanced at the clock and realized it was past eleven. "You can't just whisk him away," I finished angrily. "On what grounds?"

No one answered me. I tried to slam my door, but one of the gendarme said something, and I realized they'd written a spell on my door to keep it open.

My heart rate increased as helplessness slid through me. "This has to be illegal. Don't you need a warrant to mess with private property?"

"This is Lyceum property," the civil servant said smoothly, glancing at Madame Hadar. "The Lyceum is kindly cooperating."

Scowling, I turned to Daziel. "You don't have to go with them. We'll refuse to leave. Go to my aunt." I lowered my voice. "Or can't you—?" *Vanish.*

Daziel placed a hand on my arm. He was so much calmer than I was, his gaze steady, his shoulders back. I could see Paz, though, tucked under Daziel's collar, his little face tight. "It will be fine."

It would not be fine. If they were here for Daziel, it was because of last night. In which case, they should also take me. I'd also been involved in the binding. I grabbed my coat and stuffed my feet into my shoes, laces undone. "I'm coming with you."

"I'm sorry, miss," the civil servant said. "They would like to speak with him alone."

"That's ridiculous," I said. "Are you *arresting* him? He's a *minor*."

"I'm sorry," the man said again.

"It's all right." Daziel squeezed my hand, letting go as he stepped out of the room. His nightclothes had shifted into formal black, the lines severe and crisp. "I'll see you soon."

My breath came hard and fast, and panic welled in my throat. "I'm coming with you!"

Two of the gendarme stepped in my path, blocking the door of my apartment. I gaped at them, gaped at Daziel on the other side, who simply gave me an inscrutable nod before turning to go. "Daziel!" I cried. I turned to the two men before me, who stared above me as though I was invisible. "Are you trapping me in here? Madame Hadar!"

"It's just for a moment, so there won't be any trouble," she said, her voice quivering. "Everything will be fine."

I glared at her and at the others. Then I slammed my door as fiercely as possible and collapsed on my couch, shaking. I pulled my knees to my chest, resting my chin upon them and trying not to cry. Outside, the sky was a flat, cool gray, only a few plumes of smoke in the distance adding any texture.

It was Sunday morning. Last night had been so wonderful and terrible—the realization of the word "Ziz," the party and disaster at the Rocks, kissing Daziel. Today, my cohort would be at the Keep. We had a potential key now. We might be able to decipher everything. They'd probably be expecting me.

Instead, trembling, I packed an overnight bag. And as soon as the gendarme were gone, I set out for my aunt's.

EIGHTEEN

"THEY TOOK DAZIEL," I TOLD AUNT TIRTZAH. WE WERE IN her bedroom, where I'd been escorted by her assistant, Chava. It was an alarmingly elegant chamber, a silk rug on the polished wood floor, a massive bed, a high ceiling painted with florals. The room was bigger than my entire apartment.

My aunt sat at her vanity, wrapped in a white cotton robe, her hair still wet from showering. I paced behind her. "He didn't *do* anything, and the gendarme took him away."

Aunt Tirtzah's reflection lifted her brows. "Didn't do anything? The demon who froze the entire river?"

"He didn't freeze it. He calmed it. And there's nothing wrong about that." Except for the binding we'd performed.

"Technically, there is." Aunt Tirtzah turned from her mirror so she could level the full force of her gaze at me. "High shedim are bound by the treaty to give notice of their location if they stay in Talum for more than twenty-four hours."

Unease brewed in my stomach, clawing its way through my body. I pushed it down. "Daziel's a wild shayd, not high."

My aunt snorted. "Naomi, a wild shayd couldn't have cast that spell. Which means he lied and is a high shayd, a member of their court. He's concealed a shocking amount of power. Which makes him unpredictable. And unpredictable can mean dangerous."

But Daziel wasn't high. He'd been able to cast the spell because *I'd* cast it when we were bound together. Would telling her about the binding put Daziel in more or less danger? Would it break the treaty? I trusted my aunt, but I didn't know if she would keep this a secret. I decided to hold my ground. "He has all the markings of a wild shayd."

"A high shayd is more than capable of altering their appearance," she said impatiently. "That's why they present to us as humans. They could easily also look like wild shedim."

I needed a different angle. "Fine. But even if he *is* a high shayd, he shouldn't have been arrested. People could be dead if he hadn't done something."

"While the Sanhedrin would see student death as a tragedy, they'd understand it." Aunt Tirtzah turned back to the mirror, combing out her wet, tangled curls. "They don't understand how a shayd could cast that spell, even a high shayd. People fear what they don't understand."

I tried not to squirm. Maybe I *should* admit how we'd cast the spell, if it would make them fear Daziel less. Surely a consensual binding wasn't illegal? "Fear doesn't make arrests legal."

Her comb caught on a knot, and I took it from her, working it carefully through the strands. I'd had years of experience fixing my sisters' hair.

"Fear makes people irrational," Aunt Tirtzah said, meeting my gaze in the mirror. "Everyone is already on edge—the treaty renewal is coming up in two years, and it's negotiated by high shedim. People are going to think he's a spy. Or a saboteur."

I studied her. She was two years older than my father, but they shared so many of the same features—the texture of their hair, the curve of their noses, the color of their eyes. It comforted me, and even though I didn't know her well, it made me feel like I could ask of her what I would of my father, who loved and supported me unconditionally. And you couldn't get anything if you didn't ask for it. "He saved us. And I'm asking you for help."

She turned, gently taking the comb from one hand and unwinding the fingers of my other from the fist they'd formed. "I like Daziel, and it's clear you care for each other. But I don't know his motivations, and I'm not sure they are good. You don't, either."

"He wants to see the world," I told her. "Before he's stuck at home running the family business."

She gave me a sad smile, like she didn't believe me. "It might be wise to disentangle yourself from him now. A wild shayd is one thing; they come to the border markets and have affairs with humans. But a high shayd—they're very different from us. What do you think would happen if you, a human girl, married a high shayd? Do you think he'd stay here with you in Talum after you graduated? Would you take him home to your village?"

He's not a high shayd, I wanted to say. Still, her words wormed their way inside me, and my unease started to grow. When it came down to it, I was a poor village girl from the high plains, and Daziel was . . . not. It shouldn't have hurt, shouldn't have twisted up my stomach and made me want to crawl into bed. Yet it did.

"We don't know much about the shedim court," Aunt Tirtzah said, "but we know anyone who can cast such a spell is very high-ranking. So high-ranking, he's not going to stay in human lands. This isn't his real life. This is just an adventure to him."

My parents want me to step into the family business, I remembered him saying. *Rocks,* I'd thought, but maybe it wasn't.

What if he *was* a high shayd?

No. No, he wasn't; it was the binding that had allowed us to cast the spell. He had told me as much. Still, I stared at my boots, the worn toes, the frayed laces. I felt very small and sad. "Very high-ranking" sounded bad. He was supposed to be normal, like me. "I don't think I'm just an adventure to him."

My aunt sighed. "Maybe not. But I want you to understand what's going on. He's a member of a mercurial species. I want you to be cognizant of the fact that while you're opening up your heart, he could be using you."

"For what?"

"I don't know. And that's what worries me."

I was quiet for a moment. "You could be right," I finally said. "But there could be more context. And he still doesn't deserve to be arrested. He saved us. It's my turn to save him."

She looked so tired. "Fine. Let's go try to rescue your boyfriend."

THE SANHEDRIN'S OFFICIAL SEAT perched atop Society Hill, so it didn't take long to get there from my aunt's house—a short drive up sandstone streets, past parks, residences, and gardens. Most of the council members lived nearby to have a quick commute—helpful, Aunt Tirtzah said, when night sessions ran long or when they were summoned with little notice. As everyone had been today.

"You'll have to impress them," Aunt Tirtzah said. Chava sat across from us, flipping furiously through a notebook. My aunt sat beside me and redid my braids in a neat knot at my nape. I stared out the window at the world, still glistening from last night's storm. Branches had been knocked to the sidewalks and even here, in Talum's most exclusive neighborhood, not all cleaned up. "Many won't want to listen to you because you're young; others because you're my niece. That is separate from your request, which is already something no one will want to grant."

Nervous energy buzzed through me. "How do I impress them?"

"If I knew the answer, I'd be running the place." Aunt Tirtzah straightened my collar. I'd thrown on a neat, respectable dress of my aunt's and felt like a child playing dress-up. The weights in the hem pulled at my shoulders. I hadn't worn a dress since arriving in Talum. I wore my blue School of Humanities blazer over it, the Lyceum's emblem shining on the breast, since my aunt had said it would be good to remind everyone I was a student. It would make me more sympathetic.

We drove down a wide avenue, pausing at gilded gates. The guard gave our credentials a perfunctory check—she clearly knew my aunt—and Samuel drove us on.

I'd never been to the Sanhedrin's House of Law before, and it impressed me more than I liked. Tall cypress trees lined the drive, which ended before a winged building made of three stories of golden sandstone. Businessfolk and messengers and well-dressed civilians bustled up and down the steps.

Samuel opened the carriage door and lowered the footstep. Aunt Tirtzah descended, then me, then Chava. We trailed her up the marble stairs. She nodded assertively to the entrance guards, and I tried to look like I belonged.

I didn't. The entrance hall itself was humblingly large, two stories high and echoing with foot traffic. Whorls of paint formed sky and clouds on the ceiling. People swept about, the swish of uniforms and clatter of heels aggressively loud. It even smelled expensive, hints of jasmine and rose lingering in the air.

"Councilwoman Bat Tovah." A man appeared before us in the crisp gray uniform of a civil servant. "They're ready."

"I should expect so," she said. She followed him, and so we all did, through an archway and down one hall, then another. "The petitioner's entrance," Tirtzah said to me when we reached a modest-looking antechamber. On the far side, a white plaque with neat gold font read GREAT COUNCIL CHAMBER.

The civil servant stepped through first; Aunt Tirtzah held up a hand, so Chava and I waited. I could see only the floor inside, white marble, gleaming so brightly I thought I might slip when I stepped on it. I heard three loud bangs, like a gavel, and then the voice of the young man said, "Tirtzah bat Tovah, Naomi bat Yardena, and Chava Vilner."

We stepped into the grand hall, which I'd only seen in ink newspaper drawings before. A glass dome let in rays of sun, which streamed color across the white marble floor and walls. Rows of seats edged three sides of the room. In them sat the seventy-two members of the Great Sanhedrin—seventy-one, given my aunt's place at my side.

Directly across from us, a man sat in a larger box than any of the others. He had a face like a turnip and a great, protruding mustache. The topaz amulet resting on his black robes declared his affiliation with the Tribe of Simeon—the Chief Judge of the Sanhedrin. On either side of his box were two men in black: one who must have been the Speaker of the Sanhedrin, and another who looked to be the scribe.

I scanned the councilors. They were equal parts men and

women, and everyone wore formal tribal affiliation robes. The Naphtali councilors sat high on the left, their blush-pink robes the color of a perfect summer rose. Their presence felt like a shot of relief.

"The Sanhedrin recognizes Tirtzah bat Tovah, Naomi bat Yardena, and Chava Vilner," the Speaker intoned. He was a skeletal man with a long face and a displeased expression.

"Hello, Tirtzah," the Chief Judge of the Sanhedrin said in a tired voice. "Perhaps you can shed some light on this situation. And your absence these last few hours."

"Apologies." Aunt Tirtzah sounded unapologetic. Her voice was dry and professional, like reeds rustling in the wind. "Family duties."

"This would be the niece." The Chief Judge's gaze transferred to me. I didn't want to quail—I wanted to maintain the self-delusion that I was brave—but it turned out I hated being perceived by authority.

"Yes, Naomi bat Yardena of the Naphtali tribe. My brother's daughter. Naomi, as I wrote, was at the event. I believe you may be interested in her account."

The Chief Judge waved a hand. "Go on, then, girl."

I tried hard not to clear my throat before projecting clearly, as my aunt had instructed. "My name is Naomi bat Yardena. I'm betrothed to Daziel bar Cathmeus. I'm here to request his release."

A murmur sailed around the room, and the attention of those assembled fastened on me.

"He saved more than a dozen Lyceum students from the storm last night. I'm here to vouch for his character and take him home."

A woman to my left spoke, wearing the white of Zebulun. "We

have reports he was able to control the river itself. How do we know he—and demonkind—weren't involved in last night's flooding? In the strangeness of the winds and waters being wrong?"

I hadn't even known there'd been flooding and had no idea how to defend against such an off-base accusation. Panic surged through me. How was I supposed to debate people two, three times my age, who'd made a career of arguing? Especially when I was scared to tell them the truth?

"Perhaps we should start from the beginning," the Chief Judge said. "You say he's your betrothed. How did you come into this situation?"

Hesitantly, I explained.

The Chief Judge rubbed his forehead, glancing sidelong at a man to his left in the silver-blue robes of Dan. "Is this binding?"

"Due to the exchange of pomegranate and ring . . ." The Danite made a reluctant face. "Yes."

"Daziel clearly believes the betrothal is binding," my aunt added.

"You must admit it is a very strange thing, Tirtzah," another councilor burst out. "And to have not told any of us!"

A few people made noises of agreement, but my aunt only snorted. "Half this room knew about my niece's betrothal as soon as the shayd attended my gathering four months ago. Several have met him in person. If anyone didn't know of him, their head was buried."

"We didn't know he was a high shayd," the Chief Judge said gravely. "We were under the belief she was betrothed to a wild demon."

"As was I," Aunt Tirtzah said. "Until the events of last night, I had no idea he was high."

"You expect us to believe that?" another woman said witheringly, this one in Asher purple.

Aunt Tirtzah's chin jerked up. "Do you want to administer a truth spell on me, Melanie?"

The woman looked mad enough to spit. "Maybe we should."

"Enough," the chief said, and my head stopped pinging between the women and refocused on him. I hadn't realized this wouldn't just be about me and Daziel but about my aunt's personal relations with the Council—because these were her peers, after all, and she would have both allies and enemies. "Whether or not Tirtzah knew is less important than what we do moving forward."

"Like my niece said, you should release him. According to Law 322-B of the Matine Codex, family members are permitted to lodge foreign nationals on their own properties," Aunt Tirtzah said. "I am willing to house the shayd Daziel."

One of the older men leaned forward. "A betrothed is not a family member. And technically, your house is not your own—it's held in trust by the Judahite tribe for their representatives."

"Oh, shove it, Harry," Aunt Tirtzah said irritably, losing her professional tone. "The house is fine. You know in any legal battle, I'll win—there's precedent. And what, do you want these children to get married now so we have the legal tie? They're not yet twenty."

"She could be lying," the Asher woman who didn't seem to like my aunt said.

"I'm not lying!" I said hotly.

"She could be bespelled," the woman—Melanie—said. "Demons can do that."

"Enchanting humans is against the treaty," another woman said.

"So is a high demon staying in Talum without giving us notice," Melanie snapped back.

"And so is detaining a shayd who has broken no laws," Aunt Tirtzah said coldly. "Which Daziel has not."

"Tirtzah's right. We can't keep him locked up," the Chief Judge said. "We might as well release him into your custody. You can keep an eye on him, and we won't be accused of breaking the treaty."

"They're already going to accuse us of it, given how we treated him," a man who hadn't spoken before said.

"Reasonable need," said another. I couldn't keep track of everyone; my head was whirling trying to remember who said what, who was on our side and who against. "They'll agree."

"Since when have shedim been reasonable?" a councilor in mustard-colored robes said.

Melanie scowled. "You're not seriously considering letting out a powerful high demon?"

"We can't aggravate our own allies," another man said. "I say we release him to Tirtzah."

"Tirtzah has served for merely three years," someone in teal said. "She's hardly the best equipped to house a shayd."

"And precisely where do you think the shayd *should* be housed to prevent his people from descending in fury?" a woman asked caustically.

"I say we banish him!" someone yelled.

The room descended into outright chaos, Sanhedrin members shouting back and forth, some standing to make their point, others thumping fists against their stands. I watched with wide eyes. These were the people running our country. Weren't they supposed to have it together?

"Enough," the Chief Judge finally said. When no one listened, he banged his gavel against his desk. "Enough!"

Reluctant silence fell.

"Let us not alienate our allies. Keep eyes on them, yes. Keep them locked up? No. We'll let him go. Tirtzah—I hope you understand your responsibilities here."

"Yes, Judge."

"Good." He rubbed his head and looked at me. "You trust him, girl?"

I nodded. "Yes."

He sighed wearily. "It is what it is. Shall we bring him in?"

The Danite beside the chief shook his head. "Better to bring Tirtzah's niece to him. It should agitate him less."

"Very well." The Chief Judge waved a hand, and we were shown out.

I thought we'd be brought to dungeons or someplace grim, but it turned out to be the opposite. The Speaker of the Sanhedrin and two attendants led us up a grand staircase and down the most elegant hall I'd ever seen, with long blue carpets and gilt-framed landscapes on the walls. Our guides stopped at a tall door guarded by six soldiers. My brows shot up. "Seriously?" I muttered to my aunt.

She nudged me, a warning to stay silent.

An elaborate locking spell had been carved into the door and the walls surrounding it. This room was a prison, despite its gorgeous surroundings.

In the middle of the door, a clay tablet had been set. The

Speaker accepted a small box from one of the attendants and removed a plate with raised charaktêres. He pressed the plate into the clay, leaving behind the charaktêres' impressions. A spell to unlock the door, complicated enough he didn't wish to write it by hand. After spreading a gleaming thimble of pure neshem oil across the charaktêres, he read the spell.

The door glided open, revealing a chamber half the size of a floor at Testylier House.

Daziel looked up from where he sprawled on a four-poster bed draped in green silks. At first glance he looked so like himself I let out a huge breath, almost dizzy with relief.

But then I clocked the tension in his body. I heard it when he spoke, his voice coiled tight. "Took you long enough."

"Lord Daziel," the Speaker said, but Daziel ignored him. Instead, he was in front of me so confusingly fast the Speaker squeaked and Aunt Tirtzah inhaled sharply. The soldiers stiffened.

Daziel didn't look at any of them. He focused on me, his black eyes searching. His hands found mine, and he squeezed, as though I was reassuring to him, as though he was drawing strength from my presence. "You came."

I wasn't sure what to say. "Of course I did."

"It has been decided," the Speaker said. "You are to stay with your betrothed's family. There are conditions—"

"I'm shocked," Daziel drawled.

The Speaker flushed.

"Goodbye," Daziel said, interweaving our fingers and tugging me toward the door. He nodded to Aunt Tirtzah, who stiffly returned the greeting.

"Are you okay?" I asked. "Did they hurt you?"

He sniffed. "They locked me up. An assault to my pride and my dignity."

Serious words delivered lightly, but I could tell he meant them. I squeezed his hand. "I'm sorry."

Aunt Tirtzah spoke. "Chava's having Samuel meet us by the north entrance. Less prying eyes."

A few minutes later, Aunt Tirtzah, Daziel, and I were settled inside the carriage, Chava seated with Samuel on the outside.

"So, Lord Daziel," my aunt said as soon as the doors were closed and she'd smeared neshem across the spell for sound-proofing and activated it. "Care to tell us the whole story?"

He sat beside me, clenching my hand in his lap. He blinked innocently at Aunt Tirtzah across from us. "The whole story?"

"What a high shayd is doing in Talum," she said calmly.

"They think only a high shayd could cast the spell at the Rocks," I hurriedly explained. "It's the only explanation they could come up with." I tried to convey I hadn't said anything about the binding, but it probably came off as an eye twitch.

"My niece is quite insistent on believing you're a wild shayd," Aunt Tirtzah said. "I don't think she will believe anyone but you. Would you mind putting the matter to rest?"

Daziel's mouth pressed together. He drew back the curtain, gazing out at Society Hill as we rolled past lush gardens toward Aunt Tirtzah's home. It was early evening now, and the sun almost completely set.

"It's okay," I said to him softly. "I know you're not a high shayd. You don't have to explain anything."

He stilled. Then he turned to look at me, the gauzy curtain falling shut.

It wasn't any one thing about his expression, or the way he held himself, but all of them combined—the stiffness of his shoulders, the cant of his chin, the brackets around his mouth and the faint furrow between his brows. All the air was sucked out of me. I felt like I'd been punched in the stomach, like the floor had been stolen away from beneath me.

"What?" I gasped, staring at him. The world tilted. All my senses were misaligned, a hair off from normal. But—no. The spell had worked because we were bound. I swallowed, my throat dry. "I'm sorry. *Are* you a high shayd?"

He winced.

Oh. I blinked rapidly, my stomach roiling. If he was, then—he'd lied to me. "Oh my god. You *are*."

"Naomi—" He reached for me.

I leaned back. There was no room for rational thought in my mind, only confusion and hurt and the desire to excuse myself from this situation. I fumbled for the carriage door's handle and pushed it open.

My aunt sucked in her breath. "Naomi, stop—"

Daziel frowned deeply. "What are you doing—"

"I'm getting out of here!" My voice came out shrill, matching the high thread of panic running through me. Daziel was a high shayd? He'd *lied.* He'd lied *intentionally.* And I had kissed him; I'd thought we were as close as two people could be—I looked out the open door at the road speeding along beyond my feet.

Daziel reached across me and pulled the door closed, glaring. "You don't need to jump out of a moving vehicle!"

"A high shayd?" I shoved him hard. "You *lied* to me!"

He deflated. "Can we talk about this later?"

I didn't say anything. I didn't have anything else to say.

Aunt Tirtzah took advantage of my silence to lean forward. "What are you doing here, Lord Daziel? Why didn't you declare your presence?"

Lord. That's why they were calling him "Lord." Because he was a high shayd, part of their court.

My aunt pressed on. "You have eaten at my table and been housed by my niece, who clearly adores you, though I suspect you're going to break her heart. If that's the case, I'd like to know why."

I flinched.

Daziel was silent a moment. "I don't plan to break Naomi's heart."

"No one ever does," Tirtzah said wearily. "Yet it's so often the outcome. And while my niece is a bright, kind young woman, I'm struggling to envision a world where a high shayd lord marries her."

A pang stabbed through my chest at her words, and my stomach felt hollow. "I never expected him to marry me," I managed, trying to preserve some sense of dignity as everything crumbled around me. "It was just an arrangement."

Daziel looked away. That hurt even more.

Aunt Tirtzah's voice softened. "It's been a long day. Perhaps we should rest and talk more in the morning."

I nodded, numb. I didn't understand why he'd lied to me. I wouldn't have cared that he was a high shayd. What mattered was he'd lied, and I'd thought we were too close to lie.

We arrived at the house, and Aunt Tirtzah showed us to one of her guest chambers. It was a beautiful room, wooden framework contrasting with the gray stone walls, the parquet floor gleaming.

"We're, um . . ." I paused, then forged ahead. "We're staying in the same room?"

My aunt's lips quirked. "This isn't the plainlands, Naomi. But it's less because I'm progressive than because this is part of the negotiation."

I didn't understand until Daziel spelled it out. "You're to be my keeper. To report on my comings and goings."

I stiffened, insulted. "No."

Aunt Tirtzah looked weary. "That was part of the agreement. For his release."

"I didn't agree."

"I did, on your behalf. You're a minor. Spare clothes are in the wardrobes and night kits in the washroom. I'll have dinner sent up. If there's anything you require before morning, you can find me or Chava in my office for the next few hours, and after you can come to my room. Otherwise, I'll see you at breakfast."

She shut the door behind her, and we were alone.

NINETEEN

I'D BEEN ALONE WITH DAZIEL A THOUSAND TIMES, BUT THIS was unlike being alone in my cozy apartment, with its bookcases and warm light. This room, with its high ceilings and sparse furniture, felt unmanageable. Too big for me, too big for my thoughts. They whisked about in all directions but kept coming back to one particular question.

I took a deep breath. "I thought the spell worked because of the binding. But—you're a high shayd?"

"It did work because of the binding," he said, black eyes serious. "But . . . yes. I am."

Numbly, I sat on the edge of the bed, an elegant thing with posters and linen sheets. "Why didn't you tell me?"

An almost-weary expression flickered across his face. "Does it matter?"

"That you're a high shayd? No. That you lied to me? *Yes.*" I tried to think of a reason, a way to make this palatable. "Was it because you'd have to declare yourself to the Council? And then you wouldn't be hidden from your parents?"

Our gazes connected, and I read his thoughts in an instant. This wasn't the reason, but he was weighing if I'd believe him if he served it back; after all, I'd delivered an excuse on a silver platter. I scooched backward on the bed until my spine touched the headrest, putting space between us. "Don't lie to me," I said, my voice soft and hard at once. "Why did you tell me you were a wild shayd?"

"I didn't tell you." He bowed his head, sounding abashed. "You assumed."

"I assumed because of your feather markings and talons." I swallowed. "Are those not . . . real?"

He grimaced. "I can hide them, as high shedim usually do, if that's what you mean. But you've seen what I look like. So, no, it's not real, but it's no less real than if I fully looked like a human."

I swallowed. "Why did you do it?"

He sat on the foot of the bed, tracing the embroidery on the duvet, blue thread stark against the white linen. He said nothing.

"You have to talk to me," I said, frustrated. "My aunt says the treaty negotiations are coming up. Are you here because of them? Are you a spy? Please don't tell me you pretended to be betrothed to me because of my *aunt*." It would have been the most ironic outcome, if Daziel had been using me to get to her just like the government students had.

"No," he said immediately. "It has nothing to do with her."

"But it has to do with something?" When he returned to tracing the embroidery, new threadwork blooming under his touch, I pressed on. "You do have an agenda."

". . . Yes."

"What is it?"

"I can't tell you." His face was so compelling, so familiar and real and *mine* in a way I'd never thought it would be when I first saw it.

But he wasn't mine, not really. And he wouldn't tell me, no matter that he'd used me for months. "Do you think I'm an idiot?"

He jerked his face up, looking shocked. "Of course I don't think you're an idiot."

"Really?" I tried not to cry, trying to freeze my tears by sounding cold as ice. "I let you in so easily."

"You're a trusting person. Optimistic."

I blinked up at the chandelier, hoping the light would burn away any wetness from my eyes. "Optimistic people are stupid."

"You're not stupid."

"*I* think I'm stupid." I swallowed, my throat tight and dry. "God, I'm *so* stupid. Everyone told me I couldn't trust you. You even told me not to be so trusting. And what did I do? I let you in. I let you stay."

"Naomi—"

"*Are* you a spy?" My stomach tightened, and I could feel my grip on my emotions slipping. "About the treaty, about anything?"

He hesitated. "I can't tell you."

"Why not?" My voice rose. "Because you don't trust me? Even though you said you did. Why did you even say that? To get me to so stupidly trust you in return?" I slumped down, curling into a ball. I wanted to pull the duvet over me and block out the world.

"I do trust you. It's—I—Naomi, I *know* you. You would tell people."

"Not if you asked me not to."

"Are you sure?" His black eyes met mine. "Will you promise now not to repeat what I say?"

I hesitated. I trusted Daziel, but I was also practical, and blanket promises were dangerous.

He arched his brows. "See?"

"That's not fair."

His jaw clenched. "I'm not trying to be fair. I'm trying to—" He clamped his mouth shut, then blew out a breath, clearly trying to take things down a notch. "I want to tell you. I just want to do it right. Give me time to figure out how to talk about this."

"Why should I?" I demanded. I was too angry to deescalate. "You've had five *months* of time. Why should I wait any longer?"

His brows snapped together, and his chin jerked up. "Because I'm a little exhausted from saving all your friends right now."

His words hit me like a gale, fierce enough to bowl me over and rip the air from my lungs. I felt impossibly fragile, a glass on the brink of shattering. "I see." Instead of disappearing under the impossibly soft linens, I slid out of bed. I wanted to be as upright and proper as possible, as though it could protect me from further hurt. I spoke, as icily polite as I could manage. "Thank you, my lord. You have my gratitude."

He looked instantly ashamed. Paz poked his head out and made a chiding, chittering sound. "I'm sorry. This is bigger than me. I can't just blurt it out—"

"Got it." I couldn't be in here anymore. I crossed the room.

At the door, I hesitated, one last horrible thought invading. "My aunt suggested even most high shedim wouldn't have been able to do that spell. That you're not just high but from the upper echelons of their court. Is that true? Or was it because of the binding?"

Behind me, he was silent a long moment. "The binding made a huge difference. But . . . it is true."

And I was just a human girl from a tiny village. I heard my

aunt's words in my head: *What do you think would happen if you, a human girl, married a high shayd? Do you think he'd stay here with you in Talum after you graduated?* "What are you doing with me?" I said, and I was horrified to hear the wobble in my voice. "Do you even like me? Why did you—kiss me?"

I heard the creak of the bed, his footsteps as he came closer. "Naomi—"

He tried to catch my hand, but I yanked it away. I whirled, breathing hard, my control snapping. "Don't touch me," I said. For a moment when I saw his startled, hurt expression, vicious satisfaction flooded me. Then it drained away, and I wanted to sob. I ran.

I spent the next few hours curled up in my aunt's library, unable to concentrate. I tried to read, but my mind kept slipping.

I wished I could talk to Mom.

Instead, I silently ate the dinner Aunt Tirtzah's housekeeper brought me, then cried into my armchair and felt pathetic for another few hours. When it was late enough I thought Daziel might be asleep, I crept back to the room we'd been forced to share. He'd created a nest of bedding on the floor, and I slipped into the massive bed.

But he wasn't breathing the way he did when he was asleep. Instead, we lay there in the dark for hours, awake and unspeaking, as the moon drifted across the window and the cold seeped in.

WHEN I WOKE, DAZIEL was gone.

I could see remnants of his presence—black glitter on his pillow, the mess of his blankets. Paz blinked up at me from the top of the dresser.

"Hello," I said. I could be mad at Daziel but not Paz. "Are you with me today?"

He cheeped, and I pet the back of his neck with one finger. Feeling slightly better, I took a very long, hot shower, then put on some of the guest clothes stocked in the closet—simple drawstring pants and a boxy shirt. Paz curled up on my shoulder, and we headed downstairs.

Aunt Tirtzah sipped coffee in the dining room.

"Good morning," I said.

Aunt Tirtzah looked up. "There you are. I wasn't sure how long you'd sleep."

I poured a cup of coffee from the pitcher on the sideboard and sat. She'd prepared it the same way Dad did, with cardamom and cinnamon, and it made me briefly, achingly homesick. "Daziel's not here."

"The grand duke sent for him for breakfast two hours ago."

I blinked at her. "The grand duke?"

She lowered her paper. "Daziel is a high-ranking shayd. If he's involved in the treaty negotiations, we want to make sure he's well treated."

"After arresting him. Which . . . was not treating him well."

"These things are complicated. Eat something. You barely had dinner."

I piled my plate with tomato salad, scrambled eggs, and toast. "So he's . . . with the duke?" *Without me*, I thought. It wasn't like I *wanted* to meet the duke, exactly, but . . . it would have been nice to be invited.

"Things will be different now," Aunt Tirtzah said. "People are scared of shedim but also want their favor."

"Seems two-faced."

"Welcome to politics."

"Hm." I picked at my food. The scent of the coffee wafted up, bringing with it thoughts of home and my family. I wondered what my parents would think of all this. I wondered if they'd ever hidden anything as big as this from *their* parents. "What was my dad like when he was my age?"

"Your father . . ." She looked out the window. "You remind me of him, in how curious you are."

"Grandma and Grandpa didn't want him to be a sailor, did they?" I'd never met my paternal grandparents, who'd died when I was twelve, still estranged from my father. He had returned to Talum for their shiva and made peace with his sister then. It was one of his greatest regrets, that he'd never reconciled with them, and that they'd never met me and my sisters.

"No. Our parents were . . . difficult. They had no money but plenty of pride."

"How did you get into politics?" I'd never asked before, which embarrassed me.

"I went to the Lyceum for humanities, but I was frustrated by what the Sanhedrin of the time was doing, so I switched to government. I wanted to change the world."

"And did you? Have you?"

"Have I?" She smiled wryly. "Not nearly as much as I thought I would have by now. It takes longer than I realized." She looked back at her paper. "Won't your classes be starting soon? Samuel will drive you to the Lyceum."

"Oh," I said, taken aback. "I thought I'd take today off. Since. Yesterday was exhausting?"

Aunt Tirtzah put her coffee down. "You thought you would skip classes?"

And this was why I didn't want to live with family. "I don't have my books or papers or anything."

"Then you should probably leave now so you have time to pick them up."

SAMUEL DROVE ME HOME to pick up my things and change, and from there to the Lyceum. Instead of heading to Intro to T3, I lingered by the brass entrance gates at the land bridge, which all students had to cross through to enter the peninsula. I'd knocked on Leah's door at home, but she hadn't answered, and I had to hope I'd beat her to school since I'd traveled by carriage instead of walking.

To my relief, I saw her a minute after Samuel dropped me off, and we collided in a hug. "Are you okay? What happened?" she demanded.

It felt like a hundred years had passed since I'd last seen her. "A million things." Too many people were looking at us, so I looped my arm through hers and tugged her over to a bench beneath a willow tree, whose draping branches gave us some privacy.

"They're saying Daziel's a high demon. That he stopped the storm in its tracks at the Rocks."

"It's—sort of. He is a high shayd. That's not the only reason the spell was so powerful, though." I told her about the binding, the arrest. Going to the Sanhedrin, fighting. The kiss.

Leah listened, wide-eyed, affirmingly astonished. "How do you feel?" she asked at the end. "You kissed! Finally! But he lied. Do you like him? Do you hate him? Where are we at?"

I groaned. "I have no idea. I wish he would *tell* me why he was here. I believe he's not here for my aunt, but what other reason is good enough?"

232 ~ *HANNAH REYNOLDS*

"I don't know." Leah screwed up her nose in thought. "Okay. What *do* we know?"

"He's here in Talum," I said. "More specifically, at the Lyceum. So—maybe he's here for something we can offer?"

Leah nodded, tapping the toes of her silver boots against the ground as she thought. "The Lyceum has knowledge, I suppose that's the most obvious. Students—professors. Though it's not exactly like he's kidnapped anyone. Neshem stores? Though I'm sure there's more elsewhere."

"Knowledge is interesting," I said. "We could have something in the library . . . some book or something he wouldn't have access to otherwise . . ."

"Does he spend much time in the library?" Leah said doubtfully. "Mostly he's with you and playing knockball, right? And crocheting."

"He goes to the opera," I offered, falling back against the bench and staring up at the willow branches. "Maybe there's a magical knockball he's trying to find. But yeah, mostly he's with me, and the only thing I do is . . ."

It slammed into me, so hard and fast and sickeningly right I gasped, latching my hand over the bench's edge for support, the wood smooth beneath my palm.

The scrolls.

Daziel was a high shayd. Which he'd kept hidden so he drew less attention. Betrothed to a girl working on scrolls. Scrolls under the authority of a professor who didn't like shedim. Scrolls no one could guess the content of.

Something that looks different, he'd suggested. *Something you could recognize without needing to know the characters themselves. By recognizing a pattern.*

A pattern like a palindrome.

I looked back at Leah, who was regarding me with matching horror. "It's the scrolls, isn't it?" she asked. "He wanted to know about the scrolls."

"He knew what was in them." I felt sick. "He essentially suggested I look for a palindrome in Language X. Which we found; we found the word 'Ziz.' How did he know Ziz would be there? *No* one knows what the scrolls are about."

Leah's face was filled with empathy, her voice soft. "Maybe Daziel does."

"I have to go." I scrambled to my feet. "I have to talk to him."

Leah grabbed my hand, her eyes wide and worried. "Are you sure? I'll come with you."

"No, it's okay. And—" My voice cracked. "I'd like to confront him alone."

She squeezed my hand. "Do you think it's safe?"

You trust too easily, I heard him say. Still. "He's a liar," I said, my voice trembling. "But I don't think he's dangerous."

Leah gave me a sad smile. "This doesn't mean he lied about everything."

"It doesn't mean he was telling the truth, though," I said, then excused myself before I burst into tears.

I took the tram to the Society Hill stop, then walked uphill for half an hour past the grand gardens and estates. At least the burn from the climb distracted me from the tightness in my chest. I studied the endless bugs and beetles on my walk. Without the birds, the populations had exploded.

"The councilwoman is gone for the day," her housekeeper said when I came back, regarding me skeptically. "Shouldn't you be at school?"

I smiled tightly. "I wasn't feeling well."

The woman softened. "Have a cup of tea, then."

I took the chamomile to the courtyard garden. At home, farther to the north, nothing bloomed at the end of winter, but here, color had started to arrive. Almond trees had small pink-and-white flowers; delicate pink blossoms covered pear and apricot trees; even the cherry tree flowers had begun opening. I breathed in the fragrance, trying to clear my head, and set the white porcelain tea tray on a decorative wrought iron table, my hands shaking.

"Daziel," I said, his name tasting bitter. Why had I even expected to find him here? Maybe he planned to spend the whole day with Talum's elite. "Daziel. Daziel."

"Hello, yonati."

He stood framed between two cherry trees. His outfit was even more extravagant than usual, as though along with throwing off the deceit of being a wild shayd, he also no longer cared to fit in with the student aesthetic. Green silk pantaloons were tucked into embroidered boots; a brocade jacket framed a ruffled cravat.

"Wow," I said, brutally aware I wore the same rumpled trousers I usually did, and a boring brown shirt, my hair pulled back in a severe braid. "Fancy."

He smiled cautiously. "Like it?"

I shrugged, consumed with self-loathing. How had I ever thought he was a wild shayd? Even with his black eyes and talons, he radiated the kind of confidence and presence that only came from growing up with far too much power.

"Apparently, the current fashion is for high-waisted pants with a broad band, as set by Mr. Wasterstein, who is considered the arbiter of men's grooming." Daziel slung off the jacket and loosened his cravat. "I am less certain about the cravat, but I'm willing to give it a go."

I caught the whiff of a delicate lady's perfume. *Is that recommended by the arbiter of men's grooming too?* I almost asked but resisted. "Is that what you were doing today? Learning about fashion during your breakfast with the grand duke?"

"Partially."

"What was the other part?"

He opened his mouth as though to say more, then paused. Cocked his head. "Why did you call me?"

I studied the almond tree before me, breathing deeply. I had to do it. I addressed the pale pink blossoms. "I figured it out."

"Figured what out?" he asked, stroking a rose on the bush at his side like I might pet a dog, for comfort. The flower curled up toward him, yearning, as though he was the sun itself.

"Why you're here."

He stilled. "Did you."

I took a deep breath and plunged onward. "It's because of the scrolls."

He looked at me. Not a look of confusion or realization or surprise. Just a steady, even gaze. Which meant I was right.

Which meant he knew what was in the scrolls.

And if he knew what was in the scrolls, if he was here because of them, he hadn't *coincidentally* become betrothed to a girl attempting to decipher them.

"No lies or games," I said. "Tell me the truth, Daziel. Why are they so important?"

He inhaled deeply, steadying himself. Then he focused on me. His gaze was direct and unwavering. "Because," he said, "we think they contain knowledge about how to cure the Ziz."

TWENTY

THIS WAS NOT WHAT I'D EXPECTED TO HEAR.

"I'm sorry," I said blankly. "We're going to need to back up."

Ever since I'd started at the Lyceum, I'd heard—and participated in—speculation around the scrolls' contents. People hoped for all sorts of things—strange and powerful spells, the diaries of kings. When my cohort was overworked and exhausted, we joked it'd be grocery or to-do lists.

No one had suggested it might be a cure for a divine beast.

Why would a divine beast even need a cure?

Daziel looked upward, where clouds drifted like ships setting off. In the distance, I could hear wind chimes clanging. "The winds aren't behaving like normal. There's always been atmospheric disturbances—hurricanes, cyclones, heavy swells. But storms are becoming unpredictable, destructively so."

His dark eyes returned to mine. "We don't know *why* the winds are changing. But we do know what has shaped the winds for millennia. The Ziz." Daziel's voice was even, as though he'd had this conversation many times. "The Ziz is one of the three stabilizing forces of natural magic. Natural magic is malfunctioning. Given how the winds and air storms are most strange, we think it's the Ziz who is ill, or hurt."

I pictured the Ziz, depicted in children's books as a giant bird with the body of a lion. *A wingspan great enough to block out the sun,* went the saying. *So tall it can stand in the middle of the ocean and the water only reaches its ankles. Once it dropped an egg, which flattened cities.*

"I'm sorry," I said, rubbing my temples. Here in my aunt's garden, surrounded by manicured plants and with my chamomile tea still steaming on the round table, his words seemed preposterous. "Are you trying to tell me the Ziz is a real, physical creature that can get hurt?"

"Yes."

"No," I replied. My brain simply couldn't handle this. The Ziz was a legendary, eternal beast. Legendary, as in . . . maybe not corporeal. Eternal as in forever. "The Ziz is *real*?"

Daziel sounded puzzled. "Did you think it wasn't?"

"No . . ." I drew out the word, uncertain. "I believe in the power of the Great Beasts—like that they can impact a ship's passage or whatever. But maybe I thought of them more as—a force? Like gravity? Or sunsets?" This didn't seem like the point. "How can the Ziz get sick if it's eternal? Where do the beasts *live*?"

"I don't know."

I frowned. "That's not very helpful. How do you know the Ziz is real?"

"How do you know gravity is?"

"Because if I drop a mug, it falls."

"And if you hurt the King of the Birds and the Air, all the birds go to their wounded ruler's side. And the air starts malfunctioning."

Okay. He had a point. "What about the increased earth tremors in Ilthalit, or the maelstroms? Those aren't air."

"I suspect the Ziz being injured affects the other two Great Beasts—and their domains of land and sea. I think it could get worse if we don't figure out how to cure the Ziz."

Unease skidded throughout me. All three of the primordial beasts were affected? This seemed very bad. "Worse—how? The land and sea and sky—that's the whole world."

He met my gaze. "Yes. It is."

My chest tightened and my head spun. The whole world couldn't be in trouble. This was starting to feel too big. "Maybe something else is the problem."

"Maybe. But the only records I could find back home about similar problems with the winds ascribed them to the Ziz needing to be healed, and said human mages at Zerach had the spells to do so."

And Zerach was where the scrolls had been found. "You think the scrolls tell us how to cure the Ziz." I let the words sink in.

He shrugged. "Those scrolls were preserved for a reason."

"What are you expecting? We decipher the spell and then—what? Go heal the Ziz?"

"I wasn't going to suggest you, personally, heal the Ziz," Daziel said dryly. "But yes, I was going to take the spell and try."

I started pacing, gazing at the almond trees like their pink blooms would offer answers. This was bonkers. No one had expected the deciphered scrolls to have any bearing on anything besides scholarship. Also—"If this is so important, why haven't you been trying to speed up the decipherment?"

"Haven't I?"

I paused, nonplussed. Then I reevaluated the past five months. He *had* sped up the decipherment. Not only had he suggested I look for a pattern, but he'd let me use his magic to re-form the scrolls and given me the idea for the spell that remade them in the first place. He'd been instrumental.

And I'd just thought he was interested in what I was doing; I hadn't realized he had an agenda. I hadn't realized how much I was being led. Disappointment and sadness welled in my throat, and nausea stirred my stomach. "But—why didn't your people send in one of your own expert cryptographers?"

"We don't have one," Daziel said testily. "In this case, the Lyceum had the best chance of solving the puzzle."

That made sense, except . . . "Why didn't you *ask* us?" I cried, frustrated. "Why didn't you work with us?"

"With whom? Your professor? Who thinks so little of me?"

"Our people have a *treaty*. Go over his head. Have your leader go to ours."

"There was no time to waste if your people refused to work with us."

"Really?" I asked, coldly skeptical. "You don't think instead of spending months lying to me, we could have spent them untangling red tape?"

"It wasn't worth risking when I didn't think it would make the work move any faster."

"Oh," I said, fury starting to build. "I see. Put aside how it might have fast-tracked the project by giving us more resources—you decided it wasn't worth the risk of *telling me*? I didn't deserve to know the truth about why you were here?"

His shoulders hunched, and his thumb flicked against his signet ring, spinning it endlessly. He looked like he was searching for an answer, or like he had one but didn't know how to say it.

When he spoke, he sounded miserable. "I didn't know what you'd do if I told you. I knew if I kept lying, you'd let me stay."

I reeled back. That was honest, at least, more honest than I wanted, and probably exactly what I deserved. "You're right," I said, my voice hollow. "It worked. Congratulations."

"Naomi—"

"What now?" I stepped back. The wind picked up, the almond tree branches fluttered, a few of their pink blossoms floating down around me. "You expect me to be your own personal code breaker? To keep this a secret from everyone?"

He sounded wry. "As if you could. The second you see your cohort, you're going to tell them, thinking it's not fair to withhold this information since they've been working on the scrolls longer than you. *That's* why I didn't tell you."

I flushed. Wow. Ouch. This did, in fact, sound exactly like what I'd do. I hadn't realized how well he knew me. It shocked me, how clearly he could predict my behavior. "Is that such a bad thing?"

"What do you think the others will do when you tell them? Rule-abiding Yael. Nervous Gidon. Loose-tongued Stefan. You think they'll keep this a secret?"

"Why should it be a secret?"

"I'm afraid of losing access." His jaw worked. "What if you're taken off the project? What if it's deemed too sensitive for student hands, and you don't get to see the deciphered spell? I don't trust your government to tell mine their findings."

His words punched a hole through me, and I wrapped my arms around my stomach as though it would hold me together. He'd only wanted me for access. "Why me? You could have targeted Yael or Gidon or Stefan."

"I considered it." His voice was pained. "You left an opening."

My stomach hollowed out with horrified hurt. "Because I said I was betrothed to the demon Daziel," I whispered.

"Yes."

"But—but how . . ." What were the chances Daziel needed an in with one of just a few people, and one of them dropped his name as their betrothed? "Did you use a spell on me? So I picked your name."

He didn't say anything.

Horror slid through my body like a sheet of ice as another option occurred to me. "Is your name really Daziel?"

He looked away, then back, his eyes bleak and empty. "No."

Though I'd half expected it, it hit me like a tidal wave. I sank down on the grass, right in the middle of the garden. The perfectly good café-style chair stood a few feet away from me, but I needed to be curled around my stomach. "Oh my god."

"My name is Cathmeus." He crouched down in front of me, speaking urgently, like the words had been inside him for a very long time. "I wanted to tell you. I'm sorry," he said, words I wished weren't necessary. "I was trying to do what I thought was best. I didn't want to hurt you."

I tried to sound sharp and pithy, but instead my words came out small and sad. "Well, you did."

He closed his eyes. "I know."

I turned away, looking up at the fluttering blossoms against the sky. I wanted to scream and rage, but what good had that ever done anyone? The only thing that did any good was moving forward.

Your inevitable heartbreak? my aunt had said. *I'll accept that as collateral damage.* Brutal, I'd thought, mostly amused. I hadn't realized how brutal it would be.

The worst thing was, I understood his—Cathmeus's, Daziel's—motivation. I probably wouldn't have done what he'd done—but who knew? These stakes were higher than one person's happiness. As he'd said, he knew if he lied I'd let him stay, and if he truly thought that would help him save the Ziz, fix the magic . . . *I don't plan to break Naomi's heart,* he had said, and maybe he hadn't, but like my aunt, he probably accepted it as collateral damage. "You did it for a noble cause. To save the world. How can I be mad about that?"

He tilted his head. "Very easily."

I huffed out a breath tinged with laughter. "True. But I understand why you did it."

Daziel—I could only think of him as Daziel—reached for my hand. "Naomi. Just because I lied about my reason for coming here—I didn't lie about—"

"Don't," I said sharply, pulling back. He flinched, his hand falling to his side. Good—I wanted him to hurt like I did. I didn't want to have to be gracious and forgive him. "Let's focus on the Ziz. If it's dying, and the scrolls are our only chance to save it, we need to decipher them as soon as possible."

Daziel watched me unhappily but didn't say anything.

"You're right." I pushed to my feet. The wind was starting to pick up, and low purple clouds brooded on the horizon. "I don't think it's fair—or even wise—to keep this to ourselves. But I agree you shouldn't get cut out. We need to tell people in a way that ensures we stay in the loop. Or—can you go invisible and watch what's happening?"

Daziel stood too, managing a wry smile. "You'll be shocked to hear this, but some people, like Sanhedrin members, are better at warding me away than first-year Lyceum students."

Harsh. "Okay, fair."

"There's one other thing." He fidgeted, nervous, like when he admitted he'd eaten the chocolate croissant I'd been saving for my afternoon snack. "We don't know where the Ziz is."

This took a few seconds to sink in. "Wait, so—we decipher this spell, and then . . . don't know where to cast it?"

He nodded.

I leaned heavily against the table. "*Please* tell me your people are working on finding the Ziz, even if they're not skilled at cryptography."

He grimaced. "Remember how you thought I'd run away from home to explore Talum?"

My gut sank. "Daziel . . ."

"I'm not technically supposed to be here."

My laughter verged on hysterical. "You're kidding."

"No." His eyes were wide and nervous. "I'm trying to be honest with you."

"So—no one knows you're here? I thought the high shedim court wanted to save the Ziz."

"I hate to disappoint," he said. "But at home, I'm just a student. With a high-ranking family, yes, but I'm not a spy. You're fed up with having no agency? Me too. I'm fed up with no one doing anything about the worsening magic. I learned about the Ziz and about the scrolls, and I thought—if the adults weren't going to do something, I would."

"But—you've been saying 'we' this whole time."

"Ah." He scratched his ear. "Yes. I suppose the pluralization was . . . an evasion. I am trying not to do deceit by evasion, given your dislike of it."

I needed a nap. I needed to plant myself face first on the bed. Grabbing my mug, I headed out of the garden courtyard back into my aunt's house. "We're doomed."

"We're not." He followed, his next words coming out tentative as our footsteps echoed against the marble floors. "Was I right to tell you?"

I turned. The afternoon light spilled in from one of my aunt's tall windows to paint Daziel in stark shadows. Worry etched lines in his brow. I softened slightly. Daziel didn't care if someone told a lie or two, but he knew it mattered to me. He was trying to be honest for me.

The tight knot in my chest loosened just a little. "Yes," I said. "You were."

TWENTY-ONE

W E RETURNED TO THE LYCEUM AFTER CLASSES FINISHED. Yael, Stefan, and Gidon looked up when we entered the scroll room. "We were wondering when you would return," Yael said mildly. "Everything all right?"

I tried to smile, but it felt tight. Everything was not all right. The boy who I'd been living with for almost half a year had lied not only about his reason for coming to Talum but also about his core identity. "It's been a busy few days."

"I'll bet." Stefan inspected Daziel. "A high demon, huh?"

Daziel smiled sharply.

"What have we missed?" I asked.

"We've pulled all the words in the scrolls containing the characters we're calling Z and I and cross-referenced them with our list of ancient names containing either," Yael said. "The only noun we've thought of with both is Tzorybium. Unfortunately, no Language X words look like a match."

"So we're experimenting with words separately containing the Z and I characters," Stefan said. "There's a word starting with Z, with five letters—if that's the Tribe of Zebulun, we'd have a few more letters, but it would also mean the letters aren't a one-to-one match."

Endless trial and error. That was how decipherment often went, until you had more keys.

Which. We might.

"We have news too." I glanced at Daziel, twisting my amulet nervously, unable to get the words out.

"Do you want us to guess?" Stefan finally snarked. "Get on with it."

While the boys stared at me, Yael followed my gaze to Daziel. Then she gave me a small, comforting nod.

I steeled myself. Daziel had lied because he believed if he told the truth, he'd be excluded from the scrolls' decipherment. I didn't want that to happen. Ideally, I wanted to prove his fear had been unfounded.

I wasn't sure it had been. "Daziel has . . . information."

"Information about the scrolls," Yael confirmed.

I nodded. "We're going to tell you. You'll want to tell Professor Altschuler, and maybe others. But they might decide we shouldn't have clearance to work on the scrolls. Daziel needs to be kept involved, so every time we tell someone, we need to make them swear they'll keep Daziel involved."

"You're a fucking tease, Bat Yardena," Stefan said, throwing his infernal juggling balls from hand to hand. He looked at Daziel. "She always like this?"

"Shut up, Stefan," Gidon said, squeezing his head with both hands, as he often did when he was stressed.

"Why is it so important he's involved?" Yael asked, her voice low.

"Because he has a stake in this too." No one group of people should have knowledge on this scale over another. "Everyone has a stake. It's not the kind of thing that should be a secret, so I won't keep it one. It's Daziel's business—shedim business—just as much as it's human."

Gidon looked like he might rip his curls out of his head. "Is it about the magic being off?"

I spread my hands.

Yael pressed her thin lips together. "You're not leaving us much choice."

"Why are you the one who gets to decide what's best?" Stefan asked.

I blew out a breath. "Look, I don't love this either. I'm trying to do the best I can." As the words slipped out, I realized how closely they echoed what Daziel had said to me.

"Will it be dangerous to give this information back to Daziel or the shedim?" Yael asked.

"I don't think so. But Daziel raised the possibility the government might not want students knowing about this. They might try to cut us—and him—out."

"Hm," Yael said.

Daziel whipped out a contract and laid it before the others. "You can sign or not," he said. "I'm not trying to trick you. I just want to stay informed, because I don't trust the government—yours or mine, frankly—to move as quickly and as urgently as we should. And this should help with deciphering the scrolls."

"What are we supposed to say to that?" Stefan said, grinning slightly. He scrutinized the contract and signed first. Yael took the pen next, then Gidon, and once all their signatures had been inked, they gazed at us expectantly.

I let out a relieved breath, then took another to steel myself.

Daziel took and squeezed my hand. Part of me wanted to yank my hand away, reject him with as much ice as I could muster, but though I was mad, the comfort of his touch spread through me like a glowing warmth. "Daziel thinks the scroll is about the Ziz."

My cohort blinked.

"Sorry," Gidon said after a moment. "What?"

Yael had that narrow-eyed look of hers. "Explain."

I looked at Daziel, in case he wanted to jump in, but he appeared to be having a staring contest with Paz. "He thinks the Ziz is hurt, or sick, which is why the winds are off and why the birds left. He thinks the scrolls explain how to heal the Ziz."

They stared at me as though I'd sprouted Daziel's wings. Then they stared at him.

"The Ziz is injured," Yael said, as though processing the words, "and this is why the magic is off?"

"That's insane," Stefan said. "The Ziz can't get injured. Is the Ziz even real?"

"Counterpoint," I said. "What if it is and can?"

"The Ziz—all the primordial beasts—they're the strongest things in the world," Stefan said. "I thought they were spiritual, not corporeal. What's going to hurt them? God?"

"Each other?" I suggested.

Gidon looked confounded. "Wouldn't we have noticed if the primordial beasts had earthly bodies?"

"Humans aren't really in the habit of noticing things," Daziel said lightly. "Sometimes it's like you're trying not to."

All the humans in the room decided to ignore that.

"If this is real," Yael said, leaning forward, gripping her knees, "if the primordial beasts are capable of being injured and affecting magic—this is a big deal. It needs to be addressed. All resources—

the Sanhedrin, the Lyceum—should be on figuring out how to cure the Ziz and fix the magic."

"I told you they'd want to tell people," Daziel whispered.

"The Sanhedrin might not believe us," I cautioned. "The information comes from Daziel, and they think shedim are mischievous and untrustworthy. Also, in case they decide we can't work on the scrolls anymore, I think we should make copies before telling anyone."

I half expected the others to argue, but it turned out no one wanted to give up the chance to be the one to decipher the scrolls, especially if it meant we'd be saving a divine beast at the same time. "Fine by me," Yael said.

"Yeah, same," Stefan said.

"You think this could fix the winds?" Gidon was less hesitant and soft-spoken than I'd ever heard him. "Because my parents have a vineyard. If the Maestril doesn't come . . ."

He didn't need to finish. We all knew: If the Maestril didn't come, the soil and vines didn't dry, the grapes and olives didn't grow, the wine and oil wasn't made, and there was nothing to sell. No income for the year.

Daziel stored Paz on his shoulder and finally looked at my cohort. "I hope so."

"Then let's start," Gidon said.

BY SEVEN BELLS, WE'D replicated the scrolls. With copies, we relaxed a little. "It's time," Yael said.

The five of us traipsed down the single floor to Professor Altschuler's office. He looked up as we entered. Behind him, on the ledge of the tall, narrow window where sparrows used to land, a line of eerily neon beetles strolled across the sill. "Yes? What is it?"

Yael looked at me, and I took my cue. "We have something to tell you."

Professor Altschuler kept laughing.

I'd never heard him laugh before, but now I remembered that before he'd been a tenured professor with an office in a tower, he'd been an adventurer, leading expeditions all over the country and abroad. He must have had a thirst for adventure, and this was an adventure.

"My apologies," he said when he saw our faces, for I wasn't the only appalled student. "It's simply rare one's research has such an impact. And this is—perhaps more dramatic than I expected."

We all stared at him.

He pulled himself together. "I'll go to President Meissner immediately," he said, naming the Lyceum's president, a woman I'd only seen a handful of times, usually striding about in the distance, looking awfully important. "They'll *have* to give us funding. No grant writing, no waiting—they'll have to approve it today." He practically frothed at the mouth in excitement. "Doubtless the Sanhedrin will have to be told—Bat Yardena, have you told your aunt?"

"Uh—not yet."

"Tell her—we might be able to get an audience sooner, though I imagine they'll expedite this." He glanced at Daziel, less withering than usual. "I see why you want to be involved. Your people are concerned?"

Daziel constructed one of his haughtiest expressions. "Naturally."

~ ~ ~

THE VERY NEXT DAY, Daziel and I once more waited in the ante-chamber for the Great Council of the Sanhedrin, alongside Professor Altschuler and the president of the Lyceum. (I'd not been invited, only Daziel, but I figured I'd go along until they kicked me out.) Aunt Tirtzah hadn't accompanied us, though I'd told her everything; she'd be inside at her normal seat. *I can do you more good from there, where the other council members will remember I'm their peer,* she'd said.

"Good to meet you." President Meissner shook my hand as we waited. She was medium in height, weight, and coloring, with cropped hair and a furrowed brow. Her clothes were simply cut from expensive fabrics, and while her amulet looked modest, I'd bet the stones making up the sun and stars of Issachar were diamonds; she came from one of the tribe's preeminent families. "And, Lord Daziel, I regret it's taken this long for us to make each other's acquaintance."

He ignored her hand, as supercilious as I'd ever seen him. "You mean you did not care to until you realized I was a high shayd, not wild."

She wasn't flustered as she dropped her hand; I supposed you couldn't afford to be if you presided over an institution like the Lyceum. "Not much point arguing with wild shedim. They aren't making treaties and generally refuse to follow them, too, without a member of your court around."

A civil servant entered, heels striking sharp against the marble floor, their gray uniform crisp. They spoke to the one minding us, who said, "You may go in."

I followed Professor Altschuler and President Meissner. My hand itched to take Daziel's, but I resisted. I wasn't ready to be the one who reached out. Still, we stood so close our shoulders almost brushed as we once more faced the semicircle of representatives. I sought out Aunt Tirtzah, who gave me a reassuring nod, then the Naphtali councilors. One of them smiled.

"So." The Chief Judge tapped his desk, upon which lay what I could only assume was a letter from the Lyceum informing them of the news. "The *Ziz?*"

The president started to speak, but the Chief Judge spoke over her. "I'm sorry, Meira, we need to hear from the demon. This is too much."

"He's a shayd," I said. "Not a demon."

The chief sighed. Everyone was always sighing at me.

Daziel spoke in a light drawl. "I think Lola Hawthorne has a far superior range than Fiona Maple, but I confess, I cannot take her seriously in villain roles. She is too young to have the gravitas to carry the part."

Now I sighed.

The chief blinked, reflecting the confusion felt, I expected, by the whole room. "What?"

"You said you wished to hear from me." Daziel examined his talons. "I thought you'd appreciate my opinions on the latest operettas."

"We want them to work with us, remember?" I murmured.

He sighed. "Very well, yonati. If you insist."

"We are supposed to believe this?" the chief said to Daziel. "The Ziz exists? And needs to be healed?"

Daziel nodded.

"This is ridiculous," a man I didn't recognize said. "Why are we entertaining this?"

"Because if you don't, the winds will keep misbehaving," I said. Weren't any of them paying attention? "Don't you understand? If the Ziz dies, natural magic will be changed forever. It's not only the air being affected—which is bad enough; what if the Maestril never comes?—it's also the land and sea. What if the maelstroms disappear? We're not going to have a livable world if we don't save the Ziz." I paused, looking at the professor and the president. This was going all wrong. "I'm sorry. You should tell them."

"She's right." The Lyceum president spoke in a calmer voice than my own. "If the scrolls contain a spell for fixing the winds, this should be the highest priority of the Lyceum, the Sanhedrin, and the country. Especially if, as Miss Bat Yardena suggests, the other Great Beasts are unbalanced, and all of natural magic along with them. As such, the university is requesting extra funds for the decipherment project."

"We have no evidence other than the demon's—excuse me, young lady, *shayd's*—word, though, is that not correct?" the chief asked. "Are there any other shedim we can ask? Someone who can affirm this boy?"

Everyone looked uncomfortable. "We haven't had any shedim visitors in eight months," a Danite councilor I remembered from last time said. "Our usual contacts have not responded to our initial queries about Lord Daziel."

"Are you serious?" I remembered this speaker, too—Melanie, the one who didn't like Aunt Tirtzah. "They're ignoring us?"

Once more, the chamber erupted. I was beginning to think all the Sanhedrin did was argue. No wonder it took so long to get any policy enacted, if seventy-two people wanted to have their voices heard and the majority had to agree to get anything done.

"What if he wants the scrolls deciphered for other purposes?" someone said. "What if the scrolls really reveal a demonic spell?"

A Naphtali councilor came to my aid. "You can't assume everyone is always lying."

"Nor can we assume everyone always tells the truth!"

"Let us consider," President Meissner projected in her loud, calm voice. I wondered why she was at the Lyceum rather than a councilor. Well, maybe she was more powerful in her own way. "If it is the truth, it cannot be ignored."

"You ask for a very large sum for an 'if,'" Melanie said.

"If the Lyceum is to devote its time and effort to solving the problem of the winds, and of magic, it's reasonable for us to expect the government's support," the president said coolly. "This concerns all of us."

"Yes, yes." The Chief Judge sounded exceedingly grumpy. "Very well. We'll vote on your funds in the next budget session."

"Sir, this is giving far too much credence to the idea that this spell genuinely is tied to oddities with natural magic," an older man said.

"We should be giving credence to *any* leads on natural magic's imbalance," Aunt Tirtzah said sharply. "It's worth the cost of investigating."

"We'll have that conversation when we discuss whether to fund this," the Chief Judge said.

"One other thing," Daziel said lightly. I winced, though I'd known it was coming. "We need help finding the Ziz, so when the spell is ready, we know where to cast it."

"What?" the Chief Judge said.

"How are we supposed to do that?" another said.

"*I* know where the Ziz lives," the one who'd suggested the scrolls were a demonic spell said sourly. "Wherever the demon needs his materials delivered. Maybe he wants to raise a castle! Or bring down a mountain! We're not taking this *seriously*, are we?"

"He's a high-ranking shayd," Aunt Tirtzah snapped. "Yes, we're taking this seriously."

"He's your niece's betrothed," Melanie said. "Honestly, Tirtzah, you should recuse yourself."

"How the hell are we supposed to find a mythological crea-ture?" someone else asked.

"Enough," the Chief Judge said wearily. "One thing at a time. Meira, we'll have an answer on your funding by the end of the week. After the scroll's translated, we'll discuss finding the pri-mordial beast."

"We can't wait until then," Daziel said. "We need to be ready to go with the spell immediately—"

The Chief Judge ignored him, banging his gavel down. "Dis-missed. There is only so much world ending I can handle without getting an ulcer."

AUNT TIRTZAH STAYED FOR further Sanhedrin business, so Daziel and I walked to her house alone, me on the sidewalks like a normal person, him zigzagging from wall to lamppost. "We don't know how long it will take to translate the spell," he said, frustrated. "We can't wait to start looking for the Ziz. We have to be ready to cast it as soon as you figure out the words."

"I know."

He groaned. "This is impossible."

"You've waited five months already," I said, alarmed. "Surely a little longer won't matter."

"Five months ago, the maelstroms weren't malfunctioning nor was the river flooding, and there weren't reports of increased earth tremors in other lands."

His fraying calm worried me. Daziel had been so clear-eyed through all this. I didn't like him losing his confidence—it turned out I'd been depending on it.

If I wanted to keep the both of us from spiraling into a panic, I needed to shore up our collective morale.

I tried to mimic my aunt and the Lyceum president, the way they spoke with poise and assurance. "Nothing is impossible. We won't give up. We keep plugging away, and we keep asking for help, and we keep trying."

He jumped down, landing in a light crouch before me, then straightened. It was night now, the brass lanterns glowing, moths with their feathery wings thick about them. He looked miserable. "Why are you being so kind? When I hurt you so much?"

I shrugged. "What else am I supposed to do? Scream? Cry? We'd still have this to deal with."

He looked at me with large, mournful eyes. "You could forgive me."

I laughed, scornful to cover up how deeply I was hurt. "*Forgive* you? I thought you—you— It was all a lie."

"It wasn't all a lie. Naomi." He took my hands in his warm ones. "Nothing about how I feel for you is a lie."

I stared down at his fingers, so much larger than mine, thick and blunt and disturbingly attractive. I couldn't talk about this right now. I needed to avoid thinking about us, to focus on politics and quests and research. If I thought about us, if I thought about how he'd broken my heart, it would ruin me.

Before I could speak, the earth shook beneath my feet as though I stood on a ship. I let out a cry, and in a heartbeat Daziel had grabbed me and levitated a few feet off the ground. We stared at the pavement, and at the buildings and trees. Everything shook for ten seconds, twenty. I clutched my arms around him, feeling the beat of his heart, the breadth of his shoulders.

Daziel drifted back down when it appeared to have ended. "What the hell was that?" I asked, stumbling back from him. My body craved a repeat of the brief and sudden embrace, and I thought it best to put some distance between us.

"It felt like a quake," he said. "Like in Ilthalit."

"But *we* don't have quakes," I said, my voice high-pitched.

"They're all intertwined," he reminded me softly. "The Ziz, the Behemoth, the Leviathan. If one weakens, they all do."

The wind picked up, and the sky rapidly clouded over. I shivered, gazing up. There was no moon to be seen, and very few stars. "Then we better figure out how to find and save the Ziz."

TWENTY-TWO

A FEW DAYS LATER, TWO DOZEN PEOPLE GATHERED IN THE common room of Testylier House.

There were the residents: Leah and Jelan and Gilli, even Élodie and Birra, and the other half dozen girls, all of whom had gotten to know Daziel in the last five months. Ezra and Hiram had come with half the knockball team. Yael and Gidon and Stefan with a few friends each, most of whom I hadn't met.

"Hey, everyone." It was nerve-racking to have so many eyes upon me. I'd never done public speaking, never been interested in it. "Thanks for coming. I know I was vague about what's going on. Everyone here knows how the winds are worsening, and people are worried the Maestril won't come in two or three weeks like it should?"

Everyone nodded.

"Daziel has a theory about why." I explained about the Ziz, the magic, the scrolls. "Yes, the Ziz is corporeal, not spiritual or meta-phorical," I said, to ward off this shock in advance. "Shedim are more entwined with the natural world and magic than humans; they have knowledge we don't, including this. We need to find the Ziz so we can cure it."

Everyone blinked, then started talking at once. Just like the Sanhedrin, really. Ezra's voice rose above the rest, cutting through the confusion and wonder and getting straight to the point. "How?"

I spread out my hands helplessly. "No idea. So we're turning to you for help. If the Sanhedrin isn't going to take this seriously, we're going to put together our own council."

There were a few nervous laughs. "The Ziz is one of the Great Beasts," Birra said, like we were idiots. "If the rabbis and the sages can't find it, I don't think a handful of students will be able to, even with a shayd helping us."

"Doesn't mean we can't try," I said firmly.

"How? What do we even know about the Ziz?" one of the fourth-floor girls said.

"Maybe more than we think," Yael said, and I smiled at her. "We start with what we do know, no matter how big or small, and move forward from there."

Another fourth-floor girl, who studied art, fetched an easel, and another a few mythology books. We slowly crafted a list of what we knew.

~ *King of the Birds*

~ *Controls the wind*

~ *Real big?*

~ *Giant eggs squash cities*

~ *One of the three Great Beasts (along with Leviathan and Behemoth)*

~ *Very old??*

~ *Stands in ocean?*

"Let's go through each one by one," Jelan said from where she sat next to Gilli, her steady manner providing some much-needed calm. "See if that jogs anything in our minds. What does King of the Birds mean?"

"All the birds listen to it?" Ezra offered.

"The birds left," Yael said. "What if they knew the Ziz was hurt and went to it? They went northwest."

"Maybe we could track them," someone else said.

"Maybe someone already did," Gilli said, gnawing at the end of her pencil. "Someone must have, right? Must have charted the path they took when they left? Maybe people across islands and other countries also took note."

"Definitely." I wrote down *Find out the path the birds took.* "Anything else about the birds?"

"Birds roost," one of the knockball boys said. "High up. So maybe we want to look in the mountains?"

We worked through each bucket, teasing apart what little meaning we could. "Legend says the Ziz blocks the most violent winds," one of Gidon's friends said. "Could we learn something about its location from where winds come from? The Ver and Den winds came more frequently this year—maybe they usually get blocked at some place, and that could inform us—well, of where the Ziz usually is?"

Find out how winds work, I wrote.

"It's supposed to be in the ocean, right?" Gilli said. "The lore says sailors came across it once, and it was so giant that even though they were in the deepest part of the sea, the water only came up to the Ziz's ankles, and its head was in the clouds."

"That's very big," Ezra said skeptically. "Surely someone would have noticed."

"Maybe it just means it's in the most remote part of the ocean, which is where we should look."

By the end, we had a list of things to follow up on.

~ *Find out the path the birds took/last place birds were seen in Ena-Cinnai and direction they were flying*

~ *Find out how winds work/where winds come from*

~ *Talk to sailors about remote mountains and ocean*

~ *Pinpoint remote/high-up places*

~ *Talk to rabbis about Great Beasts*

OVER THE NEXT WEEK and a half, my friends and classmates set to work. It shocked me how much weight lifted off my shoulders with others helping. I breathed easier realizing I wasn't going to have to do everything myself. I could tell Daziel felt the same.

With others concentrating on finding the Ziz, I put my energy into the scrolls. The Sanhedrin approved funding, and the Keep became chaotic. Professor Altschuler and the rest of the linguistics department stopped by the scroll room daily, as did history professors and spellwriters and other academics, not to mention their support staffs and students.

No hints of the Maestril appeared, but the Corisoc did; the rare southern wind carried red dust that got into every nook and crevice in Talum. It clung to my skin and hair and made the whole city look like it had been dipped in clay.

"I hate this," Stefan said one evening. It was late enough no one besides our cohort remained in the scroll room, so he lay on the rug, stretching his spine after hours bending over the scrolls.

When it was just us, we'd given up any pretense of propriety. "I feel like a hamster on a wheel."

I felt like I was slowly going mad. We were giving everything we had and getting nowhere. With so many more people involved, we'd made quick progress analyzing word frequency in healing spells across a dozen languages, but it led nowhere. Our hypotheses on articles and verbs were patchy. We'd looked over the words containing *Z* and *I* and theorized what they might be and what letters their other characters might match, but everything resulted in dead ends.

It would have been different if it'd been slow progress but progress nonetheless; instead, we felt incompetent and stupid, like children turning metal puzzle pieces, unable to twist them apart.

"I feel like a blindfolded goat." Gidon picked at the red dust from the Corisoc caked under his nails.

I blinked. "A goat?"

He flicked the dirt onto the floor. "They're always bouncing around all over the place. That's how I feel. And chewing cud."

"Do goats chew cud?" Yael asked. "I thought that was cows."

"Cows, goats, sheep," I said absentmindedly. "They're all ruminants. They have four-chambered stomachs, and the cud is regurgitated from one and chewed again."

The three city kids stared at me.

"That's disgusting," Stefan said. He stretched, his shoulder bones popping. "I wish we had more Language X. It'd be way more likely we'd find other proper nouns if we had thousands more pages to pore through."

We needed proper nouns to decipher character phonetics. If we didn't have any in the scrolls, perhaps we should look elsewhere. "What if . . . we could find more examples of Language X?"

"We've already tried," Gidon said gently. "Didn't Professor

Altschuler cover this in your initial reading? He toured the northern lands two years ago, talking to international scholars, and found nothing."

"Right," I said. "But . . . what about faraway places? Places we don't share scholarship with yet?"

"How would that help?" Stefan asked. He threw one of his juggling balls in the air and failed to catch it; it rolled out of his arm's length, and he half-heartedly reached for it. "We're not going to be able to see them. I even wrote to my family in Aolong to see if they had contacts, but nothing."

A smile stretched my cheeks. "We have someone who can travel twice as far as Aolong, very quickly."

Three faces whipped up to mine. "Oh shit." Stefan sounded impressed. "You think he could?"

"Sorae." Yael immediately named an empire three thousand miles away, past even Stefan's home. I could hear the quiver of suppressed hope in her voice. "He should go to their courts. Their scholarship is impeccable. Two thousand years ago they traded all over the world. I can't believe we didn't ask him earlier. I forgot demons—shedim—can path-jump."

"Daziel," I said, not lifting my head from where I'd let it slump against the wall. "Daziel, Daziel."

He appeared. No one even flinched anymore. The red dust of the Corisoc had afflicted even him, giving his black curls a garnet gleam.

"Can you path-jump to Sorae?" I explained the situation. "If you take me with you, I'll be able to recognize the characters of Language X—"

"You can take us with you?" Yael interrupted. I didn't think she'd cut anyone off the whole time I'd known her. "I want to go."

Daziel shook his head. "I'm not taking either of you. The mirrorways are too dangerous for humans. It might not leave your mind the same."

"Would the betrothal protect me?" I asked. It'd messed with my physiology already; maybe it would help us here. "I might be fine."

He looked at me almost angrily. "I'm not risking your safety. Show me what I'm looking for and where."

It shouldn't have made me happy that he cared so much about my safety, but it did.

"Start at the universities and museums," Yael said. We made a list of everything we knew in Sorae, despite it being very little. We made him a card with the characters of Language X so he could recognize them, then a letter with an official seal we stole from Professor Altschuler's office requesting to borrow materials. Apparently we all had very flexible morals by this point. Besides, we all agreed the professor would have let us had he been here.

"Not likely you'll run into anyone at this hour, is it?" Gidon said. It was nearing eleven bells; we had just put another pot of coffee on. None of us had any intention of sleeping soon.

"It's morning in Sorae," Daziel said absently. After tucking everything up his sleeves, he touched my cheek and was gone.

I pressed my hand to my cheek, the ghost of his touch lingering. Despite my anger, I worried about him gallivanting around a foreign land on his own. I wished I'd been able to go with him.

THE NEXT DAY, THE four of us were so antsy Professor Altschuler sent us away, dryly promising he and his staff could handle the scrolls without us for a day. I couldn't concentrate without knowing whether Daziel was safe. I should have insisted on at least *attempting* to go with him.

Between classes, I passed through the front courtyard, where the winter fair had been. Now beetle corpses littered the grass matted by red dust. The school's brass gates, with their book and tree emblem, no longer gleamed. The Maestril should be arriving any day now, and everyone was wound tight with its absence. If it came, it would wipe the city clean of red dust and insects. If it didn't come, the harvests would fail.

I returned to the Keep around the same time as the rest of my cohort, and we stayed past ten bells, when Professor Altschuler finally left, shaking his head. "Your minds won't do any of us any good if you insist on exhausting yourself."

"Yes, sir," Yael said, but none of us went anywhere. Instead, we fiddled with more words, trying to guess Language X character phonetics and unsurprisingly making no breakthroughs.

Near midnight, Daziel returned. And he brought a trunk.

"What?" Yael said.

I jumped up, instinct telling me to fling my arms around Daziel, I was so happy he'd returned safe. But he wasn't mine to hug. I clasped my hands together instead.

He met my gaze with his obsidian one, and there was a pained sorrow in his smile, as though he could tell I'd wanted to embrace him but held myself back. Then he adjusted his expression with his inhuman quickness, turning to my friends with a showman's panache and sweeping his arms at the trunk. "They were very agreeable. Said these were found on an ancient Cinnaian ship excavated from a silted-up harbor some fifty years back."

He lifted the lid. Inside, a dozen scrolls nestled against a purple velvet interior.

"You wouldn't believe the amount of people I talked to," Daziel told our dropped jaws. "I had tea with a professor at his daughter's house, and he directed me to a very small university halfway across the country—anyway. A preservation spell snapped over the ship's library when water came onboard and saved the texts."

"We need the highlighting spell," Gidon choked out. My own hope and excitement were reflected in him, in all of them. If this batch of Language X included proper nouns with Z and I, we could finally theorize more of the alphabet.

Before using the finding spell, we made copies of the new texts, so we could spread neshem on the copies instead of the originals. We worked quickly, fumbling and laughing, all of us bundles of nerves barely held together. When the copies were made, we cast the highlighting spells for words containing both ׀ and ׳.

Two words glowed on the parchment.

Hope so fierce it almost hurt speared me. Stefan jumped up in the air, whooping and squeezing a smiling Yael's shoulders. Gidon made a pleased noise. I stopped trying to control every movement and whirled around and hugged Daziel tightly. I breathed him in, his familiar scent, his blazing and comforting heat. I held him tightly, as though I could use this embrace to take a print of his body. Then I let go, leaving him with wide eyes.

And then we all leaned forward.

The first of the two highlighted words glowed in the beginning of a ten-page manuscript. I blinked because I recognized it. I recognized it because it was the two letters we knew arranged in a way we'd seen before. My brain stuttered, confused and almost disbelieving of the word highlighted before us.

Ziz.

The five of us exchanged bewildered looks. "How likely is it we've found *another* spell for the Ziz?" Gidon said.

"Not likely," Stefan said.

We turned to the second word. This one was much longer, with seven characters. *Z* and *I* made up three of them, scattered throughout the middle of the word: *?Z?I?I?*

I wanted to vomit or cry. I felt like I was playing trivia at a pub. I knew this one, I *knew* it, and if it was right, we would have so many letters. "Tzorybium," I choked out.

Yael grabbed a pen, scribbling letters into our blanks: *TZ (O/R?)(I/Y?)BI(U/M?)*.

"It's not perfect," Yael said. "There's only seven characters in the Language X word and nine in ours. They might use the same character for both *Y* and *I*, but it's not a one-to-one match."

But it was *so close*, I could feel it, how painfully close we were, how we were almost at the place where we could start matching our letters to Language X. "Maybe it's Tzorybia, the adjective and language, instead of the place name." Which added *A* as an option for the last character, as well as *U* and *M*.

"Or maybe they didn't have an *O* or a *U* in their version of the name," Gidon said.

"Maybe they dropped the *R* thousands of years ago," Stefan said. "Tzoybia. Some languages don't have *R*'s."

Despite my exuberance, a wave of apprehension hovered at the edges of my mind, a wave that could pull me under into a state of helplessness. There were so many possibilities, and we had no idea which path to try first.

"Don't panic," Yael said, catching my expression. "We know what we're doing, remember? We've trained for this. We make methodical attempts, and we keep going. We're so much further ahead than we were a day ago." She gestured at the trunk Daziel had brought. "This is a gold mine."

"You're right." I took a steadying breath. We could now potentially match Language X characters to our alphabet. We were far closer than an hour ago.

We needed more ancient nouns containing the four unknown characters from our potential "Tzorybium" to test them, so we ran the highlighting spell on the manuscripts.

This resulted in so, so many words.

For a minute, the five of us stared. A gold mine, Yael had said, and she was right. Surely some of these would be proper nouns we could guess. We would have answers soon if we could stay steady and figure it out.

"We write them all down," Yael said, somehow managing not to float off in a stunned reverie like the rest of us. "Then we'll go through our ancient proper noun list and see if we can find matches."

That was the right way to do it, the academic, precise method. But I couldn't help glancing at our original scroll with the word for "Ziz," to see if anything jumped out. It did not. I glanced at the manuscript Daziel had brought in with the word "Ziz" too. Just in case.

I caught my breath.

"Look," I said, my voice a scant whisper. My heart started to pound, and a shiver danced across my neck and shoulders. One line below the word "Ziz," almost an entire word glowed—which meant we could potentially sound it out. I scribbled it down, adding our theorized characters: *B?/(M/A/U?)/T?*

The two unknown characters were the same.

"Fuck," Stefan said. "If that's an *M*—if this language doesn't use vowels and that letter's an *H*—"

BHMTH.

BEHEMOTH.

"But they use vowels. There's an *I* in 'Ziz'!" Gidon howled. "And two *I*'s in the second word!"

Stefan wrote down the word that could be "Tzorybium" again: *TZRIBIM*. "Maybe they *only* use *I*."

Energy rushed through me, the kind that meant that we were on the brink of a great discovery, not unlike standing on the cliff at the edge of the plains and the wilderness and worrying about falling, or like boarding a ship to take you to a city you'd only ever fantasized about. We were nearing a vast precipice, and as long as we could keep running, build up enough speed, we could leap to a new world on the other side.

"I hate that," Gidon said. "They're going to have some crazy grammar rule, and we're never going to find it out."

"We are," Yael whispered. She was clutching her knees to her chest, unblinking as she stared at the text. "We're going to figure it out. We're going to crack this."

The sheer belief in her voice sent a shiver down my spine. We could do this.

The others set themselves to making the list, the way Yael had suggested. But I stayed still, staring at the manuscript.

There was something niggling in the back of my mind. As if something I half remembered was trying to break free.

Something that mentioned the Great Beasts. Something I knew. Not a spell but something like a spell. Like a song, from my childhood? A poem or recitation?

I went cold, then hot.

Daziel said these manuscripts came from a ship excavated from a silted-up harbor. I was a sailor's daughter. I knew all about sailors—how they stowed belongings, what they ate, the prayers they said for safe passage. I also knew something that all ships kept on board. A rutter, a handbook used by navigators to steer the ship and provide specific directions—directions that probably hadn't changed in thousands of years because the coastlines and maelstroms hadn't changed in millennia.

I felt like I was floating. "What if it's a rutter?"

If it was a rutter, we would not only have characters we could match from one language to another—we would have words. Words we could translate from Language X to our language if the same directions were given in both.

And Gilli was a navigator's daughter. She might be able to read them.

TWENTY-THREE

GILLI COULD READ THEM.

Daziel fetched her to the Keep. She arrived in pink pajamas and her yellow School of Science blazer and a smile like a spring breeze, even as she warned us that this wasn't her forte. "I haven't looked at a rutter since I was thirteen. We should try to get one— tricky, they're not in libraries, but I can write to my mom."

Then she proceeded to identify dozens of words.

She pointed at the first paragraph. "This is probably the traditional prayer to protect the ship. The prayer *could* have changed," she said doubtfully, "but I expect it says 'Leviathan, Lady of the Sea, Ruler of the Oceans, grant us safe passage through your deep waters. Ziz, Master of the Sky, Master of the Birds and the Air, lend us swift winds and see us safe through your storms. Behemoth, Great Beast of the Land, bring us safely from shore to shore.'"

I started breathing in short little gasps; Yael closed her eyes and opened her mouth. Gidon collapsed into a chair and buried his face in his knees. Stefan punched Daziel in the arm.

"What?" Gilli looked alarmed. "Did I say something wrong?"

"You said something so right." I threw my arms around her. "You said so many words. If—if it's right—Gilli, it's a *translation*.

Enough to get us started, to give us conjunctions and definite articles and start us really, really translating. Otherwise—even if we could figure out how Language X sounded, even if we could have matched our letters to theirs, we wouldn't have known the meaning."

"Oh," she said, looking pleased. "Good."

Gilli started us rolling down a cliff until we gathered speed on our own and could make educated guesses. At some point Daziel handed over a rutter in our tongue, which no one asked too many questions about.

We spent all night working. In the morning, we'd have to tell Professor Altschuler, and we wanted to be as far along as possible before it was taken away from us. This kept us from being thorough, from doing the slow, proper analyses we'd been trained to do. Instead, we focused almost exclusively on the scroll for healing the Ziz and the rutter. We barely managed to force ourselves to pause and map out all the letters. When we did, we theorized Language X didn't use vowels the same way we did, but our consonants matched closely. We'd be able to read the language aloud, speak it to life after thousands of years of silence.

Then we dove into words. In the morning, we'd be set to detail categorizations ordered by the professor, but not tonight. We drank coffee by the jugful, until we were so jittery I thought my heart might explode. No one wanted to stop for food, so we ate whatever Gilli and Daziel brought, our eyes trained on the text. By morning, we looked chaotic—hair everywhere, faces oily, eyes twitching.

But we didn't care because the words were coming together. "Oh my god," Gidon kept saying. The syntax was similar to an-

cient Ille, one of Stefan's languages, so we could theorize how nouns and verbs worked. We could guess cardinal directions and movements and numbers. It was trial and error—we'd plug in "strong" before "wind" and then see if it held up. If it didn't, we'd try again with another word—"cold," perhaps, or "weak" or "unexpected."

By dawn, we had this:

FOR RETURNING THE ZIZ TO ITS (ORIGINAL / ENDURING?) (FORM/STATE?)

To perform the spell, the (name/description?) of the Ziz (must/should?) be (carved?) into the bone of the Ziz. It is best to do so once a (millennium). Four casters (must/ should?) (stand?) at the four points of the compass around the Ziz and read its (name/description?). They (must/ should?) (funnel/use?) fourteen (unknown) into the spell:

You are the Ziz, Master of the Sky, Master of the Birds and the Air, beast of legend. You (stand?) with your (ankles?) in the sea and your (head?) in the heavens, with wings to (block out/ inhibit?) the sun.

From there our guesses became more muddled—we suspected it was an anatomical description, which no words appeared for in the rutter.

"We're so close," Stefan groaned. "But how are we going to figure out the rest? It's impossible. We'll be able to phonetically read the characters, but we're not going to be able to understand more unless we find an ancient anatomy textbook."

It did feel impossible. There was no way for us to know, and while we could guess, our guesses were likely to be wrong. There'd be no way to read the correct spell to save the Ziz.

Unless . . .

It hit me, and I started laughing.

Only Daziel and Gilli looked concerned. The other three had suffered their own hysterical fits over the past twenty-four hours and were unconcerned with mine. "We don't need to," I said. "We don't need to decipher it."

"What are you talking about?" Stefan picked up an almond from the floor and ate it. I couldn't even judge him at this hour.

"We figured out enough. We figured out how to *pronounce* Language X. We don't need to say the spell in our tongue. We can do it in Language X."

Everyone stared at me as though I'd lost my mind. Which, perhaps, I had.

"That's madness," Yael said. "You can't perform a spell you don't understand."

"Why not? We understand what the spell is doing. It's strengthening the Ziz. We just wouldn't know what words we were saying."

"We don't know for sure about the pronunciation," Stefan said. "It might not work."

"It'd work better than totally wrong words."

"I didn't mean you *technically* can't," Yael said impatiently, ruffling her fine hair in a clear sign of stress. "I meant it's unsafe to work magic you don't understand."

"It's not safe to wait, either," Daziel said. Unlike my cohort, he'd lit up at my suggestion. Energy coiled in his body like he might spring forward any moment. "It might work."

"No," Yael said. "There's no reason to go racing off. We can wait a week, a month."

"Can we?" Support came unexpectedly from Gidon—but then, he was from a farming family. "We need the Maestril now. If we wait another month, the growing season will be ruined."

"So everyone suffers another year—that's better than an unknown spell. We don't even know where the Ziz is or what measurement the fourteen means."

"True," I said. "But maybe we can present it to the Council and pressure them to look at our possible locations for the Ziz and work on the translation in the meantime."

"We do know the measurement," Stefan said. "Language X phonetically spells out 'troyil'—I bet that's 'troyelle,' an ancient term from the Maudeli. It translates to roughly 'five swimming pools' worth of neshem.'"

We all stared at him.

"Five swimming pools?" I finally said.

"Yup."

Gidon looked like he might faint. "That's a lot of power."

"The kind used to level cities," I agreed.

"Where are we supposed to get so much power?" Gilli asked nervously, gnawing at the end of a braid.

"We're not," Yael said. "The Sanhedrin is. They have reserves they can use."

"I dunno if the Sanhedrin is going to be willing to use so much," Stefan said doubtfully. "Especially if we don't know the spell will work. I mean, that's a fuckton." He turned to Daziel. "Can you give us power to use, like you did for putting the scrolls together in the first place?"

"Not that much," Daziel said.

"Can you cast the spell yourself, then? You guys have more power than us, right?"

"We can't direct it the way you do." Daziel looked at me. "The only way . . ."

A horrible, tingling sensation skittered across my shoulders and down my spine. I knew what he was saying, could feel the realization inside me, sick and poisonous.

If you bound a demon—or a demon bound you—you could have the kind of power that raised temples and leveled cities.

"I need food," I said abruptly. "Hot food. Daziel, come with me."

The others looked startled. "Right this moment?" Gidon said doubtfully.

Yael, on the other hand, narrowed her eyes. She, at least, guessed what Daziel had meant.

"Yes." I grabbed Daziel's hand. Never mind I'd barely touched him for the last couple of weeks; this was urgent, and everything else fled my mind.

We didn't speak until we'd left the Keep. The Corisoc had coated the campus with its red dust, and in the dawn light, the marble buildings looked like dull embers.

I led us to the river, where rushing water frothed white around the craggy rocks jutting above the surface. I stepped across them, and Daziel followed, until we were isolated. Wind whipped around us, sprays of water spattering against our calves and arms. Storm clouds gathered on the horizon, turned orange gold by the Corisoc.

"You think we could cast the spell if one of us bound the other," I said flatly.

Daziel nodded. "We're greater as a whole than as two separate parts."

"I'm not binding you. Nor am I a huge fan of being bound again." I had no desire to relive the experience at the Rocks, with overwhelming magic rushing through me, making me dizzy and sick and unable to breathe. "Neither of us should be able to control the other."

He squinted toward the rising sun. "What if we couldn't? What if we could maintain our independence?"

I narrowed my eyes. He'd had that answer easily; he had a plan, or at least an idea. "What do you mean?"

"I think our betrothal lessens the aggressiveness of the binding. At the Rocks, the binding didn't feel as harsh as I expected. I suspect that in the same way natural magic recognizes us as bonded to share magic and location, it recognizes us as a unit here too. If we complete our betrothal—if you take my signet ring—I think you'll be able to draw on my magic, but neither of us will be able to control the other."

I pushed my hair out of my face. This was more complex thaumaturgical theory than any I'd learned, but I believed him. Yet . . . "If we completed the betrothal, will it be harder to dismantle?"

He hesitated. "Yes."

"How hard?"

"It could take . . . years."

Good lord. "You might be stuck with me for ages." I couldn't keep the bitterness from my voice. How noble of him. He'd strengthen the betrothal if it meant saving the world.

"We'd be saving the Ziz," he said gently. "And Ena-Cinnai."

I swallowed through my tight throat. How self-sacrificing.

"It's a moot point." I gazed out at the Lersach. All the winds were here except the Maestril, the Trio Winds churning the river into a frenzy, the rare Corisoc blowing as though it never intended to stop. "The Sanhedrin will supply us with the neshem."

He stepped closer, careful on the slippery rocks. Paz crept up onto his shoulder and cheeped a warning. "If they don't?"

"We worry about it then."

"Naomi." His eyes, his voice were searing. "If they don't?"

I bit my lip, feeling sick. What could I say? You didn't put your happiness over the needs of many. "We'd be trapped together."

"Is that how you feel?" He maneuvered even closer. "Trapped?"

"You don't want to be betrothed to me." I smiled bitterly. "I'm a means to an end."

He watched me. "You started as a means to an end. You did not stay one."

"Why should I believe you?"

"Because I mean it." His voice was fierce. His gaze locked on to mine. "Naomi, I don't think I'd be *trapped* with you. I want this betrothal. I'm sorry I lied, I know you might hate me, but I want you so absolutely. Completing the betrothal wouldn't only be for the binding. I'd do it because I *want you*."

I wanted to believe him. I wanted to more than anything in the world.

"I think you want me too," he said, his voice hoarse.

This was too much. He'd broken my heart, and I didn't know how to put it back together. "You lied to me. I should hate you."

He caught my hands and held them between us. We were so close, our bodies inches apart, breathing hard out of anger and hurt and banked desire. The wind whipped around us, pulling at our hair, pushing us closer. I had to cling to him for stability, and the burning in me shifted and bent into a different kind of heat. He brought his face closer to mine, his eyes searching. "Do you hate me?"

What I felt for him was so far from hate it almost circled back to it—it had the same strength, the same intensity. But it wasn't hate at all. "No," I whispered. "But you hurt me."

He slid his hand up my cheek, cupping my face. "How can I make it up to you?"

I didn't know—I'd never needed to forgive anyone to the extent I did Daziel. But I wanted to forgive him. I wanted to be with him.

"Prove you care." That was what I needed: for Daziel to show me he hadn't only been using me and I was more than a pawn in his elaborate plan. I needed him to make me believe he wanted me, over and over again, until my trust healed. "Prove it wasn't a lie."

"I do care," he said. "I'll keep proving it as long as you need me to."

I leaned into him, all yearning and craving and hot need. He slid his hand around my neck, lowering his lips to mine. He kissed me, a drugging, intoxicating kiss I fell into with my whole body. Heat slipped through me, winding its way with licks of fire that left me gasping. Kissing Daziel was like fire, like a storm, like ravenous hunger. I didn't want to stop.

He was the one who finally did, leaning his forehead against mine. "I'm sorry I lied. I'll never lie to you again."

I let out a half-choked laugh. "That's a really sweeping promise to make."

"Right." He considered it. "I will never lie to you on purpose? I will . . . make a concerted effort to be honest."

I couldn't help smiling. "I liked the no lying at all."

He started pulling his signet ring off his finger, but I covered his hand with my own and stilled it. "We'll wait until after the Sanhedrin answers. Then ... we'll see."

He nodded and gazed up at the sky. The clouds had blown in, low and dark and gray, heavy with rain. "We should go back before it pours."

We did, hands gripped tightly. I kept replaying his words, his touch. *I want you*, he'd said. He meant it, I had no doubt. His face as he spoke had burned itself into my mind, the perfect beauty of his eyes, the worried furrow in his brow. The heat of his body, the passion, the yearning spread beneath my skin.

But my aunt's voice: *What do you think would happen if you, a human girl, married a high shayd?*

He wanted me, but did he want to marry me? Did I want to marry him?

Yes, a tiny whisper said deep inside me. *Because you love him.*

I shut that little whisper up far away. The end of the world was not the right time to think about love.

THAT EVENING, AFTER A wretchedly exhausting day, we returned to my aunt's. As we brushed our teeth and washed our faces and put on our pajamas, nervous energy writhed through me. I was overly aware of each movement Daziel made. Curled upright in the massive bed, the privacy curtains tied to the posts, I watched Daziel gracefully sit in his nest of blankets.

Feeling both excruciatingly shy and wildly bold, I burst out, "Do you want to join me?"

Daziel froze. "What?"

My cheeks were hot enough to scramble eggs. "Not if you don't want. But. You know. You can. Sleep in the bed."

"Really."

I nodded, so many times and so rapidly I almost pulled a muscle in my neck. Also, I probably looked like a wild marionette doll. I stilled, wincing. "I just thought—I don't know. It might be more comfortable."

"Right." He studied me with a burning intensity, as though trying to read me from the inside out. "Are you sure?"

I felt like I'd swallowed a butterfly and it was trying to escape my throat, wings beating a frantic, terrified tempo inside me. "Uh-huh."

His mouth curved up in a smile. "You don't sound very sure."

"I am sure." The words scraped out past frozen lips. What if he turned me down? That, I realized, was what had me so terrified— the idea that he wouldn't want to sleep beside me, when I wanted it more than anything else in the world. "Very, very sure."

"All right." He sat on the edge of the bed, his weight shifting the mattress. He swung his legs up and under the covers, and I lay very still and flat, afraid if I looked at him, I wouldn't be able to look away. He settled in, rustling among the blankets, rearranging the pillow.

We lay side by side, all my attention focused on the scant inches between us, and how earlier today there had been none. I tried to breathe deeply and pretend I wasn't thinking about the exact arrangement of Daziel's body and how badly I wanted to roll into his side and press my mouth to his and fill all the places in me that felt empty.

Okay. Screw it. I turned on my side. Daziel already faced me. His eyes gleamed, like black paint yet to dry. It was easier to talk in the dark, with no light except the sliver of moon and spill of starlight. "You tried not to kiss me. The night after the Rocks. You held back."

"I thought if we started being physical and then you found out I'd lied to you, you'd hate me."

"Oh." Fair point. I frowned. "Why did you change your mind?"

He managed a mangled smile. "I wanted to be with you too badly."

A curl of warmth expanded in my stomach, something tender and shy and hopeful. I flopped back on my pillow and squeezed my eyes shut. "Why?"

I could hear his smile in his voice. "Because I like you."

I believed him, but I still wasn't completely relaxed. I wasn't completely sure of him. "Why?" I asked again.

The mattress shifted, and his fingertips—light as a feather— brushed the side of my face. "I like your combination of prickly and sweet. You don't like to say nice things, but you do nice things. You stock the food I like and plan things I like. You try to protect me when you think people aren't being fair. And I like how you think about what's right and just, and it matters to you. You're invested in your friends and family. You're hardworking, and I find your perseverance and dedication incredible."

My stomach swooped, in a dizzying, heady way, and I felt like I might cry. I hadn't realized how moving I'd find it, how validating, to have him say this. These were things I liked about myself. I opened my eyes.

He watched me tenderly. "I think you're very brave to not have stonewalled me when I told you everything. That would have been reasonable. But you didn't. You went forward because you understood how important saving the Ziz is. That must have been hard."

I nodded. "This is true."

He traced my cheekbone, my brow, my ear. I didn't move for fear he'd stop. "Also, you're very beautiful."

I narrowed my eyes. "Now you're just buttering me up."

"Eyes like polished wood." His voice was soft and teasing, but I could hear the earnestness in it. "Long ink-black lashes." He raised a finger to brush my bottom lip, soft as a butterfly's wing. "Perfect lips."

I closed my eyes, bright red.

I could hear the grin in his voice. "Have I embarrassed you?"

"Yes."

"I'm being honest. Look at me." He waited until our eyes were locked together. "You're stunning."

A tightness in my chest unlocked. "Will you kiss me?"

He barely had to move to bring his mouth to mine. It was different kissing like this than the other times. There were fewer barriers here: no one to perform decency for, no need to stay upright. We were in our own world, where only sensation and heart existed, and I could tell how easy it would be to let it consume me.

But I didn't. I wasn't yet ready. So I kissed him until I could tell stopping would be too difficult if we kept on. When I paused, he let out a tiny groan of disappointment but took his cue from me, kissing my forehead and rolling onto his back.

I rested my head on his chest, and we nestled into each other. He pulled me close, drawing my arm across his chest, and I wrapped my leg across his body, securely snuggled into his side.

I let out a relieved breath, released the tension I'd been holding in my body night after night, and nestled closer. I could hear him breathing, feel the thrum of his heart beneath my ear.

In the dark, and the silence, it was easy to admit how much I loved him, to feel the depth of it, how it stretched to every part of my soul, how it filled me up with intangible energy. I hoped, very much, he loved me. It felt like he did.

I fell asleep.

THE NEXT DAY, DAZIEL, Professor Altschuler, the Lyceum president, and I once more arrayed ourselves before the Sanhedrin.

"You have before you copies of our latest work on Scroll 4," Professor Altschuler said, the excitement in his voice clear. Not only had he achieved two of the biggest goals of his career—both reconstructing the scrolls and beginning to decipher them—but their meaning had weight on the shape of the world. "It shows the scroll contains a spell meant to heal the Great Beast, which, as the shayd Daziel has shared, is paramount. We request immediate help locating the Ziz and the neshem listed to perform the spell."

"This is an obscene amount of power," the Chief Judge said. He peered at the Lyceum president and Professor Altschuler. "You're sure you need this much? Maybe it's a translation error."

"We're not going to cast a spell we've never tried before on a divine being," someone else said. "Besides, this translation isn't even complete."

"As laid out on page three," Professor Altschuler said, though I could tell it hurt him to say this, "there is technically no need to translate the entire spell before performing it."

This set off a storm of protests and questions, the likes of which made my cohort's response seem like nothing. It took half an hour before everyone felt like they'd had their say explaining why performing the spell in Language X was madness. Even then councilors kept protesting and only moved on because the Chief

Judge banged his gavel and forced them to in order to keep the meeting on agenda and discuss the next impossible thing: the still-unknown location of the Ziz.

"We have six potential locations," Professor Altschuler said. He was doing an admirable job as front man for our research; his voice lent the work my friends had done credibility. I'd been shocked he'd agreed, but maybe I shouldn't have been; this was his passion too. "As you'll see on page eight."

There was a ruffle as everyone flipped through their packets. The ruffles managed to sound unfriendly.

"We've identified locations worth exploring, based on research into where birds were last seen, where the winds are shaped, and recommendations from rabbis and sailors," he said. My friends had come up with thirteen potential locations, but we'd decided to mostly give sea-based ones to the Sanhedrin. Daziel would path-jump to the land ones and explore.

"We'll discuss it," the Chief Judge hedged. "But you must understand this is a very large ask."

"As is stabilizing natural magic and saving the country," Aunt Tirtzah said. "Yet it must be done."

"We don't know if this will save anything," Melanie countered. "It's a fool's errand to waste our resources without proof."

"We could look for the creature before we agree to fund the spell," one of the Naphtali councilors offered. "Without finding it nothing else can be done. And if we find it, and it is hurt—or dying—it could lend credence."

Daziel muttered in my ear, "You'd almost think it might have made sense for them to look for the Ziz all along."

I hushed him.

"There is one way to have enough magic for this spell," a council member said. I looked toward the voice sharply. It came from a very old man swaddled in heavy robes, his face obscured by shadow. "Without wasting our own resources."

"Oh?" the Chief Judge said. "Go on."

The man stared at Daziel.

After the moment it took for everyone to comprehend the old councilor's meaning, a shocked outcry washed through the chamber. "You're suggesting we bind the demon?" someone asked in scandalized tones.

"Isn't that right, boy?" the old man asked Daziel. "Isn't that how the miracles of old happened?"

"We're not binding anyone." Aunt Tirtzah sounded furious.

"Why not?" Melanie said. "This was his idea, wasn't it? Let his magic fund it."

"It is *against* the *treaty*," a Danite I vaguely recognized said.

Voices rose; councilors thumped their fists for attention. I swallowed a sigh. We'd get nowhere now.

Daziel spoke, low-voiced so only I could hear him. "We should tell them. There's so much we need them to agree on. I'd rather they devote resources to finding the Ziz instead of finding power."

I wanted to argue. I wanted to say this shouldn't be on us, this should be something the government fixed, but he was right—it'd make it easier for them to work on one thing if they felt like we were compromising.

Only, I wanted Daziel's and my relationship to progress at the rate *we* wanted it to progress. I wanted to be with him at *our* speed, and if we completed the betrothal, do it when we wanted.

But. I loved him. And maybe he loved me. Maybe that would be enough.

"We should make it seem like we're bargaining," I said, equally quiet. "Tell them we'll only do it if they agree to look for the Ziz."

"Good idea."

Daziel's accord rang out in a suddenly silent chamber. I blinked, confused. The entire Sanhedrin had stopped talking, their argumentative expressions dropped for shock. They were staring at us. No—behind us.

"That won't be necessary," a smooth, liquid voice said.

I turned slowly. There'd been a familiar resonance to the voice, male and older, and when I saw the speaker, I knew why. A shayd. Older than Daziel, his appearance corresponding to a human man in his seventies. A blue silk bow restrained his silvered hair at the nape, and blue jewels studded his ears. A metal circle wrapped around his brow.

"Lord Khasmodai," the Chief Judge said, with a deep inclination of his head. There was a note in his voice I didn't recognize. Fear? Respect? "It has been some time."

"Has it?" Lord Khasmodai flipped his hand. "I cannot keep track."

"What has brought you to Talum?"

The shayd turned to look at Daziel. "We've lost one of our young."

"What do you mean," Daziel said in a cold, hard voice, one I suspected was born of fear instead of anger or dislike, "that this won't be necessary?"

"Ah," the man said. His gaze roved over Daziel, then flicked to me. He looked unimpressed. "I mean you will not need to go on any quests or adventures or whatnot. Because you're too late. The Ziz," he said calmly, "is dead."

TWENTY-FOUR

ONE COULD HAVE HEARD A PIN FALL IN THE CHAMBER OF the Great Sanhedrin, though no one so much as breathed loudly. All attention in the room focused on the shayd.

I was too stunned to move. My vision blurred, and my breath came in short bursts. The Ziz couldn't be dead. We were going to save it.

Daziel recovered first. "How do you know?"

"It has become quite obvious," the older shayd said. "I commend you—though your mother will not—on attempting to solve this on your own, but enough is enough. Leave the adults to their work."

"What work will that be?" Daziel asked. He sounded challenging, his chin jutted out, but I could see the flicker of both fear and desperate hope in his eyes, as though he wanted nothing more than for an adult of his own people to sweep in and make everything right.

"Why, we will have to prepare to leave Ena-Cinnai," the shayd said. "There is little else to be done—with the Ziz gone, the winds will fluctuate so wildly the land will be unlivable within five years. Other lands will face their own difficulties, so it is not yet clear where will be the best place to go, but it is best to be ready."

A Practical Guide to Dating a Demon ~ 289

A moment of dreadful silence, and then the Sanhedrin broke into wild, unstructured yelling.

"I will discuss this with the Chief Judge and the grand duke," the shayd said, his voice cutting through the noise. "You may call upon me at my usual rooms." He vanished.

Chaos remained. I looked first at Aunt Tirtzah, appalled shock on her face, then Professor Altschuler, who wore a matching expression. So much for reassurance.

"Come on." Daziel grabbed my hand. He pulled me back through the entrance door, into the small antechamber where we usually waited. No one bothered to stop us.

"Where are we going?"

"Somewhere we can talk."

But we didn't talk, not the whole fifteen-minute walk back to my aunt's, not until we reached the relative safety of our room. I threw myself on the bed, grabbing the blanket as though it, unlike the adults, could offer some measure of safety. "Who was that?" I said, still shocked. "Do you think he was right?"

Daziel paced back and forth. Paz's tiny head following him worriedly from the foot of the bed. "If he says the Ziz is dead, the Ziz is dead."

"Is he right about the rest? The country will become unlivable—the world?" My throat was dry. I found it unfathomable, a nightmare I was desperate to wake from. "What are we supposed to do?"

Daziel looked grim. "I've never known him to be wrong."

"Who is he?" I asked again, desperate to grasp the situation, to sort all the players, to find some angle to make this man less trustworthy.

"Ah." Daziel stopped pacing. "That was my father."

An entirely different kind of shock washed over me. "Are you serious?"

"Mm. Why?" He registered my alarm, which had graduated from angst on a worldwide level to deeply personal dismay. "What's wrong?"

"Your *father*. Some warning would have been nice," I said, aware I was being nonsensical; Daziel hadn't known any more than me that his father would show up in the center of the Council room. But now I had to worry about meeting Daziel's dad on top of everything else.

"He likes to be dramatic. One of the few pleasures allowed to him, he'd say." Daziel sighed. "I'm sure we'll see more of him soon."

"When?" I looked down at my outfit, practical brown as usual. I wasn't sure what one wore to meet the parent of their betrothed, but I'd have liked the chance to think about it. "Today?"

"I couldn't say."

The tone of his voice—defeated—caught my attention. "What do we do? If the Ziz is dead?"

Daziel looked on the verge of tears. "I don't know."

"But—how are we supposed to fix the winds? Bring on the Maestril? It should be here by now."

Daziel shook his head. "We can't."

We had failed.

I hadn't expected to fail. I'd known it was a possibility—I wasn't an idiot—but in my heart, I supposed, I'd thought if I worked hard, if I didn't give up, everything would be all right.

It wasn't all right.

"Abandon Ena-Cinnai?" I said. "Surely not."

Daziel came to the bed and lay down, pulling me into his arms. His voice was numb. "I don't know."

Hours passed; evening came. Eventually, we had to eat. We went to the kitchen and fixed ourselves bowls of leftover lentil soup, taking them out to the garden. "My aunt's not back yet, is she?" I asked the housekeeper, Madame Chabert.

She shook her head. "She expects to be at the Sanhedrin until late."

I half expected to be told to return, but maybe Aunt Tirtzah had decided we deserved a break—or perhaps no one needed to talk to a young shayd when an older one was around.

Daziel's *father*.

As though my thought had summoned him, the older man entered the garden—by ordinary means, Chava at his side. She gave us a strained smile and retreated.

"So, this is where you've been hiding." The man looked at me, his eyes as unnerving as Daziel's the first time I'd seen them. "With a human girl. How quaint."

Daziel straightened, his posture alarmingly perfect. "Father, this is Naomi bat Yardena."

"Hello," I said, uncertain of what to do in this situation.

"Typical-looking for a human, isn't she?" the man said. "And no style."

I flinched.

"Don't be rude," Daziel said.

Daziel's father affected surprise. "Never. Let me look at you, girl. I have an interest in human civilizations."

"Father," Daziel said warningly.

"What? I fancy myself a bit of an expert." The man withdrew a pipe from his sleeve and lit it. "I am composing an epic poem on the subject."

"On humans," I clarified, just to make sure.

"Yes." He eyed me. "All so very needy, are you not? Enthusiastic but not very inventive lovers. And hard to shake."

I flushed hot. Wow. Way to identify and go hard at my insecurities.

"Anyway, it's time to come home," the shayd said to Daziel. "Your mother is expecting you."

"Father, there's something—"

"I'm really not interested."

"Naomi and I are betrothed."

"No, you're not," his father said brusquely. "Sixty percent, maybe. Seventy percent at the most. Nothing to worry about."

"I'm not worried," Daziel said through gritted teeth. "I'm informing you."

"And I'm informing you that you haven't reached your majority. You have previous obligations."

Previous obligations?

Daziel looked frustrated. Then he shook his head, as though shaking everything away. "How did you know the Ziz was dead?"

"The birds told us," his father said. "And showed us the body."

Daziel winced. "When?"

"Two days ago. Which is why we decided to call off this little adventure of yours. You took too long."

"I would have taken less time if you'd helped."

"Well, we didn't," his father said bluntly. He glanced at me again, then looked back to his son. "You may have the night to say goodbye. You will be at my rooms in the morning, ready to go. If you aren't, I will fetch you like a child and drag you home."

He vanished.

"Cool," I said, and tried not to have a panic attack.

"Two days." Daziel sounded numb. "*Two days.* If I'd moved sooner—told you earlier—we could have cured it."

"Tried to cure it," I reminded him. "We could have failed elsewhere."

He let out a broken laugh. "But I failed here."

"Daziel." I put my hand to his cheek, made him look at me. "You can't blame yourself for this."

"Who else should I blame?" Self-recrimination filled his voice. "I made the call. I could have told you months ago."

"*You,*" I repeated, aggravated, not at him but on his behalf. "Why was it on you? It's like Yael said. This was bigger than you, than us. Your people, your government, they should have come to ours. It shouldn't be on one individual to figure out how to save everything."

Now he looked helpless. "But I could have done it. If I'd been smarter, faster. I could have saved the Ziz. And now it's lost."

"Oh, Daziel." His pain cut through me as though I'd sliced my own hand. I gathered him to me, stroking his back.

We sat in silence for a moment, disheartened and depressed. I hated seeing him this way. So I changed the subject, trying to sound lighthearted instead of disconcerted. "Your father didn't like me."

Daziel looked pained. "He isn't the most welcoming."

"He said you have 'previous obligations'?" I couldn't suppress a displeased zing.

"There's expectations in my family about what I should do with my life."

"Like what? I thought you looked after a rock garden."

He grimaced up at slowly drifting purple clouds. "For now."

Great. I should have expected this. "I don't suppose the 'no more lies' covered 'clear up past lies by omission.'"

Daziel winced. "Ah. Yes. There are one or two of those."

Our chairs jolted beneath us, and the stones of the garden path shuddered and jumped. On the table, our glasses and soup bowls skittered. Daziel leaped to his feet, grabbing my waist as though preparing to haul me into the sky, but the world stopped shaking as suddenly as it had started, leaving us standing together and trembling.

What was happening? If the Ziz was dead, were we really doomed? "Maybe one of the other scrolls also had helpful information," I said, desperate for hope.

"Maybe." He smoothed hair out of my face. "Come home with me."

"What?"

"Come home with me. To the shedim lands. It won't be easy on you, I shouldn't lie, but we're better prepared to handle strange natural magic."

My heart skipped. I had no idea how to respond. I wanted to be with him too, but I couldn't leave everything I'd ever known. "Daziel, I can't. I have school."

He laughed. "What's school with the world falling apart?"

This was not a bad point. Still, the idea of leaving struck me as wrong. "I don't know." Surely there was still some way to stop the storms, the tremors, the destabilization of natural magic. I couldn't leave everything at the height of this disaster.

Daziel must have seen the uncertainty on my face, because he switched tactics. "Let's at least complete the betrothal." His concerned gaze seared through me, with none of the mischievousness I was used to from him. "It might give you some protection. And the next few months aren't going to be safe."

"You're going to leave, then." Though his father had commanded it, it hadn't sunk in.

"He's more powerful than me," Daziel said. "I'm not sure I can resist him. And I don't know what's left for me to do."

Be with me, I almost said. Instead, feeling dizzyingly light and numb, I gathered up our bowls and headed to the kitchen. Daziel followed me there, and then we went upstairs. How could Daziel leave? When he had said he would prove he wanted to be with me?

But then, with the world ending, *shouldn't* you go home? Should I go home?

"So now what?" I asked as we crawled into bed. "We give up? We're done?"

"I don't know," Daziel said. "I hate that I keep saying that. But I just don't know."

Holding each other tight, we turned off the lights and shut our eyes. I didn't know what else to say. *Stay with me. I love you.*

But those things were scarier to say than the world ending.

Daziel fell asleep quickly, a skill I'd always envied. I lay there, thoughts whirling. Outside, I could hear the howl of the winds, feel the strange rumble of the streets. I tossed and turned, trying to sleep. I caught the edge of it, the strange drifting from where you can never remember your thoughts, and tried to let myself fall. Images flashed through my mind—Daziel, the scrolls, my friends, the river, the caves, Mom, Dad, my sisters—

A high, thin voice: *Don't let me drown.*

Another tremor jolted me awake. Great. Now I'd never fall back asleep.

I got out of bed quietly, trying not to wake Daziel. He murmured something and shifted, then lay still again.

I curled up in the armchair by the window, tucking my bare feet beneath me for warmth, craning my gaze up to see the moon. I couldn't imagine leaving Ena-Cinnai myself, let alone with everyone who lived here. It seemed impossible. And if all natural magic was thrown off, there might not be anywhere safe. I didn't know what we'd do then.

In the distance, silhouetted against the moon, soared the long, slim shape of a heron—its kinked neck, the long feathers of its plumage, the broad, distinctive wings.

I blinked. Had I really seen a bird, here in Talum, where we had no more birds?

Well, why not? The Ziz, Master of the Birds, was dead. Perhaps it no longer needed its court gathered to rend their clothes and sing a funeral song. Perhaps they'd all been released to go back to wherever they had come from. What else would they do without a new ruler to follow?

I stilled.

A new ruler. Most things did get new rulers once the old one died—kings and emperors for humans. Queens for bees.

Did mythical beasts? I'd assumed there was only one Ziz, eternal and immortal, and with its death, everything would end.

But . . .

Once it dropped an egg, which flattened cities . . .

An egg. A baby.

The Ziz controls the winds.

I thought of the winds pushing me toward the caves. Caves leading deep under the island. The wind wasn't whispering to me now. But it had.

I thought of the odd shape of Talum, of our island and the islet curving toward each other. Like a volcano had erupted, leaving a caldera. But. Not only volcanos caused depressions.

The idea was so preposterous I almost laughed. I could accept the primordial beasts being part of the physical world, but it was more difficult to accept them interacting with it so bluntly, like in the stories.

An egg. An egg that flattened cities.

But it made a strange sort of sense. Like puzzle pieces clicking together. A heavy stone dropped from the sky could leave a crater. Maybe an egg from a legendary beast could do the same.

I shoved Daziel awake. "Daziel. Daziel, what if there's an egg?"

He was sleepy and not built for waking immediately. "Hm?"

"What if that's what the wind was trying to tell me?" I hadn't thought about it recently, hadn't connected the tugging wind to the Ziz's ability to control the winds. Maybe the *Ziz* had tried to send me somewhere. "What if it tried to direct me into the caves—deep into the island. What if it sent those winds in particular? What if it was trying to send a message?"

He blinked. "And you think the message was . . ."

"That it dropped an egg here."

Daziel stared. "What?"

"Not recently. Centuries ago. Millenia. Look at Talum. We've formed around a crater. What caused the crater?"

He shook his head helplessly.

"You don't know," I filled in. "No one does; it's always been there. A volcano, some say. But what if it was an egg that fell from the sky, so large it could flatten cities?"

"I wouldn't expect the egg to survive the fall," Daziel said, but he sounded thoughtful, not disbelieving.

"Maybe it had a really thick shell."

He laughed but not mockingly. More astonished. "And the reason the wind pushed you would be . . ."

"Because I was working on the spell to heal the Ziz. It knew I wanted to heal it—or, well, I was just working on the fragments, I didn't know about the Ziz yet, but maybe it guessed. Or it didn't have much focus, like your magic doesn't, but maybe it said, 'Send someone who will help to my egg.'"

"I feel obligated to point out this is all conjecture," Daziel said.

"It's a theory. And until it's proven wrong, isn't it worth investigating? Unless you have a better idea."

Daziel shook his head, grinning wryly. "I have no other ideas."

"Then we should look. Underneath the water, maybe, between here and the islet."

"Through the caves. The wind directed you to the caves."

Which caves, though? Without the wind guiding me and opening up hidden routes in solid walls of rock, I had no idea where to start.

Or maybe I did.

"At the Rocks," I breathed. "The Rocks is all caves, and they go deep. We'll start there."

We left a note for Aunt Tirtzah—she probably wouldn't stop us, but why take the risk?—and headed for Testylier House. Thousands of stars filled the night sky, a dusting of diamonds, a whirl of white.

"If there's an egg, we might still need to cast the spell," Daziel said. It'd be the worst of ironies if the beast hatched only to die because it had no parent to care for it, especially when we had a spell designed to strengthen the Ziz's health. "Which means," he added apologetically, "we should complete the betrothal."

I closed my eyes. Of course, "I'd rather do this if we were sure. Of us."

He drew his signet ring from his finger. "I am sure of us," he said, his voice and gaze steady. "I want to give this to you, not because it will allow us to tap into a greater magic but because I want to marry you."

My heart twisted. Too many feelings overwhelmed me, joy and disbelief and hope. My protest came out weak. "Eighteen is too young to get married."

He smiled and parroted back what I'd said to others when they raised the same objection. "It can be a very long engagement. I love you, Naomi. I want to marry you."

Warmth spread through my whole body, leaving me flushed and dazzled. I couldn't believe he'd said it, the words I'd craved so badly but been too scared to say myself. "I love you too."

"You don't have to say it back," he said, looking mulish. "Just because I did."

I started laughing. A pure exhilaration made me feel as if I was going to float into the sky. "I wouldn't. I do."

Hope started to dawn in his eyes, like he'd been just as scared and uncertain as me, as though it had been a terrible risk to say the words, but he'd done it anyway, even though he hadn't known what he'd hear in return. "Really?"

"Really." I flung my arms around him, and he caught me with a surprised gasp. I burrowed my face in his neck, luxuriating in the feel and the smell of him, in the fact that he *was* mine, that he loved me, that we didn't have to let go.

He slid the ring onto my finger. "Then be with me," he said. "Stay with me."

I pressed my lips to his, trying to convey all the emotions hurtling through my body. He gripped my hips and pulled me closer, then wrapped his arms around my body until we were flush together, the two of us drenched in moonlight.

It took a while to return to business, and when we did, it was with my arm tucked through his, smiles plastered on our faces. Still, Daziel's voice was serious as he spoke. "The spell requires four casters. With you channeling my power, we'll want someone else to take your place reciting it."

I nodded. Yael, Gidon, and Stefan should be three of the four; they were intimately familiar with the spell. And any of my friends would rise to the task. But the best spellcaster I knew, the one who would easily pick up a new, complicated spell in a foreign language . . .

I groaned. The best spellcaster I knew was the last person I wanted to ask. "Maybe we can ask Professor Altschuler."

Daziel shrugged. "It's up to you. If you don't think he'd shut this down . . ."

He would definitely shut us down.

Which is how we wound up knocking on Élodie's door half an hour later. She opened it, wrapped in yellow silk from head to toe and looking like she wanted to murder someone. "Tell me you have good news."

I almost stepped back in the face of her rage. "You heard?"

"That the Ziz is dead? It's all anyone is talking about." She looked furious. "The Sanhedrin wouldn't even believe the Ziz *existed*, and now they're up in arms it's dead. It's ridiculous. Why are you here?"

"We want to go to the Rocks."

She squinted. "Your plan is to get high and dull your mind from the end of the world?"

"We think the Ziz might have dropped an egg here thousands of years ago. The cave system might allow us to reach it, deep under the river. And once we do, we want your help casting the spell to strengthen it."

"You're insane."

"Do you have something better to do?"

"No." She was already unpinning her hair wrap, her curls falling out in perfect ringlets. She took one sad look at them, then braided them back in a long plait from her crown. She ducked into her bedroom and continued talking from there. "I assume we'll be joined by the rest of your friends?"

"My cryptography cohort, yes. Meet us in my rooms in an hour."

She made a noise of agreement, and Daziel and I headed out. He went through the mirrors to wake Yael, Stefan, and Gidon. I woke Leah, since someone should know our plan. Just in case. Jelan heard the commotion and came out, which meant Gilli was also awake. They came to my rooms, and when Élodie arrived, she brought Birra. By midnight, ten of us crowded in my living room, listening gravely as I explained the situation.

"If the Ziz is dead, we're screwed." Stefan spoke through a yawn. "And if there's an egg—what, you want to cast the spell on it instead?"

"We should be prepared to," I said. "The spell is supposed to make the Ziz more itself, to keep it strong and healthy. Hatchlings usually have parents to feed them and tend them, and this one won't. The spell might give it a fighting chance."

"We can't cast the spell," Gidon said in his worried way. "We don't have the magic."

"We do," I said, hoping to put an end to this line of questioning. "It'll be fine."

Yael's head jerked up. Élodie exchanged a look with Birra. All three of them had been at the beach at the Rocks. "Naomi, no." Yael sounded like my mother.

"It's illegal," Élodie whispered.

"And dangerous," Yael said firmly.

I remembered how Daziel's magic had torn through me. How it had threatened to consume me, had been almost impossible to let go. Surely it would be different this time with the betrothal complete.

"What are you talking about?" Gilli asked. Then her gaze caught on Daziel's, and I could see her rewind back a few moments to me saying *We do* regarding having magic.

Everyone seemed to be coming to the same conclusion, mouths parting and stances stiffening. I had only told Leah, who gave me a much-needed supportive nod.

"You're not serious," Gidon said. His voice squeaked. "You're going to bind him?"

"It'll give us the power for the spell," Daziel said. "We need four casters for the four points of the compass, so Naomi can focus on handling the magic."

I nodded, deciding Daziel's strategy—simply moving on—was

the best. "Yael, Gidon, Stefan—you know the spell best. Élodie, you're the best caster in our year. If you'll come with us, we might have a shot."

"I should come too," Birra said stubbornly. "You should have a healer with you."

"Two," Gilli said quickly.

"None of you are trained in any sort of protective or combative magic," Jelan said. "I'm coming too."

Leah, looking entirely unserious in her pajamas bearing penguins wearing knit hats, shrugged. "If they're going, I'm going."

A laugh scraped out of me. "This could be a fool's errand. I don't know how to navigate the caves. We could get lost. It might not be safe."

"We'll cast a hook spell at the entrance to guide us back," Jelan said.

"The cave system's supposed to be massive," Gidon said. "How are we supposed to canvass the entire place? Find an egg no one has ever heard of, which might not even exist?"

I had no idea. But we only had one night before Daziel's father dragged him back to the shedim lands, so I would give it my damnedest effort tonight. "We try. We try, and we hope."

"If the egg's fall formed Talum," Leah said slowly, "shouldn't it be in the center of the caldera? Or—not a caldera, technically, but the point of impact between the islands, what raised the main island and the islet from the river."

"So really, we need to calculate the location, then find out how to get there," I said.

"It should be possible to write a spell on a compass," Élodie said. "To find a path to exact coordinates."

We set to work. We noted the longitude and latitude of the center point between the islands. Élodie and Yael altered a pre-existing spell to direct us toward the coordinates via a path with oxygen for as long as possible. If we went deep enough into the caves, it should lead us through them instead of aboveground.

They carved the spell on the back of a compass. "We can try it here," Élodie said, "but it might tell us to walk to the river's edge, sail to the center of the caldera—then dive. Which won't be helpful if the egg is in the caves, not the riverbed."

Sure enough, when we cast the spell, the compass needle spun and spun, then finally settled with a wobbling point to the west. Since we were so close to the shore already, Yael took the compass outside and tested following it while the rest of us scrambled to put supplies together.

Fifteen minutes later, Yael returned, windswept and out of breath. "It took me right to the water's edge," she said. "We should try casting it in the caves and hope it will show us a different path there."

Wrapping ourselves in our sweaters and blazers, we set out for the Rocks. It was deep in the night, past two bells, and the moon glowed with a lavender cast, unusually large and low in the sky. The trams didn't run this late, so we hired two dodgy carriages whose drivers didn't ask questions.

Once more, we scrambled over the glossy black rock. There was little vegetation out here, but a few scraggly trees broke through and swayed triumphantly against the wind. My gaze snagged on one where the silhouettes of a dozen small kingfishers stood out against the darkness. I glanced wildly at Leah, who gaped at me.

The birds were back. Surely that was good?

We reached the Rocks, climbing halfway down the sleek stairs to the cavern where we'd sheltered several weeks ago from the awful storm. Before us, the river spread out far to the south, disappearing into inky blackness.

Inside the cavern, we activated our glow globes, casting stark shadows against the obsidian walls. Stefan led us to a crack in the stone at the very back. "This leads to the rest of the cave system. I've gone a fair way down. I'll go first." His voice echoed in the large, damp cave, and he didn't sound as confident as usual. "There're stairs people built at some point and caves people use for smoking and hanging out, but after, it gets less . . . safe."

I shivered.

A hooking spell had already been carved into the wall, and Jelan activated it so we'd be able to find our way back. Then, single file, we followed Stefan down the rough stairs. The air here cooled, seeping through our layers, and the dark became more complete. Our glow globes struggled to push it back. Élodie tried the compass again, but it suggested we go back to the surface.

"This is as far as I know," Stefan said after five minutes of walking, stopping in a cave with a few lanterns and boxes. "There are more—I know some people who have gone farther—but not me." He nodded at the empty blackness in the far wall, indicating a tunnel leading on.

No one moved. No one wanted to, I realized, including me, but I had set this mission in motion. Taking a deep breath, I stepped forward.

Our progress slowed as we wound our way through the dark, rough caves. We tried to pick ones winding toward the river and slanting deeper into the earth, bracing our hands against the wet,

slippery wall as we crept along. Our glow globes formed a bobbing line. Daziel walked beside me, emitting a warm, burnished
light illuminating half a dozen feet on either side of him. Even so,
I felt the weight of the caves and earth above my head. How deep
had we gone? How deep did we need to go to reach below the
river itself? I shivered, the cold reaching bone deep, and inched
closer to Daziel.

Every few minutes, we checked the compass. My heart sank each
time it pointed back the way we'd come. If we couldn't get it to
work—couldn't get it to lead us through the caves themselves—
this whole expedition would be for nothing. What would we do
then? Try to rent a boat to take us out onto the river, dive down, and
see what we could find? I had very little faith in my diving abilities.

Élodie inhaled sharply, and I spun. She'd tried to spell again,
and the compass needle whirled, as though confused. Then it
settled, pointing deeper into the caves. "Finally," she muttered.

Some of the worry drained out of me, my shoulders lowering.
We *could* reach the center of the caldera from the caves.

We kept walking for another twenty or thirty minutes—time
felt endless—before puddles started to show up on the tunnel
floors. At first we jumped over them, but they became deeper and
more frequent as we went on. The first time we couldn't leap
across and had to step in icy water reaching our ankles, everyone
let out sounds of protest. Cold water submerged our shoes, and I
grimaced, trying not to shiver.

After a few minutes I became used to ankle-deep water, but
then it rose, until we routinely encountered stretches where the
water reached our knees. We took off our shoes, slinging them by
their laces around our necks. Sometimes the tunnels angled up,

and we'd be dry for a while but never long. The sound of dripping and sloshing water echoed around us.

We'd stopped talking some time ago when our tunnel opened up into a vast cavern, the largest we'd seen yet. We stood at the entrance on dry rock. It sloped down into a massive black pool of water, which filled two-thirds of the chamber.

"Now what?" Leah whispered.

Daziel raised a hand, and from it a light shot up, illuminating the whole cavern. On the far side, where water touched the rock wall, a deeper black circle indicated an opening. A tunnel to another cave.

I looked at Élodie's compass. It pointed toward the opening.

"We need a boat," Élodie said, the usual bell tone of her voice somewhat subdued.

I shook my head. No time or way to get a boat. "We'll need to swim."

Daziel looked miserable. "Must we?"

"We should have brought goggles," Gidon said. "And those globes divers wear to bring oxygen with them, in case we wind up underwater—"

"If we fail, we can go back and find those." I glanced at Daziel. Surely we'd be able to keep his father from dragging him home in the morning if we explained everything, wouldn't we? But I was scared to risk it. I thought of how close we'd been to saving the Ziz, if only we had worked faster. Two days. I thought of the tremors. We'd assumed they were from the death of the Ziz upsetting natural magic. But a tremor could also be caused by the rocking of something deep in the earth. How long did it take an egg to hatch?

"What if we get trapped?" Daziel asked, and I noticed he was breathing quickly as he stared at the black water. "What if the tunnel angles down and there's no air?"

Humans couldn't survive without oxygen. Neither could fire.

"Maybe you're right," I said quickly to Élodie. "Maybe we should go back for equipment—"

"No." Daziel shored up his shoulders. "We'll try."

"Not everyone needs to come," I said. "We'll send a small team. I'll go."

Daziel glared. "Obviously I'm going with you."

"I'll go too," Jelan said. "We'll send someone back after a few minutes."

There was a general outcry, Stefan and Élodie and Leah insisting on coming, but Yael and Jelan argued them down. Élodie reluctantly handed me the compass.

We shed down to our smallclothes. Jelan and I holding our globes, Daziel glowing, we waded into the dark, still water. It was cool, but not as freezing as I had expected, though it was unsettling to be in opaque water, in a dark cave, preparing to go deeper. The water reached our hips, sliding over us like silk, then higher still. I shivered. Beneath my feet, the stone floor was slippery.

"Ready?" I said when the water hugged my ribs. Best to jump in while we could still gain some momentum.

"Ready," the others said, and we dove forward and swam toward the dark opening.

TWENTY-FIVE

IT TOOK ONLY TWO DOZEN STROKES TO REACH THE FAR SIDE of the cave, where the water slipped under the gap. Daziel's light wasn't so strong here, and I wondered how much the water hampered him. The tunnel's roof was low—four feet above the water when we entered, then three, then two. Then one. Claustrophobia raked at me. I looked at Daziel, and he gave me a strained smile in return.

We swam another dozen yards, our dim lights battling the darkness. I didn't like thinking about what else could be down here in the darkness. *Nothing,* I told myself firmly. *Fish. That's all.*

Then the rocky ceiling lowered even more, or the water rose— in any case, there was no air left between the water and the rock. We paused, treading water. I looked at the compass, still clenched in my hand. "It was supposed to show a path with oxygen."

"Maybe it's only briefly underwater," Jelan said. "I'll go."

"It'll be easier for me," Daziel said, voice tight. "I don't need to breathe as often as you two."

"I'm not letting you go alone," I said. "Are you okay in the water? You don't seem it."

He scowled. I scowled back.

"How long can you both hold your breath?" Jelan said. "We'll go for half that length, then turn around."

"A minute?" I guessed. "A minute and a half?"

"Forty-five seconds, then," Jelan said. "When I touch your arm, we turn back, no arguing. Daziel, I trust you'll make your own call."

He nodded. The three of us looked at each other, then, on Jelan's count, inhaled as deeply as possible and dove underwater.

I swam as fast as I could, following Daziel's dimly glowing form. The water stung my eyes, cold and unpleasant, and almost immediately my lungs started to burn. I kept going.

Jelan touched my arm. Time to go back. I knew I should turn, knew it was the right thing to do, but Daziel was still swimming, and then I saw his body change directions, angling up. I pointed, giving Jelan a pleading look. She frowned but nodded.

We swam onward. My whole chest hurt. Maybe I couldn't hold my breath a full minute and a half—why had I said I could? I was going to need to suck in air any second, but I would only breathe in water; I would drown myself—

And then we were rising too, like Daziel had, but there was still more water. I'd made a horrible mistake. I had thought him rising meant he'd left the tunnel and entered air, but he hadn't; he'd entered more water, and I needed to breathe; I desperately needed to breathe; I was going to drown—

A wrist grasped my arm and pulled me upward. I broke the surface, gasping, Jelan beside me, Daziel holding on to both of us. The three of us kicked and panted, barely staying afloat, until Daziel jerked his head forward. "There's a beach."

We set out for it, throwing our bodies upon soft black sand. Daziel flung up a hand, and white-silver light slid through the cave like moonlight, illuminating everything with a cold glimmer.

We'd surfaced inside an unnervingly massive cave even larger than the one we'd left behind. If that had been a ballroom, this was a stadium, capable of housing thousands of people. Water pooled near the tunnel we'd swum through, but the rest of the massive space was filled with black, glittering sand. When I looked up, it was like we were inside a geode. Jagged iridescent gemstones covered the sides and roof.

"Neshem crystals," Jelan breathed.

For a moment, I stared, too stunned to look away. Then Daziel made a noise low in his throat.

I followed his gaze. There, in the center of the cave, half-sunk in black sand, was a giant, almost-translucent hull. It was half the length of my aunt's house and, even partially covered, taller than me.

Stumbling to our feet, we jogged closer until we reached where the egg curved into the sand. It was cerulean blue, like a robin's egg or cheerful shutters or the sea under certain slants of light. Daziel crouched down next to it, reaching out, but stopped short of touching it.

I came up right behind him, peering at the hull's surface. Cracks sidled around the edges, disappearing into the sand.

"An egg," I breathed.

Jelan stared at it, then shook herself. "I should go back. Tell the others we haven't drowned."

We hugged, and then she strode back across the sand and dove smoothly into the water. Daziel and I continued examining the egg. A pulsing light ran through it, and I thought I could almost hear something, like a melody just far enough away you thought it might be your imagination. I turned my head, so close my ear almost touched the hull.

A giant rumbling ripped through the room.

I yelped, jumping away from the egg. It was, to my horror, trembling. Daziel grabbed my arm and yanked me even farther back, and we scrambled across the black sands.

"It's ready to hatch," he said.

"*Now?*" I echoed, a mix of horror and exasperation twisting through me. "I don't know if now is the best time."

"Maybe it could tell the old Ziz was dying," Daziel said. "Maybe it knows it has to be born now."

A great tearing *boom* ripped through the cavern, and the world gave an unsettling lurch. It wasn't like when we'd been on the island's surface and everything shook. Here, the movement was greater because—as was instantly clear—it came from the egg itself, rocking back and forth. As it did, the sand around it shifted, pouring into the nooks opened up as the egg moved, creating instant quicksand.

Daziel was sucked into one. Screaming, I grabbed his arm, leaning backward, but my weight wasn't enough to do anything. His legs were trapped, the sand pulling him down suffocatingly, and the sand was up to his chest, pulling me in too, thick and raspy against my arm—

I pulled on him with all my might, and he popped free. His wings ripped out, those great webs of shadow, and he grabbed me, lifting off the shifting sands. He soared upward, cradling me against his chest.

"Wow," I said after a moment, after my heartbeat calmed enough that I could stop clutching him like I was in danger of plummeting to my death. "This is kind of freaky."

"In a hot way?" he said hopefully.

I laughed. I couldn't believe I could laugh in this moment, far under the river, floating in the air above an egg containing one of the three Great Beasts. But I laughed and I laughed until the sand stopped shifting, and Daziel floated to the ground and set me there. He took my face in his hands, looking concerned. "Are you okay?"

"Probably not," I admitted.

A moment later, our friends emerged at the tunnel's entrance, their heads popping out of the water as they gasped for lungfuls of air. They made their way to shore, sopping wet and sputtering. "What happened?" Leah cried. "We heard noises, felt the rocking— Oh shit, there it is."

"Oh shit," Stefan echoed, gaping at Daziel and his wings.

"The egg's ready to hatch," I said.

"It can't," Yael said, alarmed. "We're underneath the river. It won't fit through the tunnels."

"The egg wouldn't fit any better." Daziel considered the roof. "We could open the top of the cavern and take it directly up."

"The Lersach is up there." I started to panic. "We can't cause a hole in the bottom of the river."

"She's right," Élodie said. "This is it; these are the coordinates. We're under the middle of the river."

Everyone was silent, staring at the dark roof of the cavern. Slowly, we considered the size of the egg and the tunnels. I couldn't think of a better option. Our best—our only—plan was to make a hole in the bottom of the river and extract the egg through it.

"We need to do it while the hatchling's in the egg," Daziel said. "Right now, the hatchling's environment is protected. It has everything it needs inside the egg. Once it's hatched, it becomes fragile—"

He was right. "And moving it becomes harder. It might not be able to fly or swim—it might drown."

"If we let the water into this cavern now," Daziel said, "we could buoy the egg to the river's surface. Get it somewhere safe to hatch." He nodded at the cracks in the shell. "But we'd have to move now."

Birra spoke, her voice breaking. "If the water comes in—this place is massive, but it's still connected to the other caves. Would it flood them? Flood the city?"

If the river water rushed in here in one giant, fell swoop, the force of it might push up and through the caves and into Talum. "If we have enough magic to open the cavern roof," I said hesitantly, "will it be enough to hold the river up? And, uh, levitate the egg?"

"We might," Daziel said. "But you're going to need to protect everyone against the oncoming water, dig the egg out of the sand—I don't know if you'll be able to stop the water as well."

I looked at the others. I was in too deep, I had to try, but everyone else had to make the call themselves. "No one should stay if they don't want to. It's a big ask."

"It is," Yael agreed. She smiled, and it was so pure and girlish it took me aback. "You couldn't make me leave for anything in the world."

"Obviously I'm staying. This is badass," Stefan agreed.

Élodie's brow was furrowed, but she also nodded.

"I'll be honest," Gidon said with a high-pitched laugh. "I really don't want to stay. But I'm going to."

"You don't have—" I started.

He cut me a deadpan look. "I do. You need a fourth caster, and I know the spell. I don't have to want to do something to do it."

"I can do it," Jelan said. She, Birra, Leah, and Gilli remained. "I'm not as good a caster, but . . ." She shrugged.

Gidon lifted his chin, his face flushing. "No. This—we've been working on this spell for months. I *want* to."

I blinked rapidly. I had underestimated how brave Gidon was. How brave they all were.

"The rest of you should go, though," Daziel said. "Every additional person Naomi has to take care of during the spell is going to weigh on her. And in case the river does flood through the caves . . . go to Naomi's aunt. Let her know what's happening."

Gilli pressed her trembling lips together. "But you should have a healer."

Daziel shook his head, and unease slid through me. How difficult did he think this would be if he didn't dare risk including one other person?

Hugging tightly, our group split in two. Jelan, Gilli, Leah, and Birra dove back into the water, vanishing under the black surface. When the ripples from their passage vanished, the rest of us turned to the egg.

"Should we cast the spell on it now?" Gidon asked. "Or wait until it's hatched?"

I shrugged. "Now? I'm guessing it'll be easier to carve charaktêres on the shell than on the talons of a squirming baby bird."

"Good point," Stefan said hastily. We decided to split the spell into six and write it on the egg like we wrote spells on plywood, gauging space and size of the words so we could connect them.

But after ten minutes, the impossibility of the task became clear. The egg kept shaking, the sand shifting. The third time, Yael was almost sucked into the sand before Daziel flew her out.

"This isn't working," Yael said. "We need a new strategy."

If we couldn't stand on the sand and write . . . we would need something that wouldn't move. Or that we could move with. "We could write the spell on the top." The egg was so large and broad, all six of us could easily fit on the top of the hull.

We all considered it. The neshem crystals' glow cast strange gold and silver shadows across the blue egg. "We'd need a way to keep from falling off when it shakes, though," Élodie said.

"The shell is thick. We could carve handholds," Gidon suggested.

Everyone wore skeptical expressions, but no one offered a better suggestion. I supposed it could work. We'd have to make the handholds quick with our stylos, then keep one hand latched on as we set about writing the spell. It would be awkward and uncomfortable, and it might be our best bet.

"Okay," I said. I turned to Daziel with a dazed smile. "Fly me up?"

Once more, he opened his arms, and I stepped into them. He flew me to the top, gently landing on the peak of the curved blue hull. Even knowing how thick the shell must be, I couldn't help but be nervous I'd break it.

"Should I use your magic for the handholds?" I whispered to Daziel when we were alone. I was aware it would make these small things simple, but I was terrified to let it in until absolutely necessary.

He shook his head. Maybe he too was worried about how this would go. "Not yet."

He flew up the others, and we quickly carved handholds and began writing the spell again. The rumbles came closer and closer together, and with each one, we grabbed our handholds, feeling as though the hatchling was trying to throw us off.

By the time we finished, the egg trembled constantly. "Do we cast the spell now?" Élodie asked nervously, her knuckles white as she gripped her hold. "What if doing it causes the Ziz to hatch?"

"Maybe we try to move it first," I said, like it would be such a simple thing. I felt sick. This seemed like an impossible task. "Daziel?"

Gidon raised his head, staring at the cavern's roof and its glittering crystals. "The water won't crush us when it pours down? The riverbed won't—fall and kill us? And the Ziz."

I looked at Daziel, hoping he had answers.

Daziel tilted his head. "You *did* learn about the human-shedim wars, did you not? You're aware of what a bound pair can accomplish?"

"But you said the others shouldn't stay, and I shouldn't do the handholds," I said, confused.

He moved to stand right before me, taking my hands in his. "Because I didn't want you to handle the magic for longer than necessary. But I'm confident we can do this."

I wasn't confident, and I wasn't convinced he wasn't pretending to make me feel better, but I'd take it. I took a deep breath, steeling myself against the memory of the violent rush of power washing through me. "Then there's just the binding left."

He nodded. His wings canted forward, veiling us briefly from the others. "You can use my ring," he whispered. "That's part of why a shayd's signet is so precious. Slip it on in the other direction and say both of our names as you bind me."

Shock slid through me. No wonder he'd been so angry when I tried to take his ring. "Your true name?" I confirmed. "Cathmeus?"

He placed his palm to my cheek, his gaze as tender as his touch. "With you, Daziel is my true name."

I closed my eyes and nodded, feeling overwhelmed and scared

and hopeful. His warmth enveloped me, staving off the damp. I could hear my friends' exhausted breathing; I could smell water and stone, heavy with minerals and the slight hint of petrichor neshem carried.

I took off his ring and returned it to my finger in the opposite direction, but the words lodged in my throat. I didn't want to do this, to have Daziel's burning magic rushing through me again, but I would. I would open myself up to it instead of fighting. By feel, I brought my hands to Daziel's, brought his hands to my heart. *Okay*, I told myself. Told him. *Okay, I'm ready.* "Daziel, son of Cathmeus, son of Khasmodai. I, Naomi bat Yardena, bind you."

Heady, swift power filled me, burning like fire, flowing like a river. Yet it didn't feel as reckless as at the Rocks. My shoulders relaxed. Maybe this would be fine.

"Make a shield." Daziel's voice sounded like it came from far away. "Against the water, around us and the egg."

I nodded. "Shield us, our friends, and the egg against water or rock or anything dangerous."

I could feel the magic pulling out of Daziel, channeled through my words into a force snug over us and the egg. When I opened my eyes I could see a hint of it, a screen of golden light around us.

"Get rid of the roof. Let in the river."

The magic flowed through me, strong and steady, but not so horrible this time. Yet I hesitated to use it. To remove the cavern's roof, to let the river's water flood down upon us, seemed ludicrous. What if it didn't work? What if the force of falling water crashed down and I couldn't stop it, and it crushed us? What if it knocked us off the egg—smashed the egg—and drowned us all?

Daziel squeezed my hand. "You can do this."

I wasn't sure I could, but I didn't see what other options we had.

"Remove the roof of the cave to let the water in so it lifts the egg safely to the top of the river, and don't let the water go past this cavern. And let's extricate the egg from the sand safely too, please."

Daziel looked slightly amused, but specificity seemed like a good idea.

Then the magic ripped through me.

It hurt. It hurt worse than it had at the Rocks. I was pulling so much more of it, so much faster. I threw myself at Daziel, who seemed like the one solid, real thing in the world, clinging to him with all my might. I wanted to vomit, but I couldn't do even that.

Water rushed in.

I noticed the sound first, a sonorous roar crashing over and around us with such totality the others shouted. Sheets of water slashed down. It felt like it came from everywhere, like a suffocating curtain had fallen. It fell in a tidal rush directly onto us but slid off in a bubble around the egg. I looked up, mouth gaping, and saw nothing but black water. If the cavern still had a roof, it was obscured.

But there was no roof anymore. I'd gotten rid of it.

"Don't look at it," Daziel said. "Look at me. Hold on to the magic. Hold on to me."

I tried. I tried to look at him, at the boy who I loved. But it was hard to concentrate with the roar of water, with the thick darkness, with the surge of magic whirling within me. Daziel stroked my face, his own pained.

Then I felt the egg start to sway.

"It's working!" I heard Gidon call, thrilled. "We're rising!"

We were. Wrapped in our safe golden cocoon, we were rising atop the egg as water filled the cave below it, buoying it up and out of the sand. This was, without a doubt, more bizarre than anything I'd ever imagined. A floating magical egg? Hardly the stuff of legend to make people take you seriously.

As the egg rose, I wobbled, losing my footing. My concentration smudged, and I lost my grasp on a small piece of the magic. Water sluiced through the shield, and I heard screams.

"Ignore it." Daziel gently tugged me into a cross-legged seat on the egg. "Ignore everything. You're doing great. Everyone's fine; they're just wet."

I wrapped my arms around Daziel's shoulders, digging in hard. I pulled on his magic, channeling it through me, picturing the way he combed his golden magic at home. I tried not to focus on anything but the magic. I was combing his magic, I was the comb, it was too much, but it was okay, I could breathe through it. I had to.

Around us the water poured in torrential black streams, flooding the cavern and raising the water level, and the egg with it. We bobbed back and forth, everyone hunkered down and holding tight to their handholds. Everything around us was dark and strange, the sound slowly fading, then stopping, the rush of water vanishing as we reached the top of the cave and the waters met. The cavern had been completely filled—now we floated serenely from it into the bottom of the river itself, protected in a bubble of air. Everything was completely silent now, no rush of water, and the visibility grew as the water calmed. Light filtered down from the sky far above as we rose through blue-green darkness. Startled fish darted around us, streaks of yellow and orange and silver.

We'd made it through the first hurdle. Could I stop the water from spilling through the caves into the city? Nope, I couldn't think about the city now; I couldn't think about anything but keeping us safely on the egg and the egg rising.

Then, suddenly, the egg did not want to keep rising. Or the river didn't want us to. The current started pulling us, and the water turned wild, like we'd entered a silent submarine storm, buffeted by forces we couldn't hear but could strongly feel.

My father had told me sailing stories about having to hold the sails firm, the wheel steady, and I wondered if he had felt like I did now as I focused all my intent on urging Daziel's magic to raise us farther. I felt like I was talking to the egg too. *You can do it*, I whispered silently. *We're almost there. Just a little farther.*

Then, with a final, abrupt surge, we surfaced, the shield surrounding us pushing up and out of the river and into the middle of a storm. Rain lashed at us, and winds tore down the river. We'd emerged from absolute silence into the chaotic roar of waves and cawing.

I hadn't been prepared for the winds—I hadn't known I needed to be—and they slammed against the shield. The whole egg dipped sideways, bobbing furiously, and the others shouted and slid. "Anchor," I whispered, picturing everyone anchored firmly to the egg. Gidon slammed against the hull, and I winced. At least he wouldn't fall off.

"Naomi," Daziel said. I felt his hand on my cheek. "Bring us to land."

Yes. Right. With painful force, I brought my attention to bear, forcing my thoughts upward and out of the strange, dark murk. "Land."

Like a ship, the egg cut through the raging Lersach. My grasp on the magic slipped again, and rain poured down onto us, the protective shield broken. I scrambled for it, but it was lost. I couldn't hold it; I couldn't make myself. *Steer*, I thought. That was all that was important. Nothing else.

A scream—I turned and saw Élodie sliding off the egg, toward the water. Stefan lurched for her, grabbing her arm. Oh no. Without the shield and anchor, they had little protection besides the handholds. "Anchor," I tried again, but I was too weak to direct the magic. It was too strong. It didn't want to protect humans; it wanted to rage.

"It's okay," Daziel said. "They caught a handhold. We're almost there."

We were? I forced myself to look through the lashing rain. We were. The islet rose before us. I'd never been onshore, and it looked like a strange place, the land barren save some red succulents clinging tenaciously to the earth.

The succulents were not the strangest part. On the black isle, beneath the falling rain, thousands of birds waited. They lined the uneven rise and fall of the rocky terrain, birds of all shapes and sizes.

The wind quickened, blowing us forward. It felt reckless, unstable, and I worried I'd lost all control, but then the egg soared out of the water and onto the shore of the islet, coming to a perfect, serene rest. I looked at Daziel, relief blooming through me and a laugh slipping out at the berthing of our ridiculous vessel. "Made it."

Then—I didn't notice the transition, could barely pay attention to anything anymore—I wasn't on top of the egg; I was lying on the shore with my head in Daziel's lap. The rain had stopped as though it had never been. The predawn sky was a wild swirl of colors, vibrant blues and purples and silver.

Élodie's head came into my sight. "Is she okay?"

"I don't know."

The egg was shaking.

"It needs help," Daziel said, voice urgent. "It's too weak to break out of the shell itself. We need to help it."

"The spell," I said. "We should cast before it breaks."

Daziel frowned. "I don't know if you can handle the magic."

I didn't want to. It hurt, the amount of magic stirring inside me, like it kept hitting sore bruises and eventually it'd leave me a broken, bloody puddle. I looked beyond Daziel. "Yael."

She grimaced but directed Élodie, Gidon, and Stefan to the points of the compass. I heard her voice as she started reading the spell in the ancient language we still couldn't completely understand. The others joined in, and I directed Daziel's magic to them. I could feel it latching on, taking hold. The charaktêres began to glow as my friends' voices strengthened. Then the cracks in the egg lit up with a warm golden light, and noise came from inside. The hatchling was trying. It was trying so hard.

Yael shouted the final word in the spell. The glowing stopped. We waited.

"Cut the magic," Daziel told me. "Say 'stop.'"

I'd been waiting for him to say that. "Stop," I said, utterly relieved.

"It's not hatching," Gidon said, panic in his voice. I couldn't see his expression because my eyes were closed. "What's wrong?"

Daziel next. "It's still too weak. We have to help it."

I peeled open my eyes to see Daziel pulling at a shard of the egg—"shard" wasn't the most accurate word, for the segments were like giant plates, four inches thick at the thinnest. Stefan jumped up to help, and the two of them hefted it off and onto the sand. The membrane remained behind, tough and clinging.

Everyone—except me; I was busy trying to remember how to breathe—pulled at the egg fragments, heaving them off the hatchling. I stared at the membrane. What if it wasn't enough? What if it still couldn't get out?

But then something cut through. At first I couldn't make sense of it—it was so strange, so large. Then I could see it, tell what had pierced the membrane from inside. Talons, dagger-sharp, a foot wide, the color of gold.

I started crying. I couldn't help myself. The tears weren't there, and then they were, spilling over my cheeks in endless rivulets, hot and messy. On my hands and knees, I hauled myself to my feet. I staggered toward the egg and tore at the membrane, pulling it down so it wouldn't suffocate the Ziz. I talked to it as I went. "There you are. You're the Ziz. Just a baby right now, but you're going to be all right."

Around us, the birds watched.

My friends tore at the membrane too. It fell away with the rest of the eggshell shards, unveiling a strange creature wet with amniotic fluid. Its body resembled a land animal, four-legged with paws. But feathered wings curled up against its sides, and its head had feathers to match: It looked like a falcon's head, dark-eyed and beaked.

A baby Ziz.

A giant, ridiculous, wild-looking baby, the size of a house but a baby nonetheless. A helpless creature, alone, the only one of its kind.

"Hi there." I stood by its head. "Hi. There you are."

It opened its giant baby beak and made a strange chirp, reminding me, of all things, of Paz. Maybe it wanted its parent.

"I'm sorry." I placed my hand against its beak. "It's just you now. Well." I glanced at the birds. "You have friends."

It blinked a giant eye, the size of a serving platter. Then it opened its beak much wider and screamed.

The birds started cawing, shrieking, trilling, singing. The same cacophony I'd heard half a year ago, when all the birds left Talum in the first place.

My friends backed away from its thrashing limbs and fluttering wings. Daziel came to my side, wrapping his arms around me. I leaned into him. "Do you think it's all right?"

"Are *you* all right?"

"Oh, who knows," I said, which meant I probably was.

The birds lifted off the ground. At first, they circled us, circled the Ziz, until the air was full of them, a vast cyclone of birds, increasing in speed until I couldn't pick out an individual one.

Then, moving as though with one mind, they dove toward the Ziz, sweeping under it, over it, their beating wings somehow forming both cocoon and carrier for the creature. As one, they lifted into the sky, bearing the hatchling away. We watched them go, the cloud becoming a dot on the horizon.

When I could no longer see the birds, the last remaining energy drained out of me. I collapsed, so violently Daziel barely caught me. He carefully lowered me to the ground. I was laughing and crying, exhausted, overwhelmed, but above all, I felt wildly relieved.

I didn't know if we'd be okay. If the newborn Ziz would go wherever Great Beasts were supposed to and learn how to corral the winds. It was only a baby, and who knew how long it would take to grow powerful. But hopefully it would, one day. We had done what we could. We would have to be happy with that.

Daziel curled up behind me, holding me. My cohort and Élodie came over, collapsing beside us, looking equally wrecked. No one said anything, but we leaned into each other, and together, we watched the dawn arrive.

TWENTY-SIX

BOATS CROSSED TO THE ISLET HALF AN HOUR LATER. AUNT Tirtzah leaped from the first, running across the slick black rocks with an agility I hadn't expected. I wondered distractedly if she'd played knockball as well as admiring it, and if so, why she'd never said anything. She cut quite the figure, dashing across the rock, leading a pack of dignitaries as though the most important people of Talum always made their morning rounds jogging across islets in the dawn light.

"There you are." She sank to her knees and threw her arms around me, then extended an arm to include Daziel too, a motion that made me want to cry. "What a foolish thing to do—whyever did you not *wake* me—"

"We're all right," I said, meeting Daziel's gaze before looking back at her. "Did you see it? The Ziz."

"We saw the birds." She looked wryly impressed. "They were impossible *not* to see."

"It is an infant," Daziel's father said. He strolled through the chaos in a blue silk suit. Where had he come from? I didn't think he'd been with the other adults clustering around our friends. "I hardly think it will direct the winds as efficiently as an adult. But I suspect it will get better with each year."

"So evacuation is no longer your suggestion?" I asked.

He shrugged. "I hope not."

"How will it know what to do?" Would it be able to learn without a parent to teach it?

"How does the Maestril know to dry the soil, or the birds to migrate south?" he returned irritably. "You ask ridiculous questions."

I didn't think it'd been ridiculous, but I was glad he had—he understood natural magic better than me. If he thought the Ziz would be able to make its way in the world, I was happy.

WE WERE BUNDLED BACK home. I didn't mind; I was in shock, and all I wanted to do was curl up in a ball with Daziel.

Luckily, everyone seemed agreeable on this front. Aunt Tirtzah chased off the Sanhedrin members who wished to hear our story, putting me and Daziel and the other four in a room at her house. She only let in Leah and Birra and Jelan and Gilli. "Did the city flood?" Élodie asked.

"Very little," Leah said. "A few caves spouted water, but we haven't heard of bad damage anywhere."

Daziel curled up around me. I hadn't realized how comforting it could be lying tangled up with another person, feeling the rise and fall of their chest, the warmth of their body. I listened to the others talk but felt no need to contribute. I didn't want to do anything but listen to Daziel's heartbeat, to tuck my hand beneath him and hold on tight.

For the morning and afternoon, we slept. I woke once, ravenous, and devoured the hearty bread and lemony pesto beans my aunt had sent. Then I curled back up and kept napping.

In the evening, my friends returned to their own homes, and Daziel and I went upstairs. "Come here," I said to Daziel, crawling into bed. He slid in, and I pulled the blanket over our heads because it felt safer that way. The light through the duvet turned our world a warm yellow. "Now what?"

Daziel's eyes found mine. Our legs were tangled together, and he took my hands, drawing them into the small space between our chests. Our faces were so close our noses almost bumped. "My father still wants me to go home," he said, his voice a whisper against my cheek. "I still want you to come with me. I love you. I want us to be together. I want you to see my world."

I bit my lip. I wanted to be with him too. But I wasn't sure I wanted to be with him in the wilderness, the only human, where I didn't belong or know how to behave.

"I'm not saying it will be easy," he admitted. "My parents will probably be a nightmare and the court will be—difficult—but my friends will love you, and my siblings will love you, and there's a beauty there I think you'll love. There are mysteries even shedim don't know, and you love a puzzle. It'll be an adventure. A different kind of adventure than this but a good one."

I could. I could do all that. But also . . . "You could stay here," I said softly, because that was an option too. "Keep living with me. Go to class, play knockball. We could have a life here."

"We could," he agreed just as softly. I imagined how it would be—cozy breakfasts, laughing over coffee, studying together, exploring Talum, cheering him on at knockball. It would be a good life.

But when I met his eyes, I knew he wouldn't stay.

"You once told me I could be a bridge between our two people," he said. "If I wanted. I didn't, then. I wanted to address the immediate problem, save the Ziz. But now—I know you. I know your friends, and *my* friends. I know your aunt. And I know how much our two people don't trust each other. We don't work together. You're right—we need a bridge."

I nodded. I couldn't disagree.

He squeezed my hand. "You should be part of it. We need both of us, to span both our people."

Maybe he was right. Bridges needed support on both sides. Maybe going to the wilderness, being Daziel's betrothed, would be an incredible, empowering leap. Interspecies relations like no one had ever seen.

But it wasn't what I wanted.

What I wanted was in a small room in a tower with light streaming in, filled with dust and ancient scrolls. I wanted to finish uncovering the secrets of Language X. We were so much closer now to being able to solve it, the phonetics uncovered, and so many words known from the rutter. The work fascinated me, made me feel alive. It might take months, years, to decipher the language, but we were on the right path. I wanted to be part of it, part of uncovering a forgotten language and all its secrets. I'd wanted it for years.

"I'm not ready," I whispered. "I want to finish working on the scrolls. I'm not ready to just—be your betrothed."

He was quiet a moment, thinking, and I waited in tense silence. Then he brushed the lightest kiss across my lips. "I understand," he said, and his eyes glinted with gold. "I don't want you to leave your life behind because of me, or your passion. I want us to make a new life together. We might both have to compromise on some things—but not who we are. Why don't I come back in two months? At the graduation festival. Over your summer break, we can visit your family, and mine, and you can see what you think of my world. But I'm not asking you to leave yours behind for it."

Relief blossomed in my chest. This, I could do. Still, some of my trepidation lingered. His father alarmed me, and what did I know about a royal court? Let alone being the first human in who knew how long to enter the wilderness? "I'm scared," I admitted. "I don't know what it'll be like."

"I'll help you." He brought my hand to his mouth and kissed it. The sweetness of the gesture made tears spring to my eyes.

He leaned his forehead against mine. "And I want you to know... I know my lies, my trickery, hurt you. But what *you* did... Your support lifted a world of weight away from me. I thought I was going to have to figure out everything on my own. Having your help, your drive, your determination—it was incredible. *You* are incredible."

Emotions welled up in me, complex and tangled and fierce. They made my chest expand so much it hurt, and tears weighed heavy behind my eyes. My words came out through a scratchy throat. "Now it sounds like you're saying goodbye forever."

"I'm not," he vowed. "Only for two months."

Before Daziel, I'd been so determined to stand on my own all the time. To be the oldest daughter, to be strong and independent. I hadn't realized you could be those things *and* rely on someone else. I hadn't realized how much joy a single other person could give you, how much laughter and comfort. I kissed him. "I'll be here."

When I fell asleep, I dreamed of the strangest hesitant cheep, like a newborn baby bird learning to sing.

~ ~ ~

IN THE MORNING, WE went downstairs to a lavish breakfast. Chopped fruits and yogurt layered with honeyed granola, fried cheese and eggs, sesame bread, lavender muffins. Croissants and coffee, of course. We fell upon them like starving animals, no matter that we'd done absolutely nothing yesterday, save rest and eat.

Aunt Tirtzah, Daziel's father, and the Chief Judge of the Sanhedrin were there. Just a normal breakfast crew.

"Do we know anything about the—the hatchling?" I asked as we sat. It felt strange to call it "the Ziz" when it had just been an awkward baby, and when we had called its late predecessor the Ziz for so long.

"It was last sighted being carried by the mixed flock off the western coast," Aunt Tirtzah said. "Since then, birds have returned to Ena-Cinnai. It's being theorized they were on a death watch of sorts—for the old Ziz, but now they're returning to their normal routines."

"We're leaving this evening," Daziel's father said. "Make sure you're ready."

I spent the rest of the day with Daziel, trying to be in the present and not feel like I was about to be abandoned. I even managed to shoo him off to say goodbye to his knockball friends for an hour. Only then did I let my shoulders slump. I stepped into the garden, hugging my arms around my waist and blinking back tears.

And I found Daziel's father standing beneath a cherry tree.

Almost like he'd been waiting for this opportunity.

I told myself to be polite. I might not like him, but that was beside the point. If Daziel and I were going to have any kind of future, it would be best to get along with his dad. "Hello."

He tilted his head. He was so like Daziel in his mannerisms, but I didn't think they were anything alike in spirit. "So, Daziel wants you to come home with him."

I managed a polite smile. I didn't think he'd sought me out to offer a warm welcome.

"How charming," he said lightly. "I never suspected Daziel would find humans so amusing."

Irritation surged through me. "That's a little patronizing."

His brows arched. "A bite to you, is there?" he said, which I also considered patronizing. He smiled, and this time it was full of sharp teeth. Unlike with Daziel's sharp smiles, I genuinely found this one alarming. "You think you'll do well on top of the Shuddering Tower, girl?" he asked. "You'll wear mud-colored clothes while everyone is wrapped in rainbows. How will you keep Daziel's attention when he's surrounded by glittering gemstones who can sing the winds into silence?"

I didn't understand half of what he meant, but I knew he meant to insult, and so I fought back. "It's not my job to keep Daziel's attention. I don't exist to entertain him. We're together because we both want to be. If you'll excuse me." I turned, ready to go.

He was in front of me. "He's old enough to take up his responsibilities. You'd be a distraction."

I remembered what he'd said early on. *Previous obligations.* Though I knew I should leave—he was clearly baiting me—I couldn't help myself. "What kind of responsibilities?"

"It's time for him to marry."

"We'll marry when we're ready." I wanted, as I'd joked long ago, a very long engagement and a wedding long after my own graduation. "Our betrothal should be good enough for now."

"Not you, girl," he said, and his laugh hollowed me out. "He has been expected to marry Kaisa all his life."

For a moment, the words didn't make sense.

"You did not know?" He looked amused. "Yes, Kaisa del Amara. They will make a good pair."

"He's—no. He's betrothed to—" *Me*, I wanted to say, but I couldn't make myself.

"Oh, did you think he would marry you? You darling human child. No. Daziel is meant for greater things than . . . Well. I'm sure you have some good qualities."

My hand went to the ring on my finger. "We've completed the betrothal."

"Have you?" He looked peeved. "An irritation. But nothing that can't be handled with time and effort. Anyway, not to worry." He patted me avuncularly on the shoulder. "I'm sure he will give you something nice in return. A rosebush that flowers year-round. Drinkable gold—or is that fashionable in one of the other human realms? I can never keep track."

With a sly smile, he vanished.

When Daziel found me a few minutes later, I was sitting on a garden bench, staring numbly up at the pink-and-white almond blossoms. I shifted my gaze to him. "You're betrothed."

We knew each other so well, we'd spent so much time in each other's presence—there was no use in him pretending he thought I meant *to me*. I couldn't even try to hide the betrayal in my voice. I didn't want to.

Daziel's shoulders slumped. "My father told you."

"Have you hidden anything else?"

He hesitated. "Did my father mention who my mother is?"

Oh no. No, this was like storm clouds on the horizon, and I didn't want to unleash their rain. "Is it important?"

"Ah—you might think so?"

"If you say," I ground out, "your mother is the queen of the shedim, I will smack you."

He winced. "Then I should not say it."

"Daziel!" I cried out, jumping to my feet. "No!"

"It's not my fault." He held his hands up. "I didn't pick my parents."

"You can't be a prince." I groaned, turning from side to side as though seeking solace that refused to come. I sank back to the bench, shaking. "This is impossible."

"No, it's not." He knelt at my side, taking my hands in his own and kissing them. "It's not impossible."

"I can't be with a *demon prince*."

"Why not?"

"Because! I'm a human girl! I don't know anything!"

"You know me. I know you." He leaned forward and kissed me.

But I knew Daziel, the boy who had lived with me for half a year, wide-eyed and delighted by small things and funny and out-going. I didn't know Cathmeus. I didn't know anything about him, this prince from the wilderness, and panic started to flare in my chest. "You're betrothed."

"To you. Kaisa and I were never officially bound."

"But you can be unbound to me and bound to her."

He looked stubborn. "It's not what I want."

I let out a sharp laugh. "What if it's what I want? Daziel, I don't know if I can do this."

"You can. I'll come back. In two months. We'll talk then."

And what would we talk about? I wasn't cut out to be a princess of the shedim. I wanted to be with Daziel, and I'd like to see his home, but I wasn't born for royal courts and their intrigue. And Daziel was.

He must have seen my unease, because he brushed his fingertips against my cheek. "We'll figure it out. I swear."

"How?"

"I don't know how. I just know—if we both try, we can do it." He lifted his wrist to show me a red threadbare string wrapped around it. "Do you remember this?"

"Is that mine?" I gaped at him, astonished. "How did you get it?"

"You know the story? If you lose your bracelet, you're about to meet your true love."

"An old wives' tale," I dismissed.

"I found it before we met. It flew right into my chest. I tried to toss it away, twice, but the wind carried it back. Eventually, I put it in my pocket. I didn't even realize it was yours until you mentioned yours was gone. Then I did a small spell to check."

"Oh." I felt strange and light. "What a funny coincidence."

"Not a coincidence." He brushed his fingers against my cheek. "Do you love me?"

I scowled at him. It felt below the belt, to bring up this one irrefutable thing. It also was so upbeat and undeniably Daziel that humor bubbled in me. "Do *you* love *me*?"

His lips quirked, and he pressed a quick kiss to my mouth. "Yes. Always. Even when you're difficult."

I narrowed my eyes but couldn't stop my smile. "Fine. I love you too."

"Then we will make it work. I'm not saying it'll be easy. I'm not saying you'll love my homeland immediately—though it is indisputably more beautiful than the human lands—"

"You're not helping yourself." I smiled, but it quickly fell away. "Your father said you had to get married soon. That you have responsibilities."

He cupped my face in his hands, his gaze intent. "I love you. I have responsibilities to my family and my position, yes, but if we're building a life together, I also have responsibilities to you. One of which is making sure you're happy."

"I do like being happy."

"I thought you might."

He kissed me. At first it was an easy kiss, but then I pressed myself harder against him, and he wrapped his arms around my waist. We lost ourselves, our bodies crushed together.

When we separated, a bittersweet ache blossomed in my chest, threatening to consume me. I wasn't ready to go with him, but I didn't want him to leave, either. It felt like a wound had been opened inside me, a gaping hole it would be too easy to fall into.

"I'll come back," Daziel vowed. "In the summer, when school is closed and there is time. We'll meet each other's families. See each other's homes. And we'll figure out how to be together."

I pressed my lips together to keep them from wobbling, but I couldn't keep the tears gathered in my eyes from spilling down my cheeks. *Don't leave*, I wanted to beg. *Don't go. Stay with me.*

But it wasn't fair to beg someone to do something they could not. "I'm going to miss you so much," I said instead, and wrapped my arms around him one more time. We were heat and sorrow and love. And I didn't want to say goodbye.

When we pulled apart, we gazed at each other, as though memorizing each other's features. He traced my brow, my cheek, my lips.

"I love you. We'll see each other soon," he said, and disappeared.

I slumped, a visceral ache striking through me at his absence. Where he had been, I could see straight through to waving trees and flowers. There was no more heat, no press of his skin on mine. Only the lingering scent of him.

My vision blurred, and I closed my eyes. In two months, the school year would be over. Summer would be here. He would be back. He had promised. He had my red string bracelet, and I had his ring. We had each other, even if we weren't beside each other anymore.

When I'd recovered, I went down to the Lyceum. Campus was normal today, people carrying on like usual. Leah would be in her art history class, which took place in the basement classrooms of the Lyceum's museum, located on the Arts Quad. I climbed the steps of the grand marble building and sat, offset from the entrance so I wouldn't be in anyone's way. Before me, picnicking students filled the lawn. The sky was brutally blue, no sign of the storm from two days ago. I watched a row of blackbirds feasting upon beetles with almost an obscene zeal.

The bells tolled, the classes changing. When I saw Leah, I called her name, and she came over, plopping down next to me on the steps. "What's wrong?" she asked immediately.

"He's gone." I clutched the scarf I was wearing, the one he had made me, burying my shaking fingers in the pink and teal yarn.

"Oh, Naomi." She wrapped an arm around my shoulders. "I'm sorry."

We watched the birds swoop, watched how they filled the trees and their songs the air. I would never take them for granted again.

A warm wind danced past me, carrying the green scent of new growth and of fresh soil and of delicate, unfurling buds. In the distance, a flag I had never seen before, blue with pink-and-yellow trim, was being hoisted up the weather pole. In the distance, gold glowed on the horizon, the kind of light you only saw right after dawn or right before dusk—a golden light, a magical light, and it was spreading toward us with all the warmth of a parent's embrace.

I turned to Leah. "Is this . . . ?"

Her face was raised, her chest lifting as she inhaled. I could see the gleam in her eye, hear the quiver in her voice as she answered. "The Maestril. It's finally here."

I reached out and squeezed her hand. She squeezed back, and we sat there for a while, breathing in the spring.

Acknowledgments

The fantasy genre is my first love. As a child, I struggled to spell and read independently. It was only when I became so captivated by a book my father was reading me at bedtime that I picked it up myself. (The book was *Dealing with Dragons* by Patricia C. Wrede.) Next, I dove into the works of Robin McKinley and Diana Wynne Jones and Tamora Pierce. Fantasy novels have meant so much to me over the years, and it is an absolute joy to finally see my own in the world. Thank you for reading it. I hope it brings you the same delight writing it brought me.

I owe the existence of this book to my agent, Tamar Rydzinski, who encouraged me to return to my fantasy roots. Thank you for suggesting it, and for helping me bat this idea into shape. Without you, this book would never have been written.

Thanks as well to my editor, Gretchen Durning, who didn't blink as we jumped from contemporary rom-coms into a brand-new world. Your help turning this from a manuscript draft into the book it wanted to be was invaluable.

I am immeasurably grateful to all the resources on Jewish mythology that have influenced and informed *APGtDaD*. I knew I wanted to write about Jewish demons (given my own quirky spin), which meant learning about a subject of which I knew very little.

I started with the Talmud and Kabbalistic texts, which are rich in stories of Jewish demons. While many of the details I learned from them and elsewhere didn't make it into this novel, some did: the many ways ancient and medieval Jews tried to ward off demons; demonic characteristics and classifications; red string bracelets and magic rings and mirrors and path-jumping. I am also indebted to Howard Schwartz's *Tree of Souls: The Mythology of Judaism* and the works of Dr. Sara Ronis, author of *Demons in the Details: Demonic Discourse and Rabbinic Culture in Late Antique Babylonia* (thanks, Sara!). I took quite a few liberties with my particular Jewish demons, but I hope in some small way I captured how they fit into the Jewish mythos.

I am also indebted to the academic article that jump-started the concept of this book—"'Because He Loves Her ...' The Figure of the Demon in the Book of Tobit" by Ida Fröhlich. It in, Fröhlich writes about her work with a colleague: "Our favourite topic was demonology, especially the question of demons as obstacle to a marriage. He referred to me cases known by him from contemporary Near Eastern practice. Girls who for some reason do not want to marry refuse the marriage proposal under the cover that they are already married to a demon." With this, I was off and running.

Thank you to the team at Penguin Teen for all their varied and integral work bringing this book to life: managing editors Rye White, Natalie Vielkind, and Madison Penico; digital marketers Felicity Vallence, Shannon Spann, and Astrid Rojas; marketers Christina Colangelo and Bri Lockhart; interior designer Rebecca Aidlin; cover designer Maria Fazio; and proofreader Krista Ahlberg. Thanks as well to Monica Rodriguez and Celsie Moseley at Context Literary Agency, and to Mary Pender at WME!

Thank you, thank you to cover artist Mike Pape. This cover has killed me. It is the most beautiful thing I have ever seen. I absolutely adore your depiction of Naomi and Daziel and the way the city of Talum is captured, and I might just be staring at this for the rest of my life.

And, of course, I must thank all my friends, who have been there with me for all of this. Thanks to Monica and Cass and Emily-in-absentia, who write with me almost every weekend at Camberville's cafés; thanks to Diana, Mara, Janella, and Charlie for much-needed brunches and for talking (or actively not talking!) about publishing; thanks to Julie for endless texts; thanks to friends-my-friends, who gleefully discuss covers and titles and joys both little and big with boundless enthusiasm and generosity.

Thank you to my parents, who have always supported me. Sorry, Dad, that I wrote a fantasy novel and there are *still no dragons*.

And thank you to Alyn, for being there through my highs and lows in this process, and who told me he never reads the acknowledgments. Surprise!!!